ALSO BY TOM PERROTTA

# Mrs. Fletcher

A Novel

## Tom Perrotta

SCRIBNER

New York   London   Toronto   Sydney   New Delhi

SCRIBNER
An Imprint of Simon & Schuster, Inc.
1230 Avenue of the Americas
New York, NY 10020

This Scribner hardcover edition November 2017

For information about special discounts for bulk purchases,
please contact Simon & Schuster Special Sales at 1-866-506-1949
or business@simonandschuster.com.

The Simon & Schuster Speakers Bureau can bring authors to your live event.
For more information or to book an event, contact the Simon & Schuster Speakers Bureau
at 1-866-248-3049 or visit our website at www.simonspeakers.com.

Manufactured in the United States of America

1   3   5   7   9   10   8   6   4   2

Library of Congress Control Number: 2016059879

ISBN 978-1-5011-8433-8

# Mrs. Fletcher

"The way up and the way down
is one and the same."
—Heraclitus

PART ONE

*The Beginning
of a Great Whatever*

# The Obligatory Emoticon

It was a long drive and Eve cried most of the way home, because the big day hadn't gone the way she'd hoped, not that big days ever did. Birthdays, holidays, weddings, graduations, funerals—they were all too loaded with expectations, and the important people in her life rarely acted the way they were supposed to. Most of them didn't even seem to be working from the same script as she was, though maybe that said more about the important people in her life than it did about big days in general.

Take today: all she'd wanted, from the moment she opened her eyes in the morning, was a chance to let Brendan know what was in her heart, to express all the love that had been building up over the summer, swelling to the point where she sometimes thought her chest would explode. It just seemed really important to say it out loud before he left, to share all the gratitude and pride she felt, not just for the wonderful person he was right now, but for the sweet little boy he'd been, and the strong and decent man he would one day become. And she wanted to reassure him, too, to make it clear that she would be starting a new life just the same as he was, and that it would be a great adventure for both of them.

*Don't worry about me,* she wanted to tell him. *You just study hard and have fun. I'll take care of myself . . .*

But that conversation never happened. Brendan had overslept—

he'd been out late, partying with his buddies—and when he finally dragged himself out of bed, he was useless, too hungover to help with the last-minute packing or the loading of the van. It was just so irresponsible—leaving her, with her bad back, to lug his boxes and suitcases down the stairs in the sticky August heat, sweating through her good shirt while he sat in his boxers at the kitchen table, struggling with the child-proof cap on a bottle of ibuprofen—but she managed to keep her irritation in check. She didn't want to spoil their last morning together with petty nagging, even if he deserved it. Going out on a sour note would have been a disservice to both of them.

When she was finished, she took a few pictures of the van with the back hatch open, the cargo area stuffed with luggage and plastic containers, a rolled-up rug and a lacrosse stick, an Xbox console and an oscillating fan, a mini-fridge and a milk crate full of emergency food, plus a jumbo bag of Cool Ranch Doritos, because they were his favorite. She uploaded the least blurry photo to Facebook, along with a status update that read, *Off to college! So happy for my amazing son, Brendan!!!* Then she inserted the obligatory emoticon and launched her message into space, so her 221 friends would understand how she was feeling, and could let her know that they liked it.

It took a couple of tries to shut the hatch—the damn rug was in the way—but she finally got it closed and that was that. She lingered for a moment, thinking of other road trips, vacations they'd taken when Brendan was little, the three of them heading to Cape Cod to stay with Ted's parents, and that one time camping in the Berkshires when it rained and rained—the earth turning liquid beneath their tent—and they had to pack it in and find a motel in the middle of the night. She thought she might cry right then—it was going to happen sooner or later—but before she could get herself started, Becca zoomed up the driveway on her bicycle, moving so swiftly and silently it felt like a sneak attack.

"Oh!" Eve flung up her arms in self-defense, though she was in no danger of being run over. "You scared me!"

Becca shot her a withering *what-planet-are-you-from* look as she dismounted, but the contempt came and went so quickly it was almost like it hadn't been there at all.

"Good morning, Mrs. Fletcher."

Eve bristled at the greeting. She'd told Becca numerous times that she preferred to be addressed by her first name, but the girl insisted on calling her *Mrs. Fletcher*, as if she were still married.

"Good morning, Becca. Shouldn't you be wearing a helmet?"

Becca released the bike—it balanced on its own for a moment before toppling dreamily onto the grass—and patted her hair with both hands, making sure everything was where it was supposed to be, which of course it was.

"Helmets are gross, Mrs. Fletcher."

Eve hadn't seen Becca for a few weeks, and she suddenly realized how pleasant the interlude had been, and how she'd failed to appreciate it, the same way you fail to appreciate the absence of a stomachache until the cramps return. Becca was so petite and adorable, so totally put together—that cute little turquoise romper, those immaculate white sneakers, all that makeup, way too much for a teenager riding her bike on a summer morning. And she wasn't even sweating!

"Well, then." Eve smiled nervously, acutely conscious of her own body, the doughy pallor of her flesh, the dampness spreading from her armpits. "Something I can do for you?"

Becca shot her that frosty look again, letting her know that she'd used up her quota of stupid questions for the day.

"Is he inside?"

"I'm sorry, honey." Eve nodded toward the van. "We're just about to leave."

"No worries." Becca was already moving toward the house. "I just need a minute."

Eve could have stopped her from going in—she totally had the right—but she didn't feel like playing the role of bitchy, disapproving mom, not today. What was the point? Her mom days were over. And as much as she disliked Becca, Eve couldn't help feeling sorry for her, at least a little. It couldn't have been easy being Brendan's girlfriend, and it must have hurt pretty badly to get dumped by him just weeks before he left for college, while she was marooned in high school for another year. He'd apparently done the dirty work by text and refused to talk to her afterward, just crumpled up the relationship and tossed it in the trash, a tactic he'd learned from his father. Eve could understand all too well Becca's need for one last conversation, that vain hope for closure.

*Good luck with that.*

Figuring they could use a little space, Eve drove to the Citgo station to fill the tank and check the tire pressure, then stopped at the bank to withdraw some cash she could slip to Brendan as a parting gift. *For books,* she would tell him, though she imagined most of it would go for pizza and beer.

She was gone for about fifteen minutes—ample time for a farewell chat—but Becca's bike was still resting on the lawn when she returned.

*Too bad,* she thought. *Visiting hours are over . . .*

The kitchen was empty, and Brendan didn't respond when she called his name. She tried again, a little louder, with no more success. Then she checked the patio, but it was pure formality; she already knew where they were and what they were doing. She could feel it in the air, a subtle, illicit, and deeply annoying vibration.

Eve wasn't a puritanical mom—when she went to the drugstore, she made a point of asking her son if he needed condoms—but she didn't have the patience for this, not today, not after she'd loaded the van by herself and they were already way behind schedule. She made her way to the foot of the stairs.

*"Brendan!"* Her voice was shrill and commanding, the same one she'd used when he was a child misbehaving on the playground. "I need you down here *immediately*!"

She waited for a few seconds, then stomped up the stairs, making as much noise as possible. She didn't care *what* they were doing. It was a simple matter of respect. Respect and maturity. He was leaving for college and it was time to grow up.

His bedroom door was closed and music was playing inside, the usual thuggish rap. She raised her hand to knock. The sound that stopped her was vague at first, barely audible, but it grew louder as she tuned in to its frequency, an urgent primal muttering that no mother needs to hear from her son, especially when she was feeling nostalgic for the little boy he'd been, the sweet child who'd clung so desperately to her leg when she tried to say goodbye on his first day of preschool, begging her to stay with him for *just one more minute. Please, Mommy, just one little minute!*

"Oh shit," he was saying now, in a tone of tranquilized wonder. "Fuck yeah . . . Suck it, bitch."

As if repulsed by a terrible odor, Eve lurched away from the door and beat a flustered retreat to the kitchen, where she made herself a cup of soothing peppermint tea. To distract herself while it steeped, she flipped through a catalogue from Eastern Community College, because she was going to have a lot of time on her hands from now on, and needed to find some activities that would get her out of the house, maybe bring her into contact with some interesting new people. She'd made it all the way up to Sociology, circling the classes that seemed promising and fit her schedule, when she finally heard footsteps on the stairs. A few seconds later, Becca stepped into the kitchen, looking rumpled but victorious, with a big wet spot on her romper. At least she had the decency to blush.

"Bye, Mrs. Fletcher. Enjoy the empty nest!"

The previous summer, when Eve and Brendan were visiting colleges, they'd had some lovely long drives together. Lulled by the monotony of the highway, he'd opened up to her in a way she'd forgotten was possible, talking easily and thoughtfully about a multitude of normally off-limits subjects: girls, his father's new family, some of the options he was pondering for his undergraduate major (Economics, if it wasn't too hard, or maybe Criminal Justice). He'd surprised her by showing some curiosity about her past, asking what she'd been like at his age, wondering about the guys she'd dated before she got

7

married, and the bands she'd liked, and whether or not she'd smoked weed. They shared a motel room on the overnight trips, watching TV from their respective beds, trading the Doritos bag back and forth as they laughed at *South Park* and Jon Stewart. At the time, it had felt like they were entering a gratifying new phase of their relationship—an easygoing adult rapport—but it didn't last. As soon as they got home they reverted to their default mode, two people sharing the same address but not much else, exchanging the minimum daily requirement of information, mostly, on her son's side, in the form of grudging monosyllables and irritable grunts.

Eve had cherished the memory of those intimate highway conversations, and she'd been looking forward to another one that afternoon, a last chance to discuss the big changes that were about to unfold in both of their lives, and maybe to reflect a little on the years that were suddenly behind them, gone more quickly than she ever could have imagined. But how could they share a nostalgic moment when all she could think about were the awful words she'd heard through the bedroom door?

*Suck it, bitch.*

*Ugh.* She wanted to press a button and erase that ugly phrase from her memory, but it just kept repeating itself, echoing through her brain on an endless loop: *Suck it, bitch . . . Suck it, bitch . . . Suck it . . .* He'd uttered the words so casually, so *automatically*, the way a boy of her own generation might have said, *Oh yeah*, or *Keep going*, which would have been embarrassing enough from a mother's perspective, but not nearly so disturbing.

She probably shouldn't have been surprised. Back when Brendan was in middle school, Eve had gone to a PTA presentation on "Web-Savvy Parenting." The guest speaker, an assistant county prosecutor, had given them a depressing overview of the internet landscape and the perils it posed for teenagers. He touched on sexting and cyberbullying and online predators, but the thing that really bothered him was the insane amount of pornography that kids were potentially exposed to every day, a tsunami of filth unprecedented in human history.

*This isn't a copy of* Playboy *hidden in the closet, okay? This is an unregulated cesspool of degrading images and extreme sexual perversion available to everyone in the privacy of their own bedrooms, regardless of their age or emotional maturity. In this toxic environment, it will take constant, unwavering vigilance to keep your kids safe, to protect their innocence and guard them from depravity. Are you prepared to meet this challenge?*

Eve and the other mothers she'd spoken to were shaken by the grim picture he'd painted, but they agreed afterward that it was a little overdone. The situation was bad—there was no use denying it—but it wasn't all *that* bad, was it? And even if it was, there was no practical way to monitor your kids' every mouse click. You just had to teach the right values—respect and kindness and compassion, pretty much *do unto others*, not that Eve was religious—and hope that it provided a shield against the harmful images and sexist stereotypes that they would inevitably be exposed to. And that was what Eve had done, to the best of her ability, though it obviously hadn't worked out the way she'd hoped.

*Suck it, bitch.*

It was a little late in the day for a big sex talk, but Eve felt like she had no choice but to let Brendan know how disappointed she was. What he'd said to Becca was not okay, and Eve needed to make that clear, even if it ruined their last day together. She didn't want him to begin college without understanding that there was a fundamental difference between sexual relationships in real life and the soulless encounters he presumably watched on the internet (he insisted that he stayed away from all that crap, but his browser history was always carefully scrubbed, which was one of the warning signs she'd learned about at the PTA meeting). At the very least, she needed to remind him that it was not okay to call your girlfriend a bitch, even if that was a word you used jokingly with your male friends, even if the girl in question claimed not to mind.

*And even if she really is one,* Eve thought, though she knew it wasn't helpful to her cause.

Brendan must have sensed that a lecture was imminent, because he did his best to seal himself off in the van, tugging the bill of his baseball cap low over his sunglasses, nodding emphatically to the hip-hop throbbing through his sleek white headphones. As soon as they got on the Pike, he reclined his seat and announced that he was taking a nap.

"I hope you don't mind," he said, which was the first halfway polite thing to emerge from his mouth all day. "I'm really tired."

"You must be," she said, larding her voice with fake sympathy. "You had a really busy morning. All that heavy lifting."

"Ha ha." He propped his bare feet on the dashboard. "Wake me when we get there, okay?"

He slept—or pretended to sleep—for the next two hours, not even leaving the van when she stopped at a rest area outside of Sturbridge. Eve resented it at first—she really did want to talk to him about sexual etiquette and respect for women—but she had to admit that it was a relief to postpone the conversation, which would have required her to confess that she'd been eavesdropping outside of his door and to quote the phrase that had upset her so much. She wasn't sure she'd be able to say it out loud, not without grave embarrassment, and she had a feeling that Brendan would laugh and tell her that she'd heard wrong, that he would never say, *Suck it, bitch,* not to Becca or anyone else, and they'd end up disputing the basic facts of the case rather than discussing the issues that really mattered. He could be a pretty slippery customer when he needed to be; it was another trait he'd inherited from his father, a fellow master of denial and evasion.

*Just let him rest,* she thought, inserting a Neil Young CD into the slot, mellow old songs that left her with a pleasant feeling of melancholy, perfect for the occasion. *We can talk some other time.*

Eve knew she was being a coward, abdicating her parental responsibility, but letting him off the hook was pretty much a reflex at this point. The divorce had left her with a permanently guilty conscience that made it almost impossible for her to stay mad at her son or hold him accountable for his actions. The poor kid had been the victim of an elaborate bait and switch perpetrated by his own parents, who, for eleven years, had built a life for him that felt solid and permanent and good, and then—just kidding!—had ripped it out of his hands and replaced it with an inferior substitute, a smaller, flimsier version in which love had an expiration date and nothing could be trusted. Was it any wonder that he didn't always treat other people with the kindness and consideration they deserved?

Not that it was Eve's fault. Ted was the guilty party, the selfish bastard who'd abandoned a perfectly good family to start over with a woman he'd met through the Casual Encounters section of Craigslist (he'd falsely claimed his marital status was "Separated," a self-fulfilling prophecy if there ever was one). Eve had been blindsided by his betrayal and devastated by his refusal to get counseling or make even a token effort to save the marriage. He just pronounced it dead and buried, unilaterally declaring the past two decades of his life to be a regrettable mistake and vowing to do better on his next try.

*I have a second chance,* he'd told her, his voice quivering with emotion. *Do you see how precious that is?*

*What about me?* she'd replied. *What about your son? Aren't we precious, too?*

*I'm a jerk,* he explained. *You both deserve better.*

The whole world acknowledged her status as an innocent victim—even Ted agreed!—but Eve still felt complicit in the breakup. The marriage had been floundering for a long time before Ted found his way to Craigslist, and she hadn't done a thing to make it better, hadn't even admitted there was a problem. Through her own passivity, she had enabled the disaster, letting her husband drift away and her family fall apart. She'd failed as a wife, and therefore as a mother, and Brendan was the one who'd paid the price.

The damage he'd suffered was subtle and hard to pinpoint. Other people marveled at what an impressive young man he was and how well he'd weathered the divorce. Eve was delighted by the praise—it meant everything to her—and she even believed it, up to a point.

Her son did possess a number of good qualities. He was handsome and popular, a gifted athlete who never lacked for female attention. He'd done well in school, good enough to be admitted to Fordham and Connecticut College, though he'd ultimately settled on Berkshire State University, partly because it was more affordable, but mainly, as he cheerfully informed anyone who asked, because BSU was a party school and he liked to party. That was how he presented himself to the world—as a big, friendly, fun-loving bro, a dude you'd totally want on your team or in your frat—and the world seemed happy to take him at his word.

To Eve, though, he was still the bewildered boy who couldn't understand why his father had left and why they couldn't just make him come home. For the first couple of months after Ted moved out, Brendan had slept with a picture of his dad under his pillow, and more than once she'd found him wide awake in the middle of the night, talking to the photo with tears streaming down his face. He'd toughened up over time—his muscles turned wiry and his eyes got hard and the picture disappeared—but something had gone out of him in the process, all the boyish softness and vulnerability that had touched her so deeply. He just wasn't as nice a person as he used to be—not nearly as sweet or as kind or as lovable—and she couldn't forgive herself for letting that happen, for not knowing how to protect him, or how to fix what was broken.

They hit a traffic jam on the edge of campus, a festive convoy of incoming freshmen and their families. Inching toward the Longfellow Residential Area, they were cheered along the way by clusters of upperclassmen in matching red T-shirts who were apparently being paid to greet the newcomers. Some of them were dancing and others were holding up handmade signs that said, *Welcome Home!* and *First Years Rock!* However mercenary its origins, their enthusiasm was so infectious that Eve couldn't help grinning and waving back.

"What are you doing?" Brendan muttered, still grumpy from his nap.

"Just being friendly," she said. "If that's all right with you."

"Whatever." He slumped lower in his seat. "Knock yourself out."

Brendan had been assigned to Einstein Hall, one of the infamous high-rise dorms that made Longfellow look like a public housing project. Eve had heard alarming things about the party culture in this part of campus, but the vibe seemed reassuringly wholesome as they pulled into the unloading area and were swarmed by a crew of cheerful and efficient student movers. Within minutes, the movers had emptied the van, transferring all of Brendan's possessions into a big orange bin on wheels. Eve stood by and watched, happy to be spared another round of sweaty labor. A scruffy kid whose T-shirt identified him as *Crew Leader* shut the hatch and gave her a businesslike nod.

"Okay, Mom. We'll take this fine young man up to his room now."

"Great." Eve locked the van with the remote key. "Let's go."

The crew leader shook his head. Despite the ninety-degree heat, he was wearing a knitted winter cap with earflaps, the material so sweat-stiffened that the flaps curled out like Pippi Longstocking's pigtails. "Not you, Mom. You need to move your vehicle to the Visitors Lot."

This didn't seem right to Eve. She'd seen lots of other mothers heading into the dorm with their kids. An Indian lady in a lime-green sari was accompanying her daughter at that very moment. But even as Eve began to point this out, she realized that the other mothers must have had husbands who were taking care of the parking. Everyone seemed to agree that this was the proper division of labor—the men parked the cars while the women stayed with their kids. Eve softened her voice, pleading for clemency.

"I'll just be a few minutes. I need to help him unpack."

"That's great, Mom." An edge of impatience had entered the crew leader's voice. "But first you have to move the vehicle. There's a lot of people waiting."

*I'm not your mom,* Eve thought, smiling with excruciating politeness at the officious little shit. If she had been his mother, she would have advised him to lose the hat. *Sweetie,* she would have told him, *you look like a moron.* But she took a deep breath and tried to appeal to his humanity.

"I'm a single parent," she explained. "He's my only child. This is a big deal for us."

By this point, Brendan had tuned in to the negotiation. He turned and glared at Eve.

*"Mom."* His voice was clipped and tense. "Go park the car. I'll be fine."

"Are you sure?"

The crew leader patted her on the arm.

"Don't worry," he assured her. "We'll take good care of your baby."

The Visitors Lot was only a short drive away, but the walk back to Einstein took longer than she'd expected. By the time she made it up to Brendan's room on the seventh floor, he was already in full-tilt male bonding mode with his new roommate, Zack, a broad-shouldered kid from Boxborough with a narrow, neatly trimmed beard that hugged his jawline like a chin strap, the same ill-advised facial hair that Brendan had sported for most of senior year. They were wearing identical outfits, too—flip-flops, baggy shorts, tank tops, angled baseball caps—though Zack had spiced up his ensemble with a puka shell necklace.

He seemed nice enough, but Eve had to work to conceal her disappointment. She'd hoped that Brendan would get a more exotic roommate, a black kid from inner-city Boston, or a visiting student from mainland China, or maybe a gay guy with a passion for musical theater, someone who would expand her son's horizons and challenge him to move beyond his suburban comfort zone. Instead he'd gotten paired with a young man who could have been his long-lost brother, or at least a teammate on the Haddington High lacrosse team. When she arrived, the boys were admiring their matching mini-fridges.

"We could dedicate one to beer," Zack suggested. "The other could be for non-beer shit, lunch meat and whatever."

"Totally," agreed Brendan. "Milk for cereal."

"Arizonas." Zack fingered his puka shells. "Might be cool if we stacked one on top of the other. Then it would be like one medium-sized fridge with two compartments. Give us more floor space that way."

"Sweet."

Eve went straight to work, putting sheets and blankets on Brendan's bed and organizing his closet and dresser just the way they were at home, so he wouldn't be disoriented. Neither boy paid much attention to her—they were strategizing about maybe lofting one of the beds and moving a desk underneath, freeing up enough space for a couch, which would make it easier to play video games—and she told herself that it was completely natural for a mother to be ignored in a situation like this. This was their room and their world; she was an outsider who would soon be on her way.

"Where would we get a couch?" Brendan wondered.

"People just leave 'em out on the street," Zack explained. "We can go out later and pick one up."

"Is that sanitary?" Eve asked. "They could have bedbugs."

"Mom." Brendan silenced her with a head shake. "We'll figure it out, okay?"

Zack stroked his beard like a philosopher. "We could cover it with a sheet, just to be on the safe side."

It was almost five thirty by the time Eve got everything unpacked. She saved the area rug for last, positioning it between the two beds so no one's feet would be cold on winter mornings. It was a nice homey touch.

"Not bad," she said, glancing around with satisfaction. "Pretty civilized for a dorm room."

Brendan and Zack nodded in that subdued male way, as if they could barely rouse themselves to express agreement, let alone gratitude.

"Who wants dinner?" she asked. "Pizza's on me."

A quick, wary glance passed between the roommates.

"You know what, Mom? A bunch of guys from the floor are going out in a little while. I'll probably grab some food with them, okay?"

*Jesus,* Eve thought, a sudden warmth flooding her face. *That was quick.*

"Sure," she said. "Go ahead. Enjoy yourselves."

"Yeah," Brendan added. "This way you won't have to drive home in the dark."

"All right, then." Eve scanned the room, searching fruitlessly for another task. "Looks like that's it."

No one contradicted her.

"Okay." She smoothed Brendan's bedspread one last time. She had a slightly dizzying sense of being overtaken by time, the future becoming the present before she was ready. "Guess I better be going."

Brendan walked her to the elevators. It wasn't an ideal place to say goodbye—too many kids milling around, including a crew of student movers pushing an empty bin—but there was nothing they could do about that.

"Oh, by the way . . ." Eve fumbled in her purse and found the cash she'd withdrawn that morning. She pressed the bills into Brendan's hand, then gave him a fierce hug and a quick kiss. "Just call me if you need anything, okay?"

"I'll be fine."

She hugged him again when the elevator arrived. "I love you."

"Yeah," he muttered. "Me too."

"I'm going to miss you. A lot."

"I know."

After that, there was nothing to do but climb aboard and wave to her son until the doors slid shut. For a few seconds, the elevator didn't move. Eve smiled awkwardly at the other passengers, all of them students, none of whom responded in kind. They were chatting excitedly among themselves, making plans, bubbling over with enthusiasm, utterly oblivious to her presence. Eve felt old and excluded, as if everyone else was going to a party to which she hadn't been invited. *It's not fair,* she wanted to tell them, but they were already going down, and nobody would have believed her anyway.

# Meat Bomb

I was still a little dazed when we headed out to dinner, headachy from my daylong hangover—tequila shots will do that to you—and a little freaked out by my new surroundings, the high-rise buildings and unfamiliar faces. It was hard to believe I was finally in college, after all the endless build-up, a whole year of tours and tests and applications and interviews, the drama of choosing your future, graduating high school, saying goodbye to your friends and family and coaches, all that weepy shit.

It was exciting, I guess, to have the freedom I'd been dreaming about, the ability to do what I wanted when I wanted, no one to answer to but myself. But it was kind of a letdown, too. The truth is, I would've been just as happy to spend another year at Haddington High, where I knew everyone and everyone knew me, where I could be a varsity starter in pretty much any sport I chose, and get straight Bs without breaking a sweat. I had a slightly queasy feeling walking into town—the same feeling I got in airports and train stations—like there were way too many people in the world, and none of them gave a shit about me.

At least the fresh air did me some good. It had gotten pretty claustrophobic up in the dorm room, my mother doing that manic thing of hers, fixing everything up, offering all kinds of advice nobody had asked for, like it was rocket science to do your laundry, and she was

TOM PERROTTA

the head of NASA. When she finally got on the elevator, I felt a deep sense of relief, which isn't the way you want to feel toward your mom at a moment like that.

Zack put his arm around me, very casually, as we walked, like we'd known each other for years. It reminded me of my friend Wade, who used to do all kinds of homoerotic shit like that in the hallways. Sometimes he would even kiss me on the cheek or the side of the head, or give my ass a little squeeze, which was only funny because we were lacrosse players and everybody knew we weren't gay.

"Bro," he told me, "we are gonna have mad fun this year. Alcohol will be consumed in massive quantities in Room 706."

"Weed will be smoked," I said. "Parties will be had."

"Dicks will be sucked!" he added, in such a loud voice that these two Asian girls walking ahead of us turned and gave us a look, like we were a couple of assholes.

"Not by me," Zack assured the girls, quickly withdrawing his arm from my shoulder. "But you ladies should totally go for it, if that's your thing."

The girls didn't crack a smile. They just turned and kept walking.

"It's okay," I told him. "No one's judging you. Lots of people come out in college."

"Eat me, douchebag."

"That's hate speech, dickhead."

"*Douchebag* is hate speech?"

"Yeah. It's offensive to douchebags."

"Huh." He nodded, like that made a lot of sense. "Then I apologize."

"That's okay," I said. "We're here to learn and grow."

There were only supposed to be four of us at the pizzeria—me and Zack, plus Will and Rico, these chill dudes from our floor—but unbeknownst to us, Will had invited his camp counselor buddy, Dylan, and Dylan had brought along his roommate, this annoying kid named Sanjay.

I mean, it wasn't like there was anything wrong with Sanjay, and no, I'm not prejudiced against Indian people or anyone else. It was just awkward. The rest of us were jocks and hard partiers, and Sanjay was a skinny nerd who looked like he was about twelve years old. And that's fine, you know? Go ahead and be a nerd if that's what makes you happy. Go design your app or whatever. Just don't ask me to give a shit.

"Sanjay's in the Honors College," Dylan informed us. "Majoring in Electrical Engineering. Talk about badass."

I guess you have to give Dylan some credit. He was trying to be a good roommate, doing his best to include Sanjay in the conversation and make him feel comfortable. It was just a waste of time, that's all. Sanjay wasn't going to be friends with us, and we weren't going to be friends with him. You could take one look at our table and know that for a fact.

"Nice," said Rico, who was a white guy with curly blond hair, a former high school wrestler. His real name was Richard Timpkins, but the Spanish teacher called him Rico, and his friends thought it was hilarious, so the nickname stuck. "I thought about Engineering, but I kinda suck at math. Plus I smoke way too much weed."

"Maybe there's a connection," said Will, an ex–football player whose neck was wider than his head. "Just putting it out there."

"It's possible," agreed Rico. "Bong hits and calculus are not a winning combination."

"Actually," Sanjay said, "I'm thinking about switching to Architecture. That's my first love."

I glanced across the table at Zack, but he was already reaching for his phone, swiping at the screen and tapping away with both thumbs. His text arrived a few seconds later:

*My first love is architecture!*

I texted back: *My second is sucking cock!!!*

Zack snorted and we bumped fists across the table.

"Guess what Sanjay got on the Math SAT?" Dylan asked.

Nobody wanted to know, so the question just sort of floated away. Sanjay looked as relieved as the rest of us.

Will glared at Dylan. I don't think he was mad. He just had one of those faces that looked pissed off a lot of the time. You couldn't really blame him, I guess. He'd been one of the best high school line-backers in the state, heavily recruited by Division 3 schools, but he blew out his knee in the season opener of his senior year, and that was that. Full retirement at age seventeen.

"How come he's not living in the Honors Dorm?" he asked, as if Sanjay couldn't speak English and needed Dylan to translate.

"It's too elitist," Sanjay explained. "I don't think we should have a separate dorm from everyone else. We're all one community, right?"

My phone buzzed again. I figured it was Zack, but it turned out to be Becca.

*Hows it going college boy*
*Out w the guys,* I texted back.
*Miss me?*

I was tempted to tell her the truth—*nope, not at all*—but I took pity on her.

*Sure*
*Can we skype later*
*going to a party*
*What time*
*Ten*
*How about 9:30 you owe me for this morning!!! Ha ha* ☺

I knew this would happen. That was why I'd dumped her in the first place, so I wouldn't have to deal with this long-distance shit in college. But then last night I'd drunk-sexted her, begging to get with her one last time before I left town. She told me to fuck off, which I definitely deserved. I didn't remember any of it until she showed up at my house in the morning, and totally ambushed me, in the best possible way. *It's your going-away present,* she'd said, kneeling down in front of me and tugging on my boxers. And it was a great blowjob, too—way better than usual—but I didn't think that meant we were back together, or that I owed her for anything, though I could see how she might feel otherwise.

*Fine 9:30*
*Luv ya!*

The pizza arrived—one large pepperoni, one large sausage, and one large cheese—and of course Sanjay turned out to be a vegetarian. We started giving him shit for it, until Dylan explained that it was a religious thing, which meant, according to PC regulations, that you weren't allowed to joke about it.

"I forgot how much I love pizza," Will told us. "I didn't eat any all summer. Couldn't even look at it."

"Why not?" Rico asked.

Will shrugged. "I had a bad experience. You don't want to hear about it while you're eating."

But we did, so he told us. The day after graduation, Will had gone to a party at this rich girl's house, in the biggest McMansion he'd ever seen, with an indoor pool, a home gym, and something like eight bathrooms. The girl had been very clear that there wasn't going to be any alcohol at the party, so Will had hit the pregame hard, multiple shots of Jack plus a THC-infused lollipop donated by someone's uncle who suffered from chronic shoulder pain and had an understanding doctor. He had the munchies pretty bad when he got to the party, and it was like he'd walked into heaven—there was this amazing spread of fried chicken, lasagna, barbecue, an honest-to-goodness ten-foot-long sub, tons of great stuff. He'd already sampled a lot of it when the doorbell rang, and a delivery guy walked in with a stack of a dozen pizzas. A crowd had gathered around the buffet table, and one of Will's buddies bet him twenty bucks he couldn't eat a large pizza by himself. And not just any pizza. The one they call the Meat Bomb. Will said, *Bring it on, bitch!*

"No way," said Rico.

"It was a throwdown," Will explained.

He inhaled the first four slices like a machine. Midway through slice number five, though, he realized there was a problem.

"You know how it is. You're feeling good, totally on top of your game. And then, out of nowhere, your stomach just clenches up and says, *That's enough, bro. Do not take another bite.* But I still had three slices to go."

"You didn't eat them?" Rico said.

"The fuck I didn't," said Will. "I just kept shoveling that shit down my throat. But I knew it wasn't gonna stay there."

The spectators broke into applause when he finished, but Will didn't stick around to enjoy it. He pushed through the crowd and made his way to the nearest bathroom, only to discover that the door was locked. He pounded on it a few times, but the occupant told him to wait his turn. He didn't panic, because there was another bathroom off the kitchen. Unfortunately, that one was really popular. There were five or six people standing in line, and Will couldn't really talk, which meant that he couldn't explain his dilemma, so he just turned and headed upstairs, holding his stomach and gritting his teeth.

It was like a bad dream. Every time he found a bathroom, the door was either locked or a bunch of kids were waiting in line. So he just kept moving, hoping to find a toilet before it was too late. It was a huge house, and he pretty much gave himself the grand tour, visiting all three floors before he finally made it to the master bedroom, which was totally spectacular—a huge round bed and a wall that was all glass, looking out on a meadow—though Will didn't have time to appreciate the view. He headed straight for the bathroom, and Praise the Lord, the door was unlocked. His stomach was already lurching when he burst in there and found himself staring at six of the prettiest girls in his school, all of them in bikinis, sitting in this giant Jacuzzi.

"Oh shit," said Dylan. "Did you barf on them?"

Will shook his head. "I just gave them this sad little wave, like I was dropping by to say hello, and then I fucking bolted. I barely made it out to the hall, and that was it, the end of the road. I ducked into this little kid's room. I thought there'd be a trash can or something, but I couldn't find one, so I just yanked open a dresser drawer, pulled out all the clothes, and puked right in there. That whole fucking Meat Bomb pizza. And then I shut the drawer, wiped my mouth, and got the fuck outta there."

"Did you tell anyone?" Dylan asked, when we were finally done groaning and laughing.

"Fuck no. What was I supposed to say? Oh, by the way, your little brother might not want to open his pajama drawer . . . "

"At least you took out the pjs," Rico said. "That was thoughtful."

"What could I do?" Will had that pissed-off look again. "Eight fucking bathrooms, and I can't find a toilet to puke in? You can't blame me for that."

He shrugged and reached for another slice. Sanjay was just sitting there with his mouth hanging open, like he'd forgotten how to speak.

"Whaddaya think?" Rico asked him. "Too late to get back into the Honors Dorm?"

Zack and I returned to the room just in time for my Skype session with Becca. I asked if he'd mind giving me a little privacy.

"No problem," he said. "I'll put on my headphones."

"Think you could maybe clear out for five or ten minutes? Won't be more than that."

"Why?" He gave me a sly look. "You gonna rub one out?"

"We just need to have the talk. We were broken up for most of the summer, but then we kinda backslid. I have to let her down easy."

"Say no more, bro. I'll go see who's in the lounge. Text me when you're done."

"Thanks."

I got out my laptop and logged on to Skype. Zack was on his way out when I placed the call, but then he changed his mind and sat down next to me on my bed, just out of camera range, as Becca appeared on the screen.

"Hey, baby." She was wearing a little white tank top, tight enough to give her some cleavage, which wasn't easy with her little boobs. "How's it going?"

"Pretty good," I said. "How about you?"

"I'm okay." She was talking in a breathy whisper, way more seductive than her normal voice, which could be kinda loud and bossy. "Where are you?"

"In my room."

She licked her glossy lips. "Are you alone?"

I glanced at Zack, trying to let him know that the joke was officially not funny anymore, but he pretended not to understand. He mouthed the words *She's cute!* and pumped his fist up and down over his crotch.

"Brendan?" she said. "Is somebody there?"

I should have just said, *Yeah, it's my roommate and he's being a dick,* but I didn't want to embarrass him.

"No," I said. "Just me."

"I miss you, baby." She gazed soulfully into the camera. "I'm still thinking about this morning."

"Yeah," I said. "That was a really nice surprise."

"Just nice?"

"It was fucking awesome."

"Good." She looked a little bashful, but sort of proud, too. "I watched an instructional video on YouTube."

That made sense. She'd given me a few BJs in the past, but she was never really into it. She was clumsy and gagged a lot, and mostly just seemed relieved when it was over. But that morning she was a porn star.

"Yeah, you brought your A game."

"It was a mental thing," she explained. "I just decided to have a positive attitude. It really makes a difference."

It was ridiculous—and kind of embarrassing—to be having this conversation with Zack sitting right next to me, but there was nothing I could do about it now except try not to look at him. I didn't want to know what he was thinking, or how close he might be to cracking up.

"I thought I'd be able to swallow," she said, "but I just . . . I don't know. I'll have to keep working on that."

"With who?" I said.

24

Zack made the tiniest sound just then, a single suppressed giggle way in the back of his throat, but Becca didn't seem to hear it.

"You, you asshole. Unless you want me to find someone else."

"Practice makes perfect," I teased.

Zack was waving his hand, trying to get my attention. I could see him out of the corner of my eye, pointing at his dick and mouthing the words *I'll help*.

"Hey," she said, and her voice was normal now, like the sexy part of the conversation was officially over. "Did your mom say anything after I left?"

"No, why?"

"I don't know. She gave me this weird look when I said goodbye, like she knew what we were up to."

"Don't worry about it. She was in a bad mood all day. It had nothing to do with you."

"Good." Becca seemed relieved. "So do you like it there?"

"I think so. Just trying to get used to it, you know?"

"Well, if you ever need to talk, just give me a call." She looked down for a few seconds, so all I could see was the top of her head, that shiny brown hair that always smelled so good. When she looked up, she sniffled and wiped her eyes. "I missed you so much this summer."

Zack was leaning forward now, into my field of vision. He had this sad clown expression on his face, his bottom lip pushed way out like he was about to cry. I held out my arm where Becca couldn't see it and gave him the finger.

"I like your shirt," I told her. "It's really hot."

"Yeah?" She perked right up. "I wore it special for you. I'm wearing the red thong you like, too."

She stood up to show me, pulling down her pj pants and turning so I could appreciate her tight little gymnast butt. Zack was impressed.

"Smokin'," I told her.

"You should come home for a weekend," she said. "Or maybe I could come visit you."

Zack cast a silent vote in favor of the second option.

"We'll see," I said. "I'm probably gonna be pretty busy."

"Yeah, that's what I figured."

We were quiet for a few seconds, and I knew the time had come to say what needed to be said, to apologize for the way I'd treated her over the summer, and then to explain, as tactfully as possible, that I didn't want a long-distance relationship, and that we both should be free to hook up with other people if we wanted to. But it was hard to think straight with Zack sitting right there, flicking his tongue in the V between his index and middle fingers.

"All right," I said. "I should probably go."

She smiled sadly and nodded. But then she leaned a little closer.

"Hey, Brendan."

And then, without any warning at all, she lifted her shirt and bra and showed me her boobs, which filled the entire laptop screen. It happened and then it was over. The shirt came back down and I was looking at her face again as she blew me a kiss.

"Good night, baby."

Zack was punching the air with both hands, silently screaming the word *Yes!* over and over, like he'd just scored a goal.

"Thanks," I said. "You have a good night, too."

It was hard to stay mad at Zack. He acted totally innocent, like his eavesdropping on my private conversation was totally hilarious and not creepy at all, a great bonding experience for both of us. And he was really complimentary about Becca and very excited about her pink nipples, which he compared to *little eraser nubs.*

"Why would you want to break up with a girl like that?" he asked me.

"Because I want a clean slate."

"Just keep her on the hook. I mean, Jesus, dude. She's watching how-to blowjob videos on YouTube. That'll spice up your Christmas vacation."

"Maybe you have a point."

"Hey," he said. "If you don't want her, send her my way. I'll give her some expert instruction."

The rest of the night was kind of a bust. Zack had been invited to an off-campus house party by a friend of his older brother, and it turned out to be a lot farther away than we thought. It took us about a half hour to walk there, and the party was already breaking up when we arrived. Somebody said there was a kegger a couple of blocks away, but we couldn't find it, so we ended up trudging all the way back to the dorm.

It was on the early side, but we were both pretty exhausted. We brushed our teeth together in the bathroom, then headed back to our room, where we stripped down to our boxers and got into bed. It was like having a twin brother.

I lay there for a while in the dark, thinking that college was probably going to be okay. I knew I'd lucked out on the roommate front, and I was grateful for that. I mean, what if I'd gotten stuck with someone like Sanjay, a kid I had nothing in common with? It would've sucked, having a nerd tagging along everywhere I went, being forced to eat with him and pretend to admire his architectural drawings and superhuman test scores. It was so much easier with Zack, a bro who partied and laughed at the same stupid shit I did. I knew my mother would have preferred Sanjay, but she wasn't the one who had to live with him.

"Oh shit," I muttered.

"What?" mumbled Zack.

"I forgot to text my mom."

I got out of bed, found my phone, and wrote, *College is awesome!!!* I figured she was probably wide awake at home, wondering how I was doing. She'd been talking a lot about how sad she'd be after I left, and how hard it would be to get used to living in an empty house.

"No offense," Zack said, when I'd climbed back into my bed, "but your mom is pretty hot."

"Dude," I said. "Seriously. This is not an appropriate subject of conversation."

"I'm just saying," he said. "She's kind of a MILF, don't you think?"

This wasn't the first time one of my friends had said this about my mom. She still dressed kinda young, and had a pretty good body for a woman her age. But she was my mom, and I didn't like to think about her in those terms.

"What about your mom?" I said. "Is she a MILF?"

"My mom's dead," he said, in this really sad voice. "I miss her so much."

"Oh shit." I sat up in bed. "I'm really sorry."

"Dude," he said, laughing at my sadness. "I'm just fucking with you. My mom's alive and well. But she is definitely not a MILF."

# Department of Aging

When Eve took inventory of her life, her job stood out as the conspicuous bright spot, the sole arena in which she judged herself a success. She was executive director of the Haddington Senior Center, a thriving facility that provided an impressive array of services to the town's older residents. The Center was not only a source of companionship, mental stimulation, and age-appropriate exercise for the elderly; it was also a place where low-income seniors could come to eat a federally subsidized meal and then get their blood pressure checked by a nurse and their problem toenails trimmed by a kindhearted podiatrist. The Center ferried a busload of clients to Market Basket twice a week, and also acted as a clearinghouse for handymen, landscapers, home health aides, and the like, referring trusted local businesses to older residents in need of assistance. Eve was proud of the work she did and, unlike a lot of people she knew, never had to ask herself what the point was, or wonder if she should be doing something a little more important with her life.

When she thought about how much she liked her job, she tended to focus on activities like chair yoga, memoir-writing workshops, and Thursday afternoon karaoke. What she didn't think about were situations like *this*, when it fell on her to deliver bad news to people who already had enough trouble in their lives.

"Thank you for coming on such short notice," she began, smil-

ing in spite of herself at George Rafferty, whom she'd clearly interrupted in the middle of some filthy plumbing job. There was a smear
of grease on his face, and the knees of his work pants were darkened with what looked like years of shiny, caked-on grime. He'd
once come to Eve's house at six a.m. on Thanksgiving morning to fix
an overflowing toilet, which only made the conversation they were
about to have that much more difficult. "I know it's inconvenient."

George didn't smile back. He was a stocky, squinty guy with
rust-colored hair, a rusty beard flecked with gray, and an air of permanent impatience, as if there was always something more urgent he
needed to be attending to. He glanced apprehensively at his eighty-
two-year-old father, who was sitting beside him on the couch, making loud smacking noises with his lips.

"What'd he do this time?"

Eve heard the wariness in his voice. The last time George had been
summoned to the Center in the middle of the day, his father had
somehow managed, by standing on his seat, to urinate out the window of the Elderbus on the way home from the supermarket. It was
an impressive feat for a man his age, even if, as eyewitnesses claimed,
he'd only been partially successful.

"Mr. Rafferty?" Eve turned to the older man, who was watching
her with a vague, placid expression. "Do you mind telling your son
what happened after lunch?"

Roy Rafferty snapped to attention.

"Lunch?" he said. "Is it time for lunch?"

"You already had lunch," Eve reminded him. "We're talking about
what happened when it was over. The reason you got in trouble."

"Oh." The old man's face tightened into a scowl of futile concentration. He was one of Eve's favorites, a longtime regular at the Center, one of those chatty, friendly guys who moved through life like
a politician running for reelection, shaking everyone's hand, always
asking after the grandkids. He'd been healthy and lucid up until
about six months ago, when his wife died of a massive stroke. His
decline since then had been rapid and alarming.

"What happened?" he asked. "Did I do something wrong?"

"You went in the ladies' room again."

"Oh, shit." George stared at his father with a mix of pity and exasperation. "Jesus Christ, Dad. We talked about this. You have to stay out of the ladies' room."

Roy hung his head like a schoolboy. Eve knew his whole life story, or at least the highlights. He'd fought in Korea, and had come home with a Purple Heart and an urge to make up for lost time. Within six months, he'd married his high school sweetheart and taken over the family plumbing business, Rafferty & Son, which he ran for the next forty-five years, before handing it off to George. He and Joan had raised four kids, the eldest of whom—Nick, a high school vice principal—had died in his early fifties of pancreatic cancer. Eve had gone to the funeral.

"Mr. Rafferty," she said. "Do you remember what happened in the ladies' room?"

"I'm not supposed to go in there," he said.

"That's right," she told him. "It's off-limits for men."

"Okay," George said briskly. "We're all agreed on that. Now could you tell me what he did? I gotta get back to work."

"I'd like you to hear it from your father," Eve told him.

"My father can't remember!" George snapped. "He probably doesn't know what he had for lunch."

Eve let that hang in the air for a few seconds. It helped to have him say it out loud.

"Your father was exposing himself." She decided to leave it at that, to not specify that he was masturbating, or that he'd invited poor Evelyn Gerardi, who wheeled an oxygen tank around everywhere she went, to *come and get it*. At least he'd called her *sweetheart*.

"Oh, God." George didn't look surprised. "That's not good."

"Some of the ladies were very upset."

"I bet."

Eve turned from the son to the father. She really hated this part of her job.

31

"Mr. Rafferty, I speak for the whole staff when I say that I've enjoyed your company over the years. You've been so kind and considerate to so many people, and everybody likes you. But I'm afraid you won't be able to come here anymore. We can't allow it. I'm sorry."

"What?" George looked shocked. "You're kicking him out?"

"I don't have a choice. This is a community center. Your father needs a nursing home."

"Can't you give him one more chance?"

"We already did that," she said. "George, this isn't going to get better. You know that, right?"

"But he loves it here. This place is all he has left."

"I'm not sure you understand." Eve's voice was soft but firm. "Your father was touching himself and saying some very inappropriate things. One of the witnesses wanted to call the police and file charges. It was all I could do to calm everyone down and let me handle it like this."

George closed his eyes and nodded slowly. He must've known this moment was coming.

"What am I supposed to do? I can't watch him all day. My wife's getting chemo. She's in bad shape."

"I'm sorry." Eve had heard about the recurrence of Lorraine Rafferty's cancer. That was the kind of news that spread quickly at the Senior Center. "I don't know what to say."

"She's a fighter," he said, but there wasn't a lot of conviction in his voice. "It's in her lungs and liver."

"Oh, God. It must be really hard on you."

"Our daughter's taking the semester off. To watch her mother die." He laughed at the sheer awfulness of it all. "And now I gotta deal with this shit?"

He glanced at his father, who was sitting patiently on the couch, humming to himself, as if he were waiting for his number to be called at the DMV.

"There are resources available for people like your dad," Eve

32

explained. "We have a social worker on staff who can talk you through your options."

No one spoke for a while. George reached out and took his father's hand. The old man didn't seem to notice.

"It just sucks," George said. "I hate to see him like this."

"He's a good man." Even as she said this, Eve realized how rude it was to refer to Roy Rafferty in the third person, so she addressed him directly. "You're a good man, Roy. We're going to miss you."

Roy Rafferty looked at Eve and nodded, as if he understood what she was saying and appreciated the kindness.

"Okey dokey," he said. "How about we get some lunch?"

This happened on a sleepy Friday afternoon at the tail end of summer, no meetings or activities scheduled for the rest of the day. After the Raffertys left, Eve shut her office door and turned off the light. Then she sat down at her desk and wept.

It was hard sometimes, dealing with old people, having to cast out the unfortunate souls who could no longer control their bladders or bowels, trying to reassure the ones who couldn't locate their cars in the parking lot, or remember their home address. It was hard to hear about their scary diagnoses and chronic ailments, to attend the funerals of so many people she'd grown fond of, or at least gotten used to. And it was hard to think about her own life, rushing by so quickly, speeding down the same road.

It didn't help that she was staring into the abyss of Labor Day weekend, three blank, desolate squares on her calendar. She'd been so preoccupied by the logistics of getting Brendan off to school that she hadn't even thought about trying to make plans until yesterday. First she'd called Jane Rosen—her most reliable dinner and movie and walk-around-the-reservoir companion—only to learn that Jane and Dave had made a spur-of-the-moment decision to get out of town. They were coping with empty nest issues of their own—they'd just dropped off their twin daughters at Duke and Vanderbilt—and thought that a couple of days at an inn on Lake Champlain might rekindle the romance in their marriage.

*I'm terrified,* Jane had confided. *What if there's no spark? What if we have nothing to talk about? What are we supposed to do then?*

Eve did her best to be a good listener and a supportive friend—she owed Jane at least that much, having subjected her to countless heartbroken soliloquies during the darkest days of her own separation and divorce—but it hadn't been easy. Jane was having second thoughts about a nightgown she'd bought, pale pink and diaphanous, very pretty, but maybe not the most flattering shade for her skin tone, especially with the hot flashes coming so frequently. And sex made her so sweaty these days, though Dave insisted that he didn't mind. *I guess I'm not feeling very attractive,* she confessed. Eve murmured encouragement, reminding Jane that she was still beautiful and that Dave adored her, but it took all the restraint she possessed not to burst into laughter and say, *Are you kidding me? That's your problem? You sweat when your husband fucks you?*

After Jane, she tried the rest of her usual suspects—Peggy, the mother of Brendan's friend Wade; Liza, who'd been divorced and single even longer than Eve; and Jeanine Foley, her old college roommate—but no one was available on such short notice. Her only real alternative was to drive down to New Jersey and spend a couple of days with her widowed mother and never-married sister, who were living together in the house where Eve had spent her childhood. She was overdue for a visit, but it was always so exhausting to see them—they bickered constantly, like an old married couple—and she just didn't have the patience right now.

Eve didn't cry for long. She'd never liked feeling sorry for herself, and knew there were worse fates to endure than three sunny days with nothing in particular to do. She thought of George Rafferty, with his dying wife and brain-addled father, and knew that he would have traded places with her in a heartbeat.

*Enough of this bullshit,* she told herself. *You have nothing to cry about.* Unfortunately, she hadn't quite pulled herself together when

Amanda Olney, the Center's newest employee, opened the door and poked her head into the office.

"Quick question," she began, and then froze, taking a moment to register the dimness of the room and her boss's forlorn posture. "Are you okay?"

"I'm fine." Eve sniffled, dabbing at her nose with a crumpled tissue. "Allergy season."

Amanda opened the door a little wider. She was short and buxom, with Cleopatra bangs and multiple lurid tattoos that she made no effort to conceal, despite the disparaging comments and disgusted head shakes they never failed to elicit from the old folks. They were particularly horrified by the cobra winding its way around her left calf and shin, its forked tongue flicking across her kneecap.

"Can I help you with something?" Eve inquired.

Amanda hesitated, overcome by a sudden shyness.

"It's not about work," she explained. "I was just wondering if you were doing anything tonight. I thought maybe, if you were free, we could get a glass of wine or something?"

Eve was touched, despite her irritation. She liked Amanda and could see that it had taken some courage for her to reach out like this, however awkwardly. She was fresh out of grad school, recently broken up with a longtime boyfriend, and probably a little lonely, looking for mentorship and reassurance. But the first lesson Eve needed to teach her was that she was an employee, not a friend. There was a boundary between them that needed to be respected.

"I have other plans," she said. "But thank you."

"No problem." Amanda shrugged, as if she'd suspected as much. "Sorry to bother you."

"Not at all," Eve told her. "Have a nice weekend."

Her evening at home passed pleasantly enough, rolling along the usual track. First stop, dinner (Greek salad, hummus, pita), followed by way too much Facebook (a problem she was going to have to deal with), a couple of glasses of wine, and three episodes of *Friends* on

35

Netflix (another problem, though she figured it would eventually fix itself, once she made it through all ten seasons). She kept meaning to start *The Wire* or *Breaking Bad*, but the time never seemed right to plunge into something so dark and serious. It was the same with books, always easier to pick up something breezy and upbeat than to crack open the copy of *Middlemarch* that had been squatting on her nightstand for the past nine months, a Christmas gift from her English professor cousin, Donna, who'd insisted that it was *deceptively readable*, whatever that meant.

Aside from the shock of Brendan's absence—still fresh and omnipresent—the only real shadow on her mood was a faint but lingering sense of regret that she hadn't accepted Amanda's invitation. A drink and some conversation would have been nice, a little way station between work and home. It was true that she had an unwritten policy of not socializing with her staff, but that was more a preference than a hard-and-fast rule, based as much on a lack of chemistry with her colleagues (most of whom were married, and even more of whom were dull) as it was on some nebulous sense of propriety. In any case, it was a policy she probably needed to rethink, now that she was retired from parenting and had more than enough time to herself. At this point in her life, she couldn't afford to be ruling out potential new friends on a technicality.

The phone rang while she was brushing her teeth, and the sound made her heart leap with pleasure—*It's Brendan!* But when she hurried into the bedroom, wearing only pajama bottoms—because she couldn't find the top, and what difference did it make?—she saw that it wasn't her son at all.

"Ted?"

"Hey, I hope I didn't wake you."

"I'm awake. Is everything okay?"

"Just thought I'd check in. See how you're holding up. Hard to believe our little boy's in college, huh?"

*Whose little boy?* she thought, a reflex from angrier days. But it was true. Their little boy was all grown up.

"He seems happy there," she said. "I think he really likes his room-mate."

"Yeah, Zack." Ted chuckled like he was in on the joke. "I just talked to him. Seems like a good kid."

"You talked to Zack?"

"Just for a minute. Little while ago. I called Brendan, and he passed the phone to Zack."

That was Ted all over. Mr. Glad-to-Meet-You. Always looking for the next stranger to charm.

"How's he doing?"

"Zack?"

"No, Brendan."

"Pretty good." Ted paused, recalibrating his response. "Pretty wasted, actually. But I guess that's a given your first weekend at college."

"I hope it's not gonna be a problem."

"College kids drink a lot. I know I did." He sounded proud of himself. "I can barely remember sophomore year."

"What a great role model."

"Don't worry about Brendan. He's got a good head on his shoulders."

"I hope so." She wanted to tell him about the awful thing he'd said to Becca the other day, but she heard a child screaming on Ted's end, and a woman's soothing voice, and it didn't seem like the right time to get into it. "I really miss him."

"He misses you, too. You know that, right?"

"It's hard to tell sometimes."

"Eve," he said. "Brendan really loves you. He just doesn't always know how to communicate."

She wanted to believe this, and she was grateful to Ted for saying it out loud. His guilty conscience had made him a lot nicer than he used to be.

"What about you?" she asked. The crying had subsided for the moment. "Everything okay?"

"Up and down. Jon-Jon likes his new school. And the gluten-free diet seems to be helping a little."

Jon-Jon was Ted's four-year-old autistic son, an adorable child with severe behavioral problems. When Eve first heard about the diagnosis, she'd reacted uncharitably, considering it a form of karmic justice for Ted and his bad-girl wife, Bethany. How ironic and gratifying it had seemed at the time to see their Casual Encounter disrupted by reality. But they hadn't cracked under pressure the way she'd expected. Instead the ordeal had brought out the best in them. They were devoted to their son, totally immersed in the minutiae of his care. Ted had become an amateur expert on cutting-edge autism therapies. Bethany had quit her job and gone back to school for a master's in Special Ed. All this rising to the occasion had made it hard for Eve to sustain the hatred and contempt she'd felt for them in the immediate aftermath of her divorce.

"That's good," she said, glancing down at her bare chest. The room was chillier than she'd realized, and her nipples were hard, which made her remember how much Ted had appreciated her breasts. *They're perfect,* he used to tell her, not that it mattered much in the end. *Absolutely perfect.* "Maybe we should all stop eating gluten. Everybody who gives it up goes around telling everybody else how great they feel."

"That's because eating it made them sick."

"I guess."

The screaming started up again, louder than before, and Eve found herself wincing in sympathetic distress. Brendan had told her that Jon-Jon's tantrums could be pretty terrifying.

"All right," he sighed. "I better go deal with this. Have a good night, okay?"

"You too." She almost said *honey*, a reflex from a different era of her past. "Thanks for calling."

Eve was exhausted, but she stayed up well past midnight, playing Words with Friends against a random opponent, though that was just an excuse to keep her eyes open. What she was really doing was waiting for a message from Brendan. Over the summer he'd promised to keep in touch by sending her at least one text every single day. He was free to send more if he felt like it, or to call her, or even to arrange a Skype session if he was especially homesick. But one text per day was the agreed-upon minimum.

He'd kept his word for the past three days, texting her exactly once every twenty-four hours, even if his messages all said pretty much the same thing: *College is awesome!!!* (Tuesday); *Another AWE-SOME day!!* (Wednesday); and *Still totally awesome!* (yesterday). She was happy for him—though slightly concerned by the steady decline in the number of exclamation points he used—and grateful not to have been completely forgotten in the midst of all that awesomeness.

But no text had arrived today. It was Friday, of course, and he was drunk, as Ted had just informed her, so there was her explanation. But still—was he really going to break his promise on Day Four? Was he that irresponsible? She could have contacted him, of course, just typed out a quick *miss you xxoo*, and waited for him to respond, but that wasn't the deal. The deal was that he would reach out to her, and she wanted him to do it of his own free will, without any badgering, because he loved her and wanted to include her in his life. But she already knew, long before her match with Heather0007 was over (a decisive victory for Eve), that she was kidding herself. He wasn't going to text her tonight, and probably not tomorrow night, either. He just wasn't that kind of kid, the kind who'd think about his mother while he was out having a good time with his friends, or flirting with a pretty girl from down the hall. From now on, she'd hear from him if and when he felt like it—probably when he needed something—and she'd be lucky if it was once a week.

She must have dozed off with the phone still in her hand, because the vibration of the arriving message shocked her awake. *Thank God,* she thought, lurching upright, squinting groggily at the blurred and blinding screen, blinking hard to get the words into focus.

*U r my MILF! Send me a naked pic!! I want to cum on those big floppy tits!!!*

For a second or two, she was deeply disturbed, unable to understand why Brendan would text her something so disgusting, no matter how drunk he was. It just didn't seem possible. *Big floppy tits?* But then she double-checked, and saw, to her immense relief, that the text had come from a cellphone number she didn't recognize. It was just some anonymous jerk, a stupid prank she wouldn't even remember in the morning.

# Orientation

Those first few days of school, before the grind of classes started up, were pretty awesome. They had tons of activities for the freshmen, including this Welcome-to-BSU Field Day on the main quad with tug-o'-war and ring toss, water balloons and a Slip 'N Slide, all kinds of summer camp shit like that. And the weather was beautiful, which meant that lots of hot girls were wearing cutoffs and bikini tops, and more of them than I'd expected had tattoos that were good conversation starters. Some of the less hot girls stripped down too, and everybody tried to be cool about it, because body image and all that. Zack and I took our shirts off, because we'd both been working out over the summer and why wouldn't you, if you were ripped?

Mostly those days were about me and Zack. We did everything together, from the moment we woke up to the moment we crashed. One afternoon we hit the gym and did some lifting. We could both bench one eighty, but Zack could do five reps, and I could only make it to four. The day after that we checked out the climbing wall in the Student Center, but we'd gotten good and baked beforehand, so neither of us could manage a route higher than a 5.6.

It was pretty scary once you made it halfway up the wall, clinging to those knobby bolted-on handholds like your life depended on it, stuck in place until your forearms started to quiver and you had no choice but to reach for something higher. One time I lost my grip about thirty feet up. I fell like Humpty Dumpty, my arms swimming through the air, until the auto belay kicked in, the harness crushing my ballsack as it yanked against gravity. I was suspended up there for a few painful seconds, dangling like a limp dick until I floated slowly back to earth. Zack thought it was hilarious.

"You shrieked like a little bitch! I bet the whole school heard you!"

"Fuck you," I said. My chest felt hollow and my legs were shaky, and I guess he could hear it in my voice.

"I'm only kidding, bro." He clapped me on the shoulder, more gently than I would have expected. "Let's get some lunch."

Everybody had to meet their academic advisor at some point during Orientation Week to finalize their schedule and get one last pep talk about college. My guy was Devin Torborg from the Anthropology Department. I made the mistake of calling him "Professor," which was apparently a sore subject.

"Technically I'm an instructor," he explained, running his hand through his stringy hair, which looked like it hadn't been washed in a while. He had these little round eyeglasses like John Lennon, and his eyes were baggy and tired behind the smudged lenses. "Not currently on the tenure track. But I prefer 'Devin' anyway." He gave this sad little shrug and glanced at the folder on his desk. "So. Brendan Fletcher. This must be an exciting time for you. The beginning of a great . . ."

His voice trailed off, and he scowled like he couldn't remember the next word.

"Adventure," I said, helping him out.

"Ah," he said. "You're an optimist."

He opened the folder and examined the single sheet of paper lying inside. It must have listed my high school GPA and test scores and whatnot. He slid two fingers in between his face and his glasses and gave his left eyelid a thorough massage, clockwise first, then reverse.

"So tell me, Brendan." He paused to make a run at the other eye, working pretty hard on the loose skin, tugging it up and down and sideways. "What do you want from college?"

I knew I couldn't tell him the truth, which was that I wanted to party as much as possible and do the bare minimum of studying, but I didn't have a lie handy, so I just kind of stammered for a while.

"I . . . I . . . well, that's . . . you know. Good question. Just a degree, I guess."

"A degree in what?"

"Econ. Possibly. If I can survive the math requirements."

"Why Econ?"

"You know. So I can get a job when I graduate."

"What kind of job?"

"Any kind. Long as it pays six figures. I mean, maybe not right away, but pretty soon. That's my main goal."

He looked impressed, but only in a sarcastic way. "Good luck with that."

Then we went over my schedule, which wasn't very complicated. I had to take Econ 101, and also get the required freshman Writing and Math classes out of the way. That left room for just one elective, which I had narrowed down to either Basic Concepts in Accounting or Intro to Statistics, neither of which sounded all that exciting.

"That's one strategy," he said. "You could sign up for a practical class like that and learn something useful and so forth. But my advice would be to stretch a little, try something new and impractical, maybe even a little off-the-wall. Learn a language. Take a poetry class. Study African History or Linguistics or Drawing. There's a lecture class on Polytheism that you might want to check out. Taught by yours truly." He smiled, kind of hopelessly. "You never know. It might change your life, or at least open up some new avenues for exploration."

I didn't know what Polytheism was, and I honestly didn't give a shit. But I didn't want to hurt his feelings, so I pretended to think it over.

"Maybe next semester," I said. "I'll probably just stick to Stats this time around."

"All right. Your call." He checked the time on his phone. "What about extracurriculars? Any ideas about that? Any clubs or teams or community service organizations?"

"I'm hoping to go Greek next year," I told him. "I'm not sure which fraternity, though."

"I wouldn't know about that," he said. "Where I did my under-grad work they didn't allow frats."

I had the feeling he wanted me to ask where that was, but I didn't take the bait. Especially since he didn't seem all that impressive to me anyway, a grungy non-professor in a shithole of a basement office, wearing a Journey T-shirt under his tweed jacket, which I guess I was supposed to find amusing.

"That must've sucked," I said.

"Not at all," he replied. "I certainly didn't miss them."

Then we just sat there for a few more seconds, staring at each other. I could hear singing out on the quad, an a cappella group doing a pretty cool version of "Livin' on a Prayer." Somebody had a great falsetto. I thought it might be fun to be in a group like that, if I could sing and it wasn't so gay.

"Are we done?" I asked.

He nodded and I stood up. As I was heading for the door, he called after me.

"Brendan," he said. "You know about consent, right?"

"Excuse me?"

"It's a pretty simple concept. No means no. And an intoxicated person can't consent to sexual activity. You understand that, right?"

"Yeah," I said. "I'm not an idiot."

"All right, then. Have a great semester."

Zack was meeting with his own advisor, so I killed some time at the Activities Fair on my way back to the room. It was crowded, dozens and dozens of tables set up under a huge circus tent, a good chunk of the freshman class milling around. Apparently, anybody could start a club and get funding from the university. There were Beekeepers, Hula Hoopers, Paintballers, Vegans, Future Real Estate Professionals, Brothers and Sisters in Christ, Atheists United, Triathletes, Stroke Victims, Cancer Survivors, Bicycle Mechanics, Slavic Folk Dancers.

You could ride horses, row crew, play rugby, boycott Israel, learn to juggle or knit. Some of the people behind the tables were in costume—the Quidditch Club officers carried brooms and sported fake Harry Potter glasses, and one of the volunteers for the Muslim Student Union wore a full burka, or whatever they called it—and others just looked exactly like what their names said they were: Queer People of Color, Dungeons and Dragons Enthusiasts, Cannabis Reform Coalition, League of Young Conservatives, Bearded Hipster Alliance. I guess I must have spaced out a little, because I didn't even know where I was standing when the girl behind a table spoke to me.

"Hey," she said. "What's your name?"

"Excuse me?"

She laughed in a way that made me feel like she already knew me and liked me.

"It's not a trick question." She looked like a farm girl, freckles and a blond ponytail, and big shoulders, almost like a guy. "You know your name, right?"

"I used to," I said. "But I had a bunch of concussions last year."

She liked that, too, enough that she volunteered for a high five, which I delivered very gently, basically just pressing my palm against hers, earning a few more points in the process. I was a couple of inches taller than she was, but our hands were the same size.

"I'm Amber," she said. "Nice to meet you."

"Brendan."

"Do you know someone on the spectrum, Brendan?"

That was when I looked at the sign on her table: *Autism Awareness Network.*

"No, I—"

I was about to tell her that I'd just stopped there at random when two things occurred to me. The first was that I did know someone on the spectrum, and the second was that this girl was really pretty. I hadn't noticed at first, because I was so distracted by her shoulders.

"I mean, yeah," I said. "My half brother."

She nodded, as if she'd expected as much.

"My little brother, too." She smiled at the thought of him. "He's obsessed with Matchbox cars. It's pretty much all he cares about. Yesterday he sent me a text with a picture of two of them. Nothing else. Just two little cars."

She thought this was adorable, though it seemed kind of pathetic to me.

"Mine doesn't talk much," I said. "He just has these scary tantrums about nothing. We don't even know what he's screaming about."

"What's his name?"

"Jonathan. But we call him Jon-Jon."

"That's cute."

I agreed, mostly because she seemed so nice and had such a positive attitude. The truth was, nothing about Jon-Jon was cute. It was awful to watch him get all red-faced with rage and frustration, and not know how to help him.

"Do you have a picture of him?" she asked.

I shook my head. It had never occurred to me to take a picture of Jon-Jon.

"This is Benjy." She handed me her phone. The screensaver was a photo of Amber and her brother on the beach. I'd expected him to be a little kid, but he was a skinny teenager with an intense, almost angry expression, only a year or two younger than she was. She was wearing a navy blue one-piece bathing suit in the picture, the no-nonsense kind competitive swimmers wear. Her body was thick and strong-looking, not usually what I went for, but sexy in a way I hadn't expected.

"You can give that back now," she said, but not in a pissed-off way.

"You a swimmer?"

"In high school. But not anymore. Here I just play softball."

"Cool," I said. "What position?"

"Pitcher."

She tried to look humble about it, but I could see she was proud.

"You know what?" I said. "You look like a pitcher."

46

"Why?" She pretended to take offense. "Because of my massive shoulders?"

"I didn't say that."

"It's okay." She struck a bodybuilder pose, turning sideways and flexing her arm. "I worked hard for these muscles. And I do have a wicked fastball, if I say so myself. You should come watch us. We're pretty good."

"Maybe I will."

She gave me a look, like I was probably full of shit. But it was kind of flirty, too.

"We're not all dykes, you know."

"I never said—"

"I'm just kidding," she said. "A few of us are bi."

I must have looked shocked, because she laughed this big-hearted laugh and slapped me on the arm as a nervous-looking girl stepped up to the table.

"It was nice meeting you," she said, stepping toward the new arrival. "You should come to one of our meetings. Third Thursday of every month."

That night I got epically shitfaced. Zack and I pregamed with vodka, and then we visited a bunch of room parties in Einstein, wandering from one to the next like it was Halloween, taking a bong hit here and a shot of Jager there, a slice of pizza in a room that belonged to a skinny white dude named Evan who was supposedly a great rapper. There was dancing in a room where two girls named Kayla lived—Hot Kayla and Less-Hot Kayla—and a foosball tournament in the fifth-floor lounge.

At Will and Rico's, I drank some jungle juice that really knocked me on my ass. My father called when I was there, the first time I'd heard from him since I arrived at BSU. I must not have been making much sense, because Zack grabbed the phone out of my hand and started chatting with him like they were old buddies. All I remember after that was puking in the bathroom, and bumping into that douchebag Sanjay on my way out. He was wearing pajamas and a plaid robe, and carrying a little bucket with all his toiletries in it.

"You okay?" he asked. "You don't look so—"

"I'm fine," I said, giving my mouth one last wipe. "Ready for round two."

I went back to the room to change my shirt, but I guess I must have crashed, because the next thing I knew it was three in the morning and Zack was stumbling around in the dark, totally wasted, telling me that he'd tried to hook up with Less-Hot Kayla, but she wasn't into it, which was fine, because he wasn't really into it, either.

"I mean, if it was Hot Kayla, that would be another story, right?"

After a while he got into bed, and it was quiet again, but I couldn't get back to sleep. I was thinking about maybe getting up and seeing if anybody was still awake when Zack started jerking off. I could tell he was trying to be quiet, but our beds were pretty close together.

"Dude," I said. "Seriously?"

"Oh shit," he said. "I thought you were asleep."

"Nope. Wide awake."

"You want me to stop?"

"Nah, it's okay. Just, like, hurry it up, okay?"

I don't know how long it took after that. Maybe just a few minutes, but it felt like a long time, long enough that I said fuck it, and decided to join the party. I thought about Becca for a while, but she was already far away, almost unreal. And then I tried the two Kaylas, imagining a threeway in their room, which was kind of interesting, but only up to a point. It was Amber from the Autism Awareness Network who got me across the finish line. And the weird thing was, we weren't even doing anything. She was just standing on the beach in her one-piece bathing suit, smiling at me with her pretty face and those big shoulders, and for some reason that was enough.

"G'night," Zack said, in this soft, peaceful voice when he was finished.

"Night, bro," I said, floating on the same cloud that he was. "Catch you in the morning."

# Live and Learn

Suffering from a mild, not entirely unpleasant case of back-to-school jitters, Eve wandered through the Humanities Building of Eastern Community College, searching for Room 213. She was relieved to pass a number of "nontraditional students" like herself in the corridors, some of them even older than she was.

The chairs in her classroom had been arranged in a circle, group-therapy style. Eve chose one and sat down, not noticing until it was too late that some bored artisan had carved the words *I AM SO HORNY* into the desktop, and then highlighted the incisions with a red marker. She covered the graffiti with her brand-new notebook, and opened it to the first page. It was a heartening sight, all that blank white space waiting to be filled, the fresh start she'd been hoping for.

Once she was settled, she looked up and gave a friendly nod to the handful of students who'd arrived even earlier than she had. Only one nodded back, a worried-looking black man who appeared to be in his early thirties. The other three were staring at their phones, unaware that a greeting had been extended, let alone that they'd missed a chance to respond.

Eve already had a master's in Social Work, which she'd earned by attending night classes for four long years back when Brendan was in elementary school. Ted's resentment of her absences, and the parental responsibilities they shifted onto his shoulders, had been one of the major tensions in their marriage. His subsequent lack of interest in her work—his refusal to take it seriously—had been another, though that seemed mostly ironic in retrospect, now that he was raising an autistic child and had to rely on all sorts of specialists in the caring professions.

In any case, she didn't need another advanced degree, and had no interest in polishing her résumé. Her decision to return to school was purely personal. She wanted to read and think and reconnect with her collegiate self, which had been so much more open and fluid and hopeful than the versions that had succeeded it. And it was nice to have a reason to escape the empty house twice a week without having to convince someone else to join her.

The class she'd signed up for was called "Gender and Society: A Critical Perspective," a writing-intensive seminar that met on Tuesday and Thursday evenings from seven thirty to nine. She had no special interest in the topic; it was actually her third choice, after "Vegans vs. Carnivores: The Ethics of Sustainable Eating," and "From Jane Austen to *Downton Abbey*: The English Country House in Fiction and Film," both of which were full. But the class itself wasn't the point. The important thing was that she was here, trying something different, meeting new people, making her world bigger instead of hunkering down, disappearing into her own solitude.

At seven thirty on the dot, a tall, striking woman in a black pencil skirt and stiletto heels breezed through the door, her eyes widening in faux astonishment at the sight of the assembled students, as if this were a surprise party in her honor.

"Well, hello there," she said, in a throaty, oddly seductive voice. She was slender and athletic-looking, with narrow hips and attention-grabbing breasts bulging against the fabric of her tailored blouse. "I'm Dr. Margo Fairchild, adjunct professor." She took a moment to let that sink in. "In case you're unfamiliar with academic terminology, *adjunct* is another word for *very badly paid.*"

A handful of students, Eve included, chuckled obligingly as Dr. Fairchild entered the circle and sat down, smoothing her skirt and crossing her enviably muscled legs at the ankles.

"Let's wait a minute or two for the stragglers," she said, languidly tucking a strand of dark hair behind her ear. "There are always a few lost souls on opening day."

It was tough to guess the professor's age—anywhere between thirty and forty-five, Eve thought—though her face seemed a little older than her body. Even that was open to debate, however, because of the prodigious amount of makeup she wore, a thick, almost theatrical coat of expertly applied cosmetics that seemed more appropriate for a beauty pageant runway than a community college classroom. Eve realized that she'd been expecting someone a little more like her cousin Donna, a no-nonsense scholar who wore her graying hair in a thick braid and had a different North Face pullover for every day of the week.

Her fellow students were an impressively diverse bunch—half college kids, half older people (including a spry lady in her eighties), two black men (one of whom turned out to be Nigerian), one black woman, a Chinese immigrant man with an indecipherable accent, a young woman in a Muslim headscarf, one really cute undergraduate boy with a skateboard, and a butch woman in biker gear, complete with a black leather vest and a motorcycle helmet resting on the floor between her scuffed engineer boots. Eve was surprised to note that twelve of the twenty students were male, including a few middle-aged white guys who didn't strike her as natural candidates for a class in which students would be required to "write autobiographically and analytically about their own problematic experiences on the gender spectrum, with special emphasis on the social construction of identity, the persistence of sexism in a 'post-feminist' culture, and the subversion of heteronormative discourse by LGBTQIA voices." But this small mystery was cleared up as soon as they got started, when Professor Fairchild asked everyone to introduce themselves and talk about their reasons for enrolling in the class.

"My name's Russ," said the first guy to speak. He was wearing a Red Sox cap and a Bruins T-shirt that seemed to have been shrink-wrapped around his beer gut. "I was supposed to be in Briggsy's class, but that got, uh . . . canceled, and this was the only other writing class in the time slot, so . . ."

"Poor Hal," said Professor Fairchild, and several heads bobbed in melancholy assent. "He was such a nice person."

There turned out to be three other transfers from the same class, "The Modern Coliseum: Sports in Contemporary Society," which was apparently one of the most popular course offerings at ECC. It had been taught by Hal Briggs, a former sportswriter for the *Herald*, who had just died of a heart attack at a Labor Day barbecue, right in front of his wife, kids, and neighbors. Eve had seen his obituary in the newspaper.

"He was too young," said Professor Fairchild. "Only forty-nine."

"Were you there?" asked a bearded guy named Barry, who said he owned a sports bar in Waxford. "At the cookout?"

"No, thank God." The professor twirled a lock of hair around her index finger, as if she were still in junior high. "Briggsy and I were just colleagues. We used to play in a faculty basketball league on Sunday mornings." The memory made her smile. "He had the ugliest jump shot I ever saw."

"Was that a coed league?" asked Dumell, the black guy with the worried expression.

"I'm glad you asked that," said the professor. "That's exactly the sort of assumption our class is going to examine throughout the semester. The way our preconceptions about gender condition our responses to the social world. But I think we need to unpack your question."

"What's that mean?"

"It means I'd like you to articulate the question behind your question. In other words, what are you *really* asking?"

"Okay. I get it." Dumell nodded uncertainly. He looked a little more worried than before. "Uh, were there other ladies besides you on the team?"

Professor Fairchild had to give this some thought. "What if I told you that our players ranged widely across the gender spectrum? Would that be a satisfactory answer to your question?"

"I guess," Dumell said. "But it's kinda complicated, don't you think?"

"I do," said the professor. "And rightly so. Because there's nothing simple about gender. Nothing natural. It's an ideological minefield that we walk through every minute of every day. And that's what this class is about. How to walk through the minefield without hurting anyone's feelings or blowing yourself up."

When class was dismissed, Eve headed out of the building with Barry, the bearded bar owner, tagging along beside her, totally uninvited. They'd been randomly paired off for an in-class exercise, and had spent the better part of the past hour exchanging "gender histories," focusing, per the professor's instructions, on moments of gender-related confusion, doubt, and/or shame.

"That was pretty intense," he said. "I have ex-wives who don't know me as well as you do."

Eve didn't say so, but she doubted Barry's ex-wives would have complained about not knowing him well enough. He was a what-you-see-is-what-you-get sort of guy, a blustery jerk who began his conversation by insisting that he'd never in his life experienced a single moment of confusion, doubt, or shame in relation to his gender identity. The story of Barry's life, as narrated by Barry, read as follows: first he was a boy, and then he was a man. The path from Point A to Point B had been straight, self-explanatory, and fun to travel.

"I don't get the point of all this navel-gazing," he'd told her during the exercise. "I was born with a penis. End of story."

Eve had tried to draw him out, asking if he'd ever wished he could get pregnant or breast-feed a child. Ted had once called the ability to bear children a female superpower—he was trying to cheer her up at a particularly bloated and trying moment in her third trimester—and the description had stuck with her through the years.

"It's kind of a miracle," she said. "Feeling that little person grow-ing inside you, and then feeding it with your body when it comes out. I imagine most men would be at least a *little* jealous."

Barry chuckled appreciatively, as if congratulating Eve on a good try.

"God bless the ladies," he said. "And thank you for your service. I really don't know how you do it."

And then he'd launched into a long and needlessly graphic account of the toll that childbirth had taken on his first wife's body—especially her breasts, which were never the same afterward, he was sorry to say. He'd hoped they would bounce back, so to speak—they were her finest attribute—but no such luck. At least he'd learned his lesson. When his second wife got pregnant, he persuaded her to bottle-feed, and it was a smart decision. The baby didn't give a shit, and *mama's hooters*—those were his actual words—remained miraculously perky. She did thicken a bit around the waist, but that wasn't what caused the marriage to go south. They had bigger problems, most notably his affair with a twenty-five-year-old waitress who would soon become wife number three. With that one, he laid down the law—*no fucking kids*—and she was all right with that until she turned thirty, at which point she wasn't anymore, and that was that.

"Jesus," Eve wondered. "How many ex-wives are there?"

"Just the three. I've had a few girlfriends since then, but it's not that easy to convince someone to be Wife Number Four. Believe me, I tried."

In the classroom, Eve had listened to Barry's checkered history with scientific detachment; the point was to write a profile of the sub-ject, not to judge him on his shortcomings. Out in the parking lot, though, a sense of retroactive revulsion came over her, exacerbated by the fact that he was crowding her as they walked, occasionally bump-ing shoulders with her in a way that might have seemed friendly, or even intriguing, if he hadn't just outed himself as a heartless creep.

"I'm a big girl," she told him. "You don't need to walk me to my car."

"And I'm a gentleman of the old school. Nothing wrong with a little chivalry, right? Women say they don't like it, but in my experience they're pretty grateful if you hold the door or pick up the check or bring them flowers."

Eve didn't want to admit it, but she knew he had a point. Things had changed so much over the course of her lifetime that women her age had all these different models of behavior jammed into their heads—you could be a fifties housewife and a liberated professional woman, a committed feminist and a blushing bride, a fierce athlete and a submissive, needy girlfriend. Most of the time you could switch from one role to another without too much trouble, and without even realizing that you might be contradicting yourself.

"There's some gender confusion right there," she observed. "I guess I learned something tonight."

"Well, if you're gonna study this crap, you might as well do it with a shemale, right?"

"Excuse me?"

"You didn't know?" Barry seemed pleased by her cluelessness. "Our professor used to be a he."

"Really?"

"Yup. Margo was Mark Fairchild. He was a great college basketball player. Even played pro in Europe for a couple of seasons." He tugged his beard. "Not a bad-looking woman, actually."

Eve's surprise was short-lived. The signs were there, now that she knew what she was looking for—the voice, the hips, the incongruous breasts, the riddle of the "coed" basketball league. But she never would have guessed it on her own.

*Live and learn,* she thought.

"I've never met a transgendered person before," she said. "At least I don't think so."

"Not that I'm attracted to her," Barry added, in case she'd misunderstood his earlier comment. "I mean, to each his own, right? But that's a bridge too far for me. I wonder if she tells the guys she dates beforehand."

"How do you know she dates guys?"

"Just the general vibe I'm getting. You think she got the surgery? I'm not really sure how that works."

Eve was relieved to arrive at her car. She'd had more than enough of Barry for one night.

"All right." She clicked her remote key, and the van flashed its lights. "Guess I'll see you next class."

"Hey," he said, as she reached for the door handle. "You want to get a nightcap? My bar's right down the street. Drinks on me."

"It's been a long day," she told him. "I need to get home."

"Suit yourself," Barry said with a shrug. "I'll take a rain check."

It was too bad she didn't like him a little better, because a drink after class would have been nice. At the very least it would have given her an excuse to stay out for another hour or two, to delay the inevitable moment when she returned home and had to once again confront the enormity of her son's absence—the fact that he'd grown up and left her, and the knowledge that this was good and proper—exactly what nature intended—and that she had no right to complain.

The fact that her life had turned into *this*: this lifeless hush, this faint but elusive whiff of decay. This absolutely-nothing-to-complain-about.

She didn't linger downstairs, just poured herself a glass of wine, grabbed her laptop, and headed up to her bedroom. She locked the door behind her, not a real lock, just a hardware store hook-and-eye that wouldn't have kept out a determined intruder, but might give her a few seconds of advanced warning, hopefully enough time to grab her phone and dial 911. She'd installed it six or seven years ago, after a couple of embarrassing incidents where Brendan had wandered in while she was getting dressed. He'd insisted that these were honest mistakes, but she wasn't so sure—he was just at that age when boys get curious—and decided that a little deterrence would go a long way.

For the past few years, ever since she'd opened her account, Facebook had been an integral part of Eve's bedtime ritual. She found it soothing to scroll through her news feed one last time before turning in, paying a visit to her various friends and acquaintances, reminding herself that she wasn't really alone. They were always right there where she'd left them, the usual suspects posting about the usual stuff: recipes, pithy sayings, scanned photos from the good old days, the inevitable pets, the banal declarations, witty memes, deep thoughts, political rants, viral videos. A group from her hometown had a new thread rhapsodizing about the Freezy Cone Ice Cream Stand on Franklin Street—gone for at least two decades—that included eighty-seven comments, most of which expressed sentiments like "Yum!" and "BEST. ICE. CREAM. EVER." and "Vanilla with Rainbow Sprinkles!!!"

She forced herself to read every last one of them. That should have been enough to put anyone to sleep, but Eve was still wide awake when she finished, still as restless and aroused as she'd been when she started. So there was nothing to do but the thing she'd promised herself she wouldn't do, though it was, admittedly, a promise she'd made with her fingers crossed, knowing it would probably have to be broken.

For a sexually liberated person in her mid-forties, Eve had had, until a few days ago, a fairly limited acquaintance with pornography. She remembered thumbing through a friend's brother's stash of magazines as a teenager, being intimidated by the airbrushed beauty of the centerfold models in *Playboy*, and genuinely shocked by the "beaver shots" in *Hustler*. Her visceral distaste turned ideological in college, where it was a feminist article of faith that porn degraded and objectified women while exploiting them for financial gain. Why would you want to have anything to do with a dirty business like that?

After she graduated, she began to notice that this opinion wasn't universally shared. Lots of supposedly enlightened men she knew seemed to like porn—or at least they liked joking about liking porn—but she was surprised to learn that a number of her women friends were fans, too. Her grad school colleague Allison reported that she and her fiancé had a standing Friday night porn date that they both looked forward to all week. (Allison also had a vibrator that she'd nicknamed Black Betty and half jokingly described as the best thing that had ever happened to her.)

Succumbing to peer pressure early in their marriage, Eve and Ted had rented a movie called *Fuck My Secretary*—this was back when every video rental store had an XXX section, usually hidden in a basement or tucked away in a separate room—but they only made it through a couple of minutes before throwing in the towel. The actors had seemed like freaks, the secretary endowed with gravity-defying breasts while the boss sported an erection the size of a prize zucchini. It did absolutely nothing for Eve or Ted, so they turned off the VCR and made love, cheerfully enough, with their own serviceable, human-sized equipment. Her XXX history had pretty much stopped there. She'd never surfed for porn on the internet, and hardly ever thought about it, except in an anxious parental capacity.

Which was why it was so disorienting to find herself returning, for the sixth day in a row, to milfateria.com ("World's Biggest Buffet of All-You-Can-Eat Amateur MILF Porn!"), scrolling through the thumbnails of recently uploaded clips. *Lovely Wife BJ, Anal MILF with Creampie, Abby Loves BBC, Sexy Samantha First Time on Camera, Saucy Soccer Mom Takes It Like a Champ.* Saucy soccer mom. Eve smiled at the description and clicked on the link. That seemed worth a look.

It was the anonymous text that had led her here, the one that had arrived last Friday night. She'd forgotten all about it until Saturday morning, when she turned on her phone and saw that idiotic message staring back at her:

*U r my MILF!*

She wasn't sure why it had bothered her so much. It was probably just a harmless prank, the handiwork of a drunk teenager getting his late-night kicks. Texts like this were the digital equivalent of obscene phone calls.

*Send me a naked pic!!*

All she had to do was delete it and get on with her day. But she kept squinting at those words, floating so innocently in their cartoon bubble, as if they had every right to inhabit her phone. Before she realized what she was doing, she'd typed a reply of her own.

*I'm not a MILF, you little shit*

Luckily, her good sense kicked in before she pressed Send. There was no point in engaging with an anonymous pervert, giving him the satisfaction of a response, a reward for his harassment.

*MILF.*

She knew what the acronym stood for, of course—she hadn't been living under a rock—or at least thought she did. In her mind, it was just an updated name for the old Mrs. Robinson stereotype, the predatory middle-aged woman with a taste for younger men, maybe even boys who were Brendan's age. That was the main thing that creeped her out, the possibility that the text had come from one of her son's friends, or maybe even his new roommate.

*I want to cum on those big floppy tits!!!*

What kind of person would say something like that to a friend's mother? And what if it was Wade or Tyler or Max, boys she'd known since they were in preschool, whom she'd taken to the beach, who'd slept over at her house? It made her queasy to imagine one of them thinking about her body in such prurient detail.

*And they're not that floppy,* she thought indignantly. *They've actually held up pretty well.*

One thing that she'd learned from her web search that morning was that she'd been conflating the terms *cougar* and *MILF*, which turned out not to be synonymous at all. MILF was a broader, more passive category, basically just "any mother that is sexually desirable." What that meant, Eve realized, was that you couldn't really say, *I'm not a MILF*, because a MILF was in the eye of the beholder. The other thing she'd learned was that you shouldn't google the term if you didn't want to find yourself swimming in an ocean of porn.

There was no doubt about it—milfateria.com was part of that

"unregulated cesspool" the assistant DA had warned about so many years ago at the PTA meeting. Eve was regularly shocked and frequently disgusted by what she found there. She disapproved of the site—she would have been horrified if she'd ever found anything like it on her son's computer—and sincerely wished it didn't exist. But she couldn't stop looking at it.

A few of the allegedly "Amateur MILFs" were clearly porn stars, with huge fake boobs and full Brazilians, but the vast majority looked like ordinary people. They had stretch marks, C-section scars, pimples on their faces and butts, bruises and rashes, cellulite, underarm and pubic stubble. Some of them wore glasses while they had sex, and more than you might have expected kept their socks on. A lot of them seemed to live in drab houses or cramped apartments. While a few of the women seemed embarrassed by what they were doing, others looked straight into the camera, as if they were a lot more interested in whoever might be watching them than they were in their partners. And the men! They were (most of them, anyway) a parade of horrors—hairy and potbellied, wheezy and much too talkative for Eve's taste. They loved to narrate their orgasms in real time—*Here it comes, baby!*—as if the whole world was waiting for an update.

In the past week, Eve had spent more time watching milfateria videos than she would have liked to admit, and she'd barely scratched the surface. The site was organized by category (Oral MILF, Anal MILF, Threesome MILF, Lesbo MILF, Ebony MILF, Solo MILF, etc.), body type (Busty MILF, Shaved MILF, Big Booty MILF, Redhead MILF), but also by nationality (Turkish MILF, German MILF, Canadian MILF, Japanese MILF, Israeli MILF, Iranian MILF, and on and on), a global community of women in their thirties, forties, fifties, and even older (Granny MILF), united by their willingness to have sex in front of a camera and to share the experience with the rest of the world (unless a man was sharing it without their permission, which probably happened a lot). The sheer number of videos was overwhelming; you could never watch them all, not that you'd want to. There were so many that it seemed like only a matter of time before Eve would find herself looking at someone she knew, a high school classmate, a neighbor, maybe her old friend Allison.

Her reaction was the same every time she started a session: *Ugh!* How could they do it? How could people expose themselves like this? Just the sight of all that naked flesh was overwhelming and off-putting. She cringed at the unimaginative dirty talk and the pre-dictability of the action. She especially hated the clips that focused solely on the genitalia, the close-ups of penises and vaginas. So many assholes. She needed to see faces, to get a sense of the person she was watching. That was the only thing that mattered.

It was like a blind date or a party. Some people you liked right away, some you didn't. Some you weren't sure about. The saucy soccer mom was horrible, a giggly woman performing a clumsy striptease with the TV blaring in the background. Eve clicked out of that, tried "Swedish MILF Pink Dildo!" then "Italian Wife Deepthroat" and "Sexy Abigail Morning Fuck." None of them did anything for her.

But there was always another one. And eventually—tonight it was "Classy Lady Loves That Cock!"—something would click. The couple on her screen would seem inspired, or even blessed—you could see how alive and happy and unself-conscious they were—and maybe you envied them a little, but you also wanted to thank them for sharing this moment with you, and then that last barrier would crumble, and maybe for a minute or two you'd feel that you were right there with them, like when you heard a good song on the radio and the next thing you knew you were singing along.

PART TWO

*The End of Reluctance*

# Trouble in Sunset Acres

It was only Thursday afternoon, but Amanda Olney could already feel the weekend coming on like an illness—a mild case of the flu or some mid-level gastrointestinal distress, the kind of ailment that didn't leave you bedridden but kept you confined to the couch, unfit for human interaction. You just had to wait it out in your sweatpants, bingeing on Netflix and herbal tea, a forty-eight-hour quarantine until Monday rolled around and you could head back to work.

She understood how pathetic that sounded, exactly the opposite of how you were supposed to feel if you were a youngish single person with an office job that paid less-than-peanuts and made a mockery of your expensive education; a job, moreover, that required you to spend a good part of your life in the company of old people, some of them physically and/or mentally infirm, and many others just plain ornery. You were supposed to love the weekend, that all-too-brief window of freedom, your only chance to wash away the stink of boredom with a blast of fun. Use it to drink and fuck yourself into a state of blissful oblivion, the memory of which would power you through the work week that followed, at the end of which you could do it all over again, ad infinitum, or at least until you met the right guy (or gal) and settled down.

Well, Amanda had tried all that, and it had depressed the shit out of her. Better to be a nun than to spend every Sunday beating herself up about the bad choices she'd made on Friday and Saturday night. In fact, at this particular juncture in her life, she wouldn't have minded if the weekend were abolished altogether. She would have been fine coming to work seven days a week, barricading herself behind her beige metal desk, making phone calls and filling out paperwork, finding budget-conscious ways to keep the geezers of Haddington occupied while they ran out the clock on their golden years.

Aside from organizing events and activities at the Senior Center, Amanda was responsible for putting out a monthly newsletter called *Haddington Happenings*. One of the regular features was a chatty roundup of notable events that had transpired since the last issue— the birth of Eleanor Testa's seventh grandchild, Lou LeGrande's excellent recovery from open heart surgery, Dick and Marilyn Hauser's golden anniversary. She was adding a few items to the list—*Three cheers for Joy Maloney, who came in fifth in the Seventy-and-Over Division at last month's 5K Fun Run at Finley Park. Way to go, Joy! You're an inspiration to us all! And congratulations to Art Weber on the ten-pound bluefish he caught on Cape Cod. It was almost as big as the one that got away, right Art?*—when Eve Fletcher poked her head into the tiny windowless office.

"Hey," she said. "Did you figure out the bus thing?"

Amanda nodded, pleased to be the bearer of good news.

"It took some doing, but I finally got through to the owner and explained the situation. He says they'll give us a motor coach for the same price."

"With a working rest room?"

"That's what he said."

Eve heaved a theatrical sigh of relief.

"Thank God. There was no way I was gonna put a bunch of old people on a school bus for a trip to Foxwoods. That's a recipe for disaster."

"We're all set on our end," Amanda assured her. "The rest is up to Frank Sinatra Jr."

"I'm sure he'll be great." Eve's voice was confident, but her face expressed an alternative viewpoint. "I wish I could join you, but I have a class that night."

"No worries," Amanda told her. "I got this."

"Excellent." Eve brought her hands together in a soundless clap. "Well, enjoy the rest of your day. I'm checking out a little early."

"Lucky you."

"Not really. I'm going to a wake. Roy Rafferty."

"Oh." Amanda grimaced in sympathy. "I heard about that. Poor man."

"You wanna come?"

Amanda glanced at her computer screen. "I kinda have to finish this article."

"No worries," Eve said, retreating from the doorway. "I'll see you tomorrow."

The final chunk of the workday felt endless, that infinitely expanding space between four thirty and five, when there was nothing left to do but surf the web and pretend to look busy in case one of her co-workers wandered by in the hallway. In a more humane and rational workplace—one of those Bay Area tech companies with ping-pong tables and espresso machines and nap rooms that she was so sick of hearing about—she could have called it a day and headed out into the fresh air, but the Senior Center was old-school government work. You got paid for keeping your ass in the chair, not for the quality of your ideas or the tasks you accomplished. It was one more example of how upside-down everything was. Wouldn't it be a lot fairer if drones like her got to have the flexible hours and the hipster amenities? The people with the six-figure salaries could buy their own damn macchiatos.

On reflection, she wished she'd accepted Eve's half-serious invitation to join her at Roy Rafferty's wake. Not that it would have been much fun, sitting in a funeral home at the tail end of a beautiful fall afternoon, but at least they would have been able to drive there together, maybe go out for a drink afterward. Just a chance to hang out a bit, get to know each other a little better outside the context of work.

Amanda wasn't sure if she wanted Eve to be a mentor or a friend, but there was room in her life for both. Or maybe she was just missing her mother—it had only been six months since her death, though most of the time it felt like yesterday—and looking for a substitute, an older, wiser woman to lean on for emotional support, not that Eve was anywhere close to her mother's age, or had shown any interest in being part of Amanda's support system. If anything, she seemed a little sad herself—Amanda had totally caught her crying in her office that one time, though Eve had denied it—which just made Amanda like her that much more, and wish they could slip past the rigid, artificial boundary that separated boss and employee, and find a way to meet each other as equals.

She was clicking through a viral list she was pretty sure she'd seen before—*29 Celebs You Totally Didn't Know Were Bi*—when the phone rang. Her laptop clock said 4:52, late enough to make the call seem like an imposition, if it wasn't some sort of emergency.

"Events," she said cautiously. "Amanda speaking."

"Hello, Amanda," said the sandpapery female voice on the other end. "This is Grace Lucas."

"Okay." The name meant nothing to Amanda. "Can I help you?"

"You don't know me," Grace Lucas continued. She sounded a little off, possibly medicated. "I'm Garth Heely's wife."

*Of course you are,* Amanda thought irritably. When you had a job like events coordinator, there was always someone making your life miserable. At the moment, for Amanda, this someone was Garth Heely, an obscure local author scheduled to speak at the Senior Center's monthly lecture series in November. A retired lawyer, Garth Heely had self-published three novels featuring Parker Winslow, a silver-haired sleuth who plies his trade at Sunset Acres, a senior living community with an unusually high murder rate. Amanda had read them all—it was her job!—and they were better than she'd expected, except that the killer in all three books turned out to be a person of color—a Jamaican nurse in *Trouble in Sunset Acres*, an Indian urologist in *More Trouble in Sunset Acres*, and a Guatemalan physical therapist in *Mayhem in Sunset Acres*. When she'd pointed out this unfortunate pattern—diplomatically, she thought—Garth Heely got immediately defensive, telling her he was fed up with all this PC crap you heard nowadays, everybody so focused on the color of everybody else's skin, rather than the content of their character. Then he suggested that maybe *she* was the racist, lumping all non-white people into a single category, as if there were no difference between Kingston and Calcutta.

*Have you ever been to Calcutta?* he demanded.

Amanda admitted that she hadn't.

*Well, I have,* he said. *And believe me, honey, it ain't a bit like Jamaica!*

Amanda wasn't surprised by his attitude of aggrieved innocence. It was something she'd gotten used to, working at the Senior Center. A lot of old white people acted like it was still 1956, like they could say whatever they wanted and not have to take any responsibility for their words. Soon after she'd gotten hired, she'd called out a couple of women for using the N-word in casual conversation—they were both knitting baby sweaters—and they'd looked at her like she was making a big deal out of nothing, since there were no black people within hearing range. There rarely were; Haddington was that kind of town.

Garth Heely wasn't an out-and-out racist, just a prosperous, occasionally charming white man of a certain age, blind to his own privilege, predictably smug and condescending. The only thing that surprised her was what a diva he had turned out to be, considering that he was a writer no one had ever heard of, with an Amazon ranking somewhere in the millions.

"What can I do for you, ma'am?"

"I'm calling on behalf of my husband," Grace Lucas said. "I'm afraid you're going to have to cancel his speaking engagement."

*Oh Jesus,* Amanda thought.

Just yesterday, she and Garth Heely had butted heads about the flyers the Senior Center had designed to promote his lecture. He thought they looked boring—*guilty as charged*—and suggested that they be printed on several different shades of eye-catching colored paper, preferably pink, yellow, and light blue. Amanda explained that this wouldn't be possible, since the Senior Center's budget didn't allow for colored paper.

"Hello?" Grace Lucas said. "Are you still there?"

"I'm here." Amanda's skin felt clammy beneath her dress. She'd only been working at the Senior Center for a few months, and the last thing she needed was to walk into Eve's office and explain that the November speaker had canceled over a trivial dispute. "Please tell Mr. Heely that I misspoke. We'll be more than happy to supply colored paper for the flyers."

The silence on the other end of the line felt more puzzled than frosty. Amanda was about to add an apology to the offer when Grace Lucas finally spoke.

"Garth is dead, dear."

"What?" Amanda started to laugh, then caught herself. "I talked to him yesterday morning. He was fine."

"I know." There was a note of quiet wonder in Grace Lucas's voice. "He died right afterward. You were the last person to speak to him. He was still holding the phone when I found him."

*Oh my God*, Amanda thought. *I killed him.*

"I'm so sorry," she said.

"Thank you, dear." Grace Lucas gave a resigned sigh. "I just wish he'd been able to finish the book he was working on. He said it was going to be his best Parker Winslow yet. Now we'll never know who the murderer was."

Amanda wanted to ask if there was a non-white health care worker in the book—*There's your killer!*—but she was distracted by an embarrassing feeling of relief, the knowledge that Garth Heely's sudden death was going to be a lot easier to explain to Eve than a disagreement over colored paper would have been.

"I'm going to bury him in his blue suit." Grace Lucas's voice was dreamy and private, as if she were talking to herself. "He always looked so good in blue."

*　*　*

Wakes and funerals were an inescapable part of Eve's professional life, and she tried to approach them with a businesslike sense of detachment. She showed up in her official capacity, she paid her respects to the family of the deceased, and she went home. No fuss, no muss, no tears.

Tonight, though, she was a bit of a wreck. The news of Roy Rafferty's death had upset her deeply, coming so soon after she'd banished him for exposing himself in the ladies' room. She didn't feel guilty about her decision—as an administrator, she'd really had no choice— but the memory of it still made her sick at heart. It seemed so cruel and pointless in retrospect, humiliating a sick old man who had only a month to live, not that she had any way of knowing that at the time. All she knew was that she'd inflicted pain on someone she cared about, and that always cost you something, even if you were just doing your job. It left you feeling dirty and mean, exposed to the laws of karma. It also made her wonder if she was doing the right thing by coming here.

A lot of the wakes she went to were woefully underpopulated affairs, a corpse and some flowers and a handful of bored spectators, no one even bothering to pretend that it was a big deal. Eve was relieved to see that this wasn't the case tonight. The parking lot was packed, and so was the viewing room, an impressive line of mourners massed along the side wall, inching their way toward the open coffin. The turnout was a tribute to Roy's lifelong ties to Haddington, his membership in a variety of civic organizations, and his long and successful career as a plumbing contractor, not to mention the fact that he'd been a genuinely nice guy before the dementia kicked in.

Instead of joining the procession, Eve slipped into a velour-cushioned chair in the second to last row of the viewing room, near a group of ladies who were regulars at the Senior Center. One of them was Evelyn Gerardi, the emphysemic woman who'd been the victim of Roy's indecent overtures.

"So sad," Eve whispered. "Such a shame."

The ladies nodded in mournful agreement, murmuring that Roy was a sweetheart and a good father and so handsome when he was young. Eve turned to face the coffin, which was obscured by a wall of dark suits and somber dresses. She sat quietly for a while, trying to summon a mental image of the dead man—not the confused troublemaker he'd been near the end, but the gruff, garrulous man she'd gotten to know a decade earlier, a stocky guy with a silver-gray brush cut and an impish twinkle in his eyes. He always wore Hawaiian shirts on Friday—his favorite had pineapples and parrots on it—and he liked to flirt with the female employees of the Center, Eve included.

What she remembered best about him was the way he'd cared for his wife after the death of their oldest son, five or six years ago now. Joan had taken it hard—how could she not? Nick was still her baby, even if he'd been fifty-two years old at the time of his death—and it seemed like all the joy and vitality drained out of her after that. Roy began holding her hand in public, something he'd never done before, and treating her with immense politeness, pulling out her chair before she sat down, helping her on with her coat, checking on her in a soft and solicitous voice. That was the man Eve was here to honor, and she hoped the Rafferty family would accept her condolences without bitterness, and forgive her for the unfortunate role she'd played in the final chapter of his life.

The line had shrunk considerably by the time she got up and made her way to the viewing pedestal, breathing through her mouth to avoid the sickly odor of the funeral bouquets, which always made her a little light-headed. She hated this part of the ritual, that chilling moment when you were face-to-face with an object that appeared to be a clumsy wax replica of someone you knew but was, of course, the actual person. As usual, everything about the presentation seemed slightly off, from the gray suit Roy was wearing—in Eve's opinion, a windbreaker and a Hawaiian shirt would have been the way to go—to the pack of Camels and the bag of beef jerky that had been placed in the coffin to speed him on his way. Neither item seemed appropriate: Roy had quit smoking and sworn off red meat years ago. But the real problem was the vacant look on his face. Roy was a people person, always happy to see you, and interested in what you had to say, even if you were just chatting about the weather. Apathy didn't suit him at all.

Some people kissed the dead person's forehead, but it seemed both creepy and theatrical to Eve, not to mention vaguely unsanitary. She settled for patting him twice on the hand, very quickly.

"Goodbye," she whispered. "We're gonna miss you."

All three of Roy's surviving children were standing on the receiving line, and none of them seemed to think it odd or presumptuous for her to be there. Both of the daughters—Kim and Debbie were their names, though Eve couldn't remember which was which—hugged her and told her how much their father loved coming to the Senior Center, and how highly he'd spoken of the people who worked there. Eve assured them that the feeling was mutual, and that their father was a lovely man who'd brightened everyone's day.

George Rafferty was more reserved than his sisters, but he didn't seem like he was holding a grudge. He seemed a little dazed, or maybe just exhausted.

"Thanks for coming," he said, shaking her hand with robotic indifference. "Tough day. Good to see you. Means a lot."

Eve wasn't even sure he recognized her, which left her feeling vaguely offended as she left the funeral home. *Come on, you know who I am!* She was about to laugh at the selfishness of her reaction, but she was distracted by the cool evening air when she stepped outside, the dusky blue of the sky, and the freshly paved street in front of her, its blackness bisected by a bright yellow line, a world so inexplicably beautiful that she forgot what she was thinking about and just stood still for a moment, breathing it all in.

*    *    *

The Bikram instructor that night was Jojo, not Amanda's favorite. She would have preferred Kendra, the soulful, slightly overweight woman who read inspirational meditations about self-acceptance during Savasana at the beginning and end of class. Kendra roamed the studio like a benign spirit, the goddess of encouragement, always ready with a supportive comment. Sometimes that was all you needed, a trinket of praise to get you through the most brutal poses, Utkatasana or Balancing Stick, the ones that made you hate your body and wonder why you even bothered.

"Let's go, people!" Jojo clapped his hands as if summoning a dog. "Where's the energy? There's no such thing as halfway in Bikram!"

Jojo was a beautiful Asian man with the body of a gymnast and the soul of a drill sergeant. His adjustments were rare and brusque and sometimes borderline inappropriate, as if his lack of sexual interest in women gave him license to touch them wherever and however he pleased.

Even so, Amanda knew that complaining about Jojo was pure luxury, like whining about the prices at Whole Foods. The real miracle was that *anybody* taught Bikram yoga in Haddington. Ten years ago, when she'd left for Sarah Lawrence, there hadn't been a single yoga studio in her hometown. Now there were three—Bikram, Prana, and Royal Serenity, whatever that was—as well as a Cross-Fit gym, a decent vegan restaurant, and a tattoo parlor whose owner had a degree from RISD. Without realizing it, she'd been part of a hipster reverse migration, legions of overeducated, underpaid twenty-somethings getting squeezed out of the city, spreading beyond the pricey inner suburbs to the more affordable outposts like Haddington, transforming the places they'd once fled, making them livable again, or at least tolerable.

Another reason for gratitude: Jojo's classes were more sparsely attended than Kendra's, so she had some room to spread out, no worries about her personal space getting invaded by a rude neighbor, or slipping on a puddle of fresh-squeezed man-sweat. She hated to be sexist, but it was undeniable: men were gross at Bikram. Everybody perspired, but certain guys took it to a freakish extreme, dripping like faucets throughout the entire ninety minutes of class, the foam of their mats squishing underfoot.

Tonight there were only five males in the class, none of them familiar, thank God. A couple of weeks ago she'd found herself standing one row behind a guy she'd hooked up with on Tinder, a forty-two-year-old graphic artist named Dell, with long graying hair and a sad little belly bulging over the waistband of his Speedo. Their eyes had met in the front mirror and he'd smiled in happy surprise. She was aware of his scrutiny throughout all twenty-six postures, and it had completely ruined her concentration. And then he'd tried to chat her up in the parking lot, as if they were old pals, rather than strangers who'd fucked once, just because they both happened to be bored and lonely at the same time.

She wasn't sure why the encounter had unnerved her so much. Dell was a pretty nice guy—they'd actually done okay in bed together— and she was ninety-nine percent sure his presence at the studio was pure coincidence, not the beginning of a stalking nightmare. But it didn't matter; it was just creepy to see him there, totally out of context, as if he were an actual human being, rather than a figment of her sexual imagination. She went home that night and deleted her Tinder account, so nothing like that would ever happen again.

At the Senior Center, Amanda's tattoos were a constant source of friction with the clients, and, apparently, an open invitation to criticism, like one of those bumper stickers that read, *How's my driving?* She wished she could have supplied a toll-free number, so the irate old folks could call at their leisure and leave a message, instead of accosting her in the crafts room to inform her that she'd made a terrible mistake, that she could have been a pretty girl, and what the heck was she thinking?

*At least wear some long sleeves,* the sweet old ladies told her. *A turtleneck and some dark tights might not be such a bad idea, either.*

Something subtler, and far more frustrating, went on in the

Bikram changing room, where a number of the younger women had tattoos of their own, though of a more decorous suburban variety—a dolphin on a shoulder blade, a constellation of three or four stars around an ankle, a cheerful little bird on the nape of the neck. The first time she undressed there, she felt a sudden chill of separation, her own more drastic aesthetic marking her as an instant outsider, the badass chick with the cobra wrapped around her leg, the hand grenade on her breast, the anarchist bomb on her thigh, and the meat cleaver—the only one she truly regretted—dripping blood on her upper arm.

She tried to compensate by being extra friendly, smiling at everyone she passed, but the others rarely smiled back. Most of them avoided eye contact altogether, the same way Amanda used to avert her gaze from the anorexic woman at her old gym, the one who seemed intent on committing suicide by elliptical. You wanted to look—how could you not?—but you didn't want to be rude, so you just minded your business and pretended she wasn't there.

Five years ago, when she'd been living in Brooklyn with Blake, she would have enjoyed this outcast feeling, the knowledge that she was a little too edgy for the yoga moms and single ladies of Haddington, but she wasn't that person anymore. She was lonely and looking for new friends, and it broke her heart a little every time she showered and changed without exchanging a single pleasant word or sympathetic look with anyone.

She'd gotten so used to being ignored, she wasn't sure what to think when she emerged from the shower, a much-too-skimpy towel wrapped around her torso, and noticed a slender, pretty woman staring at her with a quizzical expression. Amanda had never seen this woman at Bikram before, but she'd been aware of her throughout the class. It was hard not to be—she was one of those front-row yoga goddesses, enviably fit and limber, observing herself in the mirror with an air of scientific detachment as she tied herself in elegant knots, barely breaking a sweat.

It was a cramped space, a single wooden bench set between two rows of lockers, with several women milling about in various states of undress, trying not to get in one another's way. Amanda had just released the towel when she sensed a presence at her side.

"Excuse me?" The woman's voice was surprisingly casual, considering that Amanda was naked, and she herself was wearing nothing but yoga pants. "I think we know each other."

The stranger was even prettier up close, with black pixie-cut hair and blue eyes that seemed pale and bright at the same time. A tiny tattoo peeked from the waistband of her pants, something dark and swirly, a tornado or maybe a comet.

"You went to Haddington?" she continued. "We were in AP English senior year?"

Her voice sounded vaguely familiar, but Amanda searched in vain for a name to connect to the face. It didn't help that she was distracted by the woman's breasts, which were small and pert, with optimistic upturned nipples. She couldn't help wondering what that would feel like, having boobs that defied gravity, and a stomach so flat it might actually be concave. She glanced with longing at her own discarded towel, lying uselessly on the floor.

"I'm sorry," Amanda said. "Your name is . . . ?"

"Beckett." After an awkward moment of silence, the woman smiled, realizing her error. "In high school I went by Trish? Trish Lozano?"

*Holy shit*, Amanda thought. *Trish Lozano*. She could see it now, the ghost of the girl she'd known hidden inside a whole new person.

"I didn't recognize you," she said. "You were blond back then."

"Of course I was." Trish shook her head. "I was such a cliché. The cute little cheerleader from hell."

Amanda wasn't sure how to respond. She'd never thought of Trish Lozano as a cliché. She was more like the platonic ideal of an American high school girl, pretty and bubbly and super-popular, always at the center of the action. And she'd been smart, too, which seemed even more unfair.

"Your name's Beckett now?"

"I changed it in college. I got into acting and Trish just seemed so blah. We were doing this all-female production of *Waiting for Godot*, and I don't know, Beckett seemed like a cool name." Trish rolled her eyes, amused by her younger, more pretentious self. "Turns out I'm a terrible actor, so the joke was on me. But I kept the name. It's a big improvement."

Amanda could feel herself nodding a little too emphatically, as if she were receiving news of profound importance, and it made her queasy to think of what she must look like, plump and flushed and naked, listening so intently to a beautiful, bare-breasted woman who called herself Beckett.

"You look great," Trish said, touching her gently on the arm. "Are you still living here?"

"It's just temporary." Amanda's face warmed with embarrassment. "I was living with my boyfriend in Brooklyn, but . . ." It was a long story, not one she wanted to go into just then. She turned toward the open locker, rifling through her clothes until she found her bra. "What about you?"

"Visiting my mom." Trish made a sour face, as if this were an unpleasant obligation, like jury duty. "I live in L.A. now. I went out there for film school and never looked back. My fiancé's a DP. You know, a cinematographer? So I think we're pretty much stuck there."

Involuntarily, Amanda's gaze strayed to Trish's left hand, the small diamond gleaming tastefully, not the least bit boastful or obnoxious. Just a fact.

"Wow." Amanda hooked her bra, then gave the underwires a little tug, getting everything in alignment. "That's exciting."

She grabbed her panties—they were black and high-waisted, with stretchy lace panels on the sides—and pulled them on. She felt a little better now that she was decent, glad it was a good underwear day.

"Do you work in the movie business, too?"

"I was a PA for a while, but now I teach at Soul Cycle. Probably do it for a few more years, till we're ready to start a family." Trish shrugged, not unhappily. "You?"

"Single," Amanda said, trying to sound matter-of-fact. "Just getting my life in order. I'm the events coordinator at the Senior Center. They actually have a pretty good lecture series."

Trish nodded, but there was a faraway look in her eyes, as if she wasn't really listening.

"This is so weird," she said. "I still think about you sometimes."

"Me?" Amanda gave a puzzled laugh. She and Trish had barely exchanged two words in high school. "Why?"

"To be honest?" Trish said. "You kinda freaked me out. You were always staring at me like I was this horrible, stuck-up, shallow person, and I couldn't understand why you hated me so much."

"I didn't hate you," Amanda said. "I didn't even know you."

"It's okay," Trish told her. "I had this epiphany in college. It just hit me one day, like, *Fuck, I was a mean girl! That's why she hated me!* Sometimes, even now, I wake up in the middle of the night, and I'm just so ashamed of the way I treated people, how fucking selfish I was, such a little princess. So when I saw you here, I just thought I should come over and apologize. Make things right."

"You don't need to apologize."

"I am so sorry," Trish said, and the next thing Amanda knew they were hugging, Trish's proud little cheerleader boobs mashing into her chest. "I am really and truly sorry for the person I used to be."

\* \* \*

Eve couldn't remember the last time she'd gone to a restaurant by herself—not a coffee shop or a hole-in-the-wall pizzeria, but an actual sit-down restaurant with waiters and cloth napkins, a place where the other diners glanced at you with pity when you were first seated at your table for one, and then did their best not to look at you after that, as if you were disfigured in some way, and shouldn't be made to feel self-conscious about it. And that was actually preferable to seeing someone you knew, giving them that sheepish little wave across the dining room—*Yup, here I am, all by myself!*—and then keeping your eyes glued to your plate for the next half hour, until either you left or they did.

But Eve had decided to do it anyway, to lean into the awkwardness and try to conquer it. Her inspiration was an article a newly divorced acquaintance had posted on Facebook—*Going Solo: Fifteen Fun Things to Do by Yourself . . . for Yourself!*—that had pointed out that too many single women deprive themselves of all sorts of pleasures out of simple fear of embarrassment, of being seen as less-than because they weren't part of a couple or a friend group. Just face up to this fear, the article suggested, and do what *you* want to do, and you might come to realize that there was nothing to be afraid of in the first place.

*Go ahead,* the writer concluded. *I dare you!*

Some of the suggested activities seemed lame—*Take a Long Hot Bath; Cook Yourself a Gourmet Candlelight Dinner*—and also beside the point, if the point was to overcome the stigma of being a woman alone in public. Others seemed unduly ambitious—*Go Kayaking; Run a Marathon*—or financially infeasible—*Take a Caribbean Cruise; Visit a New Continent.* But there were a few that landed right in her sweet spot—simple, inexpensive ways to treat yourself that required little more than the courage to get out of the house: *Sing a Song at Karaoke Night; Go to a Bar and Order a Fancy Cocktail; Take Yourself Out to Dinner.*

The restaurant she picked was Gennaro's, a homey red sauce Italian place on Haddington Boulevard. It was Brendan's favorite, always his first choice on those nights when Eve had worked late or was too tired to cook. The hostess, a high school girl with glamorous false eyelashes, led her to an out-of-the-way table near the rest room hallway. Eve didn't mind the subpar location. She was happy just to be there, surrounded by the familiar décor—the lovingly, if inexpertly, painted mural of the Neapolitan coast that took up an entire wall, the framed photographs of a Vespa and a bunch of grapes—and the comforting hum of other people's dinnertime conversation.

She wished she'd thought to bring a book for company; next time she'd know better. For now, she was reduced to perusing the old-school paper placemat—it hadn't changed for as long as she could remember—featuring a map of Italy, illustrations of the Leaning Tower and the Colosseum, and a handful of helpful facts about the country.

*Population: Sixty Million*
*Religion: Roman Catholic*
*Language: Italian*

Brendan had always gotten a kick out of that last one. *What a shocker,* he'd say. *Italians speak Italian. Never woulda guessed.* Thinking he'd appreciate the reference, she texted him a picture.

*Dinner at Gennaro's,* she wrote.

*Cool,* he replied, with gratifying promptness. *Who with?*

*Just me. Wish you were here.*

*Me too I miss that chicken parm!*

It got easier once her wine arrived, a house chianti as unchanging as the placemat. She'd only taken a couple of sips when Gennaro emerged from the kitchen and made his way through the restaurant, going table to table like a politician. He was a sweetheart, a diminutive, blue-eyed Italian with a ruddy complexion and a thick head of silver hair, one of those slender continental types who managed to look elegant even in a dark green apron. When he spotted Eve, his face broke into a big, incredulous grin.

"Ay, long time no see. Where's your boy?"

"College," she told him. "Freshman year."

"Smart kid." Gennaro tapped his skull with the tip of his index finger. "How's he like it?"

"Pretty well. Maybe a little too much for his own good."

Gennaro waved his hand, as if batting away an insect.

"Ah. He's young. Let him enjoy himself." He peered at Eve, his eyes narrowing with concern. "What about you? What's new?"

"Not much," she said. "Just work. Keeping busy."

Gennaro shrugged with good-natured resignation.

"What can you do? Gotta pay the tuition." He patted her supportively on the shoulder. "Nice to see you, pretty lady. You come by anytime, we take good care of you."

He moved on, leaving Eve slightly deflated. She knew Gennaro meant well, but there was something about that question—*What's new?*—that never failed to depress her. Maybe she was being paranoid, but it always felt like an intrusion, an indirect way of inquiring about her romantic life. And when she replied, *Just work*, that was code for *I'm still alone*, as if she were apologizing for being single, as if there was something wrong with that.

On the other hand, at least he'd bothered to ask, which implied that he thought there was still a possibility that something *might* be new. That was a point in her favor. And it wasn't even true that there was nothing new in her life. For one thing, she was taking a class in Gender Studies and actually learning something. And, oh yeah, she'd also gone and gotten herself addicted to internet porn, not that that was anything to brag about.

She understood that it was a little extreme, or maybe just premature, to call her problem an addiction—it had only been going on for a month or so—but what other label could you use when you did something every night, whether you wanted to or not? Tonight she knew she would go home and visit the Milfateria—it felt like a fact, not a choice—probably checking out the Lesbo MILFs, her current go-to category. Last week it was Blowjob MILFs—lots and lots of blowjobs—and the week before that had been a more eclectic period—spanking, threesomes, butt play—just to get a sense of what was out there.

*Addiction* was a bleak word, though, a hundred percent negative. Maybe *habit* was a better term. People were addicted to heroin. But their morning coffee was just a habit.

*I have a porn habit,* Eve thought, trying on the word for size.

There were definitely some upsides to it. She was having a lot more orgasms than she used to, which was helping her sleep better, and improving her complexion. Several people had commented on how good her skin looked. She was also picking up some techniques that might come in handy down the road, if she ever did find a partner. For example, she'd learned that her blowjob skills were seriously out-of-date. When Eve was young, a can-do attitude—really, just making the effort—had been more than enough to earn a passing grade. These days the bar was a lot higher.

But there was a big downside to porn, beyond the feminist objections that still made her uneasy. The real problem was spiritual: it made you feel like you were wasting your life. This wasn't so much a matter of lost time—though that was part of it, all those hours you squandered clicking on video after video, trying to find the one that would light up your brain—as it was a matter of lost opportunities. Watching too much porn made you feel like you were out in the cold with your nose pressed against a window, watching strangers at a party, wishing you could join them. But the weird thing was, you *could* join them. All you had to do was open the door and walk inside, and everybody would be happy to see you. So why were you still outside, standing on your tiptoes, feeling sorry for yourself?

*Thank God,* she thought, when her lasagna finally arrived.

* * *

It only took a minute for Amanda to reactivate her Tinder account. Her old matches were gone, but she didn't care about that. She used the same profile photos as before—they'd never let her down—and stuck with her tried-and-true tagline: *If you're nice, I'll show you my other ones.* She set the match distance for fifteen miles and the age range for 35–55. That was the key, in her experience. The older guys were out there, checking their phones every two minutes, just itching to be called out of retirement. And they'd happily drive through a blizzard with a flat tire if a woman in her twenties was waiting on the other end.

Amanda understood that this was a bad idea, not to mention a blatant violation of her recently instituted no-hookup policy. Tinder was like tequila—fun today, sad tomorrow—but sometimes you didn't have a choice. That unexpected reunion with Trish Lozano had really messed with her self-esteem. The thought of going home and eating a salad in front of the TV had triggered a wave of self-pity that bordered on rage.

*That's the highlight of my day? A fucking salad?*

It would have been fine, or at least marginally tolerable, if Trish had still been Trish, a grown-up version of her teenaged self, cute and predictable, flaunting a tacky rock, bragging about her fratboy stockbroker boyfriend. At least that way Amanda would have preserved her sense of intellectual superiority, the illusion that she was an adventurous bohemian who'd chosen the road less traveled.

But Trish—*Beckett*—was a completely new person, living the kind of life Amanda had always imagined for herself. *My fiancé's a cinematographer!* How the fuck did that happen? It just seemed so unfair—the girl who'd been deliriously happy in high school was the one who'd reinvented herself, moving to a glamorous city and falling in love with an artist who loved her back, while Amanda, who'd dreamed of nothing but escape, had ended up right back where she started, with only a few stupid tattoos to show for all her trouble.

*I work at the Senior Center. They have a pretty good lecture series.*

She'd felt so stupid saying that, she'd wanted to die. And then Trish had had the gall to hug her, to fucking *apologize* for her happiness, which was way worse than bragging about it.

*I am so getting laid tonight,* Amanda thought, before they'd even let go of each other.

Her match arrived in less than an hour, knocking furtively on the front door. She studied him through the peephole, amazed, as always, that this was even possible, that you could swipe at a photo of a stranger, and the flesh-and-blood person would show up on your doorstep. This one was a little heavier than she'd expected—he claimed to be an avid cyclist—but he bore an otherwise reassuring resemblance to his profile pic, which had been taken in an apple orchard on a sunny day. It showed him standing beneath a fruit-laden tree, squinting into the camera, smiling in a way that made him look worried rather than happy.

His name was Bobby and he seemed charmingly ill-at-ease in the living room, like a teenager picking up his prom date. He wanted to know if it was all right to keep his shoes on, and asked permission before sitting down on the couch. He said no to her offer of a beer, then changed his mind a few seconds later, but only if it wasn't too much trouble. Middle-aged men were often like this, tentative and overly polite. The guys her own age had more of a swagger, as if they were stopping by to pick up a well-deserved award.

"How was the traffic?" she asked.

"Piece of cake," he said. "Only a problem at rush hour."

"Well, thanks for making the trip."

"Thanks for hosting." He surveyed the décor with a skeptical expression, taking in the matching gray furniture, the gas fireplace, the vases and baskets full of dried flowers. "This your place?"

"I'm house-sitting. My parents are on a cruise. They're coming home tomorrow."

This was the lie she always told, because she didn't want any Tinder dudes ringing the doorbell at two in the morning, drunk and looking for company. Besides, the real story was too complicated— her mother's unexpected death from a heart attack at the age of sixty-two; her own return from the city to make the funeral arrangements and deal with the legal and financial crap (she was the only child of divorced parents, so it was all on her); and the fact that she'd just *stayed*, because life in the city had gotten complicated—she'd broken up with her boyfriend and was living in a temporary sublet— and here was a whole house that suddenly belonged to *her*, though she couldn't bear to redecorate or even clean out her mother's closet. At some point, if the opportunity arose, she'd tell Bobby that her dad was a retired cop, also not true—her dad wasn't retired, wasn't a cop, and in any case was no longer in touch with Amanda—but certain precautions were advisable if you were going to invite strangers into your home and have sex with them.

"I went on a cruise once," he said. "It wasn't that great."

"You couldn't pay me enough," she told him.

When he finished his beer, they went out on the back deck to smoke the joint she'd asked him to bring. She wasn't a big pothead, but weed worked faster than alcohol, and had the added benefit of making everything seem a little more unreal and a lot funnier than it would have been otherwise, which was definitely helpful in a situation like this.

"Nice night," he said, nodding at the sky. "Moon's almost full."

Amanda didn't reply. She wanted to keep the small talk to a minimum. That had been her mistake with Dell—they'd talked for an hour before taking their clothes off, and it had ended up feeling a little too much like a real date, which was probably what caused all the confusion when they ran into each other at yoga class.

"I'm divorced," he said. "In case you were wondering."

"I wasn't."

At least he could take a hint. They smoked the rest of the joint in a strangely comfortable silence, as if they'd known each other a long time and had exhausted every possible topic of conversation. For a moment—it coincided with the realization that she was very high—she imagined they were a married couple, committed to spending every remaining night of their lives together, until one of them got sick and died.

*Me and Bobby,* she thought. *Bobby and me.*

It was a ridiculous idea, but just plausible enough to make her laugh.

"What's so funny?"

"Nothing." She shook her head, as if it wasn't worth explaining. "It's stupid."

"You have a nice laugh," he told her.

They went back inside, into her childhood bedroom. The walls were pale pink, with ghostly rectangles where posters used to hang, but it all looked the same color by candlelight. He sat on the edge of her narrow bed and watched her undress.

She made a little striptease out of it, undoing the buttons on her dress one by one, very slowly. He was a good audience.

"Oooh *yeah*," he said, more than once. "You are fucking gorgeous."

The dress fell to the floor. She stood there for a moment in her black bra and panties, along with the knee-high boots she'd tugged on for the occasion. He nodded for quite a while, as if something he'd long suspected had turned out to be true.

"You're killing me," he said. "You are totally fucking killing me."

As far back as she could remember, Amanda had had mixed feelings about her body. She was shorter and heavier than she wanted to be, with big, full breasts that weren't great for yoga or running, but made a very positive impression in situations like this.

"Oh Jesus," he muttered, as she dropped her bra on top of the dress. "Look at those fucking tits."

Standing next to Trish Lozano in the harsh light of the changing room, Amanda had felt the way she had all through high school, chubby and dull and hopeless. But right now, shimmying out of her panties in the trembling yellow light, with Bobby studying her like a painting in a museum, she felt like something special.

"Want me to keep the boots on?"

"Whatever's easier," he told her. "I'm good either way."

\* \* \*

Eve wasn't sure a Manhattan qualified as a "Fancy Cocktail," but it was close enough that she felt entitled to check off a second box on her *Going Solo* checklist. And besides, even a simple Manhattan seemed plenty fancy for the Lamplighter Inn, which was the hands-down favorite dining spot of Haddington's senior citizens, who'd been holding their annual banquet here since time immemorial.

Eve would have been fine with never eating another iceberg wedge or fillet of sole at the Lamplighter for as long as she lived, but she had a soft spot for the bar, a cozy hideaway with red leather stools and a half-dozen booths that would have been perfect for a romantic nightcap, if there'd been any romance in her life. At eight o'clock on a Wednesday evening, it was pleasantly uncrowded without seeming desolate, only four other people at the bar—a grimly silent older couple who looked like serious drinkers, and a pair of blue-collar guys watching a ballgame on the muted TV. One booth was occupied as well, by two women engaged in an emergency heart-to-heart discussion.

"Do I know you?" the bartender asked. He was a nice-looking guy around her own age, with close-cropped gray hair and an appealing residue of boyishness in his face. "Aren't you Brendan's mom?"

Eve admitted that she was. The bartender held out his hand.

"Jim Hobie. I was his soccer coach way back when. He must have been in kindergarten or first grade. Our team was called the Daisies."

"Oh my God," Eve laughed. "I forgot about the Daisies. They were adorable."

In the earliest phase of youth soccer, all the teams were coed and named after flowers, and nobody kept score. That lasted for two years, and then things got cutthroat and stayed that way.

"It was pure chaos," Hobie told her. "Brendan was the only kid on our team who knew what he was doing. A couple of times we had to tell him to stop scoring goals and give everyone else a chance."

Eve studied the man's face, trying to place him on the sidelines of those long-forgotten Saturday mornings.

"I thought Ellen DiPetro was the coach."

"I was her assistant," Hobie explained. "I had more hair back then, and a little goatee, if that rings a bell."

Bells were not ringing, but it was a long time since Brendan had been a Daisy.

"You had a kid on the team?"

"My daughter. Daniella."

"Daniella Hobie. That sounds familiar."

"She was salutatorian," he said proudly. "Gave one of the speeches at graduation."

"That's right." It was a very long and boring speech, if Eve remembered correctly, about all the wonderful lessons she'd learned from participating in the model U.N. "How's she doing?"

"Great. She's a freshman at Columbia. Seems to love it."

"Wow. An Ivy Leaguer. Good for you."

"She didn't get it from me," Hobie assured her. "I barely squeaked through Fitchburg State."

"Maybe she got it from her mother."

"I don't think so. Her mom—my ex—didn't even graduate. Though I guess that was mostly 'cause I got her pregnant." He shrugged, like it didn't really matter. "I just think Dani was born smart. I could see it in her eyes when she was a little baby. Like she was just taking it all in, you know? Figuring it out. Our son—her older brother—he was nothing like that. He spent about a year trying to swallow his own fist. That was his big project."

"They are who they are," Eve agreed. "All we can do is love them."

Hobie glanced down the bar, toward the older couple. The man was holding his arm in the air, like he was trying to hail a cab.

Hobie sighed. "Excuse me."

While he was attending to his duties, Eve took out her phone and texted Brendan.

*Do you remember Daniella Hobie? I just ran into her dad. Your old coach from the Daisies.*

"What about Brendan?" Hobie asked. "What's he up to?"

"He's at BSU."

"Still playing lacrosse?"

"Not anymore."

Her phone dinged and she picked it up.

*Ugh she gave that brutal speech the daisies were so gay*

"Speak of the devil," she said, slipping the phone back into her purse.

"It's nice that he stays in touch," Hobie observed. "I don't hear much from my kids these days. Their mom and I got divorced about ten years ago."

"Same here," she said. "It's tough."

"Irreconcilable differences." Hobie laughed sadly. "She hated my guts."

"Mine was a cheater," said Eve. "Nice guy otherwise."

"Can I ask you something?" He looked a little shy, like he knew he was broaching a delicate subject. "Does Brendan have a girlfriend?"

"I don't think so. He had one in high school, but they broke up over the summer. I wasn't crazy about her, to be honest."

"Only reason I ask is because Dani never mentions boys. *Never*. If I ask her straight up, she just says she's too busy for a relationship. But then you read these stories in the paper about the kids binge-drinking and hooking up at parties and friends with benefits and all that stuff, and it sounds like a nonstop orgy."

"They're adults," Eve said. "They get to make their own mistakes, just like we did."

"Friends with benefits." Hobie shook his head in rueful amazement. "I don't even have a *job* with benefits."

"Good one," Eve said, toasting him with her almost empty glass.

He asked if she wanted a refill. Eve said what the heck, it was still pretty early. She was enjoying the conversation, which had confirmed the value of simply getting out of the house, and elevated the status of her night from small experiment to minor accomplishment.

Hobie mixed the drink with his back turned, giving her an opportunity to admire the snugness of his jeans and the tailored fit of his tucked-in white Oxford. He was in good shape for a man his age.

*A man my age,* she reminded herself.

"You're a nice surprise on a Wednesday night," he said, placing the fresh cocktail in front of her as if it were a trophy. A trophy just for showing up, like the ones they gave to the Daisies.

"I went to a wake. Didn't feel like going home."

"Sorry to hear it. Somebody close?"

"Just an acquaintance. Guy I knew from work. He was eighty-two."

"Oh." Hobie seemed relieved to hear it. "What can you do?"

In the mirror, Eve watched as the therapy session in the booth came to a conclusion, the two woman friends putting on their jackets and heading for the door. A few minutes later, the baseball fans made their exit as well. Only Eve and the old lushes remained.

"Slow night?" she asked.

"About average."

"I guess you make up for it on the weekends."

"Saturdays are pretty busy," he said. "But that's not my shift."

Eve made a sympathetic noise, but Hobie shook her off.

"My choice," he assured her. "Weekends are sacred. That's me-time. Necessary for my mental health and well-being."

He told her about the pickup basketball game he played on Saturday mornings, a bunch of Haddington High alums, former varsity players of all ages. Hobie was one of the older guys, but he could still keep up.

"Can't jump as high as I used to," he conceded. "But I still have a decent outside shot."

"Sounds like a good workout."

"The best." Hobie grinned. "Sundays I do a group bike ride with a few buddies. Usually thirty or forty miles. We did a big charity ride this summer."

It was easy to imagine him on a fancy bike, decked out in spandex like it was the Tour de France, breathing hard as he crested a steep hill, his face glowing with cheerful determination.

"My ex-husband did that a couple of times," she said. "You gotta really be in shape."

"I try," Hobie said with a touch of false modesty that Eve did her best to ignore. "What about you? What do you like to do on the weekends?"

"This and that," she said, wishing she had a sweaty and exciting activity of her own to boast about—rock climbing or kickboxing, even tennis. But all she ever did was read and watch movies and go for slow walks around the lake with Jane and her arthritic bichon frise, Antoine. In the summer there was yard work, cutting grass and pulling weeds and watering her little garden, meditative tasks she would have enjoyed a lot more if she wasn't so worried about ticks. These days she was looking longingly at the trees, waiting for the leaves to change so she could go outside and rake on a chilly autumn morning, pathetic as that sounded. "I just like to relax, I guess."

"Absolutely," he said. "That's the whole point."

Hobie turned and watched as the elderly couple dismounted their stools, the old woman assisting the old man, who needed a few seconds to get his feet properly connected to the floor.

"You guys okay?" he asked.

The man waved dismissively, as if Hobie did nothing but bother him.

"We're fine, dear," the woman said, taking her unsteady partner by the arm. "See you tomorrow."

After they'd shuffled out, Hobie explained that they lived right around the corner, which was a good thing, since they'd both had their driver's licenses revoked, with good cause.

"This is their ritual," he said. "They come here every night and drink whiskey sours. Barely say a word to each other, and then they walk home. Last year was their fiftieth."

"That's a long time," Eve said. "I guess they're all talked out."

Hobie shrugged. "Least they have each other."

Eve nodded, distracted by the realization that they were alone now. There was something undeniably porny about the situation—the handsome bartender, the lonely divorcée. She could see the video in her head, shot a little shakily from the man's point of view, the MILF looking up, licking her lips in anticipation as she undid his belt. It was an image that would have been unthinkable at any other time in her life, but now seemed weirdly plausible. There was literally nothing stopping her. All she had to do was slip behind the bar and kneel down. Hobie gave her a searching look, almost as if he were reading her mind.

"One more?" he asked hopefully. "On the house."

Later that night, after she'd watched her porn and gone to bed, Eve wondered why she hadn't taken him up on his offer. It was just a drink, a half hour of her time. He was reasonably good-looking and easy to talk to, and it had been a long time since she'd had a fun flirtation, let alone a fling. If she'd been advising a friend, she would have said, *Give it a shot, see where it leads, he doesn't have to be perfect.*

It wasn't so much the sexual fantasy that had thrown her off—that had come and gone in a flash—as it was the nagging sense of familiarity that had snuck up on her over the course of the night, a feeling that Jim Hobie was more of the same, another helping of a meal she'd already had enough of. He wasn't as obnoxious as Barry from class, or as charmed by himself as Ted had been, but he was in the same basic ballpark. She could go to bed with him, she could even fall in love, but where would it get her? Nowhere she hadn't been before, that was for sure. She wanted something else—something *different*—though what that something was remained to be seen. All she really knew was that it was a big world out there, and she'd only been scratching the surface.

*     *     *

Amanda was a wreck the next morning, not because of her sexual exertions—Bobby only lasted a couple of minutes—but because it turned out to be one of those nights when sleep wouldn't come, when there was nothing to do but lie awake in the darkness and watch the bad thoughts float by, an armada of bleak prospects and unhappy memories. It had been close to five by the time she drifted off, and then she was up at seven, nursing a headache that two ibuprofen and three cups of coffee hadn't managed to eradicate.

"Are you okay?" Eve Fletcher asked when Amanda arrived at her office for their ten o'clock meeting. "You look a little pale."

"I'm fine," Amanda insisted, suppressing the usual urge to open up to Eve, to tell her about her rough night, and ask if she had any strategies for dealing with insomnia. "Just cramps."

Eve gave a sympathetic nod. "I'm almost done with all that. I'm not gonna miss it."

Amanda would have liked to pursue the subject, to hear Eve's thoughts about menopause and growing older, but she decided that was out of bounds, too. Eve was her boss, not her friend, no matter how much Amanda wished it were otherwise.

"So you got my email about Garth Heely?"

"I did." Eve looked upset, but only for a second. "Was it a heart attack?"

"His wife said stroke."

"You know what? That's how I want to go." Eve snapped her fingers. "Quick and painless. In my own bed. That's one thing you learn, working with old people. You really don't want to die in a hospital."

Amanda murmured agreement, trying not to think about her mother. Going fast wasn't that great, either. She'd been dead for a couple of days before the neighbors even started wondering if she was okay.

"Any ideas for a replacement?" Eve asked. "We need to nail this down sooner rather than later."

"I'll email you the short list by the end of the day."

"Perfect." Eve nodded briskly. "That it?"

"I think so."

Amanda rose uncertainly. She felt like she'd forgotten something important, like there was one more thing they needed to discuss, but the only possibilities that occurred to her were Trish's perky nipples and the puppy-like whimpers Bobby made right before he came, neither of which were appropriate subjects for workplace conversation.

"By the way," Eve said, "if you still want to get a drink sometime, I'd be totally up for that."

# Julian Fucking Spitzer

When you walk into the dining hall with someone else, you kinda melt into the scenery. Nobody even knows you're there. Walking in by yourself is a totally different experience. It's like you're radioactive, like your skin is giving off this sick greenish glow. You can feel everybody staring.

*I have friends,* you want to tell them. *They're just busy right now.*

Usually I ate my meals with Zack, but he'd slipped out after receiving a booty text at three in the morning and still hadn't returned, the first time that had ever happened. He wouldn't tell me who he was hooking up with, but he usually rushed out and came back an hour or two later, tired but happy, like a volunteer fireman who'd done his duty for the town and needed to rest up for a bit. I texted him—*dude where r u*—but he didn't respond. I tried Will and Rico, too, but those guys were probably still asleep.

The Higg that morning was an ocean of strangers, so I headed past the crowded tables to the less-populated section in back. It was a reject convention back there. I guess I could have taken a book from my backpack and pretended to study—that's what the other losers were doing—but it seemed like an asshole move, like, *Hey look at me reading a textbook!* At least my breakfast was pretty good, though it was common knowledge that the Higg omelettes weren't made with real eggs—it was some kind of sludgy yellow liquid that came in a can.

One thing you realize when you're on your own is how happy the people who aren't alone look. There were a bunch of couples eating together, and most of them were pretty smiley, probably because they'd just woken up and fucked. Other people were laughing with their friends. A professor with crazy-clown hair was lecturing a bearded grad student who kept nodding like his head was on a spring.

There were two groups I couldn't stop looking at. One of them was a bunch of girls who reminded me of Becca. Super-skinny, straight hair, lots of makeup. They were all wearing short skirts and sneakers, like they were still in middle school and thought it would be fun to coordinate their outfits. They kept erupting in laughter that sounded fake and a little too loud, like they wanted everyone to look at them and wonder what the hot girls thought was so funny.

Next to them was a table of football players, seriously big guys chowing down on plates piled high with ridiculous amounts of food. Unlike the girls, they were quiet and serious, maybe discussing the upcoming game, or wondering why coach had been so pissed off at yesterday's practice. I had this weird urge to pick up my tray and join them, just so I could feel like I was part of the team again. I really missed that feeling.

There I was, people-watching and eating my omelette, and the next thing I knew my throat swelled up. And then my eyes started to water. I realized I was two seconds away from bursting into tears like a little bitch, right there in the Higg. I actually had to squeeze my eyes shut and take a few deep breaths to get a hold of myself.

Little by little I could feel the pressure letting up, the rubber ball dissolving in my throat. It was a huge relief. But when I finally opened my eyes, that douchebag Sanjay was standing right in front of me, watching me like I was a science experiment. There was nothing on his tray but an apple and a tiny container of yogurt.

"Hey, Brendan," he said. "You okay?"

I hadn't seen him for a couple of weeks—he wasn't hanging out with Dylan anymore—but it seemed to me that he was slightly less nerdy than before. New glasses maybe, or a different haircut. Cooler clothes. Something.

"Fine," I said. "Just a little hungover."

He nodded, but it was annoying the way he did it, like it served me right for getting drunk on a Monday night. *Fuck him.* I wiped my mouth and stood up, even though there were still a few bites left of my omelette.

"Gotta run," I said. "Catch you later."

I carried my tray over to the dish line and put it on the belt. I glanced back at Sanjay as I headed for the exit. He was sitting at my table, all by himself, reading a book and munching on his apple. He seemed totally fine, like he didn't even know I'd ditched him.

Losing my shit in public like that was a wake-up call. I mean, I knew I was drinking too much and fucking up in my classes. I'd flunked a unit test in Math and gotten a D on my first writing assignment for Comp—*What Does White Privilege Mean to Me?*—a grade the instructor claimed was "an act of charity" on her part. I was having trouble in Econ, too, but that was mainly because I couldn't understand the prof's heavy Chinese accent. That afternoon, he was droning on about "sooply sigh" and "deeman sigh" when I started zoning out. But instead of checking Facebook or texting Wade, I decided to be constructive for once and make a to-do list, which my dad claimed was one of the Eleven Habits of Highly Successful People or whatever. It went like this:

- Homework!
- Pay Attention in Class!!
- No Drinking on Weekdays (if poss.)
- Call Mom
- Laundry!!!
- Way Less Super Smash (vid games in gen.)
- Bday Card for Becca!
- Return Dad's Email

- Hang w ppl Besides Zack
- Break Up w Becca?
- Shave Chest & Balls
- Extra-Currics?

It had a calming effect to write it all down, to take my sense of impending doom and divide it into a dozen problems that could actually be solved, some more easily than others. I decided to start small, heading straight to the laundry room after class and washing every item of clothing I owned, plus the sheets and towels, which were pretty disgusting. It was a real morale booster, except that some of the white stuff came out pink.

That night I went to the library to do my homework, which I hardly ever did. I was trying to read this book about climate change, how it was almost too late for humanity to save itself, but maybe not quite, not if we all made a decision to change our wasteful lifestyles *immediately*. It was pretty interesting, but I had trouble keeping my focus. For one thing, I was sitting at a big table in the main reading room and the girl next to me was chewing her gum really loud. And this dude across from me kept sighing hopelessly as he erased the answers on his problem set, like he wanted the whole world to know he was struggling.

But all that was just background noise. What was really bugging me was the phone call I'd just had with my mom, which hadn't gone the way I'd expected. I figured she'd be happy to hear from me, since we hadn't spoken in a couple of weeks. But she kind of blew me off.

"I'm on my way out the door, honey. I have class tonight."

"What?"

"I told you about my class. At ECC? Gender and Society, every Tuesday and Thursday night?"

"Oh yeah," I said, though it was news to me. She'd been talking about going back to school for so long I pretty much just tuned out whenever the subject came up. "How's that going?"

"Great. It's really exciting to be back in the classroom."

For a person who was on her way out the door, she had a lot of time to rave about her class. Apparently, the teacher was a really unique person, the students were super-diverse, and the reading was challenging and thought-provoking, exactly what she needed at this particular moment in her life.

"Cool," I said, though it bugged me to hear her talking about college like it was the greatest thing in the world. I was the one who was really in college, and in my humble opinion, it was a mixed bag. Also, she was taking *one fucking class*. Try taking four, and then tell me how much fun you're having.

"Oh, by the way," she said. "One of the other students said he went to high school with you. Julian Spitzer? That ring a bell?"

I froze for a few seconds, trying to convince myself I'd misheard. But I knew I hadn't.

"I remember the name," I said, after a long pause. "But I didn't know him that well."

"He told me to say hello."

I seriously doubted that Julian Spitzer had asked her to say hello. Unless he was fucking with me, in which case I couldn't really blame him.

"Hey," I said, trying to change the subject. "I got another email from Dad about Parents Weekend—"

"You know what, honey? I really have to go. I'll call you back tomorrow, okay? Love you."

Technically speaking, I wasn't lying to my mom about Julian Spitzer. I really didn't know him that well. He'd moved to Haddington in seventh grade, too late to make much of an impression on me and my buddies. In high school he was part of the skater posse. You'd see them cruising through town sometimes, zipping down the middle of the street in a big pack, like they didn't give a fuck about oncoming traffic. I remember Julian standing up really straight on his board, hands on his hips, long hair streaming behind him like a girl's.

I didn't witness the incident at Kim Mangano's house. I was upstairs with Becca—it was the first time we hooked up—in a bedroom that belonged to Kim's little twin brothers. Meanwhile, Wade was in the kitchen, trying to talk to Fiona Rattigan, his on-and-off girlfriend who'd broken up with him a few days earlier. I guess she was ignoring him, and he got kind of upset. He grabbed her by the arm and wouldn't let go. She said he was hurting her. A couple of people tried to intervene, but Wade told them to mind their own business.

*He's abusing me!* Fiona said, in a really loud voice. I think she was pretty drunk herself. *Somebody call 911!*

Julian Spitzer happened to be in the kitchen, because that's where the keg was. When he finished filling his cup with beer, he walked over to Wade and tossed it in his face.

*Are you deaf? She asked you to leave her alone!*

It took Wade a couple of seconds to wipe the beer out of his eyes and recover from the shock, and by then a couple of our lacrosse teammates had grabbed hold of him so he couldn't do anything stupid. It was the middle of the season and our team was doing really well. The last thing we needed was for the party to get busted, and a bunch of our best players to get suspended for drinking and fighting. But Wade was furious.

For a week or two it was a big deal in school, like, *Hey, did you hear about Wade and Spitzer?* But then it just kinda died down. There were other parties, other incidents. Wade got back with Fiona, our team made it to the state quarterfinals, and then it was summer vacation. The whole beer-in-the-face thing seemed like ancient history, except that Wade couldn't stop brooding about it. We ignored him, because everybody knew that Wade could be a nasty drunk. When he's sober, he's one of the sweetest, most laid-back guys you could know.

It was just bad luck that night in August. Wade and Fiona were on the outs again, Becca and I were fighting, and our buddy Troy hated his camp counselor job, which required him to spend his days with whiny five-year-olds. We tried to cheer ourselves up by drinking a bottle of Popov vodka in the woods by the golf course, but getting wasted didn't improve our mood.

Afterward, we drove around in Troy's Corolla for a while, circling past the same familiar landmarks over and over—the high school, the cemetery, the lake, the high school again—because nobody felt like going home, and at least we could be bored together, and complain about the songs on the radio.

And then, on maybe our eighth or ninth lap around the town, we just happened to see him—Julian Fucking Spitzer, all alone on a dark stretch of Green Street. He was riding his skateboard at a good clip, pushing off with one foot and then gliding for a while, not a care in the world.

"Look at that," Troy said. "It's your little buddy."

He slowed down until we were right on Julian's ass, and then gunned it, swerving around him and jackknifing the Corolla so it blocked the road. Julian had to jump off the skateboard to keep from plowing into us. He could have run, but for some reason he just stood there, paralyzed, as Wade stepped out of the passenger seat.

"Get in the fucking car," he said. "We're going for a ride."

"What if I say no?" asked Julian.

"Just get in the car, asshole."

Julian didn't argue. It was like he'd been expecting this for a long time, and figured he should just get it over with. He picked up his skateboard and climbed obediently into the backseat. Wade ducked in right behind him, so there were three of us back there, with Julian squashed in the middle. Troy started the engine and we headed off.

"How's it going, dude?" Wade asked in a fake friendly voice. "Having a good summer?"

"Not really," said Julian.

"Awesome," said Wade. "Happy to hear it."

He slipped his arm around Julian's shoulders like they were boyfriend and girlfriend. I could smell someone's sweat, sharp and sour, but I wasn't sure whose it was. It was like we were one person back there, three bodies glued together.

"I've been looking all over for you," Wade said, in this weird flirty voice. "You never answer my texts."

Julian didn't reply. He kept glancing in my direction, pleading for help, but there was nothing I could do. This was between him and Wade.

"You shouldn't have thrown that beer in my face." Wade squeezed him a little tighter. "That was a big mistake."

"I'm sorry." Julian's voice cracked a little, like he was maybe gonna cry. "I'm really sorry."

"I bet you are," Wade agreed. "But it's way too late for an apology."

Julian nodded, like he'd figured as much. His voice was small and scared. "What are you gonna do to me?"

Wade didn't answer for a while. He took his arm off Julian's shoulders and gazed out the window at the dark houses with their neat front yards, attractive homes full of decent people.

"I'm not a bad person," he said. "I'm really not."

I could totally see his dilemma. He'd talked so much about the hardcore vengeance he was going to inflict on Julian, and now he had to deliver. You couldn't just drive around with the kid for a half hour and then let him off with a stern warning.

"You should fuck him in the ass," Troy suggested. "I bet he'd like that."

I guess it could've been worse. There was no violence, no bloodshed, no tears. Nobody got fucked in the ass. It was just the four of us standing in front of a disgusting Port-A-John near the soccer field in VFW Park. I swear, you could smell that thing from twenty yards away, a cloud of human waste and chemical perfume that had been fermenting in the sun for the whole summer. Wade held out his hand and asked Julian for his phone.

"Why?" Julian asked. "What are you gonna do with it?"

"Just give it to me, asshole."

Once again, Julian did as he was told. Wade shoved the phone into his pants pocket. Then he pointed at the Port-A-John.

"Get in there," he said.

I had my hand on Julian's shoulder. I could feel his whole body stiffen.

"No way," he said.

"Oh, you're going in," Wade told him. "I guarantee you that."

"Please," Julian said. "I already apologized."

Wade poked him in the chest. "I'm not gonna say it again."

Julian just sort of went limp. All the fight went out of him.

"That's all?" he said. "You're not gonna hurt me?"

"That's all," Wade told him.

"You promise?"

"I promise. Now get the fuck in there."

It was all very civilized. Wade opened the door to that reeking closet and Julian stepped inside.

"Enjoy your evening," Wade told him.

Julian turned to face us. The Port-A-John was slightly elevated, so it was almost like he was on stage. I guess he felt like he had nothing to lose.

"You guys suck," he said. "I hope you know that."

"Shut the fuck up," Troy told him. "You're getting off easy. If it was up to me—"

"I'm serious," Julian continued. "Guys like you are what's wrong with the—"

Wade slammed the flimsy plastic door before Julian could finish his sentence. Then he sealed it shut using the duct tape he'd found in Troy's glove compartment. He wrapped it really well, using every last bit of tape on the roll, turning that Port-A-John into a prison cell.

"Yo, Julian," he said. "I'm leaving your phone out here."

"Fuck you." Julian's voice sounded muffled and far away, though he was right next to us. "You're a terrible person. All three of you."

Wade dropped the phone in the grass.

"Catch you later, dude."

Julian started yelling as we walked away, calling us morons and scumbags and begging us to open the door, but his pleas had dwindled away to nothing long before we reached the parking lot. We tried to laugh about it in the car, congratulating ourselves on the genius prank we'd just pulled, but our hearts weren't really in it. I was about to say we should go back and let him out, but Troy spoke first.

"He can breathe in there, right? He's not gonna suffocate or anything?"

"There are vents in the side," I said. "I checked."

"Can you imagine how bad it smells?" Troy asked. "Could you actually die from that?"

"He'll be fine," Wade said. "People will be walking their dogs at like six in the morning. They'll let him out."

"That's five hours from now," I said.

"Don't feel sorry for that fucker," Wade said. "He's lucky he's not in the hospital."

I went home and got into bed, but I couldn't fall asleep. All I could think about was Julian Spitzer, trapped in that gnarly box, far from anyone who could help him. I wondered if his parents had realized he was gone, if they were maybe calling the phone that Wade had left in the grass.

I couldn't take it. Around five that morning I got out of bed and rode my bike over to the park. It had seemed so sinister the night before, a creepy place where anything could happen. But it was beautiful in the early morning, with the sun coming up and birds chirping like crazy. I could see houses through the trees, not nearly as far away as they'd seemed in the dark.

I was relieved to find the Port-A-John empty, the tape seal broken. Maybe Julian had only been in there for a little while before someone came along, or he figured out a way to free himself. Maybe I'd stayed up all night worrying about nothing.

We had a few bad days after that, wondering if he'd told any-one what we'd done, his parents or maybe the cops or even just his friends. We weren't sure if it was a crime to tape someone inside a portable toilet, but it was the kind of prank you could get in pretty bad trouble for, a serious lapse in judgment you wouldn't want to have to explain to your parents or coaches, or to a college admissions officer.

But nothing happened. We never heard a word about it.

That was the summer before our senior year. When we got back to school in September, Julian Spitzer was mysteriously absent. Some people said he'd dropped out, others that he'd transferred to private school. I was just glad he was gone, so I didn't have to see him or think about him. By the time we graduated, I'd pretty much erased him from my memory, which was why it was such an unpleasant shock to hear my mother mention his name that afternoon, drop-ping it so casually into the conversation, asking if it rang a bell.

You know how sometimes, if you try not to think about some-thing, you become that much more aware of it? That's how it was with me and that girl in the library. I kept trying to concentrate on my book—the melting glaciers and rising sea levels—and she kept chewing away, making this crackly gum-and-saliva noise that went right through me.

*Jesus Christ,* I thought. *Can you even hear yourself?*

It was actually a relief when the protesters arrived. There were maybe twenty of them, and they entered the library like a tour group, huddled together near the main entrance, whispering and looking around. Some of the kids at my table were already rolling their eyes and shaking their heads.

"Not again," moaned the chewing machine.

"Every friggin' night," said the kid with the eraser.

The protesters organized themselves in single file, stretching all the way down the center aisle. The girl closest to my table had blue hair and black lipstick. She glanced nervously at the Muslim girl next to her, who just had the headscarf, not the facemask. They lifted their arms.

"Hands up! Don't shoot!"

It was kind of lame that first time, like only half the group got the memo, and not all of them read it at the same time.

"He was a thug!" somebody shouted from one of the tables.

The blue-haired girl and her Muslim friend raised their arms higher and chanted with more conviction.

"Hands up! Don't shoot!"

I'd heard about these Michael Brown protests—they were supposedly happening all over campus—but this was the first one I'd actually seen. A lot of people were complaining about them, saying that it was really disrespectful, the way the protesters barged into classrooms and harassed the fans at sporting events. But it was kind of cool to have them invade the library like this, filling that quiet space with their chant, which became louder and more confident the more they repeated it.

"Hands up! Don't shoot!"

The line was moving now, new faces filing past me in a slow parade. To my amazement, one of them was waving at me. It took me a second to recognize Amber, from the Autism Awareness Network, and by then she'd broken from the line and was heading straight for my table.

"Dude!" she said in this jubilant voice, like I'd come back from the dead. "Where have you been? We missed you last meeting."

"Too much work," I said, holding up my book so she could see I was reading about climate change.

Even though she was out of formation, she raised her hands and shouted along with the others, begging the invisible cops not to shoot. She was wearing sweats and a hoodie, and I noticed again how strong she looked, with those linebacker shoulders, and how pretty she was, blond hair and blue eyes and farm-girl freckles, her cheeks all flushed with excitement.

"It's terrible what happened in Ferguson," she told me. "This shit's gotta stop."

I didn't know what to say to that. The more I heard about Michael Brown the more confused I got. Was he minding his business or had he robbed a store? Was he surrendering or trying to grab the cop's gun? I'd heard different people say different things, and didn't know what to believe.

"It's fucked up," I said. "That's for sure."

Amber smiled, like I'd passed some kind of test. She held out her hand, like she was asking me to dance.

"Come on," she said. "We need your voice."

I was shy at first, and worried about my backpack, which I'd left at the table.

"Hands up! Don't shoot!"

"Come on!" Amber told me. "Say it like you mean it!"

Some people heckled us, but others got up from their seats and joined the conga line as we moved through the library. We marched past the circulation desk and snaked through the stacks to the Computer Commons.

"Hands up! Don't shoot!"

It got easier the more I did it, and a lot more fun. Some people were swaying and others started raising the roof. For a little while Amber and I were holding hands, our arms aloft like we'd just won a medal.

"Hands up! Don't shoot!"

We did three circuits of the main floor and then exited through the metal detector, chanting the whole time. It felt great to step out of the library into the chilly October night, everybody high-fiving and congratulating everybody else, the moonlight shining on Amber's hair as she hugged me.

When I got back to the room, Zack was lying on his bed with these huge DJ headphones clamped over his ears. I wanted to tell him about the protest, but he yanked off the headphones and sat up before I'd even had time to shrug off my backpack.

"Dude," he said. "Can I ask you something?"

"Sure."

"Would you ever hook up with a fat girl?"

"I doubt it," I said. "That's not really my thing."

"Yeah, but what if there's a fat girl you really liked? Would you hook up with her?"

"Is this for a class?"

"No, I'm just curious."

"Depends." I sat down on my bed, directly across from him. "If she's one of those plus-sized models I might."

"Not a model. Just a regular fat girl. But she's pretty and has a great personality."

"Are you trying to set me up with someone?"

"Dude, I'm asking you a simple question."

He sounded annoyed, which was a little unfair, since I'd already answered him twice.

"Fine," I said. "I'll hook up with her. Why not, if she's as great as you say?"

Zack nodded approvingly, like I'd finally given the correct answer.

"Okay, so you hook up with this girl a couple of times and it's fun as hell, but totally casual. No strings. But then one night she starts crying, and you're like, *What's wrong?* And she's like, *Why don't we ever go out in public? Are you ashamed of me? Is it because I'm fat?* What do you say then?"

It was all so obvious, I almost laughed in his face.

"Dude, are you hooking up with a fat girl? Is that where you go at three in the morning?"

"No," he said, in that same put-upon tone. "This is a completely hypothetical scenario."

"All right," I said. "Speaking hypothetically, I'd probably say, *Bitch, maybe if you dropped a hundred pounds we could go to the movies. In the meantime, could we get back to the blowjob you were giving me? I'm tired and I have to meet my asshole roommate for breakfast in the morning.*"

"Dude, that's so mean. She can't help it if she's fat."

"Not my problem, bro."

"Wow." Zack looked impressed. "You're an even bigger dick than I am."

"Thank you," I said. "You wanna get baked and watch some *Bob's Burgers*?"

"I could go for that," he told me. "But I can't stay up too late. I'm tired and I gotta meet my asshole roommate for breakfast in the morning."

"That's funny," I said. "So do I."

We bumped fists and Zack broke out his weed, and pretty soon we were lit and laughing our asses off, talking shit about my hypothetical ex-girlfriend, the fat girl who'd been fun for a while, until she turned all weepy and started getting on my nerves.

# The Confident One

When Eve invited Amanda out for a drink, she hadn't meant it to be a date. It was a casual social thing, two colleagues hanging out after work, getting to know each other a little better. And it wasn't even Eve's idea. All she'd done was belatedly accept an invitation that Amanda had extended more than once, and that she herself had felt guilty about declining. There was no hidden agenda; she was just being polite, making amends, and giving them both something to do on an otherwise empty Friday night.

And yet it felt like a date, which was weird, because Eve didn't date women. Of course, she wasn't dating any men either, though that was only for lack of opportunity. If a man had asked her out, she would have happily said yes, unless it was creepy Barry from Gender and Society, who, unfortunately, was the only man expressing any interest at the moment, with the possible exception of Jim Hobie, the chatty bartender, though all he'd done was offer her a free drink, which hardly qualified as a romantic overture, and which, in any case, she'd declined.

But if tonight wasn't a date—and it definitely wasn't—then what accounted for the fluttery feeling of anticipation she'd been experiencing ever since she'd marked it on her calendar? And why had she chosen to wear this silky green blouse that went so well with her eyes, and then unbuttoned it one button lower than usual? The answer to these questions, Eve knew, was as simple as it was embarrassing: she'd been watching too much porn, and it had infected her imagination, making her hyper-aware of the sexual possibilities embedded in the most innocent situations. It would have been funny if it hadn't been so pathetic.

"I meant to tell you," said Amanda, who seemed quite clear about the fact that she wasn't on a date. "The maple syrup guy can't do the November lecture, so I'm scrambling to find a replacement."

"Uh-oh." Eve stretched her mouth into an expression of mock horror. "Sounds like a sticky situation."

Amanda looked puzzled for a moment, and then made a sound that resembled a chuckle.

"Sorry." Eve frowned. "Humor's not my specialty. At least that's what my ex-husband used to tell me."

"Nice," Amanda said. "I'm sure you appreciated his honesty."

"Absolutely. He was full of constructive criticism."

"Sounds like my old boyfriend," Amanda observed. "He was very concerned about my weight. If he caught me with some Ben and Jerry's, he'd pull the container right out of my hand. He'd say, *I don't want you to regret this.*"

"Really?"

"It was all for my own good, you know?"

Eve wanted to say something supportive but not inappropriate about Amanda's curves—that was one good thing about the Milfateria, it had given her an appreciation of the sexual appeal of all sorts of body types—but they were interrupted by a couple of middle-aged frat boys who wanted to know if the stool next to Amanda's was free. The guy who asked was jolly and bloated, with thinning blond hair and an alarmingly pink complexion. He made no effort to disguise his interest in the hand grenade tattooed on Amanda's left breast, only partially obscured by the neckline of her dress.

"All yours," she told the guy, scooching toward Eve to make room. Their knees bumped together, and Eve felt the subtle electric jolt you sometimes get from accidental contact. Amanda shifted again, undoing the connection.

"Ted—that's my ex—used to tell me I was a bad storyteller," Eve continued. "He said it was like a Victorian novel every time I went to the supermarket."

That didn't sound too bad to Amanda. "I like Victorian novels. At least I used to. I haven't read one since college."

"They can be kind of daunting," said Eve. "I've been meaning to start *Middlemarch* for the past year or so. Everybody always says how great it is. But it never seems like the right time to crack it open."

Amanda looked wistful. "There's so much to read, but all I do is watch Netflix and play Candy Crush. I feel like I'm wasting my life."

"It's hard to concentrate after a long day at work. Sometimes you just want to turn your brain off."

"I guess. But even on the weekends, I'll read five pages, and then I have to get up and check my phone. It's not that I want to, it's that I *have* to. It's a physical urge, like the phone is part of my body."

Eve was a little too old to have that sort of relationship with her phone, but she understood the larger point all too well. It was mortifying to be an adult and not be able to control yourself. She didn't used to be like that.

"Hey," she said. "Maybe we could find a retired English professor to talk about Dickens or Jane Austen. We haven't done anything like that for a while."

Amanda's nod was grudging at best. "We *could*. But I was hoping we could maybe try something different. Get outside the box a little."

"Like what?"

"I don't know. There are a lot of fascinating topics out there. Let's hear about global warming or immigration or the rise of feminism or the history of the birth control pill. The anti-vaccine movement. I mean, just because you're old doesn't mean you can't handle a new idea, right?"

Eve heard the implicit criticism in these suggestions. Her policy, ever since she'd taken charge at the Senior Center, had been to avoid controversy when booking the lecture series. No religion, no politics, nothing divisive or threatening. The series, as currently conceived, leaned heavily on nostalgia (FDR and the Greatest Generation, the *Titanic* and the *Hindenburg*, the Civil War and wagon train pioneers), continuing education (Backyard Wildlife, Know Your Night Sky), and uplifting human interest stories (a mountain climber with a high-tech prosthetic leg, an ex-nun turned cabaret singer), with the occasional author appearance or travelogue sprinkled in.

"I hear what you're saying. But you know who we're dealing with. A lot of the seniors are set in their ways. They don't like anything upsetting or unfamiliar. Trust me, they don't want to hear about global warming."

"I get it." Amanda nodded ruefully and tossed back the last swallow of wine in her glass. "I didn't mean to rock the boat."

"It's okay. That's why I hired you. Sometimes the boat needs to be rocked a little."

In the lesbian MILF videos that Eve liked best, there was only one basic scenario: a confident woman seduces a reluctant one. Many began with the reluctant woman grumpily washing dishes or mopping the floor when the doorbell rings. The visitor—the confident one—usually arrives with a bottle of wine, a sympathetic expression, and a bit of exposed cleavage. Cut to the two women on the couch, deep in conversation, usually sitting close together. Often their knees are touching.

*It is so good to see you,* the confident one says, stroking her friend's thigh or upper arm in a comforting, arguably nonsexual way. *But you look a little sad.*

The reluctant one doesn't deny it.

*It's been a rough day,* she sighs.

Maybe she lost her job. Maybe her husband left her. Maybe the bank turned down her loan application. But whatever the problem might be, it's nothing that can't be solved by a backrub and some cunnilingus.

Eve relaxed a little once they relocated to the restaurant section. They hadn't planned on eating, but they'd polished off the first two glasses of wine in under an hour, and neither of them wanted to drink a third on an empty stomach. It was only seven o'clock—way too early to call it a night—and a table happened to be available, so here they were.

"I love these potatoes," Amanda said.

"Should we get another order?"

Amanda dabbed at her mouth with the stiff cloth napkin, leaving a smudge of lipstick on the white fabric.

"That's very decadent of you."

"I don't get out much," Eve explained. "Might as well take advantage."

"You should've come to Foxwoods the other night," Amanda teased. "I could've used the company."

Eve grimaced. "Was it horrible?"

"It was actually okay," Amanda said. "I just felt sorry for Frank Jr. It must be depressing, doing an impersonation of your dead father. At least Nancy got to wear go-go boots and sing some songs of her own."

"She did look good in those boots," Eve said. "But I really don't think they were made for walking."

She glanced around, trying to get a bead on their elusive waiter. Aside from the iffy service, Casa Enzo was as good as everyone said, a cozy tapas place—the first ever in Haddington—with a dozen tables packed into a room that wasn't quite big enough to accommodate them. It was even louder here than at the bar, but at least Eve wasn't experiencing the restlessness that often plagued her in restaurants, the nagging sense that she was marooned at one of the boring tables while the interesting conversations were happening elsewhere.

"We should do this more often," Amanda said. "I'm usually just sitting home on the weekends, eating too much chocolate."

Eve plucked an oily green olive from the bowl. "So you're not seeing anyone?"

Amanda shook her head, more in resignation than sadness. "It's kind of a romantic wasteland around here. There aren't a lot of single people my age. At least I haven't figured out where they're hiding."

Feeling a little self-conscious, Eve removed the olive pit from her mouth and placed it daintily on her plate. There were six of them now, lined up like bullets, with bits of stray flesh stuck to the surface.

"These things are addictive," she said.

"What about you?" Amanda asked. "Are you involved with anyone?"

"Not even close. Haven't had a date in six months. Haven't had a good one in at least two years, and even that one wasn't all that great."

"Really?" Amanda seemed genuinely surprised. "How come? I mean, you're a very attractive woman."

"Thanks. That's sweet of you."

"I'm serious," Amanda insisted. "I hope I look half as good as you when I'm your age."

Eve forced herself to smile, hoping it would hide her irritation.

"Hey," she said. "Did I tell you about the class I'm taking?"

Some of the videos Eve had stumbled upon skipped straight to the bedroom, two naked women already engaged in the usual licking and groping. She clicked out of them as soon as she realized her mistake. She needed to start at the beginning and observe the negotiation, to see how the small talk turned into flirting, to hear the magic words that got the reluctant one to accept the first kiss, or allow her blouse to be unbuttoned.

The really hot part was the epiphany, the moment when the reluctant one suddenly understands that she's been seduced. All the good stuff happened then. The quickening of the breath. The parting of the lips. The silent granting of permission. The understanding that everything that came before had been leading inevitably to *this*: one mouth discovering another, a hand cupping a breast, knees spreading apart. The end of reluctance. When it was good, you could forget you were watching porn and accept it, if not as the truth, then at least as a glimpse of a better world than the one you lived in, a world where everyone secretly wanted the same thing, and no one failed to get it.

Dessert arrived and Eve did the honors, poking her spoon through the brittle crust of the crème brûlée into the golden custard below.

"Wow," she said, pushing the dish across the table. "You gotta try this."

Amanda took a little bite. Her eyes widened with theatrical wonder.

"Oh my God. If I'm still single when I'm thirty, I'm going to marry the person who made this."

"I hope you don't mind a ménage à trois," Eve told her, "because I just had the exact same thought. Except for the turning thirty part."

"I'm game if you are." Amanda glanced toward the kitchen. "But I guess we'll have to see what our husband thinks. Or wife."

"I'm sure they won't mind."

Amanda nodded, but her face had turned serious.

"So how old is your professor?"

"Around my age. But she's only been living as a woman for a few years. Before that she was a heterosexual man, a professional athlete with a wife and child. But she was an emotional wreck, self-medicating with alcohol and prescription drugs. She went on a business trip and tried to kill herself with an overdose. Apparently, she came pretty close. When she came out of the coma, the first thing she said was, *I'm a woman. I've been a woman all my life.*"

"That's so cool," Amanda said. "Studying gender theory with a trans professor. You're really lucky."

"It's pretty interesting. She's an attractive woman and there are all these middle-aged straight guys in the class. They don't know what to make of her."

"*Really,*" Amanda said, as if Eve had been holding out on her. "Any cute ones?"

Eve shook her head. "It's a motley crew. And believe me, at this point in my life, my standards are not especially high."

"Come on." Amanda smiled encouragingly. "There's gotta be someone."

Of course there was someone. There always was, at least since junior high. It wasn't a class if you didn't have a little crush on *someone*.

"It's crazy." She lowered her voice, in case anyone nearby was listening. "The only person I'm the least bit attracted to is a kid. Eighteen years old. Just a baby."

Amanda looked delighted. This was better than she'd hoped.

"That's pretty kinky," she said, as if *kinky* were a term of high praise. "I didn't know you liked the young ones."

"It's not like that," Eve said. "I just find myself watching him a lot, thinking, *If only I were your age.*"

"What's he look like?"

"He's really thin, almost like a girl. Not too tall. Long hair. Beautiful eyes."

"Smart?"

"I'm not sure." Eve had only talked to Julian once, and he hadn't said very much. "Kinda hard to pin him down. For the first couple of classes, I thought he might be gay. But it turns out he identifies as straight."

"How'd you find that out?"

"We do these peer interviews where we're supposed to articulate all this stuff people usually just take for granted."

"What did you say?" Amanda seemed genuinely curious, as if Eve's sexuality and gender identity were shrouded in mystery.

"I said straight. Cisgender. Nothing too exciting."

Amanda nodded, as if she'd figured as much. Did she look disappointed, maybe just a little? Eve wished she could qualify her answer, explain that she was very turned on by lesbian porn at the moment, and was trying to figure out what that meant. But she'd need a few more glasses of wine before she'd dream of making a confession like that.

"So would you ever do it?" Amanda asked. "Hook up with a guy that young?"

"No way." Eve grimaced at the thought. "He went to high school with my son. I'm old enough to be his mother."

"You're a MILF," Amanda said, very matter-of-factly. "It happens."

Eve was momentarily startled by the term, and the ease with which Amanda had used it in public. In her mind, it was a dirty word, not to be spoken out loud. But also a compliment.

"I don't know about that," she said, smiling modestly.

"Look at it this way," Amanda told her. "If a guy your age went out with a college girl, people would congratulate him."

"I wouldn't. I'd think he was a creep. And I'd feel sorry for the girl."

"Even if she didn't feel sorry for herself?"

"It's not gonna happen," Eve said. "It's not even in the realm of possibility."

"I'm sure the kid would be thrilled. It's like a porn fantasy come true. *I did it with my best friend's mom.*"

"They're not best friends. They barely knew each other."

Amanda scraped the last bit of crème brûlée from the bowl. Her face turned thoughtful as she sucked on her spoon.

"I wouldn't mind dating a younger guy. I've only been hooking up with older men lately, and I could definitely use a change."

"Really? How much older?"

"Mostly forties. Some fifties."

"Wow." Eve nodded in a way that she hoped came off as nonjudgmental. "Is that a preference or just a coincidence?"

"Little of both." Amanda's tongue flicked out, expertly removing a stray dab of cream from her upper lip. "They're nicer than guys my age."

"Where do you meet them?"

"Tinder, mostly." She watched Eve closely, trying to gauge her reaction.

"So you meet strange guys and have sex with them?"

Eve wanted the question back as soon as she'd asked it. But Amanda didn't seem to mind.

"They're not *that* strange," she said, smiling at her own joke.

In the videos Eve liked best, the women were friends or neighbors or former romantic partners. Some of the other scenarios were a little more problematic, playing on age and power differentials that would have raised serious red flags in real life. A teacher doesn't think a pupil's been working up to her potential. A homesick foreign exchange student needs a little cheering up. A cougarish stepmother puts the moves on her sullen, but very persuadable, stepdaughter.

In the porn world, no one seemed to have heard of sexual harassment. Doctors went down on their patients. Personal trainers fondled their clients. Underperforming employees found creative ways to save their jobs. Eve would have objected strenuously to these scenarios if a man had been involved. But with two women, it was different somehow—a little more playful, and not nearly as creepy. Just a harmless fantasy, rather than something that reminded you of an infuriating article you'd read in the paper, or a bad experience recounted by a friend.

"There was a girl in my dorm who transitioned," Amanda said. "It was an amazing thing to watch. When she showed up freshman year, she was so plain and quiet nobody even noticed her. Then she cut her hair and started dressing like a boy. Sophomore year she began the hormone therapy. Junior year her voice got deep, and it was like, *I'm not Linda anymore. Please call me Lowell.* That summer Lowell got the top surgery. By the end of senior year he was this buff, handsome dude with a scruffy beard and a motorcycle. Lots of girls I knew dated him. It got to be sort of a thing, you know? Like, cross that one off the bucket list."

Eve nodded, but the story sounded so foreign to her. When she'd been in college, there was a woman on campus with patches of dark hair on her face, but nobody thought she was cool or intriguing. People mostly just felt sorry for the poor girl, and did their best not to stare. Eve assumed she was suffering from a medical condition or some kind of cosmic misfortune. It had never even occurred to her that the bearded woman might be making a choice, moving in the direction of happiness.

"So these girls who dated Lowell," Eve said. "Were they straight or bi or what?"

"All kinds." Amanda lowered her gaze, adjusting the napkin in her lap. "I asked him out for coffee one afternoon. We had a pretty good time. When it was over, he drove me home on his motorcycle, and we made out a little outside my apartment. It got pretty heavy, but when he asked if we could go up to my room, I chickened out. I guess I wasn't ready for whatever that was gonna be, which is saying something, 'cause I was pretty much up for anything back then. But he was totally cool about it. The next time I saw him, he was dating this beautiful Turkish girl from my Milton class."

"That's so amazing," Eve said. "It's like a modern-day Cinderella story. You change your body and your name, and all your dreams come true. I wish I could do that myself."

"Really?"

"Not the man part. Just the chance to leave your old self behind. To take all your mistakes and regrets and erase them from the story. Who wouldn't want that?"

Amanda nodded, as if that made a lot of sense.

"So who would you be? If you could start over?"

"I don't know. I haven't given it a lot of thought."

"What about your name? What would you call yourself?"

"Let's see." Eve closed her eyes, and a name appeared to her unbidden, blue letters stamped on a gift shop license plate. "*Ursula*. I'd call myself Ursula."

"That's a strong name. What's this Ursula like?"

"Braver than me," Eve said. "She does what she wants. Doesn't worry so much about what everybody else thinks. Doesn't settle for less than she deserves, or apologize unless it's absolutely necessary. She just wants to live and have adventures."

Amanda smiled. "I like this person."

Eve knew she'd said more than enough, but she was on a roll. "Ursula probably doesn't work at the Senior Center."

"I'm sorry to hear that," Amanda said, but she didn't sound sorry.

"She does something a little more exciting. Maybe she's a travel writer. She wears sunglasses and has lots of affairs."

"She sounds pretty sexy."

Eve scratched at a yellowish stain on the tablecloth, hoping her face wasn't as pink as it felt. She was a little drunk, a little embarrassed, but also strangely exhilarated.

"What about you?" she said. "Who would you be?"

"Juniper." Amanda spoke without hesitation. "I'd be petite and graceful. Maybe a dancer. No tattoos. Just my own beautiful skin. And I'd be naked every chance I got. I'd leave my window shades up, let the whole world look."

"Good for you."

Amanda laughed a little sadly, like she was unworthy of her own fantasy. Eve wanted to tell her she was beautiful already, but instead she made a toast.

"To Ursula and Juniper."

"Juniper and Ursula," Amanda replied, and they clinked their tiny glasses.

By the time they left the restaurant, Eve had come full circle, back to the idea that this *was* a date, and a pretty good one at that. They'd talked for hours without hitting any dead spots, they'd drunk a little too much wine, they'd laughed and told the truth about their lives.

It was quiet as she walked Amanda to her car, a bracing autumnal chill in the air. The fluttery feeling in Eve's chest was even stronger than it had been before.

"Thanks for dinner," Amanda said. "I really enjoyed it."

"Me too."

Instead of getting in her car, Amanda just stood there, smiling shyly, like she was waiting for something else to happen. Eve wanted to kiss her, but she was paralyzed, unsure about which one of them was the confident one.

*It has to be me,* she thought.

She was older. She was the boss. But she didn't feel confident at all. She felt lost and scared, like she was floating in space, completely untethered.

And then, almost as if she were reading Eve's mind, Amanda stepped forward, opening her arms and tilting her chin at an inviting angle. Eve swooped in and kissed her on the mouth.

"Whoa!" Amanda stiffened and pulled away with a shocked expression, raising both hands in self-defense. "What are you doing?"

"I'm sorry." Eve was mortified. "I just thought—"

"Wow." Amanda laughed nervously, wiping her wrist across her mouth. The gesture seemed a little excessive—the kiss had only lasted a second, no tongue or saliva involved. "I just wanted to give you a hug."

"Oh, God." Eve hid her face in her hands. "I'm so stupid. I drank too much. I'm so so sorry."

"It's okay," Amanda told her, still sounding a little shocked. "It's no big deal."

"Yes it is," Eve muttered into her palm. "I shouldn't have done that. It wasn't right."

"Really. It's okay."

Eve uncovered her face. "Are you sure?"

"Don't worry." Amanda touched her gently on the arm. "I won't tell anyone. I promise."

Eve felt a little sick. She hadn't thought about the possibility of Amanda *telling* anyone.

"Thank you," she said. "I would really appreciate that."

She drove home in a fog of regret, wondering how she could have done something so irresponsible, so unlike herself. Was she that lonely, that desperate for sexual contact? It made no sense, taking a risk like that—jeopardizing her job, her home, her son's college education—just to pretend for a night that she was living in a porn video.

*You are so stupid,* she told herself, trying not to think about the bitter disappointment she'd felt when Amanda's lips had failed to open.

She was normally a careful person—careful to a fault—and now she'd gone and put her livelihood in the hands of a young woman she barely knew, a girl with a grenade tattooed on her chest, probably not the best decision-maker in the world. It was a terrible thing to hand someone that kind of power, even someone who claimed to be your friend.

She wanted to call Amanda and repeat her apology, let her know that it would never happen again, that their relationship would be cordial and professional for however long Amanda remained at the Senior Center. But maybe a call wasn't the best idea, not so soon. Maybe that would only aggravate the situation, make it seem like a bigger deal than it already was. But she had to say *something*, for her own peace of mind, so she sent the blandest text she could think of:

*You okay?*

*Yeah,* Amanda replied, almost immediately. *Fine.*

*Are we still friends?*

*Totally,* Amanda replied, with a smiley face added for reassurance.

A moment later, another text arrived, a single word trapped in a separate bubble.

*Ursula*

Just the name, no exclamation mark. It looked sad like that, all alone, dead on arrival.

# Parents Weekend

"This is Ellen." The freckly redhead handed her phone to the hipster Asian dude sitting next to her. "She's twenty-two and fairly high-functioning. She has a GED and works full time at CVS. She's a really good cashier, as long as the customers don't ask a lot of questions or try to use an expired coupon. She used to freak out when people made small talk, but she's trained herself to handle the common stuff."

The Asian guy took a quick glance at the screen, then passed the phone to Amber, who made a point of staring at it for a long time, because everybody's autistic sibling was uniquely wonderful and important. It was easy to see why she'd been elected president of the club as a sophomore.

"She looks so serious," Amber said. "I bet she's really smart." She passed the phone to her veep, a petite sorority girl named Cat who kept a jumbo dispenser of Purell in her purse and squirted it on her hands every five minutes. The whole room reeked of it. "What was it like for you, having a big sister like Ellen?"

The redhead's smile wilted a little.

"It was hard," she said. "For a long time I didn't understand that everybody's big sister wasn't like mine. But then I started to realize something was wrong. When I was in first grade this girl named Tierney came to my house to play Barbies. It was her first visit. Ellen barged into my room and asked Tierney what her birthday was, and then she asked about Tierney's mother's birthday, and her father's birthday, and the birthdays of her siblings. And then she said, *What about your dog? What's your dog's birthday?* And Tierney—I'll never forget it—she just looked at me, totally matter-of-fact, and said, *Why's she so stupid?* I didn't know how to answer that, so I threw my Barbie at Ellen and screamed, *Leave us alone, stupid!*"

The redhead took a moment to collect herself.

"This is a safe space," Amber said. "No one's judging you. It's a challenge to have a sibling on the spectrum. That's why we're here. To listen and support each other."

The redhead looked relieved. "The weird thing was, Ellen didn't even care that I called her stupid. I'm not sure she even heard it. She just kept talking in this robot voice she uses sometimes: *I know three people who were born on March 10th who aren't triplets and two people who were born on March 2nd who aren't twins. I've never met anyone who was born on November 8th, not even a dog or a cat.* I was just sitting there, dying inside. I looked at Tierney and I said, *She can't help it, she was born that way,* and Tierney said, *I feel sorry for you.*"

"That Tierney sounds like an ice-cold bitch," said the veep, going to town with the Purell.

"She's actually my best friend," said the redhead. "She's really nice to Ellen now. She just didn't know any better."

By that point the phone had made its way to me. The photo on the screen had been taken at the redhead's high school graduation. She was wearing a cap and gown, and Ellen was standing next to her in a shiny green dress, holding her arms way out from her body, like maybe the material bothered her skin.

"That's great to hear," Amber said, and for some reason she was staring straight at me. "That's how we change the world. One person at a time."

We were about an hour into the meeting at that point, and already I was itching for it to be over. There are only so many stories you can listen to about somebody's autistic brother or sister.

I was only there for Amber, who I hadn't seen since the night we protested in the library. I'd texted her a bunch of times in the past week, trying to get her to meet me for coffee or pizza or whatever, but she kept putting me off, saying that she'd see me at the October meeting of the Autism Awareness Network and we could make a plan then. She was so insistent about the meeting that I started to wonder if she saw me more as a new recruit than as a guy she might want to hook up with, but I liked her enough that it was worth a couple hours of my time to figure out which it was.

So far things were looking pretty good on the hookup side of the equation. She had let out a happy little squeal when I walked through the door, and then led me around the room, introducing me to her friends like I was some kind of VIP.

"This is Brendan," she told the veep. "He's the first year I was telling you about. Brendan, this is Cat."

"Hey, Brendan." Cat looked me up and down, like she was thinking about buying me. "Amber was hoping you'd come."

"Shut up!" Amber told her, her cheeks a shade pinker than normal. Instead of her usual sweats and hoodie, she was wearing skinny jeans and a tight top and sexy platform sandals, the kind of clothes you'd wear to a party, or on a date. She had nice small boobs—I hadn't really gotten a good look at them before—that went really well with her athletic build.

"All I meant is that we need more men in the group," Cat said with a smirk, reaching into her purse for the Purell. "I wasn't trying to insinuate anything."

"It's true." Amber glanced at the Asian hipster, who was standing in a circle of girls, basking in the attention. "Usually it's just Kwan. I'm sure he'll be happy to have a bro."

"I don't know," I said, because Kwan was giving me the stink eye, like I'd crashed his party. "Looks like he's doing fine without me."

Cat headed over to the refreshment table, leaving me alone with Amber.

"I'm so glad you came," she said, placing her hand on my forearm, super-casual, like she didn't even know she was doing it. But I knew.

I felt it way down in my balls, a warm surge of power, like someone had just turned a key and started the engine.

After the break, a girl named Nellie told us about her brother, who was really smart but flapped his hands and grunted a lot, which made it hard to take him anywhere. Three girls in a row said they had siblings with Asperger's. This other girl, Dora, said she was the only normal kid out of four siblings. The other three were all diagnosed PDD-NOS, and one of them was totally nonverbal. Amber suggested that Dora stop using the word *normal* and substitute *neurotypical* instead.

"It's less hurtful that way," she explained. "And besides—in your family, it actually seems like autism is the norm, right?"

Dora shrugged. "My mom always calls me her normal one. That's how she introduces me to strangers. *This is Dora. She's my normal one.*"

The hipster, Kwan, had a brother named Zhang who acted out too much to go to a regular school. He was totally hyper and would run around in circles whenever he got worked up. The only thing that calmed him down was playing the piano. When he was seven years old, he sat down and played "The Entertainer," from that old movie *The Sting*. It came out of nowhere. No one in the family had seen the movie, and Kwan's parents were first-generation immigrants who only listened to European classical music. But Zhang totally nailed it.

"My parents were so happy that day," Kwan said. "It was like, *Oh my God, our son's a genius!* They were really proud of Zhang, which was amazing to see, because they were usually pretty ashamed of his condition, and didn't know how to help him. They hired a piano teacher who specialized in kids with special needs, and did everything they could to encourage his gift."

Kwan stopped talking and looked around, in case anyone had any questions. He was wearing cuffed jeans, a tight plaid shirt with the sleeves rolled up to his biceps, and a beige fedora, but I liked him anyway.

"That's so cool," Cat said. "Does he play classical or jazz?"

Kwan shrugged. "He plays 'The Entertainer.' Over and over and over. Every fucking day of his life. Every time I call home I hear him in the background, banging it out: dada dada DA DA da DA DA! I hate that song."

My little half brother was autistic, but I hadn't grown up with him. I was already in high school when he was born, and I wasn't getting along with my father at the time, or with my stepmother, Bethany, who I liked to think of as The Evil Bitch Who Ruined My Life. I realize now that it was stupid to blame her for the divorce; it wasn't like she brainwashed my dad and kidnapped him from my mom and me. Whatever my dad did, he did because *he* chose to do it. Because he *wanted* to. I still remember the day he explained that to me. He took me out for ice cream, put his arm around my shoulders, and said, *Look, Brendan, if you have to hate somebody for what happened, hate me, okay? Don't take it out on Bethany. She's an innocent bystander, just like you.*

The custody agreement said he'd get me two weekends a month, but he didn't complain if I blew him off for a sleepover at a friend's house, or even if I just needed to stay home and catch up on my schoolwork. I was playing three sports at the time—football, basketball, and lacrosse—so mostly he just came to my weekend games and took me out to dinner afterward. That was pretty much our relationship right after the divorce—my dad and me at Wild Willie's or Haddington Burrito Works, talking about whatever game I'd just played, acting like everything was perfectly normal, like this was how it was supposed to be.

I saw him even less right after Jon-Jon was born. There wasn't one specific day when he sat me down and said, *There's something seriously wrong with your brother.* It was more like a steady drip of bad news. They didn't know why he wasn't talking, why he ignored his toys, why he wouldn't look his father in the eye or smile at his mother. The doctors had concerns about the severity of his tantrums.

By the time they were openly using the word *autistic*, I was getting along better with my dad, and even with Bethany, who had turned out to be a nicer person than I'd given her credit for. She was a lot younger than my mom and had been pretty hot when my dad married her, but she'd aged a lot in the past few years. You could see in her eyes how hard it was, having a kid like Jon-Jon, and you couldn't help but feel a little sorry for her.

There was a brief period during my junior year when we tried to be a two-weekend-a-month family. I'd pack my bag, and my dad would pick me up on the way home from work and bring me to his new house.

The only problem was that Jon-Jon freaked out whenever I showed up. He didn't just get upset—he totally fucking lost it. Bethany would be all fake cheerful when I got there, like, *Hey, Jon-Jon, look who's here. It's your big brother! Can you say hi to Brendan?* Jon-Jon wouldn't even look at me. He just waved his arms around and screamed like I was a monster who was coming to eat him. Sometimes he'd throw himself on the ground or start punching himself in the head, which was a terrible thing to see, because he wasn't fooling around. Once he got going on a meltdown like that, he could keep it up for hours. When he finally wore himself out and fell asleep, the rest of us would have a little time to hang out in peace, except it wasn't really peace, because we were all so rattled by what had just happened. We'd play a game or two of Yahtzee and then Bethany would head up to bed, and my dad and I would watch an episode of *Scrubs*, which we both loved. Those were some of the best father-and-son times I can remember, the two of us sitting on the couch, cracking up about something completely ridiculous that J.D. said to Turk. It felt really good, just being in the same place, enjoying the same thing. When the show was over, he'd kiss me good night—something he never used to do before the divorce—and we'd both go up to bed. Then I'd wake up the next morning, head downstairs for breakfast, and Jon-Jon would start screaming all over again.

It was hard on everybody, so we eventually gave up and went back to the old way—me and my dad getting together for the occasional dinner, talking about sports and TV shows and college and girls. He was easy to talk to, a lot easier than my mom, though that was probably just because he was a guy, and because he never gave me the feeling that he was judging me, or wishing I was a different person than I actually am. I always made sure to ask him about Jon-Jon, and he always said something positive, like *He's getting big*, or, *He really likes his new teacher*, but I never pressed for details. Jon-Jon's life was a mystery to me. I had no idea what he did all day, what he thought about, or why he hated me so much. Mostly I just lived my own life without thinking about him at all.

I wasn't planning on going into my whole family history at the meeting, but Amber just sort of coaxed it out of me. After a while I forgot about the other people in the room. It was just me talking and Amber listening.

I told her how my father had invited himself to Parents Weekend, catching me totally off-guard. I thought that was a great idea—I hadn't seen him since the week before I left for school—but said he'd have to work it out with my mom, because she was planning on coming, too, and they didn't usually do stuff like that together.

*I'll talk to the boss,* he said. *Throw myself on the mercy of the court.*

I have no idea how he managed it, but he called a week later and said he'd gotten the thumbs-up. The plan was for my dad to come on his own, because it didn't make any sense to bring Jon-Jon to an event like Parents Weekend. He hated long car rides, responded badly to new environments, and was often freaked out by unfamiliar faces. It would be easier for everybody if he stayed home with his mom and followed the usual routine. Easier for everybody except Bethany, I guess.

*It'll just be us guys,* my dad said. *Maybe we can go to the football game. If Zack wants to join us, he's more than welcome.*

Zack was totally up for that. He and my dad had talked on the

131

phone a few times, and Zack told everybody what a chill guy he was, way chiller than his own parents, who, he was happy to report, were staying home in Boxborough for the weekend. His little sister was competing in an Irish step dance competition, and that was a big deal in his house.

*You ever see that shit, bro? It's like these girls are all dancing with a stick up their ass, and smiling like it's the best feeling in the world.*

We had the whole day planned. Commandos game in the afternoon, barbecue on the quad for dinner, and then this student talent show that people raved about. They did it like *American Idol*, with these smart-ass professors acting as judges. Apparently, one of them was a total dick, just like Simon Cowell, and everybody loved him.

*Who knows?* Zack said. *Maybe your dad'll get drunk with us.*

*Yeah, right.*

*I'm serious, bro. You think he still smokes weed?*

*Dude, he's not gonna smoke weed with us. Trust me.*

*We should take him to a party,* Zack said. *Maybe we could get him laid.*

*Don't even go there,* I said.

For the whole week leading up to Parents Weekend, that was the big joke in our room, all the wild shit we were gonna do with my dad. I knew none of it would happen, but it was fun to think about, and put us both in this goofy, stoked-up mood, like something big was about to happen.

And then, the day before Parents Weekend, I got the phone call.

*Change of plans,* he said. *I'm really sorry.*

*You're not coming?*

*No, no. I'm still coming. But I'm bringing the gang.*

*The gang?*

*Bethany and Jon-Jon.*

*Oh.* What was I supposed to say? You couldn't tell your dad not to bring his wife and kid. *All right. Sure.*

*You okay with that?*

*I guess. I mean, I only have three tickets for the football game, and one of 'em is for Zack.*

*Yeah,* he said. *I'm not so sure about the football game. Think I can take a rain check?*

They showed up around eleven on Saturday morning. I hadn't seen Jon-Jon in about six months, and I almost didn't recognize him. He was a lot bigger than I remembered. He was really cute, blond hair and blue eyes, and those long eyelashes that everybody who met him commented on. Bethany had dressed him in khakis and a button-down shirt and a little denim jacket. He looked like a model in a Gap Kids catalogue, but that wasn't the main thing. He just seemed more together than the kid I remembered. He was actually looking in my general direction and not screaming his head off.

*Look,* Bethany told him. *It's your big brother. Brendan's in college. This is where he lives. Why don't you say hi to Brendan.*

Jon-Jon took this all in.

*Hello,* he said, addressing the word to my knees. His voice was soft and mechanical, and the word sounded almost foreign, but still, he fucking said it.

*Wow,* I said.

*I know.* Bethany looked so happy. *He's doing great. We finally found the right school.*

*He was pretty good in the car,* my dad added. *Hardly complained at all.*

They came in and I introduced them to Zack, who totally rose to the occasion, making small talk like an Eagle Scout. Jon-Jon was standing in the middle of the room, lost inside his head, while the rest of us chatted about how nice the dorms were compared to the ones my father and Bethany had lived in back in the day. It was the usual story—they got treated like shit and we got treated like kings.

*I saw the lounge on the way in,* my dad said. *That's a big TV!*

*And that communal kitchen,* Bethany said. *Jeez. I wouldn't mind living here for a few months.*

At some point, Jon-Jon took a couple of steps in my direction. I thought he was maybe gonna hug me or sit on my lap, but he was just coming to examine the fabric of the couch I was sitting on, the one Zack and I had found on the street at the beginning of the semester. It had a weird texture, kinda fuzzy but also a little slick—almost greasy—and Jon-Jon seemed fascinated by it. He reached out his hand, very slowly, and started stroking the armrest, as if it were a living thing. For a while, the conversation stopped, and we all just watched him.

*I think he likes it here,* Bethany told us.

Before lunch we went for a walk. Zack stayed behind, claiming he had work to do, so it was just me, my dad, Bethany, and Jon-Jon. There were lots of official tours available throughout the weekend, but my dad and Bethany didn't think Jon-Jon was ready for something like that. Better to go at our own pace and not bother anyone else, even if that meant they had to listen to my feeble attempts to impersonate a college student who actually knew what he was talking about.

*Uh . . . I think that's a science building. Maybe Chemistry. I'm really not sure. Could be Sociology.*

*Yeah, so this is the new gym. It's a lot nicer than the old one. That's what everybody says. I guess the old one smelled really bad.*

*So those are bike racks. Maybe I'll bring my bike next year. I just need to inflate the tires.*

*I'm not sure who that statue is. Some dude from the nineteen hundreds. Guess I should read the plaque.*

I felt like a dumbass, blathering on like that, but my dad and Bethany seemed happy enough. Whatever I said, one of them would repeat it to Jon-Jon in simplified language. *Look at the bicycles . . . Look at the statue . . . That's where people go to exercise.* Sometimes Jon-Jon would look where they were pointing, but most of the time he would stare at whatever he felt like staring at. A tree. His own hand. Nothing at all.

I could see why they were in such a good mood. Given the way things usually went with Jon-Jon, it was a minor miracle to be outside on a beautiful day, walking around a public place like a relatively normal family. I met Bethany's eyes a couple of times, and she gave me this shocked, excited look, like, *Oh my God, can you believe this?* I felt pretty good about it myself. It wasn't the fun day that I'd planned, but it was still kinda nice in its own way.

We were walking toward the library, Bethany and Jon-Jon trailing behind my dad and me. I was telling him about my Econ class, leaving out the part about my D average, when he turned to check on his wife and son.

*Oh shit,* he said.

It didn't seem like a big deal at first. Jon-Jon had stopped walking. He was just sort of frozen in place, staring up at the sky. Bethany stood right beside him, looking at my dad with a worried expression on her face.

*What's wrong?* I asked.

My dad shook his head and starting walking toward Jon-Jon, moving slowly and carefully. He spoke his son's name in a soft voice, but Jon-Jon didn't seem to hear it. His attention was focused like a laser beam on the small plane that was flying overhead at a low altitude, trailing a banner that read, *WELCOME PARENTS!*

*He hates airplanes,* Bethany explained. *It's one of his things.*

The plane was directly overhead, buzzing like a giant insect. Jon-Jon let out a yelp, quick and shrill, like someone had jabbed him with a pin. Then he did it again, this time even louder. I could see people turning in our direction, squinting in confusion. Jon-Jon slapped himself in the head.

*I'm sorry,* Bethany told me. *He was being so good.*

It was hard enough to deal with one of Jon-Jon's meltdowns in the house, but it was way worse with all those strangers around. A gray-haired lady in a BSU sweatshirt wandered over, asking if the poor thing was okay. Bethany fished a business card from her purse and handed it to the woman. They'd gotten the cards printed up the year before, after an epic tantrum at Target.

*Please don't be alarmed,* it said. *Our son Jonathan has been diagnosed with autism and sometimes needs to be physically restrained to avoid injury to himself and others. We love Jonathan very much and only want to keep him safe. Thank you for your understanding.*

The plane banked away from us, moving toward the football stadium, but I don't think Jon-Jon even noticed. He was rocking from side to side, moaning and clutching his head. And then he punched himself. Hard, right above his ear. Like it was somebody else's head he was punching, somebody he hated.

*Please don't do that,* Bethany told him.

My father sat down on the grass and hugged him from behind, trying to pin his arms, but Jon-Jon fought like crazy to break free, thrashing and screaming like a trapped animal.

The struggle only lasted a few minutes, but it felt a lot longer. Every time it looked like my dad had Jon-Jon under control, one of his arms would slip free, and he'd start punching himself again. And then my dad would have to grab that arm without losing control of Jon-Jon's other limbs. It almost looked like a game, except that Jon-Jon was drooling and my father's nose was bleeding from a backwards head butt. Even so, he just kept speaking quietly the whole time, telling his son that he loved him and that everything would be okay. A pretty good crowd had gathered by then, and Bethany was handing a card to each new arrival, apologizing for the disturbance.

"They sound like great parents," Amber said, when I'd finished with the story.

"Yeah," I said. "They're really patient with him."

"What about you?" she asked. "How did you feel while that was happening?"

"I just felt sorry for them," I told her.

That part was true. I really did feel bad for my dad and Bethany, and even for Jon-Jon, because I knew he couldn't help himself. What I didn't tell her was how sorry I felt for myself, and how jealous I was of my little brother, even though that was totally ridiculous. Jon-Jon had a hard life, and I would never want to trade places with him. But that whole time, while he was screaming and thrashing around, I kept thinking how unfair it was that my father loved him so much and held him so tight—way tighter than he'd ever held me—and wouldn't let go no matter what.

# The Human Condition

At the end of the Tuesday night seminar, white-bearded Barry raised his hand and invited the whole class to reconvene for a nightcap at his sports bar.

"I don't know about you guys," he said, "but all this talk about gender makes me thirsty!"

The initial response to Barry's overture was lukewarm—it was late, people had work in the morning—but public opinion shifted when he added that drinks would be on the house.

"Now that you mention it," said Russ, the fanatical hockey fan, "I could definitely go for a free beer."

"That's the spirit," said Barry. "What's the point of being in college if we don't socialize outside the classroom? That's like half your education right there."

"Does that include hard liquor?" Dumell ruefully patted his midsection. "I'm watching my carbs."

"Within reason," Barry told him. "I'm not breaking out the Pappy Van Winkle."

"Don't worry about that," Dumell assured him. "I'm a cheap date. Just ask my ex-wife."

Eve had no intention of joining the party. She'd been dodging Barry's invitations to get a drink after class for the past two months and didn't want to offer him the slightest encouragement, not that he needed any. Barry was one of those guys who didn't know the meaning of rejection; he just kept trying and trying and trying. His persistence might have been flattering if it hadn't felt so smug and entitled—so steeped in male privilege—as if there was no possible way she could outlast him in a battle of romantic wills.

Hoping to avoid any unpleasantness in the parking lot—Barry sometimes lurked outside the exit and then attached himself to Eve as she walked to her car—she ducked into the ladies' room and killed a few minutes in the stall, playing several turns on Words with Friends (random opponent, not very good) and then peeing, not because she needed to, but because she was already sitting on a toilet and it seemed foolish not to. She washed her hands with excessive diligence and checked her face in the mirror—an unbreakable, though less and less rewarding, habit—before leaving the rest room and almost colliding with Dr. Fairchild, who was standing outside the door, her lanky basketball player's frame augmented by businesslike heels.

"Eve." She sounded concerned but vaguely reproachful. "Are you okay?"

"Fine. Why?"

"You were in there for quite a while." The professor heard herself and grimaced, mortified by her own rudeness. "Not that it's any of my business."

"Great class tonight," Eve said, trying to cut through the awkwardness.

Dr. Fairchild gave a distracted nod and then asked, with some urgency, "Are you going? To the bar?"

"I wasn't planning on it."

"Oh." Dr. Fairchild couldn't hide her disappointment. "I was hoping you were."

"Are *you*?"

"I was thinking about it. Might be fun, right?"

*Huh*. Eve hadn't given a lot of thought to the professor's idea of fun, but it hardly seemed like drinking at a sports bar with guys like Barry and Russ would be high on her list.

"It's been a long day," Eve explained. "I'm kinda wiped out."

"I just—" Dr. Fairchild flipped her hair over her shoulder, first one side, then the other, her favorite nervous gesture. "I really don't want to go there by myself."

"You won't be by yourself. Sounds like a bunch of them are going."

"I know." A pleading note had entered the professor's voice. "It's just a lot easier to walk in with a girlfriend. Especially at a place like that."

Eve was puzzled, but also touched, by the professor's use of the word *girlfriend*. Until this moment, they'd never even had a conversation outside of class.

"I guess I could get a drink," she said. "Just one, though. Tomorrow's a workday."

"Thank you." Dr. Fairchild leaned down and gave Eve a hug. "I really appreciate this."

"No problem. So I guess I'll see you over there?"

Dr. Fairchild's smile was also an apology. She knew she was pushing her luck.

"Could you maybe give me a ride?" she asked. "That way I can't chicken out."

Ten minutes later, they were parked outside of Barry's bar, a squat brick building that had the unappealing name of *PLAY BALL!* emblazoned on the front awning, with a baseball bat standing in for the exclamation point. Dr. Fairchild didn't seem in any hurry to leave the car.

"I have very big feet," she said. "It's not easy to find cute shoes in my size."

"Those are nice," Eve observed. "You can't go wrong with black pumps."

"You should see my red stilettos. I can barely walk in them, but they look really hot. I just don't have many opportunities to wear them at the moment."

"I've pretty much given up on heels," Eve told her. "At my age, I'd rather be comfortable."

"You're not that old."

"Forty-six. Not young, that's for sure."

"I'm not that much younger than you," Dr. Fairchild pointed out. "I guess I'm trying to make up for lost time. I missed out on my best years."

In the bright public sphere of the classroom, Eve never had a problem accepting Dr. Fairchild as a woman. In that context—a teacher interacting with students, deconstructing outmoded concepts of masculinity and femininity—she seemed like an embodiment of the curriculum, her theory and practice a continuous whole. In a minivan outside a sports bar, however, the professor's gender identity seemed a little more precarious, as much wish as reality. It was partly the timbre of her voice in the darkness, and partly just the size of her body in the passenger seat, the way she filled the available space.

*I can see who you were,* Eve thought. *One self on top of the other.*

As soon as this uncharitable image occurred to her, she did her best to erase it from her mind. She wasn't the gender police. Her job—her *responsibility*—was to be kind and supportive, and not to judge the success or failure of somebody else's transformation.

"You look really pretty," she said.

"I'm trying." Dr. Fairchild's chuckle was tinged with anxiety. "Every day's an adventure, right?"

"I wish."

"At least that's what my therapist tells me. I think she's just trying to cheer me up."

"Is everything okay?"

Dr. Fairchild stared out the windshield while she considered the question. The only thing in front of them was a brick wall.

"It was my daughter's birthday last weekend," she said. "Her name is Millicent. She just turned eight."

"That's a sweet age."

"We threw her a party, my ex-wife and I. And some of the other parents came by at the end, and it wasn't like they were mean to me or anything. But I could see I made them uncomfortable, and my daughter saw it, too. They stood as far away from me as possible. Like whatever I had might be contagious."

"I'm sure they didn't mean anything by it," Eve said. "It just takes people time, you know?"

Dr. Fairchild examined her manicure. "If it wasn't for Millie, I'd probably just move to New York or L.A. Just get far away from all this suburban bullshit."

"If that's what you want to do, you should do it. New York's not that far."

"It's too expensive," Dr. Fairchild said. "And it's not like it's gonna make any difference. Doesn't matter where you live. You're always just kind of alone with your shit, you know?"

"It's the human condition," Eve told her.

Dr. Fairchild turned away from the wall.

"You're as bad as my therapist," she said, but it sounded like a compliment.

\*    \*    \*

Julian Spitzer wasn't old enough to drink legally—not even close— but none of the adults objected when he poured himself a glass of beer from the communal pitcher, and then another one after that. That was the upside of going out to a bar on a Tuesday night with a bunch of middle-aged people. You just sort of slipped in under the radar. Nobody bothered to check your fake ID or otherwise give you a second glance, especially if you happened to be sitting with the owner of the bar, which, he had to admit, was pretty fucking cool.

The downside of this situation was that he was stuck at a dump called PLAY BALL!, surrounded by people twice his age who were talking among themselves about the kind of unbelievably boring crap people that age liked to talk about—dental benefits, kale, lower back pain. He might as well have been hanging out with his parents, except that his parents never would have seated him directly in front of a pitcher of Bud Light or whatever weak-ass beer this was and then pretended not to notice while he imbibed to his heart's content.

This wasn't the kind of news you could ethically keep to yourself, so he snapped a pic of the half-empty pitcher and shot it off to his friend Ethan, who was having a blast at UVM.

*Dude I'm getting WASTED with a bunch of old farts from my Gender and Society class! How fucked up is that?*

Until he typed this message, Julian was unaware of the fact that he was in the process of getting *WASTED*. But once he saw the word *WASTED* throbbing like a prophecy inside the green text balloon, it struck him with the force of undeniable truth. Because, really, why shouldn't he get *WASTED*? He'd been in college for almost two months and this was the first time he'd partied with his fellow students, or with anyone else, for that matter. It had not been a very exciting fall.

His phone pinged right away: *That's what you get for going to community college, asshole!*

Dumell, one of two black guys in the class—he was the African-American, not the Nigerian—heard the chime and elbowed him in the arm.

"Message from your girlfriend?"

"One of 'em," Julian replied.

Dumell chuckled. "How many you got?"

"Hard to keep count."

"Listen to you, player. I bet they love it when you roll up on your skateboard."

"What can I say?" Julian told him. "I'm a fuel-efficient lover."

Dumell considered the metaphor.

"Guess that makes me a gas-guzzler," he said. "Old-school Detroit. Ten miles to the gallon highway. But it's a smooth ride, if you know what I'm saying."

Barry, their host, pounded on the table, sparing Julian the need for further banter.

"Welcome, fellow scholars," Barry said. "I'm glad you all could make it. And I'm especially delighted that our esteemed professor has decided to grace us with her presence. Dr. Fairchild, it's a privilege to have you in my humble neighborhood tavern. You really class up the joint."

Dr. Fairchild blushed and waved off the compliment as the students drank a toast in her honor. Julian made a point of clinking glasses with everyone at the table—Barry, Dumell, Russ, the professor, Eve (Brendan Fletcher's mom, weirdly enough), the hilariously named Mr. Ho (who spoke very little English), and Gina (the chatty motorcycle dyke). Aside from Barry, who was one of those *I'm-an-asshole-and-proud-of-it* guys, Julian liked them all just fine, and he was even feeling okay about Barry, considering that he was picking up the tab.

*Fuck you,* he texted Ethan. *These are my people.*

Julian knew he was too smart for Eastern Community College. Everybody said so—his parents, his teachers, his friends, his former guidance counselor, who was a bit of a dick, but still. He had the GPA and the SATs to get into a good four-year school, and his parents had the money to pay for it, or so they said. It was just that senior year of high school had been a total bust—he'd been seriously depressed for most of it—and he hadn't been able to complete his applications in a timely fashion.

He didn't start feeling better until the beginning of summer—they'd adjusted his meds for the fourth or fifth time, and finally stumbled on the magic formula—and by then it was way too late to get in anywhere decent. His parents and shrink agreed that it would be wise for him to take a few classes at ECC, *to get his feet wet,* as they insisted on putting it. If he liked it and got good grades, he could transfer somewhere better for sophomore year, somewhere *more commensurate with his abilities.*

Julian hadn't expected much from community college, and for the most part ECC had lived up to his low expectations. His Math class was a joke, way easier than high school. He regularly dozed off in Bio and still got A-pluses on the first two tests. Gender and Society was the only exception to this general rule of mediocrity. It was a wild card, a night class full of rando adults, taught by a female professor who'd been born a male and had *transitioned*, as she liked to say, in her late thirties, which definitely enhanced Julian's academic experience. It was one thing to have a professor tell you that gender was socially constructed, and another to hear it from a person who had actually done construction work.

There was a lot of funky jargon in the reading assignments—*cisgender* and *heteronormative* and *dysphoria* and *performativity* and on and on—but he didn't mind. It was one of those classes that actually made you *think*, in this case about stuff that was so basic it never even occurred to you to question it, all the little rules that got shoveled into your head when you were a kid and couldn't defend yourself. Girls wear pink, boys wear blue. Boys are tough. Girls are sweet. Women are caregivers with soft bodies. Men are leaders with hard muscles. Girls get looked at. Guys do the looking. Hairy armpits. Pretty fingernails. This one can but that one can't. The Gender Commandments were endless, once you started thinking about them, and they were enforced 24/7 by a highly motivated volunteer army of parents, neighbors, teachers, coaches, other kids, and total strangers—basically, the whole human race.

*Any hot chicks?* Ethan texted.

*Ha ha,* Julian replied.

Sad to say, it was slim pickings in Gender and Society. The only halfway hot female close to his own age was Salima, the Muslim babe, and she wore a fucking headscarf. The rest of her clothes were normal enough, and she had a cute round face, but that headscarf was black and forbidding. When they'd interviewed each other, she told him she didn't drink, date, or dance—which explained her unfortunate but totally predictable absence at the bar—and was saving herself for marriage to a good Muslim guy. She said she was happy being a woman, except that just once she'd like to know what it felt like to punch someone in the face.

*Only three ladies at the table. A dyke, Brendan Fletcher's mom, and my professor*

*The tranny?* Ethan texted back. *Holy shit!*

Julian snuck a guilty glance at Professor Fairchild, who was deep in conversation with Mrs. Fletcher. Early in the semester, he had unthinkingly used the word *tranny* to describe his teacher, before she'd had a chance to explain how offensive it was, and now his friends wouldn't stop using it, no matter how many times Julian asked them not to. They insisted that *tranny* was just a harmless abbreviation, and called Julian a pussy for scolding them about it.

*She's a nice person,* he wrote.

*Hot?*

They'd been over this ground before.

*Not especially*

Professor Fairchild wasn't a freak or anything, far from it. She was what his mother would have called an *attractive older woman*. She wore tasteful conservative suits like a lady lawyer on TV, always with a colorful scarf tied around her neck. Lots of makeup and nice perfume. A little manly around the jaw, but otherwise pretty convincing.

*What about Fletcher's mom?*

This was a harder question. Mrs. Fletcher actually *was* kind of pretty, as much as he hated to admit it. Not in a young woman way, but *pretty-for-her-age*, which he didn't know exactly, beyond the obvious fact that she was old enough to be his mother. She had a nice face, maybe a little sad around the eyes, or maybe just tired. There was some gray in her hair, and she had a little belly, but she had a decent body overall. Excellent boobs, and she still looked pretty good in jeans, which was a lot more than he could say for his own mom, despite her Paleo diet and yoga addiction.

*She's okay,* he texted back. *Except that she gave birth to a raging asshole*

\* \* \*

The bar wasn't all that crowded on a Tuesday night, but it was pretty noisy, with classic rock blasting in the background, songs that Eve remembered from high school—Aerosmith and Led Zeppelin and

"Little Pink Houses"—more than a few of which inspired Barry and Russ to trade high fives or break out their air guitars. Eve hated most of those songs—*cock rock*, her college friends used to call it—but the lyrics were permanently engraved in her memory, courtesy of every boyfriend she'd ever had.

*Snot running down his nose! Greasy fingers smearing shabby clo-hoes!*

That awful Jethro Tull song came on while Professor Fairchild told Eve about her mother's death, which happened just a few months after Margo—they were on a first-name basis now—had completed her transition. It was one of those freak things, a stubborn cold that somehow turned into drug-resistant pneumonia. Her mother went to the emergency room, complaining of a nagging cough and short-ness of breath, and twelve hours later she was on a ventilator, unable to speak, drifting in and out of consciousness. She rallied a little right before she died, just long enough to scribble a final message to the daughter who had once been a son.

*You are confused,* she wrote, in a weak and trembling hand. *You need to wake up and smell the coffee!*

"Those were her dying words." Margo tried to smile, but couldn't complete the mission. "Right after I told her how much I loved her. *You need to wake up and smell the coffee!* I'll never forgive her for that."

"You should try," Eve told her. "It's unhealthy to resent the dead."

Margo knew this was true. "I wish I could talk to her one more time. Just to make her understand that *this* is me. Not that sad little boy living inside the wrong body. But she'd probably just hurt my feelings all over again. She used to say such horrible things."

"I know how that goes," Eve said. "I work with older people. You wouldn't believe the stuff that comes out of their mouths."

"Oh, I believe it," Margo said. "But my mother was a school-teacher. She was not an ignorant woman. She just refused to accept my experience and acknowledge my pain."

"She loved her little boy." It was strange how clear this was to Eve, though she'd never even met the woman. "She didn't know how to think about you any other way."

Margo drank the last sip of wine in her glass.

"She never really knew me. My own mother. Isn't that terrible?"

Margo buried her face in her hands. After a moment of hesitation, Eve reached out and began rubbing the professor's shoulder, aware as she did so that everyone else at the table was watching them with a mixture of concern and discomfort.

"Something wrong?" asked Dumell.

Eve shrugged—of course something was wrong—but Margo raised her head and told him that she was fine.

"Don't mind me," she said, wiping her eyes and mustering an embarrassed smile. "I just get emotional when I drink."

"There's only one cure for that." Barry waved his hand, signaling to the bartender. "Yo, Ralphie! Another round for my friends."

*　*　*

Russ had switched to Diet Coke, and everyone else at the table was drinking wine or hard liquor—trying to get the most bang from Barry's buck—so Julian had the second pitcher all to himself. It was a lot of beer for one person, but he was approaching a level of intoxication where finishing it on his own seemed like a matter of personal honor. To make it official, he texted a pic to Ethan before he poured the first glass: the sweaty plastic vessel filled to the brim, his own liquid Mount Everest.

*60 oz bro wish me luck!!!*

"You texting or listening?" Dumell asked.

"Both," said Julian, but he put down his phone and turned his full attention back to his real-life companion, who was telling him about Iraq, which was not a subject Julian got to hear about every day, at least not from someone who'd actually been there.

Not that it was all that exciting, apparently. Dumell said it was mostly boring as shit, due to the fact that he was an auto mechanic, not a combat soldier. He spent most of his tour sweating in a repair shop, changing oil and brake pads, replacing spark plugs and rotating tires, the same routine tasks he now performed every day at Warren Reddy Subaru in Elmville. Every once in a while, though, he got sent out in a tow truck to pick up a disabled vehicle that had been hit by an IED or an RPG.

"That's when shit got real," he said. "You're driving through that desert, totally fucking exposed, just waiting for something to explode. Every pothole feels like the end of the world, know what I'm saying?"

Weirdly, Julian thought he did, though he'd never been near a war zone, and had never seen anything blow up that was bigger than a firecracker, except on a screen.

"Anything bad happen?"

"Not to me. Just did my job and came home."

"Must've been a relief."

"You would think so. But I didn't . . . *readjust* too good. Couldn't sleep, couldn't hold a job. Marriage fell apart. Scared all the time. Like I was still out in the desert, driving through a minefield."

"That sucks."

"PTSD," Dumell explained. "That's what the doctors say. But it doesn't make any sense. I was lucky. Came home in one piece. Ain't got shit to complain about."

Julian was intimately familiar with this line of thinking. It had played on a loop during the black hole of his senior year. *My life is good. People love me. I have a promising future. So why can't I get out of bed?*

"Doesn't matter," he told Dumell, surprising himself with the conviction in his voice. "You feel what you fucking feel. You don't have to apologize to anyone."

Dumell squinted for a few seconds, as if he was trying to get Julian into focus. But after a moment, his expression softened.

"Guess you know what I'm talking about, huh?"

"Kind of," Julian told him. "I got PTSD from high school."

\* \* \*

Eve stopped drinking after her second glass of the house white—a watery pinot grigio—but Margo happily accepted Barry's offer of a third.

"What the heck," she said. "I'm not teaching tomorrow."

It was close to eleven, and Eve started thinking about the logistics of a graceful exit. It would have been simple, except that she felt responsible for getting Margo back to campus, where she'd left her car. She was about to broach the subject when Margo turned to her with a wistful smile.

"This is nice," she said. "It's just what I hoped it would be."

"What do you mean?"

Margo gestured vaguely, sculpting a roundish object with her hands.

"Just *this*. Going out with a girlfriend and talking about . . . stuff." She laughed sadly. "I always thought I'd have more women friends after I transitioned. I mean, don't get me wrong. I have friends. But not too many of them are cis women."

"It's hard," Eve said. "Everybody's so busy."

Margo tapped a manicured fingernail on a damp cocktail napkin. "I think I watched too much *Sex and the City*, and read too many novels about amazing female friendships. These women who talk about everything, and help each other through the hard times. I never had friends like that when I was living as a guy."

"My ex-husband didn't have any friends like that, either. Men just don't need that much from each other."

"But you do, right? You have friends you can confide in. Talk about your love life or whatever. Share your secrets."

"A few," Eve said, though she hadn't done a great job of maintaining those friendships in recent months. She hadn't told Jane or Peggy or Liza about her porn problem, and she certainly hadn't mentioned her crush on Amanda. The only person she could imagine confiding in about her feelings for Amanda was Amanda herself, and that wasn't possible at the moment. They hadn't really talked since their fateful dinner at Enzo, even though they saw each other every day at work. When they did communicate, they were both a little guarded, very proper and professional, as if neither one wanted to venture into any gray areas, or get anywhere near the other's personal boundaries.

"You know what the problem is?" Margo said. "I missed out on the bonding periods. I didn't grow up with a tight group of girls, didn't have any women roommates in college, didn't get to swap sex stories with co-workers at lunch. No Mommy and Me classes, no hanging out with a neighbor while our kids had a playdate. The only woman I could ever talk to like that was my ex-wife, and she refuses to be my girlfriend. She wants me to be happy, but she doesn't want to go clothes shopping or hear about the cute guy I have a crush on. Can't really blame her, I guess."

"That's gotta be complicated," Eve said.

Margo nodded, but her mind was elsewhere.

"When I was a guy, I used to get so jealous when women went to the bathroom together. One of them would get up, and then her friend would get up, too. Sometimes two friends. It was like a conspiracy. And I'd be like, *What's going on in there? What kind of secrets are they telling each other?*"

"Nothing too exciting," Eve said, though she'd actually had some interesting bathroom experiences over the years. Sophomore year of high school, Heather Falchuk pulled up her shirt and showed Eve her third nipple, a little pink island at the bottom of her rib cage. Her college friend Martina, a recovering bulimic, used to have Eve accompany her to the bathroom so she wouldn't be tempted to purge after a big meal.

"I know it's stupid," Margo said, running her finger over the lip of her wineglass. "It's just one of those things I always wanted to do."

\*   \*   \*

Julian had made it through two-thirds of the pitcher when the extent of his inebriation made itself clear to him.

"Oh, shit," he told Dumell.

"What?"

Julian's laughter sounded hollow and faraway in his own ears. "I'm pretty fucking wasted, man."

"I can see that. You been sucking it down pretty good."

"Can I tell you a secret?" Julian leaned toward Dumell. It felt to him like something important was happening. "I never had a black friend before. You think that makes me a racist?"

Dumell thought this over, scratching the corner of his mouth with the tip of a thumb.

"I hope you're not driving home," he said.

Julian shook his head and pointed to the floor.

"Got my trusty skateboard."

"Where you live?"

"Haddington."

"That's five miles away."

"Yes, sir."

"You really commute on that thing?"

"It's better than nothing."

Dumell didn't dispute this. "Is it fun?"

"Fuck yeah. You know that hill on Davis Road? Over by Wendy's? Sometimes I'm going faster than the cars. Feel like a superhero."

"Ever have an accident?"

"Nothing bad. If I see trouble coming, I just hop off."

"I get that," said Dumell. "But you can't always see it coming, right?"

Julian picked up his glass—it was half-full—and then put it down without drinking.

"Only bad thing that ever happened, some jock assholes from my high school kidnapped me."

"Kidnapped?"

"They threw me in their car, drove me to a park, and duct-taped me inside a Port-A-Potty."

Dumell's eyes got big. "You shitting me?"

"Nope."

Julian shot a venomous glance across the table at Mrs. Fletcher, but she didn't notice. She was too busy sucking up to the professor, who was apparently her new best friend. Mrs. Fletcher's dickwad son had been one of the kidnappers.

153

"Why would they go and do that?" Dumell asked.

"Why? Because one of these jocks was being an asshole at a party, so I threw a drink in his face."

"Crazy motherfucker," chuckled Dumell. "How long were you stuck in there?"

Julian shrugged. It had only been a couple minutes—his house key cut right through the tape—but it felt like forever. The stench of that open toilet had been seared into his nostrils for months afterward. He could still smell it now if he tried hard enough.

"Too fucking long," he said.

Julian shot another hateful look at Mrs. Fletcher. He wanted to say something mean, to let her know what a horrible bully she'd brought into the world, but she was standing up now, not even looking in his direction as she headed off to the rest room with Dr. Fairchild in tow.

"Damn," said Dumell, who was watching the women walk. His voice was low and appreciative. "She looks good."

"Which one?" asked Julian.

"Damn," Dumell repeated in that same soft voice, which wasn't really an answer.

\*　　\*　　\*

With only one stall and limited standing room, the women's rest room at PLAY BALL! wasn't ideal for girl talk. Eve made a magnanimous *after you* gesture, inviting Margo to avail herself of the facilities. She checked her phone while she waited—there were no texts or emails of note—and reminded herself that it was rude to speculate about the particulars of the professor's anatomy.

*It's not important,* she thought. *Gender's a state of mind.*

Margo flushed and emerged with a slightly tipsy smile on her face.

"Mission accomplished," she announced in a singsong voice, turning sideways so Eve could slip past. "Your turn."

Eve really did have to pee, but she was overcome with a sudden attack of shyness the moment she sat on the toilet. She had no problem going with strangers nearby, but it was harder when people she knew were within hearing range. It was all because Ted, in the early days of their relationship, had once teased her about the force of her stream.

*Jesus,* he said. *Who turned on the faucet?*

Years later, when their marriage was falling apart, Eve had mentioned this incident in a couple's therapy session, to which they'd each brought a list of unspoken grievances. Ted had no recollection of making this comment, and was mystified that it could have bothered her for so many years. *It was a dumb joke,* he told her. *Just let it go already.* But here she was, seven years divorced, and still brooding about it.

"Eve," said Margo. "Can I ask you something?"

"Sure."

"What do you think of Dumell?"

"Dumell?" Eve repeated, trying to buy some time. The truth was, she hadn't given a lot of thought to Dumell. They hadn't interviewed each other yet, and he didn't talk much in class. She didn't even know if Dumell was his first name or his last. She mostly just thought of him as *Worried Black Guy,* though she'd been impressed tonight by how attentive he was being to Julian Spitzer, who looked like he was getting pretty drunk.

"Yeah," said Margo. "Do you like him?"

"He seems nice." Eve discovered to her relief that it was easy to pee while holding a conversation. "Kinda low-key."

"I think he's handsome," Margo said. "He's got really nice eyes."

Eve wiped and flushed and exited the stall. She understood her role now.

"So," she asked, washing her hands in that slightly theatrical way she adopted when other people were watching. "Do you have a crush on him?"

"Maybe." Margo was gazing into the cloudy mirror, applying her lipstick with the concentration of a surgeon. "And by *maybe* I mean *definitely.*"

"Wow."

"I can't stop thinking about him."

"Is that allowed?" Eve inquired. "The teacher-and-student thing?"

"Who cares?" Margo scoffed. "Do you have any idea what they pay me? Anyway, we're all adults, right?"

If they were going to swap secrets, this would have been the time for Eve to mention Amanda, to bond with Margo over their illicit crushes, but she wasn't drunk enough to say it out loud.

"I'm just glad he's tall," Margo said. "I don't think it would work with me and a short guy. I mean, there's no reason why it shouldn't, but a lot of men get freaked out by tall women."

"They're such babies," Eve said. "What doesn't freak them out?"

Margo nodded, but without much conviction.

"I've never actually been with a man before," she confessed.

"Oh," said Eve. "Wow."

"I liked women when I was a man. At least I tried to. But now . . . that's not really working for me anymore. I think I'm ready to branch out."

"Good for you." Eve gave her an encouraging squeeze on the arm. She wanted to say, *I know exactly how you feel,* but once again the words stayed put.

"So what should I do?" Margo asked. "How do I seduce him?"

"Maybe you should just talk to him first. Get to know him a little."

"I was afraid you'd say that."

"Or you could sit on his lap and stick your tongue in his ear. That works, too."

*   *   *

Something happened to Julian in the men's room. He wasn't exactly sober going in—nowhere near it—but he could still walk and think straight. But when he came out, he was totally fucking *WASTED.* It was like that whole second pitcher caught up with him in the course of a single piss.

Getting back to the table was an adventure worthy of a video game, and Dr. Fairchild seemed to have taken his seat.

"'Scuse me," he told her. "No offense, but that's my spot."

Dumell pointed across the table. There was an empty chair next to Mrs. Fletcher.

"Why don't you sit over there?" Dumell told him. "Spread the love."

Dumell was giving him a badass military stare, like, *Just do it, motherfucker.* Julian wasn't so hammered that he couldn't take a hint.

"Chillax, bro." He winked at Dumell and then gave him a thumbs-up, which he realized, even as he was doing it, was a little too much of a good thing. "I got your back."

There was something else he wanted to say, but he couldn't remember what it was, and the next thing he knew Mrs. Fletcher was standing next to him with her arm around his shoulders, offering to drive him home. Julian didn't want to leave just yet, but Barry said he didn't have a choice.

"You overdid it, kiddo. It's time to go."

"I'm not drunk," Julian protested, but even he didn't believe it.

They escorted him out to the parking lot like a criminal, Barry on one side, Mrs. Fletcher on the other. It was actually a relief to get out of the bar, to breathe some fresh air.

"I drank that whole pitcher," he told them. "All by myself."

"You're a champ." Barry helped him into the passenger seat of Mrs. Fletcher's minivan. "You're not gonna get sick, are you?"

"No way, Jose."

"All right." Barry nodded solemnly before he shut the door. "Don't let me down."

Mrs. Fletcher smiled at him as she slid the key into the ignition. Not a happy smile, but one of those *What are we gonna do with you?* smiles. It was weird being in the van with her. Like she was his mom. Or maybe even his girlfriend. Why the fuck not?

*Brendan would not like that,* he thought.

"How old are you?" he asked.

"Buckle your seatbelt," she told him.

He felt okay at first, except that the world kept lurching at him through the windshield. Too many trees and headlights and storefronts. It was better to focus on Mrs. Fletcher's face. She had a nice profile.

"You think they're gonna hook up?" he asked.

"Who?"

"Dumell and Dr. Fairchild. I think he likes her."

Mrs. Fletcher turned and looked at him, as if he'd said something interesting.

"Did he tell you that?"

"Kind of."

"Well," she said, after a brief hesitation. "It's none of our business if they do. They're both adults."

Julian nodded. He liked the sound of Mrs. Fletcher's voice. And he liked the tight shirt she was wearing, the way her boobs swelled against the buttons.

"What about us?" he said. "We gonna hook up?"

"You're drunk," she told him.

"You're really pretty. Do you even know that?"

"Julian," she said. "Let's not do this, okay?"

"Why not?"

"I'm forty-six years old," she told him. "You're not even old enough to drink."

He wanted to tell her that age didn't matter, but something went badly wrong in his stomach, and he had to ask her to pull over.

"Right now! *Please.*"

She heard the urgency in his voice and swerved to the side of the road. He jumped out of the van, hand clamped over his mouth, and puked into a nearby storm drain, which was better than leaving a disgusting puddle on the sidewalk for dogs to sample in the morning.

"Oh, fuck."

He was down on all fours, gazing through the metal grate into the dark abyss below, when he realized that Mrs. Fletcher was crouching next to him, rubbing his back in a slow circle, telling him to relax, that he'd feel better when he'd gotten the poison out of his system.

"Poor baby," she said.

"You have great boobs," he told her, right before he puked again.

PART THREE

*Gender and Society*

# A Bouquet of Red Flags

For the most part, Amber and her mom got along really well. They texted each other several times a day and spoke on the phone at least twice a week. And these weren't short calls, either. Once they got started, they could talk for an hour straight without coming up for air.

Unless there was something urgent to discuss, their conversations followed a well-worn path. They always began with an update about her brother—what he was eating, how he was sleeping, how things were going for him at school, how many new Matchbox cars he'd acquired—because Amber missed him a lot and still felt guilty about going away to college, leaving her mom to care for him as if she were a single parent, even though her father lived in the house. He'd never really bonded with Benjy; he acted like there was no point in even *trying*, and everybody let him get away with it, including Amber.

When they'd exhausted the topic of Benjy, her mom would ask a few questions about Amber's schoolwork, and then Amber would reciprocate, giving her mom lots of room to ramble on about anything that occurred to her, no matter how trivial—the weather, a story in the news, the quality of the produce she'd bought at the supermarket. There was always some discussion of her mom's allergies and a segment devoted to any unusual activity in the neighborhood: who got a new car, whose dog was in a clown collar, who had switched from oil heat to natural gas. Amber listened patiently, because she knew how lonely her mother was, and how small her world had become.

It was the least she could do.

At the same time, Amber dreaded these phone calls, because they inevitably drifted to the awkward subject of boyfriends—specifically, her mother's inability to understand why Amber didn't have one. It made no sense: Amber was pretty, she was smart, she had a big heart and a warm personality. Yes, her mother understood that she had a demanding schedule—academics, softball, the various clubs and organizations she belonged to—but young people could always make time for a little romance. Amber's mother certainly had, when she was her daughter's age. She'd been a very popular young lady, if she had to say so herself.

*You should go on some dates,* her mother would say, as if this were a brilliant idea that had just occurred to her, rather than a suggestion she'd made a hundred times before.

Trying to keep her frustration in check, Amber would explain, for the hundredth time, that no one went on *dates* anymore, that it wasn't a thing people her age actually did.

*I literally do not know a single person who's been on a date,* she would protest. This wasn't *literally* true, but she didn't want to muddy the waters of the argument with a more nuanced position.

And then came the Big Significant Pause. Every frigging time.

*Amber, honey? Is there something you want to tell us? You know your father and I will support you no matter what.*

It was all because she'd gone to her senior prom with Jocelyn Rodriguez, a softball teammate and one of the few out kids in her high school. Neither one of them had a date, so they decided to go as friends. Lots of girls did that. But they looked so good together, so totally *plausible*—Joss in a tux, with her short hair slicked back, Amber girly in a pink dress—that everyone simply assumed they were a couple, Amber's parents included. Even Joss seemed to think so, because she was pretty disappointed when Amber wouldn't make out with her during the slow dances.

*Jesus, Mom. How many times do I have to tell you? I like guys. There just aren't any good ones here.*

*Well, that's your problem right there, honey. You're going in with a bad attitude. You have to give them a chance.*

At that point in the conversation, Amber was tempted to list all the guys she'd hooked up with during freshman year—eight or nine, depending on how you looked at it, and every one an asshole in his own special way—but she didn't want to be slut-shamed by her own mother. And besides, she was done with all that. No more drunken hookups. No more getting naked with sexist jerks who had no interest in her as a human being.

*Maybe if you dressed a little more feminine,* her mother would say. *You look really pretty in dresses. Those skinny jeans aren't always so flattering.*

It was like they were actors in a play that never ended, doomed to keep performing the same depressing scene over and over again. But that was about to change, Amber thought, as she took a deep breath and reached for her phone.

\*   \*   \*

Becca was supposed to visit that weekend. It was all set. She'd arranged for a ride from Haddington with a girl in her class who had an open invitation to crash at the Sigma house, and Zack had agreed to sexile himself for a couple of days, not that it was much of a sacrifice on his part. His on-and-off relationship with the mystery girl (who was supposedly not fat, though that's how I always thought of her) was back on again, and he hardly ever slept in our room anymore anyway. Most of the time it felt like I was living in a single, which would have been great, except that I missed having him around. Even when he was there, things weren't the same. I mean, we got along fine, but we didn't joke around or laugh as much as we used to. He seemed a little distant, way more interested in whatever text he'd just received than in anything I had to say. It was pretty fucking annoying.

*Dude,* I asked him one night. *Are you in love or something?*

*What?* he said, chuckling to himself as he tapped out a reply.

*Forget it,* I told him. *It's not important*

I was excited about seeing Becca after all this time, but also kinda nervous. She was the one who'd been pushing for a weekend visit—I was fine with waiting until Thanksgiving—but now that it was a done deal I figured I'd make the best of it. I was juiced about getting laid, because after almost two months at BSU, I'd had exactly zero sex (except solo), which did not seem like an auspicious start to my college career.

But fucking a girl is one thing, and spending a whole weekend with her is another, and Becca and I had never been one of those couples that hung out together very much, or had a lot to talk about when we did. So I can't say I was all that crushed when she Skyped me on Wednesday with her eye makeup smeared from crying and told me that the visit was off. Her parents had talked it over and decided that she was too young to be spending the weekend with a college guy—even if the college guy was actually her high school boyfriend—and wanted to know why, if I was so keen on seeing their daughter, I didn't just come home for the weekend and hang out with her there.

"Damn," I said. "That really sucks."

"I know. I wanted to sleep with you so bad."

"Yeah, me too."

She sniffled and wiped her nose, staring at me with this wounded bird expression.

"It's not such a terrible idea," she said.

"What?"

"You could take the bus, right? And your mom would be really happy to see you."

"You want me to come home?"

"Why not? I'll split the cost with you, if that's what you're worried about."

"It's not the money."

"Then what's the problem?"

I knew I was in dangerous territory. There was no non-asshole way to tell her the truth, which was that I was happy enough to see her if I didn't have a choice, but even happier not to if I did.

"Let me think about it," I said. "I'll text you tomorrow."

And then, like ten minutes after we hung up, Amber called. I hadn't heard from her since the meeting of the Autism Awareness Network, where I'd humiliated myself by crying like a little bitch.

"What are you doing on Saturday night?" she asked.

"I'm not sure."

She made a sound like the buzzer on a game show.

"Wrong," she said. "We're going on a date."

\* \* \*

Amber was painfully aware of the mismatch between her politics and her desires. She was an intersectional feminist, an advocate for people with disabilities, and a wholehearted ally of the LGBT community in all its glorious diversity. As a straight, cisgender, able-bodied, neurotypical, first-world, middle-class white woman, she struggled to maintain a constant awareness of her privilege, and to avoid using it to silence or ignore the voices of those without the same unearned advantages, who had more of a right to speak on many, many subjects than she did. It went without saying that she was a passionate opponent of capitalism, patriarchy, racism, homophobia, transphobia, rape culture, bullying, and microaggression in all its forms.

But when it came to boys, for some reason, she only ever liked jocks.

It kind of sucked. She wished she were more attracted to men who shared her political convictions—the tree-huggers, the gender nonconformists, the vegan activists, the occupiers and boycotters, the Whiteness Studies majors, intellectual black dudes with Malcolm X eyeglasses—but it never seemed to work that way. She always fell for athletes—football players, shotputters, rugby forwards, heavyweight wrestlers, even an obnoxious golfer, though he was definitely an outlier—almost all of them hard-drinking white guys with buff, hairless chests, marinated in privilege, unable to see beyond their own dicks. And of course they used her like a disposable object, without regret or apology, because that's what privilege *is*—the license to treat other people like shit while still getting to believe that you're a good person.

What was it her father always said? The definition of crazy was doing the same thing over and over and expecting different results? Well, that was the story of Amber's love life so far, and she'd had enough. She'd vowed over the summer to stop the madness, to either start choosing her partners more wisely or, if need be, to opt for celibacy and self-respect over empty sex and the self-hating sadness that came with it.

And then, as if the universe were testing her resolve, she met Brendan at the Activities Fair on the very first day of her sophomore year. He was a bouquet of red flags—a handsome, self-confident, broad-shouldered, inarticulate, politically oblivious lacrosse player— the exact type of guy she'd sworn to avoid. But it didn't matter: her heart did its usual, incorrigible somersault and gave the middle finger to her brain. It amazed her how weak she was, like a smoker who'd vowed to quit, but couldn't get through a single day without lighting up.

To her credit, she put up more resistance than usual. Freshman year, she would have texted him right away, inviting him to hang out, maybe smoke some weed and watch a movie. At the time, it had seemed like the feminist thing to do—why shouldn't a woman pursue sex as freely as a man?—but for some reason it always ended up with her staring pathetically at her phone, wondering why Trent or Mason or Royce (the asshole golfer) hadn't even sent her a *thanks for the blowjob!* text, as if that would have made her feel any better.

With Brendan, she hung back, playing hard to get, as her mother would have quaintly put it, waiting for him to make the first move. She didn't text him, didn't orchestrate a "chance" meeting in the Higg, didn't even friend him on Facebook, though she did do a fair amount of stalking. He posted lots of shirtless pictures of himself, and, she had to admit, he looked really good without a shirt.

It turned out to be an effective strategy for not hooking up, especially since Brendan made no attempt to contact her, either. But even at a big school like BSU, they couldn't avoid each other forever. About a month into the semester, she'd walked into the library with the newly formed Student Coalition Against Racism and Police Brutality, and there he was, cute as ever, reading a book about climate change.

He'd surprised her in the best possible way. She couldn't imagine any of her former hookups joining her to protest the shooting of Michael Brown, or weeping in front of a roomful of strangers at a meeting for people with autistic siblings. He seemed like a decent guy, and maybe even boyfriend material, definitely worth taking a chance on.

*What are you going to do on your date?* her mother had asked.

*We're going to a movie. After that we'll probably go to a party where everyone gets naked.*

*Ha ha,* her mother said. *Very funny.*

*　　*　　*

I didn't *hate* the movie. It just wasn't the kind of movie you were meant to *like*, and not the kind you normally went to on a date. But Amber was really into feminism, and one of her good friends, a Vietnamese girl named Gloria, was in charge of the Women's International Documentary Film Festival, so there we were.

It was an eye-opener, that's for sure. The movie focused on a bunch of depressing third-world hellholes where women were treated like garbage. In one African country, young girls got raped all the time and nothing ever happened to the men who did it. There was this one victim—she was twelve, but looked older—who was raped by her "uncle" who was not actually her uncle. He was a family friend, and a very important man in the village. The white people who were making the film convinced her to press charges, but it backfired. She and her mom ended up getting kicked out of their house and the rapist denied everything.

*I am not that kind of person,* he said, like the accusation had hurt his feelings.

There were other stories—girls sold into prostitution by their own parents, girls forced into sweatshops to support their families, girls who were "engaged" to be married to disgusting old men before they'd even reached puberty, girls who were genitally mutilated while their own mothers held them down. I could hear Amber sniffling next to me and I reached for her hand. She turned and gave me this sad little smile.

After a while I just kinda zoned out. There's only so much misery you can take in one sitting. Normally, in a situation like that, I would've checked my texts or played a game of Hitman, but the girl who introduced the film had made a big deal about asking everybody to turn off their phones and devote their full attention to the screen.

*Please,* she said. *This is important. Please don't look away.*

The movie was long, which meant I had a lot of time to think. I thought about my mom, and how happy she would've been to know that I was watching a serious documentary like this, getting educated about the world, which to her was the whole point of being in college. And I thought about Becca, who wouldn't have lasted five minutes in that theater, because why should she pretend to care about stuff that happened to people she didn't know in places she'd never heard of? I understood why she felt that way—part of me even agreed with her—though I knew it was selfish, and not the kind of thing you were allowed to say out loud, especially not at the Women's International Documentary Film Festival.

Amber was quiet after the movie ended. We left the lecture hall and headed outside. It was a chilly night with a light drizzle coming down, but I think she was as grateful as I was for the fresh air. We were still holding hands, and I wondered if I should try to kiss her. But then I looked at her puffy eyes and stunned expression and realized that it probably wasn't such a good idea.

"What did you think?" she asked.

"About the movie?"

That made her laugh just a little.

"Yeah," she said. "About the movie."

If I'd been totally honest, I would have told her that the movie had made me realize just how lucky I was. To be a guy. To be an American. To have a healthy body and enough money that I never had to wonder where my next meal was coming from, and to know that I would never have to sacrifice my own happiness and freedom for anyone else's. To wake up every morning knowing that something fun could happen. The movie made me want to get down on all fours and kiss the ground. But I knew that was the wrong way to go.

"It fucking broke my heart," I told her.

*   *   *

Amber had been looking forward to the party all week. A lot of her friends from the Feminist Alliance were going to be there, and everybody was excited. It was one of those rare situations where you could have fun and make an important point at the same time, at least that's what they were all telling themselves. But now, after the movie she'd just seen, the party suddenly seemed ridiculous, a bunch of privileged college kids pretending that they were making a political statement, fighting the patriarchy by getting drunk and taking their clothes off.

"You okay?" Brendan asked, laying his hand gently on her shoulder. They were standing out on the quad, getting rained on.

"Just sad," she said, touched by his concern. He'd sat through the grueling film without a single complaint, and had held her hand through the worst of it. "The world's so fucked up."

"Tell me about it."

Amber didn't regret watching the movie. You couldn't turn away from the truth just because it ripped your guts out. You had to look cruelty and injustice in the eye, to acknowledge the humanity of people less fortunate than you, and accept your obligation to help improve their lives. It was the least you could do.

But it was so little. It was almost nothing.

Some part of her just wanted to say *Fuck it*—drop out of school, say goodbye to softball and Women's Studies and Autism Awareness and Slut Walk and her hilarious roommate, Willa—say goodbye to *America*—and get a job with some NGO that built schools for girls in Afghanistan, or fought human trafficking in Thailand, or provided free surgery for African women with obstetrical fistula. Do something useful, instead of wasting her time reading books and watching movies and liking meaningless shit on Facebook. It would be hard on her mother, though, and she'd really miss Benjy, who would only understand that she was far away, not why she'd gone. Her generous motives would be lost on him.

"You want to get a drink or something?" Brendan asked.

Before she could answer, her phone buzzed. It was Cat again. She'd texted three times during the movie.

*Where rrrrr uuuuu???? You better get that big fat booty over here so I can spank it bitch!!!!*

Amber smiled in spite of herself. Cat was the only person in the world who could talk to her like that and get away with it. And besides, it was ten thirty on a rainy Saturday night, and she had to accept the fact that, right now, there was nothing she could do to help anyone but herself lead a better and happier life.

"I know where we could get a drink," she told him.

\*   \*   \*

The party Amber took me to wasn't a full-blown naked party. It was an underwear party, sponsored by the Feminist Alliance, so of course it had an uplifting name, which in this case was EVERY BODY IS BEAUTIFUL!—a statement that is totally not true.

When we arrived, a feminist at the door handed us nametag lanyards. Instead of your name, you were supposed to write down something about your body that you didn't like. The idea was that you were supposed to celebrate your flaws and not be ashamed of them. Just get it out in the open, so people could tell you you were beautiful anyway.

Amber didn't hesitate. She uncapped the Sharpie and wrote *DIS-TURBINGLY LARGE SHOULDERS* on the card as easily as if she were signing her name. Then she handed the marker to me. I was stumped for a second, because I'd been working out and felt pretty good about my body. All I could think to write was *CALVES COULD BE BIGGER*, even though they were perfectly fine, too. Amber laughed when she saw what I'd written.

"That's it?" she said. "Your calves could be bigger?"

I shrugged. The only other thing I could have gone with was *SMELLY FEET*, because I did have an occasional problem in that direction, though I didn't really think it qualified as a physical flaw.

"Mine's not that different from yours," I pointed out.

I could tell she didn't agree, but she nodded anyway and pulled her dress over her head in this totally matter-of-fact way, which gave me an instant half-boner. I had to turn away and stare at a chubby dude in tightey whities until it was safe to start undressing. Weirdly, the chubby dude had listed his flaw as *TWITCHY EYELID*, which seemed a little beside the point. When I was done, we put our shoes and clothes into a trash bag and shoved it behind a couch.

"You think it's okay there?" I asked. "I don't want to walk home in my underwear."

Instead of answering, Amber grabbed my wrist and pulled me into the crowd. She was wearing regular cotton panties, black with a white border, and a V-neck black top that looked like a sports bra but was lacier in the front. Her body was just like I'd imagined it, strong and sleek, no hourglass but a nice round ass I was happy to follow wherever it led.

The house was pretty dark. Some rooms were lit by candles, others had lava lamps, and the dance floor had these swirling disco lights and flashing strobes. It made being half-naked a lot less problematic than it otherwise would have been. In a funny way, you ended up paying more attention to people's lanyards than their actual bodies. It was really interesting to see what people were ashamed of—

*MUFFIN TOP, UNIBROW, HUGE NOSE, MAN BOOBS, ASS ACNE*—and then kind of casually try to check out whatever flaw they were talking about. Sometimes you could spot the problem right away, and other times you had to take their word for it.

Amber knew a lot of the people there, so mostly I just nodded and smiled while she introduced me to her friends—*ECZEMA, TOE-NAIL FUNGUS*, and *RIGHT ONE WAY BIGGER*, among others. Most of the people I met were nice enough, though a bunch of them seemed skeptical that my non-bulging calves qualified as a bona fide problem. The only person I'd met before was Cat from the Autism Awareness Network, who was alarmingly skinny with her clothes off—all ribs and elbows and hip bones—though, I had to admit, kind of sexy in her leopard-print bra and panties. She was also wearing blue flip-flops and white surgical gloves, all of which added up to an eye-catching package.

"Hey Brendan." The sign around her neck read, *FURRY ARM HAIR.* "Good to see you again."

"You too," I said, squinting at her completely hairless forearms.

"I wax," she explained. "A *lot*. Otherwise I'd look like an orangutan."

"What's with the gloves?"

She shrugged and drank some jungle juice from a solo cup.

"Too many bodies." She gave a small shudder of revulsion. "Way too much skin and sweat and . . . *ugh*."

We smiled at each other for a couple of seconds, stumped for conversation. She turned and looked at Amber, who was talking to a black girl who had amazing abs and suffered from *ASHY SKIN*. The black girl was wearing gym shorts and a bikini top, which seemed like cheating to me, since neither one qualified as actual underwear.

"Amber really likes you," Cat told me.

"I like her, too."

"You better not hurt her," she said, poking her latex-covered finger into my sternum. "Otherwise you'll have to answer to me."

\* \* \*

Amber's room was on the sixth floor of Thoreau Hall. It was even smaller than her first-year double in Longfellow, but at least it wasn't in the basement.

"We're in luck," she told Brendan. "Willa's away for the weekend."

"Cool." He was busy checking out the posters on the pale green walls: Malala, the Dalai Lama, Andy Samberg. "Nice place."

She hadn't planned on bringing him home after the party. She'd meant to take it slow, maybe just make out a little, plant a seed for the future, but dancing with someone in your underwear turns out not to be the best strategy for taking it slow. They'd gotten into some pretty heavy grinding toward the end, and it had been an amazing feeling, to be that close to fucking with so many people around.

She dumped her coat on Willa's bed and then took off her dress, because why not? She'd already undressed in front of him, and he'd clearly liked what he saw. The party had done wonders for her mood—totally turned the night around—and given a welcome boost to her self-esteem. It had been so moving to be part of that community, one imperfect human among many, all those people admitting to their vulnerabilities, making one another feel safe and loved and beautiful. She took her bra off, and tossed it to Brendan.

"Heads up!"

His reflexes were a little slow—it must have been the weed they'd smoked on the upstairs balcony, their bare skin steaming in the night air—but he managed to make a one-handed grab after it bounced off his chest. Then he just stood there for a second, staring at the bra like it was an object he'd never encountered before.

"You okay?" she asked.

"Yeah," he said. "Awesome."

He was such a *boy*, she thought—sweet and clueless and weirdly passive. Amber was only a year older, but she was a woman, and had been one for a long time. She didn't mind the imbalance. She liked being in charge, the only adult in the room.

"I have one question," she said. "Why are your pants still on?"

\* \* \*

It should be a big deal the first time you hook up with someone new. A momentous occasion. I remember it felt like that the first time I fucked Becca. My hands were literally shaking when I put on the condom.

What you don't want is for your mind to be elsewhere, stuck on something stupid that has nothing to do with the girl you're with, especially if she's down on her knees, giving you a blowjob that you didn't expect, and didn't even have to ask for.

What you don't want to be thinking about just then is your ass-hole roommate, and the way he'd dissed you at the party.

In a funny way it was Amber's fault. She'd been grinding on me so hard on the dance floor, I thought I was gonna bust a nut right there. I told her I needed to pee, but she knew exactly what the problem was and thought it was pretty funny.

"You do what you have to do," she told me. "I'll be right here."

To calm myself, I took a solo lap around the house, upstairs and down, with my hands crossed—casually, I hoped—in front of my crotch. It was a pretty big place, with a balcony on the second floor and a rickety deck off the kitchen. There was also a small sunporch off the living room, and that was where I found Zack, playing quarters with two people I didn't know. One of them was a girl in a wheelchair.

"Yo, dude," I said. "Didn't know you were coming to this."

"Oh, hey." Judging from the look on his face, he didn't expect to see me there, either. "Brendan, wow."

He put his hand on the wheelchair girl's arm—she was sitting right next to him—and whispered something in her ear. She turned to me, a funny little smile forming on her face.

"Holy shit." She sounded pretty drunk. "The famous roommate."

176

"That's me," I said. "The famous roommate."

"I'm Lexa." She had straight dark hair and a cute face, though one eye seemed kinda squinty or something, like it had frozen mid-wink. The sign around her neck read, *LEGS DON'T WORK*.

"I'm Brendan."

"Riley," said the other dude at the table. He was short and angry-looking, with ridiculously big biceps, pimply shoulders, and a tag that read, *VERY SMALL BLADDER*.

"Riley and I went to high school together," Lexa explained. Her skin was golden-bronze all over, like she'd just gotten a spray tan. "Up in North Ledham."

"Go Raiders," said Riley, without much enthusiasm.

We all shook hands, and then I turned to Zack, whose nametag read, *UNCONTROLLABLE FARTING*.

"At least you're honest," I told him.

"Tell me about it," said Lexa, who was wearing a shiny maroon bra and matching panties. She had a nice body—big boobs and a tiny waist—though I was distracted by the clear plastic tube that snaked out of her underwear and around her back. I couldn't tell where it went and didn't want to look too hard.

"You love it," Zack told her.

"Yeah," she said. "Your uncontrollable farting is a huge turn-on."

"It's a popular fetish," he said. "You should google it sometime."

"Already have," she told him. "You take a nice picture."

Zack high-fived her—*Good one!*—then looked at me. "Where's Becca?"

"She couldn't come. I'm here with that other girl, Amber?"

"The softball player?"

"Yeah, we went to a movie and—"

"We playing or bullshitting?" Riley grumbled.

"Shut up," Lexa told him. She smiled at me and pointed at the shot glass on the table. "Wanna join us?"

Her invitation was totally sincere, and I would have been happy to play a round or two. But I could tell Zack didn't want me there. He didn't shake his head or give a warning glance, nothing that obvious. He just kind of looked down and away, like there was something on the floor that required his full attention, a dead bug or a speck of dirt.

"Not tonight," I told her. "Maybe next time."

*       *       *

Amber felt a familiar vacancy taking shape in the pit of her stomach, an empty space that, if something didn't change, would soon be filled with regret.

It didn't make sense. Things had been so hot on the dance floor. Their hands all over each other, the easy way they'd moved to the music, the sweet dirty things he'd whispered in her ear.

And now . . . *this*. No connection at all. Just a strange dick in her mouth and fingers drumming impatiently on the top of her head, like he wanted to get it over with. She glanced up at him, checking in, hoping for a little guidance, but he didn't notice. He was lost in thought, staring straight ahead at nothing, his expression frozen somewhere between confusion and anger.

She wondered if maybe she'd moved too fast. They'd only made out for a minute or two before she'd decided to go down on him. The kisses had been uninspiring—stiff and distant—and she thought she needed to try something a little more drastic to change the energy.

She was just about to call for a time-out when his fingertips tightened suddenly on her scalp. He pushed into her and gave a soft grunt of approval, his first real sign of life.

*Finally,* she thought.

She picked up the pace and he responded to the new rhythm, thrusting to meet her. It was encouraging, but also a little worrisome, because she didn't want him to come just yet. She wouldn't have minded if she'd thought he might reciprocate with any degree of skill or patience, but Brendan didn't seem like the type. She'd only ever been with one guy who gave decent oral, and that had been a one-time deal. When it was over, the guy—a wrestler named Angus—

never responded to any of her texts, and acted like he didn't know her when they bumped into each other on campus.

"You like that, don't you?" Brendan asked in a soft, dreamy voice.

Amber made an affirmative noise, the best she could do under the circumstances.

"You like that big cock in your mouth?"

*Ugh.* She ignored the question. For some reason, she detested the word *cock.*

"Suck that cock, slut."

*Whoa,* she thought. That was not okay. She tried to tell him, but his hand had slid down the back of her head, and his grip had tightened.

"Suck it, bitch."

She couldn't move, couldn't pull away. Couldn't even breathe. He thrust forward again, and Amber started to gag.

\*   \*   \*

I mean, I would have understood if it was just Zack and Lexa on the sunporch, but that kid Riley was already there, so it wasn't like I was spoiling some big romantic moment. I tried to tell myself that Zack was embarrassed by Lexa, but that didn't make any sense, either. They were at a party together, out in public in their fucking underwear, and they looked like they were having a great time. No, the only person Zack was embarrassed by was me, and I'd done nothing to deserve it, not a damn thing.

*Fuck him,* I thought.

It wasn't fair to me, and it wasn't fair to Amber. She'd been down on her knees for quite a while, giving it a hundred and ten percent, and I could see that she was starting to sweat a little.

*Focus,* I told myself. *Get your head in the game.*

Amber was doing a great job, don't get me wrong, but for some reason I wasn't feeling it, not the way I had with Becca on the day I left for college. I could almost hear her voice, the way she looked up at me and said, *This is your going-away present,* and we just kept talking like that the whole time, saying whatever crazy shit popped into our heads.

I know it's a little sketchy, thinking about one girl while you're with another, but you can't control what goes through your head at a time like that. And it worked, you know? I went from zero to sixty in a couple of seconds, and there was no stopping after that. I kept my foot on the gas, the highway wide open in front of me, not a car in sight.

And then Amber punched me in the nuts.

It was no accident. She hammered me in the scrotum—a short, brutal uppercut—when I was about ten seconds away from the finish line.

My knees buckled and I hit the floor, curling into the fetal position, waiting for the agony to subside.

"What the fuck?" I said, when I was finally able to talk. "Are you crazy?"

Amber was standing now, hugging herself so I couldn't see her chest.

"You were choking me," she said.

"No, I wasn't."

"I couldn't breathe, Brendan. I couldn't even move my head."

The pain had faded a little, but it returned in a sickening wave. I looked around for a wastebasket in case I had to puke.

"I don't know what you're talking about."

"And don't you ever call me a slut." She lifted her foot like she was gonna kick me, but then she put it back on the floor. "I don't know who you think you are."

"I was just talking dirty. I thought you liked it."

"Why would you think that?" Her face was really pink. "You have no idea what I like."

I forced myself to sit up.

"I'm sorry. I just got carried away."

"Get the fuck out," she told me.

"Come on, Amber. Don't be like that."

"Like what?" She grabbed my pants off the floor and threw them at me. "Like a person with self-respect?"

She'd been pretty calm up to that point, but then her mouth stretched out and she started to cry. I could tell she didn't want to do it—didn't want to show that weakness in front of me—and she just kind of sniffled really hard and pulled herself together. The tears just stopped. I'd never seen anyone do that before.

"Can't we talk about this?" I said.

But Amber was done talking. She stood there in her black-and-white panties, hugging herself and shaking her head no, like there was no point in discussing anything with me, like I wasn't worth the effort.

# One Woman's Story

Amanda waited by the main entrance, doing her best to tune out the usual lecture day jitters and focus instead on her own sense of personal accomplishment, a feeling she rarely got to enjoy in her post-college life.

*I did this!* she reminded herself. *I made this happen!*

Technically, this was the third monthly lecture she'd overseen, but she'd felt no ownership stake in the September or October offerings—dry-as-dust tributes to the Queen of England and the Versatile Soybean, respectively—both of which she'd inherited from her predecessor. They'd been such demoralizing experiences that Amanda had seriously considered quitting her job after each of them, or at least writing a heartfelt letter of apology to everyone who'd attended, herself included.

But instead of quitting, or poisoning her work life with bitterness and negativity, she'd behaved like an adult. She'd gathered her courage and discussed the situation with her boss, and together they'd found a way to effect constructive change. Eve deserved a lot of the credit, of course. She was the one who'd floated the possibility of inviting her professor to deliver the November lecture, but she'd only done so in response to Amanda's pitch for a more edgy, out-of-the-box approach.

Bringing a transgender guest speaker to the Senior Center was exactly the sort of bold move Amanda had been advocating, an announcement to the entire town (and beyond) that the monthly lecture series was under exciting new management, and people might want to start paying attention.

Eve was excited, too, and their shared sense of anticipation had brought them closer together, helping them to get past any lingering awkwardness related to the surprise kiss outside the restaurant. It was a relief to Amanda, and not just for professional reasons. She'd been feeling bad about the way she'd reacted that night, flinching as though Eve had been attacking her, rather than making a slightly clumsy but not completely unwelcome overture. It wasn't that Amanda wished she'd gone to bed with her, or even kissed her back, because she knew it was a terrible idea to get involved with your boss. She just wished she'd been a little nicer about saying no, because she really liked Eve, and had actually been flattered, and even a little turned on, at least in retrospect—at the time she'd simply been flustered—because she sometimes found herself replaying the kiss in her mind when she was bored, and occasionally using it as fuel for more fully developed fantasy encounters that totally got her off, not that Eve needed to know about that.

"Excuse me," said an elderly woman in a dark green tracksuit with pale green piping. Amanda had met her a couple of times, but couldn't remember her name. Bev or Dot or Nat, something truncated and nearly extinct. She wore her hair in a cap of tight white curls and had a Halloween-themed Band-Aid pasted on her cheek. "What is this?"

Bev or Dot or Nat jabbed her finger at the hardback poster resting on an easel near the front desk. It featured a blown-up head shot of Margo Fairchild, smiling blandly, like an upscale realtor.

NOVEMBER MONTHLY LECTURE
WEDNESDAY, 7 PM
MARGO FAIRCHILD, Ph.D.
*ONE WOMAN'S STORY*

"She's a local professor," Amanda explained. "A very inspiring person."

The woman with the three-letter name squinted at the poster for a few seconds—long enough for Amanda to be engulfed by a powdery floral cloud of perfume—and then shook her head. She looked deeply irritated, though Amanda had spent enough time with old people to know that their expressions didn't always match up with their moods.

"What's it *about*?" she demanded.

Amanda hesitated. She'd wanted to use the word *transgender* somewhere on the poster and in the press release, but Eve had overruled her, on the grounds that it might alienate or frighten potential audience members.

*Let them come with an open mind,* she'd advised. *Margo will win them over.*

"It's about taking control of your life," Amanda replied. "Finding happiness on your own terms."

The woman thought this over.

*Viv,* Amanda suddenly remembered. *Her name is Viv.*

Viv nodded, apparently satisfied.

"Better than soybeans," she said, and headed on her way.

\* \* \*

The music was so loud, Margo barely heard the *ding!* of the incoming text, another message from Eve Fletcher, who was, understandably, starting to get worried.

*On my way,* Margo texted back, after a brief strategic delay, because it was less embarrassing than the truth, which was that she'd been sitting in the parking lot of the Senior Center for the past fifteen minutes, hiding inside her Honda Fit, listening to "Shake It Off" over and over again. *There in 5.*

She could imagine how silly she looked, a middle-aged transgender woman—with a Ph.D.! Tonight's guest speaker!—singing along to a teen anthem as old people hobbled past, heading toward the lecture hall where Margo would soon address them. But the thing was, she didn't really feel middle-aged. In her heart, she was a teenager, still learning the ins and outs of her new body. Still hoping for her share of love and happiness and fun, all those good things that the world sometimes provided.

Her phone dinged again, but this time it wasn't Eve. It was Dumell. *You go, girl!*

Margo smiled. He was so sweet. Such a kind, gentle, fragile man. And handsome, too. He scared her a little. Not in a bad way, but because she liked him so much, and didn't want to screw things up. They'd been on two dates so far, the best dates she'd had in her entire life. They'd talked about everything—Iraq, basketball, families, the pros and cons of various antidepressants and anti-anxiety meds, and how strangely normal it felt when they were together, despite the fact that they were a peculiar couple on so many levels. They'd kissed—there'd been quite a bit of kissing—but they hadn't slept together, not yet. It was coming, though, right around the next corner, if one or both of them didn't chicken out.

*Will I see you later?* she asked.

*Unless you go blind,* he replied, signing off with a winky face. She shot him a smile in return.

It was past time to get out of the car, but she couldn't help herself and pressed play for one final encore. She felt safe in the car, and the song was so good. She loved the video, too, all those people dancing at the end, not only the lithe, gifted professionals, but the regular folks, bald and chunky and self-conscious and plain, with their eyeglasses and cardigan sweaters and perfectly ordinary bodies, all of them trying to rid themselves of whatever it was that held them back and knocked them down and made them wonder if they would ever find what they were looking for. They were Margo's people.

Taylor Swift wasn't actually one of them—she was just pretending, the same way Jesus had pretended to be a man. That was why she stood in front of the line, ahead of the others rather than among them. Because she was the teacher, the role model. She'd already shaken off the haters and the doubters and activated her best self.

She was there to show the world what happiness and freedom looked like. You glowed with it. You did exactly what you wanted to. And whatever costume you wore, you were still yourself, unique and beautiful and unmistakable for anyone else.

*Someday,* Margo thought. *Someday.*

\* \* \*

Eve's office was small and functional—pale walls, metal desk, industrial gray carpeting—the kind of office you got when taxpayers were grudgingly footing the bill. Even so, it was the biggest office at the Senior Center, and the sign on the door said *Executive Director.* Margo was duly impressed.

"Wow," she said. "Look at you. The big cheese."

Eve chuckled dismissively, but she appreciated the phrase. She *was* the big cheese in this little pond, and she was glad that Margo had a chance to observe her in her natural habitat.

"That's right," she said. "I'm not just a part-time community college student. I'm also a mid-level municipal bureaucrat."

"Don't listen to her," Amanda said. "Eve's a great director. Everyone loves her."

It was a pro forma compliment—an employee sucking up to her boss—but Eve felt a blush coming on anyway. Her relationship with Amanda was still a little unsettled, every interaction colored by the memory of that misguided after-dinner kiss and the awkwardness that had followed. Amanda had been nothing but gracious about it—mostly, she acted as if it had never even happened—but Eve had been unable to banish it from her mind, or find a way to behave normally in Amanda's presence.

"I'm not surprised," Margo said. "Eve's a sweetheart."

"Okay, okay," Eve murmured. "Enough already."

She was about to suggest that they head over to the lecture room, but Margo had shifted her attention to Amanda's outfit—a black-and-white polka-dot dress over lime-green tights.

"I love your dress." She stroked Amanda's sleeve, getting a feel for the fabric. They were a striking pair—Margo tall and angular in a conservative navy suit, a colorful silk scarf knotted around her throat; Amanda short and voluptuous, deeply feminine, despite her aggressive tattoos and lace-up Doc Martens. "Where'd you get it?"

"Thrift store," Amanda replied, with the smugness of the successful bargain hunter. The dress was adorable, with a Peter Pan collar and big white buttons down the front. "Fourteen dollars."

"You're kidding."

"Nope. A little shop called Unicyle. Best-kept secret in Haddington."

"I need some fun clothes," Margo said, a little wistfully. "I just hate shopping alone. Sometimes it's nice to have a second opinion."

"I'll take you," Amanda said. "Anytime you want."

"Watch out," Margo laughed. "I might take you up on that."

Eve was happy to see them getting along so well. It was always gratifying when friends from different parts of your life hit it off, a reflection of your own good taste. She just hoped she'd be included if they ever did go on a shopping adventure. She hadn't done anything like that in a long time, a group of friends wandering through the mall or checking out the shops in a quaint suburban town, stepping out of changing rooms with dubious or hopeful expressions. Then they'd stop at Starbucks or a wine bar for a postmortem, shopping bags resting by their tired feet. It was such an appealing fantasy, exactly the sort of innocent female camaraderie Eve needed in her life. But it was hard to reconcile with the guilt she was feeling toward both of the women in her office, the suspicion that she was unworthy of their friendship.

Her offense against Amanda was clear-cut, easy to define: it was sexual harassment, as much as it pained her to use the term—a violation of trust, a misuse of authority, the kind of thing you could rightfully lose a job over. With Margo, the betrayal was a bit murkier, more private and indirect and possibly more forgivable, though it didn't actually feel that way at the moment, probably because the transgression was so fresh in her mind.

It had happened the night before, right after she'd come home from class. All she'd done was google the phrase "transgender woman." She'd told herself she was acting out of simple curiosity—a perfectly reasonable impulse—except that she didn't end up clicking on the sober informational links that would have led her to helpful articles on hormone therapy, Adam's apple surgery, antidiscrimination laws, or anything else decent and aboveboard. Oh, no. She'd gone straight to the smut, as usual, to the Hot Brazilian Trannies and the Slutty Thai Ladyboys and the Dirty Chicks with Dicks, insisting to herself the whole time that she was disgusted by what she saw—the exploitation of vulnerable people, the reductive sexualization of something that went way beyond sex—though not so disgusted that it stopped her from sampling several videos, and then watching an eight-minute clip called *Tranny Seduces MILF* three times in a row, despite the fact that the characters were speaking Portuguese with no subtitles, though in Eve's defense, they weren't saying much besides *Oy!* and *Deus!*

It was pretty hot, she had to admit, though in a very uncomfortable way. A true jolt to her system, one of those mind-expanding moments when you found yourself aroused by something that had never even been on your erotic radar. A beautiful dark-haired woman with an erect penis speaking a mysterious foreign language. There was something almost mythological about it.

On a moral level, Eve was pretty sure that she hadn't done anything truly wrong. She was just a human being watching other human beings do what humans sometimes did. She'd wanted to *know*, and now she did. *Oy!* It was nothing personal. *Deus!* It had nothing to do with Margo, and nothing to do with herself.

And yet, at the same time, she knew it did. *Tranny* and *MILF*. *MILF* and *Tranny*. They were just labels, a shorthand to organize the chaos of the world. But the labels have a funny way of becoming our names, whether we agree with them or not. *Margo* and *Eve*. *Me* and *you*. She must have looked puzzled or upset, because she was suddenly aware of a strange silence in the room. She looked up and saw both of the friends she'd wronged staring at her with concerned expressions.

"Eve?" Amanda said. "Are you okay?"

"Fine." Eve mustered a businesslike smile and clapped her hands once, softly. "Guess we better get this show on the road."

* * *

Julian was worried. November always felt like a setback, what with the clock change and the sudden onset of darkness, the bitter wind and that ominous sense of *falling behind*. It reminded him too much of last year, the paralyzing sadness that had set in with the cold weather, day after day when he saw no reason to get out of bed, not even to take a shower. That was rock bottom, flopping around like a hooked fish in the tangled sheets, smelling his own sour stink and not caring enough to do anything about it. He didn't think it was going to happen again, not with these new meds, but you never knew. That was the scary part. *You never knew.*

It was a chilly night to be out on a skateboard, with a damp headwind that made the air itself feel like an obstacle. By the time he rolled into the parking lot, his face was pretty much frozen in place. He hesitated for a moment, exhaling vapor clouds and staring at the front of the building, which was bigger and more impressive from this angle than it was from the road. Several old people were making the arduous journey from the parking lot to the well-lit front entrance, moving in super-slow motion.

Julian picked up his skateboard and joined the herd. He understood just how pathetic this was—he had no intention of mentioning it to Ethan or to anyone else, even as a joke—but he also accepted the sad truth of his life: *he literally had nothing better to do.* He was eighteen years old and had come to the fucking Senior Center in search of a good time. Only fifty years ahead of schedule.

Dr. Fairchild had mentioned the lecture yesterday, and invited the whole class to come out—it was free and open to the public— if they weren't already sick of the sound of her voice. *It'd be nice to see some friendly faces in the crowd,* she'd told them. Mrs. Fletcher would definitely be there—she ran the Senior Center and had organized the whole thing—and Dumell said he was hoping to make it, too, but only at the tail end, because he had a class on Wednesday nights.

Julian was hoping that maybe they'd all go out for a drink afterward, though he promised himself that he wouldn't get sloppy drunk like the last time, when he'd ended up on all fours on Haddington Boulevard, barfing into the sewer while Mrs. Fletcher rubbed his back and told him to let it all out. He'd emailed her the next day, apologizing profusely for the inappropriate comments he'd made about her body—not untrue, but totally out of line—and she'd assured him that there were no hard feelings.

He entered the lecture room behind a bulky old man in a windbreaker and baseball cap. The poor guy had a bum leg that he dragged along behind him. Every step he took, it was like he was drawing a new line in the sand.

The room was pretty full, probably close to a hundred people. Julian glanced around, hoping to spot one of his classmates—Russ or Barry, or even Mr. Ho—but all he saw was a bunch of white-haired geriatrics craning their necks and squinting in his direction, as if they'd ordered a pizza an hour ago and were wondering if he might be the goddam delivery guy.

The man in front of him limped into a row with two empty seats on the aisle and Julian followed, because an aisle seat seemed like a smart idea, in case he felt the need to make a quick exit. He bent down and stashed his skateboard under the folding chair. Straightening up, he noticed that his neighbor was watching him with an amused expression.

"Don't see too many of those things around here," the old guy observed. His nose was swollen and veiny, and his baseball cap said *U.S.S. Kitty Hawk*.

Julian nodded politely, not wanting to get into a big discussion while they waited. The old guy stuck out his hand.

"Al Huff," he said. "I live on Hogarth Road."

Julian was sorry he'd sat here.

"Julian Spitzer. Sanborn Avenue."

They shook. Al's hand was soft and dry, weirdly puffy.

"You here for the lecture?" he asked.

Julian couldn't help himself. He glanced around, then spoke in a confidential tone.

"Who cares about the lecture? I came for the ladies."

Al's laugh was loud, but a little wheezy, half cough.

"Me too," he said. "Maybe one of us'll get lucky."

Julian said the odds were on their side, but Al wasn't listening anymore. He was twisting in his seat, trying to look over his shoulder. Julian followed his gaze and saw that Dr. Fairchild had entered the room, along with Mrs. Fletcher and a younger woman, and the three of them began moving toward the stage in single file. Except for the absence of music, it felt almost like a wedding procession, the audience watching in rapt silence as the guests of honor made their way down the aisle. Mrs. Fletcher nodded to Julian as she passed, and Dr. Fairchild's face blossomed into an expression of happy surprise at the sight of him. The younger woman—she was short and a little heavy, but kind of sexy—gave him a puzzled glance, as if she wondered what the hell someone his age was doing there. When Julian turned back around, he saw that Al Huff was scowling and shaking his head.

"What a shame," he said. "What a goddam shame."

*  *  *

Margo took a deep breath and forced herself to smile. It was a good crowd, bigger than she'd expected, at least two-thirds women. She hadn't even begun her speech and one elderly gentleman was already snoring in the second row, making a soft gargling sound that came and went at random intervals.

"Good evening." She tapped her fingernail on the bulb of the handheld microphone. "Can everyone hear me okay?"

The response was mostly affirmative, though there was some disgruntled murmuring scattered through the room, probably due more to individual hearing impairments than any problem with the sound system. Margo glanced at Eve, who gave her a thumbs-up from the front row.

"I'll try to speak slowly and clearly," she said, scanning the crowd for allies. She was glad to see Julian Spitzer—extra credit, not that he needed any—but she made a conscious decision not to look in his direction for moral support. He was an outlier in this group, totally unrepresentative of the demographic she was hoping to connect with. Instead she found an equally encouraging face to focus on—it was a trick she'd learned in public speaking class—in this case, a plump, pleasant-looking woman in a lavender turtleneck, sitting in the fourth row, dead center. She wasn't smiling, exactly, but she had a patient, benevolent expression, like a proud grandmother at a piano recital.

"Thank you so much for coming out tonight. You're the first group of seniors that I've ever addressed."

Usually Margo spoke to young people, mostly high school students, because they needed to be exposed to transgender role models, and if not her, then who? She remembered how lonely she had been as a teenager, detached from the world by a secret that she could barely admit to herself, let alone her parents or teachers or friends. What she wouldn't have given back then to hear a trans adult tell her that she wasn't alone, that happiness and wholeness were possible, that you could find a way to become the person you knew in your heart you truly were, despite all the undeniable evidence to the contrary.

The teenagers she spoke to were usually on pretty good behavior. They laughed at her jokes and applauded politely when she was done. But Margo wasn't fooled. She knew the bullies were out there, smirking and muttering insults under their breath, hating her because hating was so much fun, and feeling superior was its own reward. It always took something out of her to stand in front of them, to offer herself up for their condescension and mockery, but she did it. She did it because those kids were the future, and even the worst of them could have a change of heart, or at least be shamed into silence.

But these old people in front of her tonight, they weren't the future. They belonged to the past, and Margo had learned from bitter experience—not just with her mother, but with a whole generation of aunts and uncles and family friends and neighbors and acquaintances—that very few of them were willing to examine their fundamental beliefs about gender, let alone revise them so they could make room for trans people in their hearts and minds. It had gotten to the point where she had stopped even trying to argue with her older relatives; it just wasn't worth the effort and the heartache. You just had to wait them out. They'd be gone before too long, taking their narrow-minded, uncharitable ideas along with them.

That was why she'd initially declined Eve's invitation to speak at the Senior Center. But then Eve had performed some tricky PC jujitsu, calling Margo out for ageism and hypocrisy, for doing to seniors what society had done to LGBT people for so long. She reminded Margo that older people were a vulnerable and often stigmatized part of the community, and that it was both morally wrong and politically counterproductive to write them off as a lost cause. After all, they vote. And they have children and grandchildren, the power to give or withhold their love and approval.

Margo looked directly at the woman in the lavender turtleneck. The woman didn't resemble Margo's mother—she seemed soft and easygoing, where Donna Fairchild had been sinewy and judgmental—but she was about the same age, and shaped by the same social forces. She could have been her mother's friend or co-worker. It was close enough.

*I'm talking to you,* Margo thought. *I hope you'll listen.*

"Good evening, everybody."

She stepped out from behind the podium, letting the crowd take a good look at her body, giving them time to register all the particulars—her unusual height, her pretty hair, her full breasts and narrow hips, her long muscular legs. It was something she was still getting used to, this need people had to scrutinize her from head to toe, as if all of life were a beauty pageant, and every woman a contestant. She even did a little twirl, because the judges liked to see your back as well as your front. It wasn't fair, but Margo knew better than anyone that fairness and gender rarely intersected.

"My name is Margo Fairchild," she announced, "and I used to be a man."

\* \* \*

Julian was trying to concentrate on the slide show, a series of photos that documented Dr. Fairchild's early life—baby pictures, the bright-eyed toddler, birthday hats and Halloween costumes and presents on Christmas morning. Cub Scouts and Little League and a smile with a missing tooth.

"I was an adorable little boy and a very good son," Dr. Fairchild explained. "Everyone said so."

Al Huff let out a groan of despair.

"It's a mental illness," he said.

Al had been delivering this sort of commentary for the entire lecture, in a loud voice he seemed to think was a whisper. It was a huge disruption, but no one in the nearby rows seemed to mind. They acted like it was perfectly normal, like Al had a God-given right to express every single thought that passed through his mind, no matter how stupid or offensive.

Julian glanced around, checking for empty seats. A few were available, but none of them were near the aisle, and he wouldn't be able to move without forcing a bunch of old people to stand up and let him pass, drawing a ton of attention to himself in the process.

"I had a growth spurt in seventh grade," Dr. Fairchild announced, and you could see it in the pictures. All at once, Mark was a gangly adolescent with pimples, braces, and a mortified smile. "There were times when I woke up in the morning and could tell from my pajama pants that my legs had gotten longer while I slept. It was a nightmare. People kept telling me, *You're turning into a handsome young man*, which was the last thing I wanted to be. But there didn't seem to be any way to stop it from happening. It had a biological momentum of its own, like my body was telling me, *You'll be a man whether you like it or not."*

Julian's phone vibrated in his pocket. He pulled it out and saw that it was a text from Ethan, who'd been bugging him to come to Burlington for the weekend to smoke some weed and check out the campus, in case he wanted to transfer sophomore year.

Julian put the phone away without responding. It was cool that Ethan had invited him, and it should have been a no-brainer to say yes. Why wouldn't he want to go away for the weekend, sleep on a dorm room floor, get a taste of real college life? But for some reason the thought of the trip made him anxious, all that pressure to be normal and have a good time with kids his own age. In Julian's experience, guaranteed fun usually just left him more depressed than he'd been in the first place.

"Good Christ," said Al. "I can't even look at this."

The picture on the screen showed young Mark in a basketball uniform, looming over his scrawny teammates.

"The only good thing that happened to me in junior high was that I started playing basketball in a serious way," Dr. Fairchild observed. A flurry of images followed, documenting Mark Fairchild's career as a high school superstar. Some of the photos came from newspapers and yearbooks; others were candid shots taken at school or home. In every one of them, even those taken in classrooms or on a living room couch, Mark was wearing a basketball uniform or a warm-up suit with long pants and a zippered top.

"I felt like myself on the court. That was the only place. Everywhere else I felt like a big mistake."

To illustrate this point, a prom photo appeared, Mark Fairchild tall and handsome in a classic black tuxedo, his arm around a pretty girl in a shiny pink gown. The girl was beaming with happiness, Mark not so much.

"I remember that night so clearly. I was miserable in my tux. I wanted to be in a gown like the one my date was wearing, to feel the skirt swish against my legs while I danced. I just wanted to feel pretty on my prom night, to be seen for who I truly was."

"That's wrong," Al muttered. "It's unnatural."

Julian had finally had enough.

"Dude," he snapped. "Could you please be quiet? People are trying to listen."

Al wasn't offended. In fact, he seemed genuinely interested in Julian's opinion.

"Do you think that's natural?" he asked.

"There's nothing natural about gender," Julian informed him. "It's a social construction."

Al shook his head. "I don't know what that means."

Julian was sorry he'd opened his mouth. Luckily his phone buzzed, saving him from further explanation.

"Excuse me," he said, reaching into his pocket.

It was Ethan again, reminding him to bring a sleeping bag.

*I'm not coming,* Julian wanted to write, but he couldn't think of a good excuse.

*I have plans?*

*I hate the bus?*

*I don't want to sleep on the floor?*

He was still staring at the empty text bubble when he noticed that someone was crouching beside him in the aisle. It was the young woman in the polka-dot dress, Eve Fletcher's employee. She was looking at him with a sour expression, as if he were the troublemaker who was ruining the lecture for everyone else.

"Excuse me." She nodded toward Al, who was ranting about a man being a man and a woman being a woman. "Could you please tell your grandfather to keep it down?"

\* \* \*

Eve was trying not to cry; it didn't seem like something the executive director should do at a public event. It was hard, though—the

197

slide show was breaking her heart, the inexorable progress of a child moving through time, changing with every picture, yet somehow remaining the same person. Mark Fairchild had been a beautiful boy—so confident, so *happy*, or so it seemed. But there was Margo standing right beside the screen, insisting that it had all been a lie and a more or less constant torment, a nightmare she didn't know she could escape until much later in her life.

Of course Eve's thoughts turned to Brendan—how could they not? She was overcome by an almost desperate longing to see her son's face, to put her arms around him, to hear his voice, to assure herself that he was okay. She'd been a fool to surrender Parents Weekend to Ted, to volunteer for her own deprivation. She could feel her only child slipping away from her, and understood that she'd been complicit in the process. They hadn't spoken on the phone in almost two weeks, and their text exchanges had been brief and unrevealing, just the usual banalities and apologetic requests for money. It wasn't that she'd forgotten him, but she had allowed him to fade in her mind, to become peripheral. And it had happened so quickly, with so little resistance from either of them. She'd justified it by reminding herself that a little distance was good, that he was growing up, becoming independent, and that she was reclaiming a little of her own life, and maybe some of that was true, but the expanding lump in her throat suggested otherwise.

"This is my mother," Margo said, as an old high school yearbook photo filled the screen, a pretty young woman with dark hair and an enigmatic smile. "Her name was Donna Ryan when this picture was taken. A few years later she became Donna Fairchild."

A wedding-day picture replaced the yearbook photo, the bride admiring herself in an oval mirror. And suddenly the bride was a bald, emaciated woman in a hospital bed, staring at the camera with a bleak, defeated expression.

"If she were alive today, she'd be seventy-four years old. She died too young."

Donna washed the dishes. She fed a baby with a tiny spoon. She stood beside Mark on the day of his high school graduation. Her head only reached to his shoulder.

"I fooled a lot of people," Margo said. "But I never fooled her."

Another picture appeared, this one an overexposed snapshot from the late seventies or early eighties: Donna Fairchild, neither young nor old, standing on the beach in front of an empty lifeguard chair, wearing dark sunglasses and a blue bathing suit with a ruffled skirt. Her face was blank, unreadable.

"I loved that bathing suit," Margo said. "I loved it a little too much for my own good."

Donna remained frozen on the screen throughout the entire anecdote that followed. It happened when Margo was in fifth grade, and still thought of herself as Mark. One day Mark pretended to be sick so he could take a day off from school. Previously, his mother, a second-grade teacher, had stayed home to care for him when he was feeling ill, but on this particular day, Donna decided he was old enough to stay home alone, which was exactly what he'd been hoping for. As soon as his mother left for work, Mark went straight to her bedroom and found the blue bathing suit with the ruffled skirt. It was right where he'd expected, in the second drawer from the top.

"I thought I just wanted to touch it. But touching it wasn't enough."

Mark was only eleven and hadn't begun his big growth spurt, so the suit fit surprisingly well, everywhere except the chest, which had a droopy, deflated appearance. It looked a lot better once he stuffed the padded bra cups with paper towels. In fact, it looked amazing.

"I'm pretty sure I hypnotized myself. I must have stared at my reflection in the mirror for fifteen or twenty minutes. It was like I was seeing *me* for the first time."

Mark eventually left his mother's bedroom, but he didn't take off the swimsuit. He went downstairs, opened a bag of potato chips, and turned on the TV. He figured he had at least four hours before he had to worry about anyone coming home and finding him like that.

"It was such a luxury," Margo said. "Just being alone in the house. That *never* happened."

It was a beautiful hot day, late September or early October, and Mark headed out to the back deck to do a little sunbathing, an activity very popular among the girls at his school. He brought a portable radio and some Bain de Soleil, and he tugged down the shoulder straps of the bathing suit to avoid an unsightly tan line.

"It was so relaxing. The sun and the music. I guess I just let my guard down and fell asleep."

It must have been a deep sleep, because he didn't hear the car pulling into the driveway or his mother entering the house and calling his name. She'd been worried about him, and had come home on her lunch break to see how he was doing. What she found was the daughter she didn't know she had, wearing a matronly bathing suit that did her no favors.

"For a long time, my mother didn't say a word. She just kept staring at me and shaking her head. *No, no, no.* I remember how pale she looked, like she'd just received terrible news about someone she loved, an illness or an unexpected death. When she finally did manage to speak, she asked me if this was my idea of a joke, if I thought it was *funny* to wear her clothes. It's clear to me now that she desperately wanted me to say, *Yes, Mom, it was just a stupid joke.* But I was so scared and ashamed, all I could do was tell the truth. *I love this bathing suit. It's my favorite.* She ordered me to go upstairs, take it off, and never touch it again. Or any other article of her clothing, for that matter."

They never discussed the incident, at least not directly; they weren't that kind of family. But Donna had seen what she'd seen, and it had frightened her.

"She had a code word," Margo explained. "She called it my *nonsense.* Whenever my parents left me home alone—and believe me, they didn't do it very much—my mother would say, *You better not get up to any of your nonsense!* If she ever caught me looking sad, she'd say, *Is this about that nonsense?* And when I finally got engaged to be

married, she said, *I hope this means you're done with all that nonsense.*"
Margo shook her head, amazed by her mother's stubbornness. "Even
on her deathbed, after I'd transitioned and was living as a woman,
she looked at me and said, *Are you ever gonna stop with this nonsense?*"

Eve knew it was rude to text in the middle of a presentation, but
she couldn't stop herself. She pulled out her phone and sent a quick
message to Brendan.

*I miss you.*

"I'm sorry, Mom," Margo told the photograph. "I can't stop my
nonsense. I'm your daughter and I love you very much."

*   *   *

I couldn't wait for Thanksgiving. I just wanted to go home, sleep in
my own bed, eat some decent food, sneak onto the golf course with
Troy and Wade, polish off a couple of blunts and a bottle of shit
vodka, just like the old days. We'd get completely annihilated on
Wednesday night and then drag ourselves to the homecoming game
on Thursday morning, where we could brag about our hangovers
to people we hadn't seen in three months, though it felt *way* longer
than that. Becca would be cheering on the sidelines—the last football game of her career—and I was hoping maybe I could catch her
in a sentimental mood and convince her to give me another chance.
I loved the way she looked in that stretchy little dress they all wore,
red with a big white H on the front.

*H is for hot,* I used to tell her.

*H is for ho,* I used to tell my friends.

The only thing I dreaded about going home was having to talk
about my *college experience*, pretending it was the greatest thing ever,
parties on top of hookups mixed in with challenging classes and
inspiring professors and lots of cool new friends, when the truth was,
it had pretty much all turned to shit in the past couple of weeks. I
was on the road to failing Econ and Math, Amber wasn't responding
to my texts, and Zack was hardly ever around. He was spending all
his time with Lexa, sleeping in her room, pushing her wheelchair all

over campus, like he was her fucking caretaker instead of her boy-friend. One day I bumped into him at the Student Center Chick-fil-A and asked him point-blank if he was pissed at me, but he said he wasn't. I told him it didn't feel like that, and asked why he'd never said a word to me about Lexa.

"I thought we were friends."

"We are," he said, though he didn't sound all that happy about it. "But honestly? The way we talk about girls? The shit we say? I didn't want to do that to her. She deserves better."

"What are you talking about? I would never make fun of a dis-abled person."

"It's not you, bro. It's me."

"What's that supposed to mean?"

He took a while to answer. I could see him thinking it over, trying to get it right.

"No offense, dude, but the person I am when we're together? I just don't want to be that guy anymore."

All right. So he was in love or whatever. Good for him, I guess. It didn't really bother me, except that I hated being alone in our double, especially at night, when I had work to do, and I always had work to do, not that I ever did any. When Zack was around, we would procrastinate for hours, trash-talking and playing video games, and it would feel great, exactly like college was meant to be. But on my own it just seemed kinda pathetic, like I was a loser with no friends who was failing half his classes. I started keeping the door wide open, in case somebody I knew walked by and felt like saving me from my solitary confinement.

That's what I was doing that boring-as-shit Wednesday night, sit-ting on the ratty couch Zack and I had found on Baxter Avenue, playing Smash on auto pilot—I was Captain Falcon—just killing time, waiting for *something* to happen that would give me an excuse to get off my ass and out of that depressing room. I remember how my heart jumped when the phone buzzed—I was thinking, *hoping*, Amber, Becca, Zack, Wade, in that order—and how disappointed I was when I paused the game and realized it was just a text from my mother.

*I miss you.*

I mean, it was sweet, don't get me wrong. I was glad she missed me. But it didn't really help with my situation.

*Miss you too,* I texted back.

And then I looked up and saw Sanjay standing in my doorway, staring at me with his big sad eyes. Somehow, just from that look on his face, before he even said a word, I could tell that bad news was coming.

*    *    *

Somewhere in the middle of the slide show, Margo felt the audience slipping away from her. No one laughed at her jokes; a handful of spectators were behaving badly, disrupting her talk with loud whispers and possibly derisive comments, some of which drew appreciative snickers from their neighbors. The applause at the end of the main presentation barely rose to the level of basic politeness.

But it wasn't until the lights came back on for the Q&A that she realized the extent of her flop. She could see it in the faces staring back at her—some blank, some icy, many others disgusted or confused.

"Go ahead," she said. "Ask me anything. There's no such thing as a stupid question."

The silence that followed took on an embarrassing density. Then, mercifully, she noticed a hand inching upward in the center of the crowd. It belonged to the woman in the lavender turtleneck, her imaginary ally, whose face no longer seemed quite so sweet or supportive.

"Some of us ladies were wondering," she said in a frail voice. "Which rest room do you use?"

*Really?* Margo thought. It wasn't just the question that depressed her, it was the loud murmur of approval that followed it. *After everything I just told you,* that's *what you want to know?*

"I use the women's room," she said, forcing herself to smile. "I think I'd cause quite a stir if I wandered into the men's room."

The seniors took a moment to discuss the matter among themselves. Margo noticed another hand jabbing into the air, offering her a lifeline.

"Next question. Over there."

The words were already out by the time she realized that she'd called on Julian Spitzer's neighbor, the loudmouth who'd made such a ruckus during the slide show. He rose with some difficulty and gazed at her for a long time with a weirdly expectant expression, his arms spread wide, as if he himself were the question.

"Mark," the man finally said. "Don't you recognize me?"

Margo winced, but maintained her calm. "I'm sorry, sir. I don't go by that name anymore. Please call me Margo."

"You really don't know who I am?" He removed his baseball cap, giving her a better look at his face, but it didn't help. Margo had spent so much time trying to forget so many things that huge swaths of the past were lost to her. And that was okay.

"I'm sorry. You'll have to help me out."

"Al Huff." The man's tone was reproachful, as if he shouldn't have been forced to say his name out loud. "*Coach* Huff. From St. Benedict's? We played you twice in the state tournament, '88 and '89? You were such a great player, Mark. Best pure shooter I ever saw at the high school level."

"Oh, wow." Margo nodded in fake recognition, trying unsuccessfully to connect the Coach Huff she remembered—former Marine, lean and athletic, a motivator and disciplinarian—with the old man standing in front of her, his face bloated with alcohol and disappointment. If she remembered correctly, Al Huff had resigned under a cloud, some kind of recruiting scandal, ten or maybe even fifteen years ago. "It's good to see you."

"You killed us with that buzzer beater in the semis." He shook his head, as if the memory still stung. "Just broke our backs. I'll never forget that."

"Coach Huff is a local legend," Margo informed the crowd. "St. Benedict's was our arch-rival and always one of the best teams in the state."

A few people clapped for the local legend, but Al Huff didn't seem to notice. He opened his arms a little wider.

"Mark," he said. "What the hell happened? Why would you do this to yourself?"

Margo tried to smile, but she couldn't quite pull it off. Moments like this always knocked her off-balance, times when she realized that other people—some of them near-strangers—were more invested in the young man named Mark Fairchild than she herself had ever been.

"Coach," she said. "This is who I am."

Al Huff looked at the floor and shook his head. When he spoke it sounded like he was close to tears.

"You need help, son. You can't live like this."

"Thanks for your concern," Margo said, a little frostily. "But I'm doing just fine. I'm happier right now than I've ever been in my life."

As if to underline this declaration, Dumell chose that moment to arrive. He entered through the back door, unzipping his leather jacket in slow motion as he glanced warily at the old white people in the audience, and then at Margo. He grinned when their eyes met, and gave her a sheepish little wave, apologizing for his tardiness. She wanted to blow him a kiss, but settled on a fleeting smile before returning to her duties.

"Any other questions?" she asked.

\*　\*　\*

Sanjay had warned me about what to expect on the way over, so I wasn't exactly surprised when I walked into the Student Center and saw my face up on the wall. But it still felt like a kick in the gut.

It was crowded in there, lots of kids milling around, checking out the paintings and sculptures, all of them made by undergrads in the Visual Arts Program. Most of it was the standard crap you'd find at any high school art show—still lifes with fruit and wine bottles, self-portraits of hot girls, black and white photographs of poor people. What made it a college art show were the little cards that accompanied each item, which listed the name of the artist and the title of the piece, along with a brief Statement of Intent.

The "project" I was part of was the biggest and most eye-catching work in the show. It took up an entire wall of the gallery and was the first thing you noticed when you walked in: two rows of bigger-than-life portraits, each one with a little caption underneath. The card identified the artist as Katherine Q. Douglass, class of 2017, and the title of the work as *My Call-Out Wall*. The Statement of Intent read, *I asked a few of my friends to call someone out for behavior that damages our community and threatens our safety. This is an interactive project. Feel free to add your own call-out to the Call-Out Wall!*

The portraits themselves were pretty good—acrylic on canvas, according to the card—not perfect, but I recognized myself without any problem. There were ten faces in all, nine of them dudes, along with one unlucky blond girl, who was actually pretty cute. Two of the guys were black; one was Asian. There were no names attached to the faces, only a brief description of the offense the person supposedly committed. A ginger-haired dude *GROPED ME ON THE DANCE FLOOR.* The Asian kid *THINKS HE'S WHITE.* The blond girl *LIES RIGHT TO YOUR FACE.* A fat kid I'd seen around was a *CULTURAL APPRO-PRIATOR.* One of the black dudes—I'm pretty sure he was a football player—was an *EXTREME HOMOPHOBE.* A bro in a knit cap was a *GASLIGHTER*, whatever that was. Three guys were labeled *RAPIST.*

"I'm not sure this is legal," Sanjay told me. "It's got to be a violation of due process or something."

"Whatever," I said, because I really didn't give a shit about due process.

"You want to get out of here?" he asked.

I knew I should leave, but I couldn't stop staring at my face on the wall. It looked so *real* up there, just as real as the one I saw in the mirror every day. Even worse, I was grinning like an idiot, as if I were thrilled to be included in the art show and had no objection to the words written beneath the painting, a brief summary of my entire life:

*HUGE DISAPPOINTMENT.*

I smelled a sharp, medicinal odor and turned to see Amber's friend Cat standing right beside me, rubbing sanitizer into her hands.

"Wow," she said. "Look who's here. You've got some nerve."

I was surprised by the coldness in her voice. Cat had always been pretty nice to me. She nodded toward the wall.

"I had a hard time with your eyes. They're a little asymmetrical."

"You did this?"

She shook her head, like I should have known better.

"I told you not to hurt her."

\*    \*    \*

Eve hadn't planned on company, but she was relieved to see that the living room looked fine. The throw pillows on the couch were plump and perfectly spaced, one per cushion, exactly as God had intended. There were no slippers abandoned on the rug, no mug of yesterday's tea or crumpled kleenex marring the pristine surface of the coffee table. Even the TV remotes—all three of them—were resting in front of the flat screen in perfect alignment, arranged in descending order of size. It was, if anything, a little too neat and fussy, as if she'd stepped inside a museum exhibit documenting the uneventful life of a woman of exactly her age and circumstances. But better that than a dirty sock on the arm of the wingback chair or a beige bra slung over the newel post.

"What a lovely home." Margo surveyed the décor with what seemed like sincere admiration, and maybe even a touch of longing. "Thank you so much for inviting us."

Dumell and Amanda echoed this sentiment, while Julian Spitzer lingered near the door, skateboard tucked under his arm, nodding in dubious agreement.

"You're welcome," Eve told them. "Make yourselves comfortable." Shifting into hostess mode, she ducked into the kitchen to see what she could round up in the way of snacks and beverages. The answer, unfortunately, was not a whole lot. On the plus side, there was an unopened bottle of Australian Shiraz on the counter; wine was one thing she rarely forgot at the grocery store. On the minus side, the refrigerator held only a single beer, a Dos Equis Amber she couldn't remember buying, along with a bottle of Hard Lemonade that must have been over a year old. The food situation wasn't much better—half a sleeve of not-quite-fresh Stoned Wheat Thins, a block of cheddar that had hardened around the edges, a handful of baby carrots that seemed okay if you didn't look too close, and a tub of hummus she wouldn't have foisted on her own worst enemy.

She found a platter and arranged the crackers in a semicircle around the brick of cheese, which looked a lot better after some minor cosmetic surgery. If nothing else, the carrots added a splash of color. The hummus went straight into the garbage, where it should have gone days ago. Removing the cork from the Shiraz, she heard a reassuring burst of laughter from the living room, and realized that it had been a long time since she'd had this many people in the house.

She'd made the invitation on an impulse, after the lecture room had cleared out. The five of them were standing around, trying to figure out where to go for dinner. It was a frustrating conversation—Dumell didn't like Thai food, Amanda avoided fish whenever possible, Julian wasn't hungry—without any resolution in sight. Margo, the guest of honor, wasn't even participating. She looked tired and rattled—who could blame her?—and it suddenly occurred to Eve that she might not be in the mood for a big night out.

*I have an idea,* she said. *Why don't you all come to my house? I can order some pizza and we can decompress.*

And now here they all were, laughing and making themselves comfortable.

*How about that?* she thought, as she grabbed the wine and the snack platter, and went to join her friends in the living room.

\* \* \*

Amanda didn't mind taking one for the team. Somebody needed to go to the liquor store, and it might as well be her. Dumell had been the first to volunteer, but Margo had looked so happy, snuggling up to him on the couch—she kept patting his leg and poking him in the shoulder, as if checking to make sure he was real—that it seemed like a shame to separate them. And besides, this was still kind of a work thing, even if she was technically off the clock.

She was glad to get out for a bit, to leave the others to their wine and chitchat. She wasn't in a super-social mood, not after the debacle at the Senior Center. It was just so disheartening, to get yourself all pumped up with optimism—a sense of ownership and personal fulfillment—and then have to sit there and watch your One Big Idea crash and burn.

She glanced at Julian, her fidgety but mostly silent passenger. "Want some music?"

"Whatever," he said. "You're the driver."

*Come on, dude,* she thought. *Help me out here.* He'd seemed happy enough to accompany her on the liquor run but apparently didn't feel obligated to contribute anything in the way of conversation.

"You like Prince?" she asked.

"He's okay."

*Whatever.* She pressed play, and the atmosphere inside of the car was instantly transformed by the spare, sultry sound of "When Doves Cry," possibly the sexiest song ever written. It seemed a little too intimate for the circumstances, but there was no way she was gonna turn it off.

"I've been going through a Prince phase lately," she told him. "I sort of forgot what a genius he is. So many great songs."

Julian gave one of those noncommittal therapist nods, like it was interesting that she felt that way, not that he necessarily agreed with her.

"What kind of music do you like?" she asked.

"I don't know. All kinds, I guess."

*Jesus.* It had been a long time since Amanda had hung out with a college freshman, so she wasn't sure if this was standard behavior or not. Maybe terse, grudging replies were the most you could hope for. At least he was cute.

"Is this weird for you?" she asked. "Hanging out with a bunch of old people?"

"You're not that old."

"Ha ha," she said. "You seemed a little uncomfortable back there. I thought you might need a break or something."

"It wasn't the people," Julian explained. "It just kinda freaked me out to be in that house."

"Why's that?"

"You know her son? Brendan?"

"Not well."

"I went to high school with him." Julian gave a shudder of disgust. "Such a fucking asshole. It gave me the creeps, walking in there and seeing his picture on the wall. Felt like I could *smell* him."

"I get that." Amanda had only met Brendan once, but that was enough. "I didn't like him much myself."

"Nothing against Eve," Julian assured her. "She's really nice."

"Eve's great," Amanda agreed. "Everybody loves Eve."

\* \* \*

Sanjay really needed to go. He had work to do, a big problem set in CS and a dense chapter in his Architectural History textbook. Sitting in a coffee shop listening to someone else's problems was not a productive use of his time.

"This totally sucks," Brendan said. "I don't know what to do."

Sanjay wasn't sure how to respond. He had no experience with a situation like this, and absolutely nothing of value to contribute, which made it even crazier that he'd gotten himself stuck in the role of advisor.

"Maybe you should apologize," he suggested.

"I already did," Brendan said. "She won't even answer my texts."

The worst part of it was, Sanjay didn't even like Brendan, or any of those other guys he'd met for dinner his first night of college. His roommate, Dylan, was okay, but the rest of them were jerks. It would have been fine with Sanjay if he'd never spoken to any of them ever again.

But then he'd walked into the art show after dinner, and had seen Brendan's portrait up on the Call-Out Wall. It seemed wrong to publicly shame someone like that, and Sanjay thought Brendan should know about it. That's what he would have wanted if it had been his own face up there, not that it ever would have been. The problem was, you incurred an obligation when you made yourself the bearer of bad news. You couldn't just stand up and walk away whenever you felt like it.

"I didn't even do anything," Brendan muttered. "She punched me in the nuts, and I'm the bad guy?"

"She punched you?"

Brendan shrugged, like the details didn't really matter. "You wanna get drunk? I got some vodka back in my room."

"I don't drink."

"We could smoke some weed."

"I don't do that, either."

Brendan looked perplexed. "What *do* you do? I mean, for fun. On the weekends?"

"My sister's a senior," Sanjay told him. "She has a car and she drives home every weekend to see her boyfriend. I usually go with her."

"So you hang out with your buddies?"

"They're all away at school. I just do my work and watch movies with my parents. They like having me there. And the food is way better than the crap we get at the Higg."

"Sounds pretty chill," said Brendan. "I haven't seen my mom since the day I got here."

"I bet she misses you."

"Yeah. She just sent me this."

Brendan picked up his phone and did some swiping. When he

found what he wanted, he held up the screen so Sanjay could see his mother's text and his own reply.

*I miss you*

*Miss you too*

Sanjay nodded. "Moms are the best."

"Totally," said Brendan.

He stared at the phone for a few more seconds before putting it back in his pocket. Sanjay took advantage of the lull to scoot his chair away from the table.

"I hope you don't mind," he said, rising from his chair. "I really need to go to the library."

"It's cool," said Brendan. "Do what you have to do."

* * *

Sometimes, Eve thought, a casual gathering like this just sort of gelled into a spontaneous party, which was, by definition, better than a party you had planned, precisely because no one saw it coming. It was a tribute to the people involved, the chemistry of their individual personalities combined with a collective desire to salvage *something* from what otherwise might have seemed like a wasted evening, not to mention a big assist from the pitcher of margaritas Amanda had whipped up in the kitchen, using a jug of cheap tequila and a pre-made, neon-green industrial mixer that was tastier than it looked.

It was a conveniently small group—maybe a little *too* small—and they all seemed to be vibrating on the same wavelength, cracking jokes and laughing a little too loudly, toasting Margo for her excellent scarf collection, Dumell for service to his country, Amanda for the alcoholic beverages, and Julian simply for showing up, representing the millennials. There was a palpable sexual charge in the air—you couldn't have a decent party without it—mostly generated by Margo and Dumell, who, as the night went on, had graduated from hand-holding and whispered endearments to a full-on make-out session on the couch.

Eve knew it was rude to stare at the lovers, but she found it difficult to avert her gaze. Ever since she'd been aware of herself as a sexual being, going all the way back to middle school, she'd been aroused by the sight of people kissing in public, and the familiar effect was intensified in this case by the fact that Amanda was sitting only a short distance away in the wicker chair, and their eyes kept meeting in the awkward interludes that occurred while the happy couple was going at it. Most of these glances felt completely innocent—two friends rolling their eyes, sharing a moment of amused solidarity—but a few of them went deeper than that, lingering moments of silent, searching connection that made Eve wonder if a door she'd thought was closed might have swung open again.

*I should kiss her,* she thought, even though she'd vowed never to go down that road again, never to embarrass or expose herself the way she had that last time. *I bet she'd let me.*

This reverie was disrupted by the sudden realization that she was being watched, that Julian was staring at *her* with the same sort of longing that she herself was directing toward Amanda. She turned in his direction, raising her glass in a silent toast, not wanting him to feel left out. He returned the gesture, gazing at her with soulful drunken sincerity.

Things were starting to get a little awkward when Margo finally extracted herself from a marathon kiss, brushing the hair from her eyes and blinking like she didn't quite know where she was. She let out a long, slow, calming breath and straightened her skirt.

"Enough of *that,*" she said, fanning her face with one hand. "Anyone feel like dancing?"

\* \* \*

Amber went to a house party with Cat and some of her artist friends, but she left on the early side, unable to connect with the festive mood. Everybody there was really excited about the Call-Out Wall—they thought it would be great to make it a permanent installation in the Student Center—and they found it hilarious that Brendan kept texting her, begging for a moment of her time, sounding more and more pathetic with each successive message.

Amber could appreciate the poetic justice of the situation—let him see how it felt to be silenced and powerless for once in his life, to be defined by other people—but it wasn't as gratifying as she'd hoped it might be. In fact, the more she thought about Brendan the guiltier she felt, as if she'd done something bad to him, which was totally frustrating, because he didn't deserve her sympathy or anyone else's. It was just like her—just like a girl—to feel sorry for a guy she had every right to despise, and then to turn the blame back on herself.

She could have taken Cat's advice and blocked his calls. That would have solved the problem of her constantly buzzing phone, and spared her his manipulative cries for help. But it seemed kind of harsh, and even a bit cowardly, to call someone out and then cut off all possibility of communication, as if they had no right to respond, as if they were dead to you.

Amber was tired and a little depressed. She just wanted to go to bed and forget this day had ever happened. But there was only one way she was going to be able to do that, and there was no use pretending otherwise. With a small shudder of resignation and distaste, she picked up her phone and touched her finger to his name. He answered in the middle of the first ring.

"Wow," he said. "Took you long enough."

"What do you want, Brendan?"

"I don't know. Just to talk, I guess. I've been having a rough night."

"Well," she said, a little defensively. "I've had some rough nights lately myself."

A nicer person might have picked up on her cue and asked what was wrong, maybe even expressed a little sympathy, but this was Brendan she was talking to.

"The art show," he said. "That was really fucking brutal."

"I'm sure it was. But you have to—"

"Do you really think that about me?" He sounded genuinely curious. "That I'm a huge disappointment?"

Amber hesitated. She'd known that Cat had been working on the Call-Out Wall all semester, but she hadn't realized that Brendan was a part of the installation until two days ago, when she'd helped transport the paintings from the art building to the Student Center. She was startled when she pulled off a sheet of bubble wrap and saw his happy face with the words *HORRIBLE HUMAN BEING* written beneath it like a final verdict.

*What the hell is this?*

*It's my gift to you,* Cat told her.

*He's not a horrible human being. He's just—*

*Those were your words,* Cat reminded her. *That's a direct quote.*

Amber didn't deny it. She'd said that about Brendan on the morning after their disastrous date, when she felt raw and betrayed, and Cat had been there for her, the way she always was, offering support and validation when Amber needed it most.

*I was pissed. I just needed to vent.*

*You spoke your truth,* Cat said. *Don't take it back now.*

*It doesn't feel right,* Amber had insisted.

Reluctantly, Cat proposed some alternate captions—*DATE RAPIST? MISOGYNIST?*—but Amber didn't think those were accurate, either.

*He was just a . . . huge disappointment, that's all.*

*All right,* Cat said. *You're being way too nice, but I'll change it if that's what you want.*

*That's what I want,* Amber had said, and she wasn't about to retract her words a second time, or give Brendan a reason to think he'd been forgiven. She couldn't even think about that night without feeling sick and degraded.

"Dude," she told him. "You got off easy. It could have been a lot worse, believe me."

"Amber," he said. "I'm really sorry."

"It's a little late for that."

"I know. I'm just saying."

"All right," she sighed. "I should go. I'm wiped out."

"Wait, Amber. I was just wondering—" His voice turned small and hopeless. "Could I come over and hang out with you for a while?"

"Are you fucking kidding me?"

"Not to hook up," he assured her. "I just don't want to be alone right now."

She almost laughed, but she could hear the pain in his voice.

"I'm sorry, Brendan. Our hanging out days are over."

"Yeah," he said. "I kind of figured that."

Amber ended the call and wiped away an embarrassing tear. It was so stupid and unfair that someone could treat you so badly, and still make you want to hug them. She thought she might call Cat and commission a portrait of herself for the Call-Out Wall:

*JUST WANTS EVERYONE TO BE HAPPY, EVEN THE PEO-PLE WHO DON'T DESERVE IT.*

\* \* \*

Dumell hated to be the bad guy, but it was a weekday and he had to work in the morning.

"Last dance," he whispered in Margo's ear. "Then I got to take you home before I turn into a pumpkin."

"I believe it's your car that turns into a pumpkin," she told him.

They were glued together like prom dates, swaying under the spell of "Sexual Healing," which felt just then like an uncanny coincidence, a not-so-subtle message from the universe, even though it was just another song on Amanda's iPhone, part of a crowd-pleasing soul- and Motown-heavy playlist that had kept them going for the past hour and a half.

"That's even worse," he said, making unsolicited eye contact with Julian, who was very drunk, lurching around the room with his hands up, like the music had placed him under arrest. "I still owe money on that car."

Margo laughed and kissed him again. The woman loved to kiss. It was dark and she smelled good and her warm body felt just right pressing up against him. Dumell reminded himself that nothing else mattered.

*Don't be scared,* he thought. *There's nothing to be scared of.*

Fear was tricky, though. It had a way of sneaking up on you, making you question yourself and worry about the future. *What would people say? What would they think? Do I really want this?*

They rotated a little, and now he was looking at Eve, who was dancing with Amanda, though they weren't actually touching each other. Eve had one hand in her hair and the other on her hip. Amanda had her eyes closed and her mouth open, head tilted upward like a blind musician. Dumell wondered if maybe something was going on there, 'cause it sure felt like it.

*Good for them,* he thought.

He slid his hand down Margo's back, tracing the ravine of her spine all the way to the gentle swell at the bottom, the beginning of a different landscape. He tucked his thumb inside the waistband of her skirt, tugging down a little bit, a promise for later.

"Mmmm," she said, like something tasted good.

He'd had only one bad moment the entire night, right when the music started up. Margo was normally a graceful person, with the physical control of an athlete, but you wouldn't have known it from watching her on the dance floor. In motion, she seemed bigger and more masculine than she'd been on the couch, uncomfortable in her own body, not the person Dumell wanted her to be. It must have shown on his face, because she stopped and asked him what was wrong. She had a slightly spooky ability to read his expressions, to register every flicker of doubt or hesitation.

"Nothing," he told her. " 'Cept you dance like a white girl."

Margo had laughed with relief, as if that were the sweetest thing anyone had ever said to her. She loosened up after that and so did he. But he was still a little off-balance, unsettled by the knowledge that his feelings could—and sometimes did—turn on a dime, that he might not be able to follow through with what he'd started, that his courage would fail in the clutch the way it had so many times before, that he might hurt someone who'd trusted him. All he had to do was think himself outside of this room and this little group of people, to imagine the faces of his family, his ex-wife, his co-workers, the guys in his unit, some of them smirking, others shaking their heads, as if they had a right to judge. Who the fuck were they? They didn't know Margo, or what she'd been through, or how she made him feel. Shit, most of them didn't even know Dumell. Not really.

He felt her stiffen in his arms. She tried to smile, but her face was pale and defenseless.

"Everything okay?" she asked.

The song was still playing, but they weren't moving anymore. They were just standing there, looking at each other from across a very narrow divide.

"It's all good," he said, right before he kissed her.

\* \* \*

The only problem with hosting a successful party, Eve thought, was the letdown you felt at the end of it, when the music stopped and the lights came on and the guests started asking for their coats. Margo and Dumell were the first dominoes to fall. Eve hugged them good-bye with a smile that was the product of pure willpower.

Amanda was already busy in the kitchen, rinsing dirty glasses and loading them into the dishwasher, preparing for her own departure. Hoping to postpone the inevitable, Eve asked her to mix one last batch of margaritas, only to be reminded, by her own employee, that they had to work in the morning.

Eve winced. "Let's not talk about work, okay? Work is sooo boring. All I ever do is work."

Amanda opened her mouth, but no words came out. She looked so cute in her polka-dot dress, her face all flushed and glistening.

"You're such a great dancer," Eve told her. "Really sexy."

"So are you. I had no idea."

Eve waved off the compliment. "I'm out of practice. I have to get out more. I spend way too much time at home, staring at my computer screen. It's not good. I need to live in my body, you know? Just get out of my head a little."

"We all do." Amanda placed the last glass in the rack and closed the dishwasher door. "It was a great party. I think Margo really enjoyed it."

Eve agreed, but didn't want to be diverted from her purpose.

"Just one more drink. What's the big deal?"

Amanda exhaled a skeptical breath. "I'm gonna be pretty hungover as it is."

"Call in sick. I won't tell the boss."

Before Amanda could respond, Julian wandered in from the living room, phone in hand, his long hair tucked girlishly behind his ears.

"What's up?" he said, with just a hint of a slur. "You guys talkin' about me again?"

"I should drive you home," Amanda told him. "You're way too drunk to ride a skateboard."

"What?" Julian looked offended. "You're drunker'n I am."

"Not even close, dude."

"Really?" He squinted at her. "You're not drunk?"

"Maybe a little," Amanda conceded. "I would say I'm mildly inebriated."

Julian smirked. "Tell that to the breathalyzer."

"I live like five minutes away. I'm not gonna get pulled over."

Skateboards. Breathalyzers.

"Why don't you just sleep here?" Eve said. "There's three bedrooms upstairs. I have spare toothbrushes if you need them. My dentist gives them out free with every checkup."

"Mine too!" Julian was excited by the coincidence. "You go to Dr. Halawi?"

* * *

The bed in the guest room was perfectly comfortable. There were more than enough blankets, the windows weren't drafty, and the shades blocked out the moonlight much more effectively than the flimsy curtains in Amanda's own bedroom. The pajamas Eve had loaned her were soft and fit reasonably well, despite the difference in their body types. There really was no good reason why she couldn't fall asleep, especially after all the tequila she'd drunk.

It was just nerves, the by-product of a long and sometimes stressful night—the lecture, the party, new people, more dancing than she'd done in a long time. She was all wound up, her senses on high alert. It didn't help that she was also super-horny, a condition that afflicted her whenever she slept in a strange place—a hotel, her grandmother's house, a friend's apartment in the city, a bare-bones Airbnb, a tent in the woods, even a sleeper car on a train, which was something she'd experienced exactly once in her life. Being in a bed that wasn't her own instantly flooded her brain with thoughts of sex.

Or, in this case, the absence of sex.

She'd really believed that something was going to happen with Eve. They'd been flirting all night, lots of meaningful glances and not-quite-accidental contact on the dance floor. And then Eve had convinced her to sleep over, encouraging her to get even more drunk than she already was, and to go ahead and play hooky from work in the morning. It had felt like a pretty straightforward seduction, one person pressing, the other resisting, then wobbling, then giving in.

And then . . . Nothing.

*Why'd you make me stay if you weren't going to do anything?*

They'd had their opportunity. Right after Amanda had brushed her teeth, Eve had knocked on the guest room door and presented her with a little bedtime care package—a bath towel, a pair of clean pajamas, a bottle of Tylenol. Eve had already changed into her sleeping clothes, sweatpants and an oversized T-shirt that said, *Haddington Youth Lacrosse*. It felt so intimate seeing her boss in that context, her face tired and sweet, softer without makeup. *I thought you might need a few things.* Julian was in the bathroom— they could hear the water running—so it would have been easy for Eve to slip into the room and stay for as long as she wanted. But for some reason, she lingered shyly in the doorway.

*Sleep tight,* Eve told her. *I'll see you in the morning.*

Right now, though, the morning felt like an eternity away, and

Amanda was dreading the thought of it. It would be so awkward, waking up hungover in Eve's house, heading downstairs with bad breath and a splitting headache, dressed in yesterday's clothes. A walk of shame, but without any shameful fun to make it worth the embarrassment. And then what were they gonna do? Eat breakfast together?

*I can't,* she thought. *I just can't.*

Better to just slip out now, leave a note on the kitchen table so Eve wouldn't worry. She wondered if she should knock on Julian's door on the way out, see if he was awake and wanted a ride home as well.

He was a sweet kid. He'd really opened up to her on the way back from the liquor store, telling her about his clinical depression, his hatred of high school, his fears of going away to college, the difficulty he had talking to girls his own age.

She knew exactly what was weighing him down: that helpless feeling that you were wasting your precious youth and it was your own damn fault. It was something you never quite recovered from, and it usually led to some stupid mistakes down the road, many of which were worse than a few regrettable tattoos. She wished she could climb into a time machine and make herself twenty again, just so she could be his girlfriend for a while, let him know how great he was, build up his confidence for the future. It sounded like a good idea for a TV show, a modern-day feminist superhero:

*Amanda Olney, Agent of Sexual Justice.*

\* \* \*

Brendan's room was a jock shrine. Trophies from a lifetime of athletic excellence—Little League baseball (All-Star!), Pop Warner football (County Champs!), middle school swimming (2nd Place, Backstroke!), Haddington Youth Lacrosse (Most Valuable Player!)—were crowded on top of the dresser, right below a framed photo collage that must have been assembled by Brendan's ridiculously hot cheerleader girlfriend, Becca DiIulio, since it included two different images of Becca looking fine in a bikini (one orange, one pink), the latter of which was actually autographed in silver marker, as if she were a fucking movie star: *Luv ya, Becca xxxooo!* There were three pics of Brendan with sunglasses and no shirt. He was the kind of dick who made muscleman poses for the camera and wasn't being ironic about it. Just to rub it in, he had a roll of LifeStyles condoms stashed in his sock drawer—Julian couldn't help taking a peek—eighteen in all, because you never knew when the whole cheerleading squad might show up and beg to be fucked, one right after the other.

Eighteen condoms. A little whimper of defeat leaked from Julian's throat. He hadn't bought eighteen condoms in his entire life. For a minute, he thought about searching for a sharp object—a safety pin or some nail scissors—and poking a few strategic holes in Brendan's lifestyle, but he quickly detected the flaw in this plan: all it would do was populate the world with more little Brendans, which would not be doing the world a favor.

It would be doubly weird if Brendan had a kid, because that would make Eve a grandma, and Eve didn't look like anyone's grandma. Julian had been lusting after her all night—she was wearing a snug gray pullover, just a hint of cleavage, and a fuzzy light blue skirt that he badly wanted to touch. She and Amanda were so into each other on the dance floor that Julian had expected them to start making out, though they never actually did, which was too bad.

After he finished his depressing inspection of the room, Julian turned off the light and climbed into bed. Eve had assured him that the sheets were clean, but even so, it was kind of disturbing—this was Brendan Fletcher's mattress and Brendan Fletcher's pillow, the soft place where Brendan Fletcher rested his empty head and dreamed his vapid dreams. Julian wasn't sure whether to feel disgusted or triumphant. It had to count as a small victory just to be here, to have penetrated so deeply into enemy territory.

Did it qualify as revenge to jerk off in Brendan's bed while fantasizing about his mother? At the very least, it was fun to imagine Brendan's reaction to the news.

*Hey Brendan, your mom is sucking my dick.*

*Hey Brendan, your mom's got amazing boobs.*

*Hey Brendan, your mom's a really nice person.*

*No, wait . . .*

*Hey Brendan, your mom likes it doggie style.*

*Hey Brendan, I'm going down on your mom.*

That was the one he settled on. He was going down on Eve, and she was totally into it, doing the whole porn star moaning thing, like the whole world needed to know how good he was making her feel. He imagined that she was shaved down there, though he had no idea.

*Hey Brendan, your mom tastes like strawberries.*

There was a soft knock at the door.

*Oh shit.*

He let go of his dick just as the door creaked open.

"Hey Julian," Amanda whispered. "You asleep?"

\*   \*   \*

Eve woke with a vague sense of unease. She held her breath and listened. There was something unfamiliar—even slightly alarming—about the silence that surrounded her.

*Calm down . . .*

She had these night frights every now and then—the panicky suspicion that an intruder had broken into the house—and they were always false alarms.

*It's probably nothing . . .*

And then it came back to her, a tiny explosion of relief.

She had company.

*Thank God.*

Maybe Amanda needed a glass of water. Maybe Julian was sick. They'd all had too much to drink, never a recipe for a good night's sleep, though Eve herself had managed to doze off without too much trouble.

It was nice to have guests in the house. Comforting, and also validating—this was exactly what she'd hoped for after Brendan left

223

for college, during those first melancholy and disorienting days in the empty nest. She'd made a vow to create a new life for herself, to meet some interesting people, to make some new friends and have a little fun. And the miracle was, she'd actually done all these things, and it hadn't even taken that much time or effort. She'd signed up for one class. She'd accepted an invitation. She'd thrown a party. She'd opened her heart, and the world had responded.

*How often does that happen?*

Not very often, she knew, which was why she hadn't pushed her luck with Amanda, though she'd very badly wanted to. New friends were rare and valuable, worth a lot more than a fleeting sexual adventure that would only cause pain and confusion down the road. She could tell that Amanda was disappointed—she'd looked so bereft, standing in the guest room doorway—but Eve knew she'd made the right decision—the *adult* decision—the one that would be best for both of them in the long run. Someday they'd have to talk about it, when they weren't drunk and sleeping under the same roof. She was sure that Amanda would understand.

There was that noise again. It wasn't loud, but it was followed a second later by a groan of distress that sounded like it had come from Brendan's room. Eve threw off the covers. It was a familiar feeling, padding down the hallway in the darkness. Standing outside her son's door, straining her ears for the sound of slow, steady breathing that would let her know that everything was okay. But that wasn't what she heard.

"Ooooh fuck! You're amazing!"

"Shhhh."

"Sorry."

"Shhhh."

*You've got to be kidding me . . .*

The last time this happened, Eve had retreated in horror. But that was her son, not her friends. This time she opened the door—just a crack—and peered inside.

It was dark, but she could see pretty well.

Amanda was on top of Julian, her polka-dot dress unbuttoned to the waist. Her breasts were shockingly large, her tattoo a blotchy shadow. She turned and looked at Eve. She seemed oddly calm, not the least bit embarrassed.

"Sorry," she said. "We didn't mean to wake you."

"It's not your fault." Eve opened the door a little wider. "I'm a light sleeper."

Amanda continued her gentle rocking. It was beautiful to watch, and weirdly familiar, like a memory from a dream or a video. Eve took a step forward.

"Is this okay?" Julian asked.

"It's okay with me," Amanda said.

Eve moved closer. Her foot landed on something strange, a snake-like object that turned out to be a roll of condoms. She was glad to know they were being safe.

Amanda reached for Eve's hand.

"Ursula," she said, as their fingers intertwined.

Eve bent down and kissed her; this time there was no confusion, no rejection, no need to apologize. It was a long, slow, welcoming kiss, and it didn't stop until Julian lifted his hand and placed it, very tentatively, on Eve's breast.

"Is this okay?" he asked again, gazing up at her with a worried expression.

Eve thought for a second.

"I hope so," she said.

Julian looked relieved.

"You're a really nice person," he told her.

\*　\*　\*

I was going out of my mind, drinking alone in my room, scrolling through my useless contacts. I left two messages for my dad, but I guess he'd already gone to bed, and my mom didn't pick up, either. Becca ignored my invitation to Skype. Wade had a midterm he needed to study for, and Troy's phone was running out of juice. Will and Rico had dropped some acid, and they weren't making any sense. Dylan's phone went straight to voicemail, so I finally tried Sanjay, because I couldn't think of anyone else, and he picked up right away.

"What are you doing right now?" I asked him.

"Just working."

"Let's go get some pizza or something."

"I'm not hungry."

"Come on," I said. "Please? Just one fucking slice."

"Brendan, are you okay?"

"No, dude." I tried to laugh, but it came out weird. "I am not okay."

He told me I should find my RA, or maybe go to Health Services. He said it might help if I talked to someone. But I didn't feel like talking to anyone.

"I hate this fucking place. I just want to go home."

It felt good to say it out loud, but then I started to cry. It took me a while to get it under control.

"I'm sorry," I said. "I'm a fucking mess."

Ten minutes later we were in Student Lot C, buckling ourselves into his sister's Subaru wagon, which wasn't really his sister's. It belonged to their parents and Sanjay had his own set of keys.

"You really don't have to do this," I told him.

"It's okay," he said. "I know how it feels. I get homesick all the time."

The highway was pretty clear at that time of night, mostly big trucks barreling along in the right lane. Sanjay was a decent driver, not as timid as I thought he'd be. He was also pretty easy to talk to, and knew a lot more about sports and music than I'd thought he would, which was a relief, since it was a long way to Haddington. Talking helped pass the time and kept my mind off the fact that I was a *Huge Disappointment*.

He told me about his girlfriend, this Korean-American math whiz named Esther. She was a senior in high school, applying early decision to Harvard. Sanjay was hoping she'd get rejected and end up at the Honors College at BSU so they could finally be together like normal people.

"Her parents are super-strict," he explained. "She's not allowed to date or go to parties. She would go to the movies with her friends, and I would go to the same movie with mine, and then the two of us would go sit by ourselves and make out. But then some girl from her church saw us, and after that she wasn't even allowed to go to the movies. I could only see her at school."

They kept things on the DL until the end of Sanjay's senior year, when it was time for the prom. Sanjay organized this crazy stunt where one of his friends dressed up as a UPS guy and came into Esther's AP Calc class with this big box on a hand truck. He said, *Special delivery for Esther Choi!* And then Sanjay burst out of the box with a rose in his teeth and the word *PROM?* scrawled across his forehead. Everybody clapped, and Esther hugged him and said yes, of course she'd be his date. But then she called him in tears that same night and said her parents wouldn't let her.

"That sucks," I said.

Sanjay nodded. "It sucked so bad."

I must have dozed off after that, because the next thing I knew we were off the highway, driving through Haddington, past all the familiar landmarks I hadn't seen in such a long time. I directed Sanjay to Overbrook Street and we pulled up in front of my house. I unbuckled my seatbelt and gave him an awkward one-armed hug.

"Thanks, dude."

"Take care of yourself," he told me. "Maybe I'll see you in a couple days?"

"Yeah," I said. "Maybe."

I got out of the car and watched him drive away. Then I stood on the sidewalk for a while. My house looked sleepy and peaceful, the way it always did when I got home late. I hadn't told my mom I was coming home, so I was surprised to see that she'd left the porch light on, almost like she was expecting me.

PART FOUR

*The MILF*

# *That* Happened

E ve was deeply relieved, and not at all surprised, when Amanda
gave her notice in late January. The only real surprise, given the
mess they'd made of their friendship and work relationship, was that
she'd lasted as long as she had.

"I got the library job," she said. "Director of Children's Events. I'll
be in charge of story time, arts and crafts, author visits, holiday celebra-
tions, stuff like that. Kind of like here, just with kids instead of old people. It pays a little better than what I'm making now, so that's a plus."

"That's great," Eve told her, but then she caught herself. "I mean,
I'm really sorry to be losing you. That goes without saying. You're a
valued member of our staff. Everybody's going to miss you so much."

"I'll miss you, too. You were such a great boss."

She sounded completely sincere, though nothing, Eve knew, could
have been further from the truth. She'd been a terrible boss—completely
irresponsible, not to mention legally culpable—and she'd put Amanda
in an impossible position, giving her no choice but to leave.

"Thanks again for the recommendation letter," Amanda continued. "I think it made a big difference."

"I meant every word. You have a bright future ahead of you."

She'd used that exact phrase in her letter: *Amanda Olney has a
bright future ahead of her.* She was also *a model employee* and *a beacon
of good cheer in the office*, not to mention a *self-starter who revitalized*

231

*the Lecture Series during her brief but eventful tenure.* And now she was looking for *new challenges more commensurate with her exceptional abilities*, opportunities the Senior Center *regrettably couldn't provide.* Eve had understood, even while composing the letter, that she was laying it on a little thick, but she figured it was the least she could do.

"My last day is February 13th," Amanda told her. "That's a Friday. Just my luck."

"Day before Valentine's," Eve added, unhelpfully.

Amanda nodded, well aware of this fact.

"You doing anything? For the holiday?"

Eve shook her head. "You?"

"Nothing." Amanda shrugged, as if it were no big deal. "Just whatever. I'm not a big fan of Valentine's Day. It's always kind of depressing."

That was when it descended, the gray cloud that followed them wherever they went, the Big Awkward Thing that couldn't be discussed or undone. It seemed completely impossible that it had even happened, except that she could—and all too often did—visualize it with mortifying clarity, though only in choppy fragments, involuntary bursts of memory that made her wince and blink, as if a flashbulb had gone off a little too close to her face: Amanda whimpering through gritted teeth; Julian moaning *oooh fuck, oooh fuck* over and over; all three of them breathing hard, encouraging one another, working together as a team.

It was so stupid and frustrating. They should have been able to get past the weirdness, to find a way back to being friends and coworkers who could meet for an occasional drink, go to the movies on Sunday afternoon, or keep each other company on the loneliest night of the year. Maybe there were women somewhere who could have done that, friendly colleagues who'd blundered into an ill-fated sexual adventure and then found a way to laugh it off, people who just shrugged and said, *Well,* that *happened,* and went back to being the way they were before. That would have been a healthier way to deal with it, instead of dying a little inside every time you saw the other person, as if the two of you had buried a body in the woods or something.

And it wasn't like they were in any danger of repeating their mistake. Whatever desire they'd felt for each other had consumed itself in that single, regrettable burst of flames, and now there was nothing left. They'd learned this the hard way after the staff Christmas party, when they tried to spark it back to life with a tipsy kiss in Eve's office that had left them both empty and discouraged.

*I don't know,* Amanda said. *I'm just not feeling it.*

Eve nodded, conscious of a sad taste in her mouth. *Let's pretend it never happened.*

Unfortunately, they weren't good pretenders. They couldn't remember how to talk to each other like normal human beings, or find a way to build a fence around their error. In the end, it was easier not to have to see each other at all.

"Good luck," Eve said from behind her desk. "I hope you like your new job."

Amanda scowled at the floor for a moment, as if troubled by what she saw there. Then she looked up.

"I'm not ashamed of what we did," she said. "I want you to know that."

"That's good," Eve told her. "Because you have nothing to be ashamed of."

Unlike Amanda, Eve didn't have the luxury of a clear conscience. She had no problem absolving her partners of responsibility—they were young (Julian was barely legal, for God's sake), they'd been drinking, they were free to do as they pleased, no responsibility to anyone but themselves. That wasn't true for Eve: she was the boss, the homeowner, the host, the adult in the room. The one who should have known better. Nothing but selfishness and bad judgment had compelled her to walk down the hall, barge in on Amanda and Julian's private moment, and turn their duet into a threesome. And no, she hadn't been checking up on Julian to make sure he was okay. Maybe she'd started out worrying that something might be wrong, but by the time she poked her head into the bedroom, she already knew what was going on. She'd *heard* them in there.

She just didn't want to be left out.

That was all it was—simple loneliness. She couldn't bear the thought of retreating to her room, shipwrecked again on the desert island of her bed. Didn't want to lie there feeling sorry for herself— she'd wasted so much time feeling sorry for herself—while they had all the fun. So she'd behaved like a child and invited herself to the party, without a thought for the consequences.

It had taken her a while to understand how badly she'd screwed up, mainly because it could have been *so* much worse. By the time Brendan showed up, with no warning whatsoever—he'd let himself in with the spare key they kept hidden in a fake rock beneath the azalea bush—the main event was over, thank God. Amanda had gone home, too embarrassed to spend the night, and Eve had returned to her own bedroom to process what had just occurred. Only Julian remained at the scene of the crime, and that was all Brendan saw when he turned on the light: a kid he vaguely knew from high school sleeping naked in a tangle of sheets and blankets, a roll of condoms unfurled on the floor, two wrappers torn and empty. Brendan seemed more confused than upset, calling out, *Mom? Mom?* over and over, until Eve finally emerged from her room, clutching the lapels of her fuzzy pink robe. By that point Julian was already tugging on his jeans, talking to Brendan in a calm but frightened voice, assuring him that everything was cool, though it obviously wasn't. Eve felt terrible about sending him home on his skateboard in the middle of the night, but it seemed like the best thing for everyone to get him out of the house as quickly as possible.

Then she lied to her son—what else could she do?—telling him that she'd thrown a little party for her fellow students, and that Julian had hooked up with one of the other guests, a girl named Salima from their Gender and Society class. This was a ridiculous, deeply unfair story—Salima was a modest young Muslim woman who would never have gone to a party where alcohol was served, let alone had sex with Julian—but Brendan was mercifully uninterested in the plausibility of her alibi. He waited for her to finish, and then announced in a matter-of-fact voice that he was dropping out of college, which Eve assumed was a melodramatic way of saying that he was homesick or had failed a test. They were both exhausted and embarrassed, for their own individual reasons, and agreed to postpone further conversation until they'd gotten some sleep and could think more clearly. But first Eve went back up to his room and changed the sheets on his bed, even though he insisted it wasn't necessary, because she knew that it absolutely was.

The closeness of that call—the dizzying, weak-kneed feeling of disaster barely averted, of having been spared an unspeakable humiliation—had thrown her off her game in the days that followed, kept her from being as firm with Brendan as she should have been. She should have insisted that he return to school *immediately*, that he buckle down and study hard and finish what he'd started. She should have made it clear that quitting wasn't an option. But she couldn't locate her inner tiger mom, couldn't find a good-faith way to access the voice of parental authority at the moment when she needed it most.

Instead she listened and sympathized—as if she were his friend instead of his mother—letting precious days go to waste while she gently interrogated him about what had gone wrong at school, and why he was refusing to go back. They spent hours hashing it over, but he never managed to give her a convincing explanation. His laundry list of grievances always struck her as vague and insufficient: his classes were boring, this one professor had a crazy accent, everyone was so PC, Zack was never around anymore, the food sucked, he didn't have any friends. There had to be more to the story, but Brendan was a master at shutting down the conversation. If she pressed him too hard for specifics, he'd pull out his phone and start swiping at the screen with an expression of surly impatience, as if he were a busy corporate executive who didn't have time for this nonsense.

Desperate for professional guidance, Eve called BSU and spoke to an academic dean named Tad Bramwell. He told her what she already knew—the university offered counseling services for students who were struggling emotionally and tutoring for those who were having trouble with their course work—but he reminded her that it was Brendan's responsibility to avail himself of these resources. At Bramwell's urging, she also spoke to her son's faculty advisor, Professor Torborg of the Anthropology Department, who didn't seem overly concerned about her son's plight.

"Freshman year's a tough adjustment," he told her. "Not every incoming student is willing or able to meet the challenges of college work."

Eve bristled at his tone.

"Brendan's very intelligent. He's just a little lazy sometimes."

"Well," Torborg said, after a diplomatic pause. "You know him better than I do."

"You're his advisor," she reminded him. "Maybe you have some advice?"

Torborg gave the matter some scholarly contemplation. "I think it's totally up to Brendan."

"That's it?"

"It's his choice. If he wants to be in college, he should probably start acting like it. And if he doesn't, he should probably find something else to do."

"What if he doesn't know what he wants?"

"Then he should take some time off and figure it out," Torborg told her. "That's my recommendation. I took a gap year after high school and it was one of the best experiences of my life. I went backpacking all over Southeast Asia—Thailand, Vietnam, Cambodia, Nepal . . ." He paused for a moment, savoring the memory. "God, Nepal was beautiful."

"Sounds nice," Eve said, right before she hung up. "I hope you took some pictures."

Ted came over the following evening for an emergency family dinner, the three of them gathered around the kitchen table for the first time in seven years. It felt unexpectedly normal—comforting, even—to have him back in the house, everyone in their assigned seats, order temporarily restored in the universe.

At the same time, for all the familiarity of his presence, Ted seemed like a different person, not just older and heavier—Eve was pleased to note these changes, though both things could also be said about her—but calmer, too, no longer radiating the impatience that had always seemed like such an essential part of his personality. He even chewed more slowly than he used to.

"This is delicious." He jabbed his fork at Eve's sausage mac and cheese. "I don't get to eat like this at home."

"I forgot about the gluten," she said. "I hope you don't mind."

"Do I look like I mind?" Ted grinned at Brendan. "Your mom's a great cook. Always was."

As gratified as Eve was by the praise—he hadn't always been so effusive—she was a little irritated by his air of relaxed good cheer, as if this were a pleasant social occasion rather than a family crisis. It was a part of their marriage she remembered all too well—that feeling of being out of sync with Ted's moods, of always having to swim against his tide.

"How's Jon-Jon?" Brendan asked.

"He's okay." Ted nodded thoughtfully, affirming his own statement. "Doing a lot of drawing at school. He's very interested in circles. Other shapes, not so much."

"He seemed pretty good," Brendan said. "On Parents Weekend."

"That was fun," Ted agreed. "Just bad luck with that plane."

Eve had heard about Jon-Jon's tantrum on the BSU quad. She couldn't imagine what that would feel like, to see your child in such pain and not know how to help him, and all those strangers watching.

"You know what I did last week?" Ted said. "I went to an indoor batting cage. Haven't done that for years."

"I used to love that," Brendan said.

"Let's do it," Ted told him. "We can go to Five Guys afterward. Make a night of it."

"Cool," said Brendan, though Eve doubted it would ever happen. Ted was great with the plans, but less impressive with the follow-through.

It went on like that for a while, Ted and Brendan talking football and debating the finer points of *The Walking Dead,* a show they both loved that Eve refused to watch. She couldn't help feeling a little jealous of their connection. The conversation rarely flowed like this when it was just her and Brendan at the table.

"Well," she said, when everyone's plate was clean. "Can we maybe talk about the elephant in the room?"

"*Really?*" Brendan muttered. "The elephant in the room?"

Ted accepted the parental baton with obvious reluctance.

"Tough semester, huh?"

Brendan nodded, unable to hold his father's sympathetic gaze.

"You want to go back and finish up?" Ted posed the question in a soothing voice, as if he were addressing a child. "It's only another month or so."

Brendan shook his head.

"Any particular reason?" Ted asked.

Brendan closed his eyes and shrugged, a gesture more suited to an eighth grader than a college student.

"I hate it. I'm not learning anything."

"Well, whose fault is that?" Eve snapped.

Ted silenced her with a cautionary hand. Somehow he always got to be the good cop.

"You sure about this?" he asked.

Brendan nodded. Ted sighed and looked at Eve.

"All right," he said. "I guess that's that."

"*That's that?*" Eve repeated the phrase in disbelief. "That's all you have to say?"

"I don't know what else—"

"So it's just sixteen thousand dollars down the drain?"

"Eve," he said. "Don't make this about the money."

"I'm sorry to be so mercenary. What do you think this is about?"

"Our son," Ted told her. "It's about what's best for our son."

Eve nodded, as if impressed by his superior wisdom.

"Wow," she said, knowing even as she spoke that she wasn't helping anyone. "*Our son* is lucky to have such a devoted father."

Ted ignored the barb—it was as if she hadn't even spoken—which was another thing he did that drove her crazy.

"Look," he said, doing his best Mr. Reasonable. "It's a big school. Maybe it's just a bad fit."

This was a valid point, Eve knew, but that didn't make it any less irritating.

"Don't blame me," she said. "I wasn't the one—"

"Nobody's *blaming* you," Ted told her. "Jesus. I'm just saying, people don't always make the right choices in life. That doesn't mean they have to be stuck with them."

Eve tried to laugh but nothing came out.

"Do you even hear yourself?" she said, but the question went unanswered.

Ted had shifted his attention to Brendan, who had one hand clamped over his mouth, as if he were about to be sick.

"You okay?" Ted asked. "Are you choking?"

Brendan shook his head and burst into tears.

"I'm sorry," he sobbed through his fingers. "I fucked up."

Eve couldn't remember the last time she'd seen him cry. At least five years, she thought. Maybe longer. But the sound was instantly familiar, like an old song on the radio. Ted reached across the table and patted him on the arm.

"Take it easy," he said.

Brendan struggled to catch his breath. "I'm sorry I . . . disappointed you."

"Hey, hey." Ted shook his head. "Don't say that. Nobody's disappointed."

*Speak for yourself,* Eve thought. Ted was staring at her with raised eyebrows, requesting a little support.

"It's okay," she said after a moment, reaching out to pat Brendan's other shoulder. "Everything's gonna be okay."

The next morning, Brendan filled out the paperwork to formally withdraw from BSU. The day after that they drove to campus and moved him out of his dorm room. Zack wasn't around to help, didn't even show up to say goodbye. It didn't take long to load Brendan's stuff into a big orange bin, take it down in the elevator, and cram it into the maw of the van. It barely fit, just like at the beginning of the semester—the oscillating fan, the lacrosse stick, the toiletries, the laundry bin, the rolled-up rug, the suitcase and the garbage bags full of clothes. It had all looked so hopeful back in September, an emblem of the future. But now it just looked shabby and depressing, like they'd found a bunch of crap on the sidewalk and decided to take it home.

# Somebody Loves Me

Valentine's Day felt like just another Saturday in winter, which was bad enough in itself. Eve kept herself reasonably busy during the daylight hours—food shopping, laundry (there was so much more to do now that Brendan was home, especially since he'd gotten into CrossFit), bill-paying, a solo afternoon walk around the half-frozen lake. When she got home, she roasted a chicken with fingerling potatoes and brussels sprouts, a delicious, lovingly prepared meal that she ended up eating by herself, because her son had plans he'd forgotten to mention.

"Sorry," he said. "Thought I told you."

"Nope."

"My bad."

*Yeah,* she thought. *Your bad.*

"Who are you going out with?"

"Chris Mancuso," he said. "I don't think you know him."

"Why can't you eat here and then go out?"

"We're gonna get pizza and watch the hockey game. Is that a problem?"

"Fine. Do what you want."

"Jeez, what's the big deal?" he asked. "When I was away at school, you ate by yourself every night."

It was true, of course. She'd happily eaten alone in the fall, because that was how it was supposed to be. His absence was part of the necessary and proper order of things. His *presence* now was the problem—a huge backward step for both of them—along with his uncanny ability to take up more than his share of space in the house while giving so little in return.

"You're right." She waved him toward the door. "Go have your fun. Don't drink and drive."

"I know, I know," he said in a weary voice, as if he were a mature adult who could be counted on to make good decisions. "Enjoy your chicken."

She lingered at the table for as long as possible—she owed herself that much—and then dragged her feet on the cleanup, doing her best to stave off that troubling moment when there was nothing left to do, the official beginning of what she already knew would be a melancholy and restless night.

It had been like this all winter long. She found it difficult to relax after dark—couldn't curl up with a book, or settle down long enough to watch a movie from beginning to end. She was full of nervous energy, a nagging, jittery feeling that there was somewhere she needed to go, something else—something urgent and important—that she needed to do. But that was the catch: there was nowhere to go, and nothing to do.

All the freedom she'd experienced in the fall, that giddy sense of new horizons, all that was gone. She wasn't a student anymore, puzzling over feminist theory, drinking and dancing with her friends, exploring her sexuality, making stupid but sometimes exhilarating mistakes. She was just plain old Mom, chopping onions, feeling neglected, cleaning lint from the filter. Her life felt shrunken and constricted, as if the world had shoved her back into an all-too-familiar box that was no longer large enough to contain her. Except that the world hadn't done any shoving. She'd volunteered for her confinement, climbing in and pulling the cardboard flaps down over her head.

She told herself that she'd done it for Brendan's sake. After all, *he* was the college student in the family, not her, despite the fact that she'd completed her first semester with flying colors, earning a solid A in Margo's class, and high praise for her final paper, which explored the fraught relationship between radical feminism(s) and the transgender movement.

*This is excellent!!!* Margo had scrawled on the back of the essay, in sloppy, barely legible cursive that Eve couldn't help but think of as manly, even though she knew it was a faulty mental reflex, a kind of residual transphobia. But Brendan came first: he was the one who really needed to be taking college classes during the spring semester, and ECC was the logical place for him to do it. Eve understood that it was a tricky moment in his academic career—his confidence at an all-time low—and it had felt right to give him some space, to spare him the embarrassment of attending the same college as his mother, of possibly bumping into her at the library—if he ever actually *went* to the library—or having to compare his grades to hers.

It had seemed like a minor sacrifice at the time—a brief hiatus from her continuing education—but it turned out to be a much bigger loss than she'd anticipated. Without a class to get her out of the house—to focus her thinking and provide her with a community of like-minded people—her intellectual life ran out of steam and her social life went into a coma. She felt like a teenager, grounded indefinitely for one stupid mistake, though she was also the parent who had imposed the punishment, which meant that, as usual, she had no one to blame but herself.

\* \* \*

Chris wanted the last wing in the basket. I told him to go for it.

"These are pretty good," he said.

I agreed, and had a big pile of bones on my plate to prove it. But I felt kinda guilty, too, because my mom had cooked a whole chicken at home, and here I was eating hot wings at the Haddington House of Pizza.

"There was this place at my school, Pennyfeathers? Their wings were fucking awesome. Dude, they'd deliver until like two in the morning on weekends." He got this faraway look in his eyes and nodded for a long time. "I miss those wings."

Chris missed a lot of things about college. His frat brothers, his rugby teammates, this amazing ice cream place that had waffle cones dipped in chocolate, all the bars on 12th Street that didn't care if you had a fake ID, and now these wings from Pennyfeathers.

"Those were good times," he told me.

Chris and I knew each other a little from the Haddington High football team, but he was two years older, a varsity starter back when I was still warming the bench. I'd heard he'd gone to one of those small colleges in Pennsylvania, so I was pleasantly surprised to spot him in the hallway at ECC, where I hardly ever saw anyone I knew from high school (the only exception was Julian Spitzer, who seemed to pop up every time I turned a corner, though we always walked right past each other like we'd never met, like I hadn't found him sleeping in my fucking bed that night, a memory that still gave me the creeps). Chris explained that he was home for the semester due to some disciplinary bullshit and said we should grab a beer sometime. I thought he was just saying it to be nice, but he repeated the offer when we bumped into each other at CrossFit, and it wasn't like I had anything else going on.

"I guess you'll be happy to get back there," I said.

"I don't know if I'm going back." He wiped his mouth with a napkin, but he missed a greasy streak on his chin. "It'll suck without the frat."

"What do you mean?"

"They shut us down. Five-year suspension."

"Why?"

"Because of the kid. You didn't hear about it?"

"I don't think so."

"Huh." He seemed surprised that it wasn't a matter of common knowledge. "This freshman pledge died of alcohol poisoning at our house. It was all over the internet."

"Holy shit. Were you there?"

"Kind of. I mean, I was playing air hockey in the game room, just minding my own business. I saw this kid staggering around, but he wasn't the only one. All the pledges were shitfaced." He pulled the visor of his baseball cap lower, like a celebrity who didn't want to be recognized. "I guess he went outside to puke and everybody forgot about him. My buddy Johnny found him in the yard the next morning."

"Jesus. How much did he drink?"

"A shitload of vodka shots."

"Like how many?"

"I don't know." Chris sounded pissed. "It was a fucking drinking game. Everybody makes it sound like it was our fault, like we poured it down his throat. But he was totally into it. Screaming and high-fiving everybody. Having the time of his life."

He stopped himself, like he realized that probably wasn't the best way to put it.

"We had to write apology letters to the parents, which was brutal. And then there were hearings, and the whole frat got suspended. Didn't matter if you were involved or not. And now if I want to go back I have to reapply. For my senior year. Can you believe that shit?"

"Wow," I said. "I just thought you failed a class or something."

"That would at least make sense."

"So what are you gonna do?"

Chris took another napkin from the dispenser. Instead of wiping his face, he unfolded it very carefully and laid it over his plate, like he was covering his bones with a blanket.

"I might join the Marines," he said. "Just get the fuck out of here, you know?"

*　*　*

Facebook wouldn't let her forget what day it was for a second, flooding her news feed with images of hearts and flowers, a seemingly endless torrent of saccharine memes, happy couple photos, and loving tributes to loyal partners.

> *Thank you, Gus, for twenty-two years of red roses!*
> *A romantic dinner for two at the Hearthstone Inn. So blessed . . .*
> *This wonderful man didn't just make my DAY! He made my LIFE!*
> *I love you, Mark J. DiLusio!!!*
> *Snuggling by the fire with my handsome hubby on V-Day*
> *Somebody's gonna get a little surprise tonight . . . #feelingnaughty*

She tried her best to be a good sport, issuing a handful of half-hearted likes and offering a supportive comment when she could, but she gave up after a few minutes of resentful scrolling. It wasn't that she begrudged her friends their happiness—she wasn't that kind of person—she just wished they'd be a little quieter about it, a little more private.

*You won,* she thought. *There's no need to gloat.*

She knew that the winners didn't *think* they were gloating—in their own innocent minds, they were just celebrating the holiday, sharing a sweet sentiment with people who cared—but it was hard for Eve not to take it personally, not to feel like a weepy high school girl stuck at home while everyone else was slow-dancing at the prom. It had been a lot easier to be a loser back in the days before social media, when the world wasn't quite so adept at rubbing it in your face, showing you all the fun you were missing out on in real time.

\* \* \*

I wasn't crazy about the idea of partying with a bunch of high school kids—it's kinda awkward once you graduate—but Chris really wanted to go. He was friends with the girl who was hosting and said she was totally chill and down-to-earth, despite the fact that she went to the Hilltop Academy, a local prep school that cost almost as much as an Ivy League college.

246

"How do you even know her?" I asked. Kids from Haddington High and kids from Hilltop didn't usually mix.

"Summer camp. She was my junior counselor. We flirted a lot, but we never hooked up. I'm hoping to take it to the next level."

"That's cool," I said. "You mind if I just drop you off? I'm not really in a party mood."

"*Dude*," he said, like I'd failed to live up to his expectations. "Just come in and have a beer. If you don't like it, that's fine. But don't be a pussy about it."

His friend's name was Devlin and she lived up in Haddington Hills, in what looked like a fairly normal house, except that it was like four times bigger than any house I'd ever been in. She was half-Asian and very cute, dressed in a short black skirt and white knee socks. A construction paper heart on her shirt said, *Are You My Valentine?*

"Oh my God." She gave Chris a fierce hug, like he'd just returned from the dead. "It's so good to see you."

"You too," he said. "This is my buddy Brendan."

She gave me a stern look, her heart all crooked from the hug. "You're going to have to help me talk him out of it."

"Out of what?"

"Joining the Marines. It's crazy."

"Good luck with that," Chris told her. "Brendan's joining up with me."

She squinted in dismay. "Really?"

"Why not?" I said. "Somebody's gotta do it."

I was just goofing around, following Chris's lead, but Devlin didn't know that. She told some of her friends, and pretty soon it spread through the whole party. That was all anybody wanted to talk about, which was fine with me, because it spared me the embarrassment of having to explain that I'd flunked out of BSU and was currently living at home with my mom and taking classes at community college.

Most of the girls I talked to were firmly opposed to my enlistment—

a couple said they were pacifists, and others just thought it was too dangerous, or that it made more sense to join the Peace Corps, to help people instead of trying to kill them. Some of the guys were more gung ho, and wondered if I'd given any consideration to the Special Forces, because those dudes were the true badasses, the Rangers and the Seals and Delta Force.

The best conversation I had was with this light-skinned black kid named Jason, a middle-distance runner who was heading to Dartmouth in the fall. He'd taken a summer school class on Contemporary War Literature and told me about a bunch of books he liked—the only one I'd heard of was *The Things They Carried*, which I'd read in English class junior year—and then we switched to movies. Our tastes were pretty similar—we both liked *Lone Survivor* and *The Hurt Locker* and also *Tropic Thunder*, which wasn't really a war movie but was still hilarious.

"Not very PC, though," he said. "I know I'm not supposed to laugh at Robert Downey Jr. in blackface, but damn. Funny is funny, right?"

"Absolutely," I said, and we clinked our bottles.

Jason was one of the few guys at the party with a paper heart pinned to his chest. His said, *Somebody Loves Me!* He tapped it with two fingers.

"All right," he said. "Gotta get back to my girl before somebody steals her."

After that I danced with Devlin's friend Addison, whose heart said, *Make Me an Offer*. I hadn't been out on the dance floor since my date with Amber, and it felt really good to be moving in the dark, getting all sweaty and goofy with a bunch of cool people I'd just met. It was almost like I was back in college, except that it was a better college than BSU, and I was a better person, too, a thoughtful guy with interesting opinions and a solid plan for the future.

I'd only had two beers, so I wasn't close to drunk, but I did need to find a bathroom. Addison told me it was down the hall, just past the den.

I got a little distracted on my way. It was a long hallway, and the walls were lined with photographs of Devlin and her little brother and her mom and dad, a good-looking family who seemed to live their lives near water—beaches, lakes, swimming pools, fountains— and were always laughing about something when the picture got taken.

The first room I stuck my head into was a home office, and the second had a yoga mat on the floor, along with a big red exercise ball. I found the den on the third try—bookshelves, fireplace, leather chairs.

"Sorry," I said, because there was also a couch, and it was occupied by Jason and the girl he was making out with. They were going at it pretty good, and my arrival had startled them. "I was just trying to . . ."

"Trying to what?" Jason said, after an awkward moment of silence.

I didn't answer. I was staring at the girl. She was staring right back, looking just as confused as I was.

"Becca?" I said. "What are you doing here?"

*　　*　　*

Eve closed her eyes and let out a heavy sigh, the way she always did before she started watching porn. It was somewhere between an admission of defeat and an attempt to clear her head, to create a mental space free of judgment and open to erotic suggestion.

She had cut way down on her porn consumption in the past few months—that was one upside of Brendan's return—but she still found herself visiting the Milfateria from time to time, usually on nights like this when she was bored and lonely and looking for something to cheer her up, or at least distract her for a little while.

*I deserve some pleasure, too,* she reminded herself, which wouldn't have been such a terrible status update—not to mention an epitaph on her fucking tombstone—if only she'd had the courage to post it.

She didn't think Brendan would be home anytime soon, but she went upstairs and latched the bedroom door behind her, just in case.

Then she took off her jeans, got into bed, and started searching, clicking on any thumbnail that caught her eye.

In the Milfateria, at least, no one knew it was Valentine's Day. The people in the porn videos just did what they did, all day, every day, with boundless energy and unflagging enthusiasm, regardless of the calendar. They fucked on Christmas; they fucked on Earth Day and the Fourth of July and Thanksgiving; their fucking was not affected in the least by wars or terrorist attacks or natural disasters. They never got sick, never got tired, never got old. Some of them were probably dead, Eve realized, not that she'd have any way of knowing which ones. But here they were on her screen, going at it with abandon, having the time of their lives.

*Good for you,* she thought. *Keep on doing what you're doing.*

She was happy for them, but she wasn't especially aroused, which was not an uncommon occurrence in recent weeks. She just didn't know what she wanted anymore. The lesbian MILF stuff made her nervous, and she hadn't been able to find a new category to take its place. Some items on the menu seemed a little too familiar, while others were *waaaay* too specific. Usually she ended up sampling the Homemade MILFs, ordinary women having fairly straightforward sex, mostly with their husbands, if you could believe the brief descriptions that accompanied the videos.

The problem was, Eve had become a lot more interested in the women than she was in the sex. She kept trying to figure out who they were, and how they'd ended up on her laptop. Had they volunteered, or had their partners pressured them? Did it occur to them that their kids might someday watch the video? Their parents? Their neighbors and co-workers? Were they in denial, or did they simply not care? Or maybe they were proud, like they were finally getting a chance to show the world their best selves.

She must have clicked on twenty different videos, looking for something that would get her out of her head and into her body, but nothing worked. It was sad to fail at masturbation—again, no one to blame but herself—but at least it was better than failing with a partner. You didn't have to fake anything, or apologize, or offer comfort, or pretend it was no big deal. You could just close your computer, shake your head, and call it a night.

\* \* \*

I tried to find Chris before I left the party, but someone told me he'd gone upstairs with Devlin. I figured he was all set, so I headed to the mudroom to grab my coat. That was where Becca caught up with me.

"I'm sorry, Brendan." She was standing in the doorway, looking like her usual put-together self—all her buttons buttoned, every hair in place—which was not how she'd looked in the den. "I should have told you."

The coats were in a big pile, and half of them were black ski jackets, just like mine.

"Whatever," I said, tossing aside a girl's red parka. "I guess you weren't as busy as you expected."

I had tried to start things back up with her in early December, a few weeks after I came home from BSU, but she claimed she was swamped with schoolwork and college applications, and didn't have time for a relationship.

"I've been meaning to text you," she said.

It was hard to look at her just then, not only because I'd kinda forgotten how hot she was, but also because she was wearing a paper heart that said the exact same thing as Jason's: *Somebody Loves Me!*

"How do you guys even know each other?" I asked.

"Instagram," she said. "He's a really nice guy."

I found my coat. I knew it was mine because my mom had written my initials on the inside label before I left for college.

"I know," I said. "I talked to him before."

I tried to slip past her on my way out, but she grabbed my arm.

"Brendan?" she asked. "Are you really joining the Marines?"

"I'm thinking about it."

She stared at me for a few seconds, like she was trying to picture me in my dress blues.

"You know what?" she said. "I think that would be really good for you."

I didn't feel like going home, so I drove around for a while. When that got boring, I went to the high school and sat on the top row of the bleachers, looking down on the football field. Wade and Troy and I had done that a few times over the summer. It was kind of a nostalgia thing, a way to remember our glory days.

It wasn't very cold for February, I guess because of climate change, though maybe it was just a weather pattern, the Gulf Stream or whatever. I didn't know as much about that stuff as I should have. I'd read a chapter for my Comp class that made it sound like the end of the world, but it didn't feel like that in real life. It just felt like a pretty nice night.

Now that the shock had worn off, I realized that I wasn't that upset about Becca. I wanted to be mad at her for lying to me back in December, but I knew she was just trying to be nice, letting me down easy with that bullshit about being too busy for a relationship. And I couldn't blame her for hooking up with Jason, though I did wish she'd found someone a little more ordinary, who didn't make me feel like such a loser by comparison.

The only girl I was really upset about was Amber. I'd sent her a bunch of texts in December and January, just checking in, trying to start a dialogue, but she threatened to block me if I kept bothering her. I hadn't tried to contact her since then, so I figured maybe she'd calmed down a little. I thought about telling her I was joining the Marines—that would at least get her attention—but there was no way I was actually going to enlist. I had zero interest in shaving my head, and even less in going to Afghanistan.

I had a hard time thinking of what to say. I'd already apologized to her a bunch of times, and it hadn't gotten me anywhere. I couldn't think of anything funny or charming or even interesting, so I just wished her a Happy Valentine's Day and left it at that. She didn't reply, but my phone said she'd looked at the message, which I figured was better than nothing.

*　　*　　*

Eve was fast asleep when her phone dinged, shocking her back into consciousness. She sat up and threw off the covers, her groggy brain sorting through disaster scenarios as she tapped in her security code.

The text came from a number she didn't recognize. It was three words long, a sad little joke from the universe.

*Happy Valentine's Day!*

She took a moment to breathe, and get her heart rate under control.

*Who is this?*

There was a brief pause, and then a pleasant *bloop!*

*Its me Julian*

The glow from the screen was painfully bright. Eve's fingers felt fat and clumsy as she typed.

*How did you get this number?*

*Class list . . . last semester*

Was that possible? Eve couldn't remember putting her cell number on a class list. But maybe she had. In any case, another text had already arrived.

*Am I bothering you?*

She wasn't sure how to answer that. It was sweet of him to remember her on Valentine's Day. But not in the middle of the night. That wasn't okay. Except it wasn't the middle of the night, according to her bedside clock, just a few minutes after eleven. In any case, Julian had already moved on to the next question:

*R u in bed?*

And the next:

*R u naked?*

Eve tugged on the blankets, covering her bare legs. She wasn't naked, but she was pretty close. Just underwear and a T-shirt, not that it was any of his business.

*Julian . . . please don't do this.*

There was a longish pause.

*Dont you miss me?*

This was an easier question. Of course, she missed him, just like she missed all her new friends from the fall—Amanda, Margo, Dumell, the whole short-lived gang. And she owed him an apology, too, for everything that happened on that night in November, and for ignoring the emails he'd sent her in the days that followed. But this wasn't the time or place for either of those conversations.

*Have you been drinking?* she asked.

*Im kinda wasted*

*Where are you?*

His reply arrived in multiple parts, a rapidly accumulating stack of bubbles.

*Vermont*

*Visiting my friend at UVM*

*This girl was hitting on me at a party*

*and I kept thinking*

*Id rather be with u*

Eve laughed, because it was so crazy for him to be thinking of her under those circumstances. Except it wasn't completely crazy.

Not crazy at all, come to think of it.

*This girl,* Eve wrote, because she suddenly needed to know. *Was she pretty?*

*I guess*

*What did she look like?*

Julian took another moment to gather his thoughts.

*u r hotter . . .*

*Waaay fucking hotter*

*That's sweet,* she told him, adding a smile emoji. *I'm flattered.*

Two more messages arrived just as she'd sent hers off.

*I jack off all the time*

*thinking of u*

Eve grimaced. A murky sound escaped from her throat.

*Julian . . . This isn't a good idea.*

*Im so fucking hard right now*

She closed her eyes and tried not to think about that.

*I could send u a pic,* he added.

*Good night, Julian. I'm turning off my phone now.*

He didn't protest, didn't even try to change her mind.

*night eve*

She didn't really turn off her phone, but he didn't text her again, which was too bad in a way, because she really did miss him, and thought he would've liked to know—not that she ever would have told him—that she was touching herself and thinking about his body. The orgasm that had eluded her before was suddenly within easy reach—right there at her fingertips—and a lot more intense than any she'd had in recent memory.

*Thank you,* she would have liked to tell him. *Thank you for that.*

# Dirty Martini

Eve knew it was time to start dating again—it was one of her top three New Year's resolutions—but it was hard to get motivated, to convince herself that she'd have any more success this time around than she'd had in the past.

Feeling the need for moral support, she invited her closest friends—Peggy, Jane, and Liza—for a pep talk/brainstorming session at the Haddington Brasserie and Lounge. It had been months since they'd had a girls' night out—everyone had been so busy in the fall— and they all jumped at the opportunity to escape their houses on a weeknight in late winter, to drink a few glasses of wine, and put their collective romantic wisdom to work on behalf of such a good cause.

As excited as they were to strategize about the revival of Eve's love life, they began where they always did, with a quick update on their kids, which was how they'd all become friends in the first place: young mothers in the schoolyard, on the sidelines at soccer games, at school plays and award ceremonies and graduations, a whole era of their lives—it had felt so permanent while it was happening— suddenly behind them. Just a chapter, and not the story itself.

Jane was missing her daughters, the smart, sweet-natured twins, both of whom were thriving in college. Liza's son, Grant, had just embarked on a semester at sea, and the pictures looked amazing. Peggy was thrilled to report that Wade had survived the fall term, buckling down after a couple of disastrous midterms, and earning Bs and Cs on all his finals, which was better than anyone had expected.

"That's great," said Eve. "You must be so proud of him."

Peggy nodded reluctantly, apologizing for her pride. Jane and Liza regarded Eve with identical sympathetic expressions.

"Brendan's *fine*," she said, deflecting their pity. "He just had a hard time. He was partying too much and . . . I don't know. Something didn't click. He still has some growing up to do."

"He'll get it together," Liza said.

"On the bright side," Jane added, "at least he's back home. That must be nice."

"I guess. But I was just getting used to having my own life again. I don't want to lose that. I just want to get out and have some fun, you know?"

Eve's friends were full of encouragement, confident that she would find love on the internet, or at least meet some appealing prospects. You just had to go into it with a positive attitude.

"My sister's friend, Denise, met a great guy on Match.com," Jane said. "They just got married. The husband's a little older, a retired dermatologist. They travel all the time. Couldn't be happier."

"When you say a little older," Eve inquired, "are we talking late fifties, early sixties?"

"More like mid-seventies," Jane replied. "But he's in good shape."

"Stop right there," Eve said. "I don't want to date a guy in his mid-seventies. I don't care *how* active he is."

"The point is, Denise hired a dating coach, and that was why things worked out so well. The coach helped her write her profile, recommended a professional photographer to take her pictures, and advised her on how to respond to the men who reached out. She held Denise's hand every step of the way." Jane looked at Eve. "Just something to consider."

"Out of curiosity," Eve said. "Do you know what that would cost?"

"A lot," Jane admitted. "But Denise said it was the best investment she ever made."

Peggy patted Eve's wrist. "You don't need a coach. You've got us."

"I could definitely use some help with my profile," Eve said. "I always sound so boring. I mean, what am I supposed to say?"

"Just be honest." Jane counted on her fingers. "You're a good mom, a great friend, really good at your job . . ."

"See?" Eve slumped in her chair. "You're making my point. I'm falling asleep just thinking about me."

"Don't stress about the profile," said Liza, who'd been divorced longer than Eve, and had tried every internet dating site in the known universe, to no avail. "Trust me. The only thing that matters is your picture. You need to find a good photographer, and wear something tight and low-cut. That's what I would do, if I had a figure like yours."

"She's right," agreed Peggy. "Go to a salon and get a blow-out. Maybe hire a stylist to do your makeup. You only get one chance to make that first impression."

Broadly speaking, Eve was happy with her hair. It was thick but manageable, and unlike some other parts of her body, it had weathered the transition into middle age without losing too much of its youthful bounce and luster. She had to color it, of course, but that was her only serious intervention. In her mid-thirties, she'd briefly experimented with a sassy, athletic bob, but it didn't work, probably because she wasn't a sassy, athletic person. She'd quickly returned to her tried-and-true collegiate hairstyle—long and straight, parted in the middle, a folk singer at the coffeehouse—unless she was at work, in which case she opted for the professional discipline of a bun or a scraped-back ponytail or a tortoise-claw clip.

It was a safe and familiar look, and she'd begun to wonder if that might be a problem. Because she understood on some level that Liza was right, that you needed to make a bold impression if you were going to succeed in the cutthroat world of online dating, especially once you'd crossed the Rubicon of forty. And Eve had a growing suspicion that the Joan Baez/social worker hairdo she'd been sporting for most of her adult life wasn't going to do the trick.

"All right," she announced, settling into the salon chair. "Let's try something new for a change."

Her haircutter—he went by Christophe, though his given name was Gary—was pleased. "What would you like?"

"You're the expert. You tell me."

He studied her in the mirror, nodding with quiet confidence, like he already had a plan.

"Nothing crazy," she warned him.

He began by changing her hair color—it was naturally dark, mahogany bordering on black—to a luminous shade of golden brown that really brought out the hazel in her eyes. Then he shifted her part from the middle to the side and began to snip away, first crudely, to adjust the length, and then with more deliberation, framing her face in a series of artful layers that looked deceptively simple and natural, highlighting the graceful oval of her face and the elegant curve of her jawline—she'd had no idea that her jawline was elegant—while also concealing some of the less fetching regions of her neck. When he'd completed the blow-dry, Eve stared at herself in amazement.

"Oh my God," she said, as Christophe undid the velcro fastener on her smock. "You're a genius."

He waved off the compliment.

"This was you all along," he told her. "You just needed to come out of your shell."

All that afternoon, Eve kept returning to the mirror, waiting for the usual post-haircut remorse to set in, but instead of the sinking feeling she knew so well—*What was I thinking? Why do I even bother?*—all she experienced was a renewed sense of pleasant surprise.

Just to make sure she wasn't crazy, she took a selfie and posted it on Facebook, along with the matter-of-fact caption *New Do*. The response was instantaneous and overwhelmingly positive, twenty plus likes in the first ten minutes, and lots of supportive comments from her female friends.

It was gratifying, but only for a little while. Her mood darkened as evening set in, another Saturday night with nothing going on. What was the point of getting a fabulous new haircut if no one was going to see it except Brendan, who didn't even notice until she hung a sign around her neck?

"I got my hair done this morning," she said. "What do you think?"

He assessed her for a second or two, then gave a curt nod of approval.

"Nice," he said. "Did what's-his-name do it? The French dude?"

"Christophe."

"He's gay, right?"

"I think so. Does it matter?"

"Not in a bad way," he said. "It's just, the guy has a gay name and a gay job. It would be kind of confusing if he was straight. This way's better for everyone."

Brendan left around eight, climbing into a battered Toyota driven by one of his CrossFit buddies. As soon as he was gone, Eve went upstairs and changed into a tight skirt and tailored blouse and the one pair of special-occasion high heels she still owned. She took a selfie of her reflection in the full-length bedroom mirror, her mouth set in a sultry pout that didn't look as ridiculous as she'd thought it would. Just for laughs, she undid two more buttons on her blouse and took a photo with the edge of her black bra showing, not that she would ever post an image like that on social media. It was just for herself—an ego boost, irrefutable proof that she could still be sexy if the occasion called for it.

Now that she was all dressed up, it seemed crazy not to go out— just for a quick drink, a little human contact. Nothing fun or interesting was going to happen if she stayed home, that was for sure.

The Lamplighter Inn was a lot busier than it had been on her previous visit, the Saturday crowd younger and louder than she'd expected. Feeling instantly self-conscious, Eve took the last open stool at the bar and ordered a dirty martini from a baby-faced bartender who looked like she'd just graduated from college.

"Is Jim Hobie working tonight?" Eve asked.

The bartender gave her a suspicious look. She was wearing a cropped shirt, and Eve could see a tattoo of a black rose peeking out from the waistband of her jeans.

"Hobie only works weeknights. You know him?"

"Not that well. Our kids went to school together."

The girl nodded and swiped Eve's twenty off the bar. When she returned with the change, she frowned like there was something on her mind.

"I know it's none of my business," she said, "but you should be careful. Hobie's a nice guy, but he says a lot of shit that he doesn't really mean. And then he acts like he never said it in the first place."

"Okay." Eve took a sip of her cocktail. "Thanks for the warning."

The girl laughed sadly and rubbed her tattoo, as if it were a sore spot.

"I don't know what I was thinking."

"Join the club," Eve told her.

"What do you mean? Did you and him . . . ?"

"No," Eve said. "I just meant, you know, you're always hoping for the best and . . ."

The girl laughed. "You get Hobie."

"Exactly." Eve shrugged. "But it doesn't mean you were wrong for hoping."

It wasn't a bad night in the end. She stuck it out for two drinks, and chatted with a couple of not-completely-horrible guys around her own age—a divorced home inspector and an ex-cop who'd retired on full disability, though he seemed to be in perfect health—both of whom were reasonably attractive and had nothing of interest to say. But at least she'd tried, that was the important thing.

She left the bar a little after ten and got into her car. While she waited for the engine to warm up—it was another frigid night—she took out her phone and looked at the pictures she'd taken earlier in the evening. They were really good—not just the haircut and the clothes, but the look on her face, and even the way she was standing, with her hand on her hip, and her head canted at the perfect, self-possessed angle. Everything felt right and true, just the way she wanted it.

*There I am,* she thought.

She selected the second photo—the sexier one—and texted it to Julian. She'd been wanting to do it all night. It was exciting to finally press Send, to turn the fantasy into action.

He didn't answer right away, so she pulled out of the parking lot and started toward home. She'd only gone a couple of blocks when her phone chimed. Eve was adamantly opposed to texting and driving, so she forced herself to wait until she'd pulled into her driveway to read his reply.

*Great pic! But you missed a few buttons*

*Just a minor oversight. I thought you might like it.*

She got out of the car and went inside, her heart beating at a rapid clip. There was nothing quite like the suspense of waiting for a flirty text—as if the whole world was on pause, holding its breath until the next little *ding!* started it up again. She'd just locked the door behind her when he replied.

*I fucking love it!*

She sent him a blushing-face emoji that must have crossed with his follow-up:

*Could u take one with your shirt off?*

Eve laughed out loud, a melodic, two-martini chuckle.

*Don't get greedy,* she told him.

# An Invitation

As always, it was work that kept her grounded, reminding her that she could still make a positive impact in her community, and in the world. It was hard to feel sorry for herself at the Senior Center, where she encountered so many people who were dealing with problems that made her own seem trivial—chronic arthritis, early-stage Parkinson's, severe hearing loss, the death of a beloved spouse, a Social Security check that didn't cover even the most basic monthly expenses. The resilience of the elderly—their sense of humor and reluctance to complain, their determination to make the best of a bad (and almost always worsening) situation—was both humbling and inspiring.

That winter, Eve threw herself into the day-to-day life of the Center with renewed energy and commitment, delegating fewer tasks to her staff and playing more of a hands-on leadership role than usual. She personally revived the Mystery Novel Book Club—it had faded away after the death of its founder and guiding spirit, a retired English teacher named Regina Filipek—selecting *Gone Girl* as the first title and leading a lively, if occasionally frustrating, discussion of the book's many byzantine twists and turns with a group of seven mostly enthusiastic readers.

She was also drafted into the Tuesday morning bowling league, joining a team called the Old Biddies as a temporary substitute for

Helen Haymer, who was suffering from a severe case of vertigo that had left her housebound. None of the Biddies' opponents minded that Eve was a ringer, thirty years younger than the woman she'd replaced. This was partly because they were tickled by her presence at the bowling alley—as executive director, she was a bit of a celebrity—but mainly because she was such a weak bowler compared to Helen, a former school bus driver with a 150 average, one of the highest in the league (Eve was lucky to break a hundred on a good day). She hadn't played organized sports in high school—she'd grown up right before the golden age of girls' athletics—and was surprised by how much fun it was to be part of a team, cheering on her fellow Biddies when they rolled a strike, bucking them up after the gutter balls, patting them on the back and reminding them that it didn't matter, that there would always be a next time.

Tuesday mornings quickly became the highlight of her work week. She came into the office in her most comfortable jeans, took care of her email and any other business that couldn't wait, and then filed onto the Elderbus along with her fellow bowlers. They trash-talked the whole way to Haddington Lanes, where the seniors pretty much had the place to themselves. It was an invigorating break from the daily routine, full of laughter and high fives and soft drinks.

Right before her fifth outing, Eve's teammates presented her with an extra-large T-shirt with the words *FUTURE BIDDY* emblazoned on the front. Eve wore it proudly, and bowled her highest game ever, a completely respectable 117. Later that day, she called to check on Helen Haymer, and was sorry to hear that the vertigo wasn't getting any better, though not quite as sorry as she probably should have been.

Eve was thinking about Amanda as she left work on a rainy Wednesday evening in early March, curious to know how she was doing at the library. She wondered if it would be okay to reach out to her with a brief, friendly email, just to say hi and let her know that she hadn't been forgotten. It was probably a bad idea, but the silence between them felt wrong and unfinished, like a phone left off the hook.

Amanda had been on her mind a lot in the past few days because Eve needed to find her replacement ASAP—in an era of tight municipal budgets, you had to fill a job opening quickly or risk having the position eliminated—and the hiring process was in full swing. More than fifty applicants had submitted their résumés, many of them seriously overqualified for the low-paid, entry-level post. At least a dozen had master's degrees—mostly in Social Work or Nonprofit Administration—and two had completed law school, only to realize that there were already too many lawyers in the world.

Eve had drawn up a short list of five candidates, and had interviewed three so far. They were all perfectly fine—competent, professional, appropriately dressed. They had relevant experience and impressive letters of recommendation. Hannah Gleezen, the young woman she'd spoken to that afternoon, was fresh out of Lesley College, and had spent the past six months doing an unpaid internship at an assisted living facility in Dedham, where she'd called out Bingo numbers, organized a hugely successful Scrabble tournament, and led a holiday sing-along that had been a real morale booster for the residents. She was earnest and bubbly, and Eve had no reason to doubt her sincerity when she said that she really *liked* old people and believed that her generation had a lot to learn from their elders.

"I don't see it as me helping *them*," she'd said. "It's more of a two-way-street type of thing."

Eve could have just hired her on the spot. The seniors would love her, and so would the staff. She was the complete antithesis of Amanda, who'd confessed in her interview that old people freaked her out, not only because of their casual racism and homophobia and their love of Bill O'Reilly—though all that was bad enough—but also because of their broken-down bodies, and the terrible clothes they wore, and even the way some of them smelled, which she knew was unfair, but still.

It had been a gamble to hire her—Eve knew that from Day One—and it hadn't paid off in the end, but that didn't mean it had been a mistake. She was proud of Amanda for trying to shake things up at the Senior Center, and proud of herself for taking a chance on such a wild card. She didn't want to settle for a replacement who didn't have that same spark, a bland, safe choice that would look like an apology—or worse, a betrayal of everything Amanda had stood for—so Eve had shaken Hannah's hand and said she'd get back to her in a week or so, after she'd met with the remaining candidates.

The rain was cold and insidious—she could feel it snaking under her collar and rolling down her back as she made her way across the parking lot—but she thought she detected a faint undercurrent of spring in the air, the faraway promise of something better. It was late, almost six thirty, and the lot was deserted except for her minivan and a car she didn't recognize—a newish Volvo sedan—parked right beside it, so close to the white divider line that it felt like a violation of her personal space.

The Volvo's lights and wipers were on, which seemed a little ominous, and made it hard for Eve to see through the windshield. Squinting into the glare, she squeezed into the narrow space between the two vehicles. As she clicked her key fob—the van's dome light flashed on to greet her—the passenger window of the Volvo slid down.

"Eve." Julian was leaning across the interior console, wearing a green army coat with button-down epaulettes, his head and shoulders torqued at an awkward angle. "What's up?"

As she turned to face him, her shoulder bumped into the van's side-view mirror.

"Jeez," she said. "Did you have to park so close?"

"Sorry." Julian looked embarrassed. "I'm out of practice. I don't drive very much."

It was true, she realized. She'd never seen him behind the wheel before.

"Can I . . . *help* you with something?" Her tone was frostier than she'd intended. It was disorienting to see him here, at her place of work, without any advance warning. Not a practice she wanted to encourage.

"Not really," he said. "I was just hoping we could talk."

A car drove by on Thornton Street, and Eve felt suddenly exposed, as if she'd been caught in the middle of an illicit transaction. She cupped her hands around her face and leaned in closer.

"It's raining out."

"Come in." He nodded at the passenger seat. "The heater's on."

Eve knew this was her own fault. She never should have sent Julian that picture the other night. It was a stupid, reckless thing to do. And now she had to deal with this. With *him*. And talking to him—clearing up his understandable confusion, apologizing for the mixed messages she'd sent—was the least she could do.

"Just for a minute," she said. "I need to get home and make dinner."

The door didn't open all the way, on account of his terrible parking job, so it took some doing for Eve to slip into the Volvo. She felt calmer once she was inside, no longer visible from the street.

"I missed you," he said.

Eve nodded, acknowledging the sentiment, but not quite returning it. They examined each other for a little too long, reacquainting themselves after the winter-long separation. He'd grown out some stubble on his cheeks and chin, a scruffy hipster look that added a couple of years to his face.

"I like your hair," he said. "It's really pretty that way."

"Thank you."

"I liked it before," he added quickly, in case she'd taken his compliment the wrong way. "But this is better. You look really hot."

Eve let out a cautionary sigh that was directed more to herself than to Julian, a reminder not to drift off course, to wander into a conversation that would be a lot more enjoyable (and dangerous) than the one they needed to have.

"Julian," she said. "That's really kind of you. But I'm old enough to—"

"I don't care," he told her.

"Look." She shook her head in weary self-reproach. "I know I've done some things that have muddied the waters between us, and I'm really sorry about that. But we're not a couple. We can never be a couple. I think you know that as well as I do."

He conceded the point without a fight.

"I totally get that."

"Okay, good." Eve smiled with relief. "I'm glad we're on the same page."

Julian stared through the windshield—the wipers were still arcing back and forth—with a brooding intensity that reminded Eve of her high school boyfriend, Jack Ramos, a sad-eyed baseball player with an explosive temper. Jack had burst into tears when she broke up with him, and then ordered her to get the fuck out of his car, a yellow VW bug that smelled like dirty socks. There were no cellphones back then, and it had taken her an hour to walk home in the dark. But that had seemed like a reasonable price to pay, because the breakup had been her choice, and she was relieved to be done with him.

Julian reached across the console and took her hand. She was so surprised that it didn't occur to her to resist.

"I was just hoping we could hook up sometimes," he said, stroking her knuckles with the pad of his thumb. It was a nostalgic sensation, a memory made flesh. "Nobody has to know but us."

Eve laughed. She hadn't seen *that* coming. Belatedly, and with some regret, she extracted her hand from his.

"Julian," she said. "That's not gonna happen."

"Why not?"

She groaned in disbelief. "I don't even know where to start."

"Just give me one reason."

"Are you kidding me? I mean, really. How would we even—"

"My parents are on vacation."

Eve didn't understand him at first. She thought he was changing the subject, conceding defeat.

"They'll be gone all week." He paused, giving her a moment to catch up. "Come by any night you want. Early, late, I don't care. Just text me and come on over."

Eve couldn't even imagine it. What was she supposed to do? Walk up his front steps and ring the doorbell? Stand there in full view of the neighbors and wait for him to let her in? But it was almost like he read her mind.

"I'll leave the garage door open. You can just pull right in. There's a string with a key on it hanging from the ceiling. You can reach it from the driver's-side window. Give it a tug, the door goes down automatically. No one'll even see you."

Eve didn't know what to say. It sounded like a good plan, simple and totally plausible, if the person pulling the string had been any-one other than herself.

"You've given this some thought," she muttered.

Julian looked at her. His face was serious, full of adult longing. It was like she could see right through the college boy to the man he would one day become.

"It's all I fucking think about," he told her.

# Coyote

E ve had no intention of sneaking out for a tryst with a nineteen-year-old boy whose parents were away on vacation. Leaving aside the difference in their ages, which was a deal-breaker in and of itself, everything about the scenario felt tawdry and vaguely demeaning—the open garage door, the ticking clock (*offer valid for one week only!*), the whole booty-call/friends-with-benefits aspect of what he was proposing. It smelled like a surefire recipe for regret, if not disaster. Even the memory of their semi-illicit rendezvous at the Senior Center—the cold rain, the car and the van side by side in an otherwise empty parking lot, the brief interlude of hand-holding—made her feel foolish and a little uneasy in retrospect.

She remembered reading an advice column a few years back in which the expert suggested the following rule of thumb: *If you're thinking about doing something you won't be able to confess to your spouse or best friend, then DON'T DO IT! YOU ALREADY KNOW IT'S WRONG!* This was solid, unimpeachable advice, and it definitely applied to her current dilemma. With the possible exception of Amanda—to whom Eve wasn't currently speaking in any case—there was no one she could imagine confiding in, no responsible adult she knew who wouldn't be horrified to hear what she'd already done with Julian—*to* Julian?—let alone the proposition that was now on the table.

Luckily, this wasn't a major problem, because there was nothing she needed to discuss. She wasn't going to drive to his house and pull into the garage, nor was she going to tug on a string (the key on the end was a nice detail, very Ben Franklin) and wait for the door to descend so she could sneak inside and compound her previous mistake—which at least had the virtue of being unpremeditated—with a more serious and deliberate error, stupidity in the first degree.

She simply wasn't going to do that.

And yet, for something that was totally out of the question, she found herself thinking an awful lot about it in the days that followed. His desire—the simple fact of it—exerted a kind of gravity on her that she hadn't anticipated, and found surprisingly difficult to resist.

He was waiting for her.

Nobody else was.

That had to count for something.

It would be so easy to make him happy, which also had to count for something, because it wasn't like she was making anyone else happy, least of all herself. Besides, what was the alternative? Updating her Match.com profile and getting some professional photos taken? Wading through hundreds of boastful profiles of guys she wouldn't want to meet in a million years? And the ones she did want to meet, *those* guys probably wouldn't give her a second look, if they ever condescended to give her a first. Months could go by before she got asked on a date. Years could pass before she went on a good one. Maybe even a lifetime.

And the thing was, these men on the internet, the ones she was hoping to someday maybe just possibly meet, they were purely hypothetical. Julian was real. *He was waiting for her.* Yes, he was young— *way too young*, she was well aware of that unfortunate fact—but there was something to be said for youth, wasn't there? The stamina, the gratitude, all the clichés that were clichés because they were true. Even his lack of experience was touching, because it wouldn't last forever. And he was beautiful—there was no other way to put it—at a time when there wasn't nearly enough beauty in her life.

It was painful, to be offered a gift like that, and have no choice but to return it unopened.

Julian was a gentleman; he didn't press too hard, but he didn't let her forget, either. He texted her a question mark on Thursday night, and *all alone* on Friday. At midnight on Saturday, he sent a photo of himself sitting up in bed, narrow-shouldered and shirtless, with a comically forlorn expression on his face.

*No one came to my party*

She couldn't stop thinking about him on Sunday. She thought about him on her afternoon walk—it was a mild day, and she took a rare second lap around the lake—and she thought about him while cooking a hearty dinner of roast pork, scalloped potatoes, and kale with white beans. She wished she could invite him over, set a heaping plate in front of him, and watch him while he ate. With his parents out of town, he was probably subsisting on ramen noodles or yesterday's pizza.

Instead it was just Eve and Brendan at the table, and Brendan seemed a little down. She wasn't sure what was bothering him. They'd barely spoken in the past week—their schedules were out of whack—and she felt guilty about neglecting him, allowing her attention to drift into more selfish channels.

"Did you work out today?" she asked.

"Yeah," he said. "Mostly cardio."

Eve took a bite of the pork. It was perfectly cooked, tender and garlicky.

"Were your friends there?"

"A few."

"I'd love to meet them sometime."

"Sure." He took a sip of water and set his glass back on the table. Then he picked it up again and took another sip. "I mean, I mostly just see them at the gym, so . . ."

"No pressure," Eve assured him. "What about school? How's that going?"

Brendan gave a listless shrug. He'd registered for two spring-term classes at ECC—Accounting Basics and Intro to Political Science— but he hardly ever talked about them, and claimed to do all his homework in the library, which supposedly explained why he never had any studying to do at home.

"It's kinda boring, to be honest."

"What is? The textbooks? The professors?"

"I dunno," he mumbled. "The whole place. It's like I'm back in high school, just with all the losers. The ones who weren't smart enough to get into a real college."

*And whose choice was that?* Eve wanted to ask him.

"It's not a bad school," she said. "I had a great class there last semester. The professor was excellent, and some of the other students were really smart."

Brendan looked up from his plate. His face was blank, but she could sense some hostility in it nonetheless.

"I know. You only told me a hundred times."

He was probably right about that, Eve realized. And guilt-tripping him wasn't going to help. That had never worked with Brendan.

"You know who I saw at the supermarket?" she said. "Becca's mom. I guess Becca's got her heart set on Tulane."

"Am I supposed to care?"

"She was your girlfriend. I just thought—"

"I'm done with Becca," he said.

Eve was curious about their breakup, and its role in his disastrous fall semester. It seemed like an important missing piece of the puzzle.

"What happened to you two? Did you have a fight or something?"

"Not really." Brendan shrugged. "We just . . . I don't know. We never got along that great."

"Well," Eve said. "You weren't very nice to her."

"Me?" Brendan looked offended. "What did I do?"

Eve had been waiting for this opening for a long time.

"Remember the day you left for college?" she began. "When Becca came over to say goodbye?"

Brendan gave a cautious nod, but before she get could any further, her phone emitted a loud chirp, alerting her to an incoming message.

"Somebody just texted you," Brendan said. He seemed grateful for the interruption.

Eve felt a warm blush spreading across her face. The phone was lying facedown on the table, right next to her plate. She wanted to pick it up, but she couldn't, not if it was Julian.

"Aren't you gonna check?" he asked.

Luckily, it was just a harmless group text from Peggy—a picture of her next-door neighbors' chocolate lab puppy with a slipper in its mouth—so she didn't have to lie. She showed Brendan the puppy, and replied with a heart emoji. Her phone chirped again almost immediately; it was Jane, adding a photo of her late and much-loved beagle to the thread.

*R.I.P. Horace,* Eve wrote. *He was a sweet dog.*

By the time she looked up, Brendan was already at the sink. He rinsed his plate, and stuck it in the dishwasher.

"Good dinner," he said, and then he was gone.

Julian didn't text her at all on Sunday night. Eve tried to tell herself she was relieved, that he'd finally gotten the message implicit in her silence, but she couldn't stop checking her phone, and had an unusually hard time falling asleep.

Monday's silence was even worse. She wondered if something was wrong—if she should maybe give him a call, make sure he wasn't sick or depressed—but the clearer part of her mind understood that this was exactly the reaction he was hoping for. They were in a battle of wills now, and Eve just needed to hold out for a little while longer, until the window of opportunity closed, and they could both get on with their lives.

*Stay strong,* she told herself. *Don't do anything stupid.*

She followed this wise counsel until about eleven thirty that night, when she slipped out of bed and tiptoed downstairs in her nightgown and slippers. After a brief stop in the kitchen, she grabbed a fleece from the coat rack and pulled it on as she headed out to the van.

The back streets of Haddington were desolate at that hour, uninhabited except for a lone coyote prowling on Lorimer Road. It was scrawny and dejected-looking, all ribs and tail. The animal stared forlornly at Eve as she passed, as if it would have appreciated a ride across town.

She'd only been to Julian's house once before, on the night she drove him home from Barry's bar. It was a nice place, a brick-fronted ranch with a picture window and a wide front lawn. All the lights were off.

The garage door was open, just like he'd promised, but Eve parked in front of the house, right behind the Volvo. Leaving the engine running, she grabbed a small, red-and-white picnic cooler off the passenger seat and carried it across the lawn and up the steps to the front door. The cooler had two Tupperware containers inside—one with leftover pork, the other with potatoes—along with an ice pack and a post-it note telling him to have a great day. She left it on the welcome mat, where he'd be sure to find it in the morning.

Eve struggled at the bowling alley on Tuesday, regressing from an unspectacular 98 in the first game to a truly abysmal 77 in the second. Her teammates patted her on the back, telling her that she would bounce back next time, because everyone had bad days and you never stayed down for long.

"I hope so," Eve said. "I don't think I can do much worse."

As the afternoon wore on, she found herself glancing at her phone with embarrassing frequency, and feeling deeply resentful of Julian. How could you not acknowledge a gift of food left on your doorstep? It seemed a little rude, and totally unlike him (more like something Brendan would do, now that she thought about it). She wondered if her original intuition had been right—maybe Julian *was* sick and bedridden. Or maybe he'd left the house through the garage, and hadn't even noticed the cooler, though that seemed unlikely, given the location of the Volvo. Unless he'd gone out on his skateboard; that was another possibility to consider. She kept on telling herself that she had better things to think about, but her mind refused to believe it.

The mystery was resolved that evening, when she got home from work and found the picnic cooler resting on her welcome mat. It seemed like a sweet, thoughtful gesture until she slid back the lid and saw that the food was still there, untouched inside the Tupperware. Even her post-it note had been returned, its banality and fake good cheer impossible to miss now that it was directed back at her:

*Have a great day!*

She hadn't meant to offend him. She'd thought of the food as a peace offering, a clever way of breaking her silence—letting him know that he was on her mind—without actually saying anything that would get her into trouble. But to him—she could see it so clearly now—it had been a taunt. She'd walked right up to his front door—so close, *right there*—but hadn't gone inside. She'd withheld herself, and given him some greasy leftovers instead. No wonder he was upset.

*My bad,* she thought.

Eve couldn't sleep. Her brain was foggy. She stared at her message for a long time before pressing Send.

*I'm sorry. I shouldn't have done that.*

It was 2:14 in the morning, but Julian answered right away.

*Why didn't you come in?*

*Lights were out. Didn't want to wake you.*

*I'm awake now*

*It's late. I have to work tomorrow.*

*I cant stop thinking about u*

Then, because she didn't respond:

*My parents get home on Thursday*

Then, in case she hadn't done the math:

*Tomorrow's our last chance*

Then, because she *still* hadn't responded:

*I want you so fucking bad I'm going crazy*

Eve stared at her phone. She could feel his desire all the way from outer space, bouncing off a satellite, beaming straight into her hand.

He was still waiting.

He'd been waiting all week.

That had to count for something.

*All right,* she told him. *You win.*

*I do??? What's the prize???*

Eve was suddenly exhausted.

*Go to sleep, Julian. I'll see you tomorrow.*

# Garage Door

Eve felt surprisingly alert and well rested in the morning. She'd only slept for a few hours, but it had been a deep and restorative sleep, the best she'd had in days. All the agitation she'd been feeling—the cumulative weight of her indecision—had fallen away. What remained was a fizzy, almost buoyant feeling of anticipation.

*I'm doing this,* she told herself. *It's going to happen.*

She knew she'd be working late, so she chose her underwear with care, in case she decided to head straight to Julian's from the Senior Center. It wasn't too elaborate—just a red lace bra and matching panties—but it looked pretty on her. She knew he'd approve.

*You win,* she thought.

She could see it in her head, a romantic scene from a foreign movie. A beautiful woman of a certain age pulling into a dark garage, the door sliding down behind her. She tiptoes through the silent house, heading upstairs, into a candlelit bedroom where a sensitive young man awaits her. She stands in the doorway, basking in his appreciative gaze, and slowly begins to unbutton her blouse . . .

*This is the prize.*

Her clothes on the floor. Their bodies coming together.

But then what? What would happen when it was over, when she got dressed and went home? That part of the movie was a black hole, the one thing she couldn't afford to think about if she was going to make good on her promise—to do the thing she badly wanted to do—because he was waiting for her, and it was their last chance, and she was the prize.

It helped that it was the second Wednesday of the month—the day of the March lecture—which meant that she was a lot busier than usual, taking care of the last-minute tasks that were normally the responsibility of the events coordinator. She had to run to Staples to pick up the hard-backed poster to place near the main entrance—she'd forgotten all about it—and stop at the supermarket to buy cookies and soft drinks for the reception. She had to set up the folding chairs in the lecture room and make sure the sound system was working, all the while fielding several calls from the guest of honor, a New Hampshire–based journalist named Franklin Russett, who'd written a book called *Sweet Liquid Gold: In Praise of Maple Syrup*. Mostly, though, she was trying to drum up an audience, buttonholing every senior she saw, reminding them of the start time, and talking up the speaker, who was in high demand on the regional lecture circuit.

She was glad that Amanda wasn't here for this. Franklin Russett and maple syrup represented everything she'd hated about the lecture series, and had hoped to disrupt. But they'd tried it Amanda's way, and it hadn't worked. A lot of seniors had been upset by Margo's presentation—they'd found it *disturbing* and *inappropriate* and even *appalling*—and the complaints had made it all the way to the Town Council. Eve knew the entire program was under the microscope; she needed to repair the damage that had been done to its reputation and protect the funding that had allowed it to become such a beloved institution in the first place. All she wanted was a return to form—an upbeat talk about an insipid subject, a reasonably pleasant evening that no one would ever have to think about again.

There were four rest rooms at the Senior Center—the main men's and women's rooms, an employees-only facility, and a spacious, wheelchair-accessible bathroom that was in almost constant use throughout the day. It was the go-to spot for diabetics to inject themselves with insulin, and for people with ostomy pouches to attend to their sanitary needs. Sufferers of constipation or diarrhea also appreciated the privacy afforded by a single toilet and a locked door, as did a large group of people (mostly men) who liked to hunker down with a crossword puzzle while nature worked its leisurely, unpredictable magic.

This popularity had a downside, however. The toilet in the accessible bathroom was notoriously temperamental—easily blocked and prone to overflow—and it had been malfunctioning with increasing frequency in recent months. Eve had formally requested funding for a replacement, but the council was dragging its feet, as usual. So she wasn't exactly surprised when Shirley Tripko—a grandmotherly woman who looked like she wore pillows under her clothes—approached her a couple of minutes before seven to let her know there was a "problem" with the handicap rest room.

"Would you mind informing the custodian?" Eve asked. "I have to introduce our guest speaker."

"I already informed him." Shirley's voice was tense, a little defensive. "He needs to talk to you."

"All right," Eve sighed. "I'll be there in ten minutes."

"He said *right now*."

"Are you serious?"

Shirley bit her lip. She looked like she was about to cry.

"I didn't do anything wrong," she said. "I just *flushed*. That's all I did."

Eve stood in the doorway of the accessible bathroom, trying not to breathe. The toilet hadn't simply overflowed; it appeared to have erupted. The custodian, Rafael, was gamely trying to mop up the mess.

"Did you try the plunger?" she asked.

Rafael stared at her with dead eyes, his face partially concealed by a surgical mask. He was also wearing rubber boots and dishwashing gloves, the closest the Senior Center came to a hazmat suit.

"No good," he said in a muffled voice. "Better call the plumber."

Eve groaned. An after-hours emergency call was a huge—and expensive—pain in the ass.

"Can it wait until morning?"

Rafael cast a wary glance at the toilet. It was filled to the brim with a nasty-looking liquid, still quivering ominously.

"I wouldn't," he said.

A wave of fatigue passed through Eve's body. A phrase she'd never spoken out loud suddenly appeared in her mind.

*Shit show,* she thought. *My life is a shit show.*

"All right," she said. "I'll take care of it."

She calmed down a little once she got the introduction out of the way and returned to her office. On the bright side, there was a full house in the Lecture Room; her advance work had paid off. And the toilet thing was manageable. All she had to do was call the plumber and get the problem fixed.

*It's okay,* she told herself. *It's under control.*

Her usual contractor—the ironically named Reliable Plumbing—didn't return her call, and Veloso Brothers said they couldn't get anyone there until ten at the earliest. Eve didn't want to wait, so she tried Rafferty & Son. She made the call with some trepidation, fully aware of the thinness of the ice she was standing on, asking a favor of a man whose late father she'd banished from the Senior Center not so long ago. Luckily, George Rafferty wasn't a grudge-holder. He was cordial on the phone, and said he'd be right over.

"Thank you," she told him. "You're a lifesaver."

Eve barely recognized him when he appeared at the main entrance fifteen minutes later, toolbox in hand. He'd shaved off the reddish-gray beard that had been his most prominent feature for as long as she could remember. He looked younger without it, not nearly as imposing.

"You're lucky you caught me," he said. "I usually go to yoga on Wednesday night, but I got hungry and ordered a pizza instead."

Eve was impressed. He didn't seem like a yoga guy.

"Bikram?" she asked.

"Royal Serenity." He rolled his shoulders and massaged his trapezius with his free hand. "Doctor recommended it for my back."

"Does it work?"

"Sometimes. Gets me out of the house."

Eve nodded, murmuring sympathetically. She remembered that George's wife had died in the fall, just a month after his father. She'd meant to send him a note, but hadn't gotten around to it.

"I'm sorry," she said. "About Lorraine."

"That was hard," he said, shifting the heavy toolbox from one hand to the other. "Really tough on my daughter."

"How's she doing?"

"She's back at school. It's gonna take her a while." He gave a vague shrug, and then put on his game face. "So what do you got for me?"

Eve led him down the hall to the shit show. Rafael had made it more or less presentable—the walls had been scrubbed, the floor carpeted with paper towels—and had even posted a warning note on the door, complete with skull and crossbones: *Broken Toilet!!! Do NOT Use!!! You WILL Regret!* George peered inside and nodded with an air of professional melancholy.

"All right," he said. "Lemme get to it."

Eve slipped into the auditorium and caught the tail end of the lecture. Russett was explaining the difference between Grade A and Grade B maple syrup, which was a matter of color and sweetness and the time of year in which the sap was gathered. Paradoxically, many syrup connoisseurs preferred the cheaper and darker Grade B to the more refined Grade A.

"It's a heated controversy," Russett explained. "But whichever kind you buy, you can't really go wrong. In my humble opinion, real maple syrup always gets a grade of D . . ." He paused, letting the audience wait for the punch line. "For Delicious." He grinned and held up his hand. "Thank you very much. You've been a wonderful audience."

The post-lecture receptions never lasted long. Most of the seniors just grabbed a cookie or two on their way out the door; only a handful stuck around to chat with the speaker. By eight thirty the room was empty, and Russett was on his way back to New Hampshire.

Eve tidied up a bit—she decided to leave the folding chairs for the morning—and went to check on the plumbing situation.

"All set," George told her, drying his hands on a paper towel. "You're good to go."

"What was the problem?"

"Adult diaper." He tossed the crumpled towels in the trash can and wiped his hands on his pants. "Someone must have shoved it down, really wedged it in good. Maybe with a coat hanger or a stick or something. I don't know. It's way too big to flush."

"They get confused sometimes," Eve said. "Or maybe just embarrassed."

"Poor bastards." George shook his head. "That's gonna be us one day."

Eve locked up and walked across the parking lot to her minivan. The sight of it annoyed her—the bulging, shapeless body, the cavernous interior, all those seats that never got used.

*I need a new car,* she thought. *A tiny one.*

She sat in the driver's seat for a minute or two and tried to compose herself, wondering why her nerves were so jangled. The lecture had been a success, the toilet was fixed, and it wasn't even nine o'clock.

*Everything's fine,* she told herself. *Right on schedule.*

It was just hard to switch gears, to make the superhero transition from her responsible, professional self to the beautiful older woman in the foreign movie, the one with the lacy red underwear beneath her sensible outfit.

What she really needed was a drink. Just a quick one to clear her head, to get herself into a more relaxed and open frame of mind. She thought about stopping at the Lamplighter for a martini, but a detour seemed like a bad idea.

*Just go,* she told herself. *He's been waiting all week.*

Maybe his parents had some alcohol on hand. It was probably good quality, too, given the neighborhood they lived in and the car the father drove. She could pour herself a tall glass of vodka over ice, Absolut or Grey Goose. They could sit at the kitchen table and talk for a while before heading upstairs.

*Nice,* she thought. *Raid their liquor cabinet before you sleep with their son . . .*

It was a bad idea to think about the parents. Mr. and Mrs. Spitzer, enjoying themselves in St. Barts, not a clue about what was happening in their lovely home.

This had nothing to do with them.

It was between her and Julian, and it was their last chance.

She turned the key. The engine hesitated for a moment—it was long overdue for a tune-up—and then sputtered erratically to life. She shifted into reverse and started moving.

She circled his house twice—the first time she got spooked by a passing dog walker, the second by nothing at all—before finally working up the nerve to pull into the driveway. She sat there for a while with her foot on the brake, staring straight ahead, gathering her courage.

An overhead light was on inside the garage, which made her a little uneasy. She was pretty sure it had been dark in there on Sunday night when she'd dropped off the cooler. But then it struck her that Julian was being polite, welcoming her into his home, rolling out the red carpet.

The garage in Eve's house was a disaster area, a jumble of broken and rusted and outgrown objects, the relics of Brendan's childhood and her life with Ted. The Spitzers' garage was enviably clean and well organized by comparison—bare cement floor, assorted tools hanging from a peg board, wall-mounted bicycles, shop vac and lawnmower, water heater with shining copper pipes.

Julian's skateboard, wheels-up on a workbench.

The famous string with the key on it.

*Just reach up and give it a tug.*

The interior was spacious, the entrance wide. You could just glide right in, no worries about clipping your side mirrors or pulling up far enough for the door to close behind you.

She would have done it, too, except that something smelled a little off inside the van, and she'd begun to wonder about the source of the odor. She brought the back of her hand to her nose and gave it a quick sniff, but all that registered was the sweet chemical tang of liquid soap—not a great smell, but nothing to worry about.

Continuing her investigation, she tucked her chin and tugged at her shirt collar, sampling the air trapped between her skin and her blouse. A familiar, dispiriting fragrance wafted up, a distinctive compound of sweat and worry mixed with sadness and decay.

*Ugh,* she thought. *I smell like the Senior Center.*

Of course she did. That was where she'd spent the past twelve hours. It was always on her skin at the end of the workday, trapped in the fabric of her clothes. But today there was something else on top of it, the subtle but unmistakable scent of a plumbing emergency, a rotten cherry on the sundae.

She told herself she was just stopping at home for a quick shower, that she'd return to Julian clean and refreshed in fifteen or twenty minutes, smelling the way a seductive older woman was meant to smell. But this conviction faded as she drove across town. By the time she walked through her own front door and saw Brendan playing a video game on the couch, she knew she was defeated. All her courage was gone, replaced by a sudden wave of anger.

"Don't you have any homework?" she asked.

Brendan didn't answer. He was totally engrossed in his stupid game, flinching and tilting his body from side to side as he banged away at the controller, trying to kill all the bad guys.

"Turn that off," she snapped.

"Huh?" He looked up, more surprised than annoyed.

*"Now."*

He obeyed. The gunfire ceased, but the silence that followed was just as unnerving.

"You need to treat women with more respect," she told him.

Brendan blinked in confusion.

"What?"

"I'm not deaf. I hear the way you talk sometimes, and I don't like it. We aren't sex objects and we're not *bitches*, do you understand? I never want to hear that word in this house again."

"I never—" he protested.

"Please," she told him. "Don't insult me. Not tonight. I'm not in the mood."

He stared at her for a long time, still clutching his useless controller. And then he nodded.

"Sorry," he said. "I don't mean anything by it."

"Life's not a porn movie, okay?"

"I know that." He sounded genuinely hurt that she might even think he thought it was. "Jesus."

"Good," she said. "Then please start acting like it."

Julian texted three times while she was in the shower, wondering where she was and what was wrong. Eve didn't know what to tell him.

*I smelled bad.*

*I'm a coward.*

*I'm way too old for you.*

All these things were true, but none of them would make him feel any better. She remembered how awful it was at that age—at *any* age—to get your hopes up and then to come up empty.

*Poor kid.*

She lay down for a few minutes, but she wasn't tired anymore. She got up and stood in front of the full-length mirror in her fuzzy pink bathrobe. Then she undid the belt of the robe and let it fall open.

*Not too bad,* she thought.

Her body wasn't what it used to be, but she looked okay. Her stomach not so much, but it was easy enough to frame the image so only her head and chest were included.

*Not bad at all.*

The first picture was too dark, so she turned on her bedside lamp and tried again. This one was much better. Her hair was wet and her eyes were tired, but she looked like herself, which was a fairly rare occurrence.

In real life, her breasts were a bit droopier than she would have liked—no longer *perfect* or *amazing*—but the way the robe fell alongside them, you couldn't really see that.

In the photo, her breasts were lovely.

In the photo, she was smiling.

*This is just for you,* she told him. *Please don't show it to anyone else.*

After she sent the text, she went to her contacts and blocked his number, so she could never do anything like that again.

PART FIVE

*Lucky Day*

# Red Carpet

Eve got married in early September, around the beginning of what would have been Brendan's sophomore year of college, if Brendan had still been going to college. The day dawned gray and drizzly, but the sky cleared in late morning and brightened into a glorious afternoon, which was a huge relief, because the ceremony was taking place in her own backyard.

A few minutes after four o'clock, she stepped out onto the patio, wearing a pale yellow dress and clutching a bouquet of peonies and garden roses. The guests were gathered on the lawn, standing on either side of a narrow, slightly wrinkled red carpet that had been unfurled on top of the grass.

She paused for a moment to savor the tableau, to imprint it on her memory. There weren't a lot of people in the yard—only forty or so, with more on the groom's side than the bride's—but the faces turned in her direction formed a map of her life, old and new. Her sister and mother had made the drive up from New Jersey in the morning and had done nothing but complain about the traffic since their arrival. Jane and Peggy had come with their husbands; Liza completed the friend group, the self-proclaimed fifth wheel. She'd been sweet and supportive over the past few months, repeatedly congratulating Eve on her good fortune, though it clearly pained her to see her best divorced buddy rejoining the ranks of the married, leaving her to face the harsh world of middle-aged dating on her own.

*Don't forget me,* she'd whispered at the end of the previous week's bachelorette dinner, after too many glasses of wine. *Promise?*

*I won't,* Eve told her, and it was a promise she intended to keep.

Ted and Bethany had surprised her, not only by RSVP'ing an enthusiastic *Yes!!!,* but also by bringing Jon-Jon, who looked adorable in his little blue blazer, eyes wide, arms rigid at his sides. He was doing okay, observing the scene with some apprehension, but no outbursts or tantrums so far, knock on wood. And if he did start screaming, Eve thought, then so be it. She wasn't some starry-eyed twenty-five-year-old who expected everything to be perfect on her Special Day.

Aside from Jon-Jon, the only other child present was Margo's eight-year-old daughter, Millicent, who'd come to the ceremony straight from a soccer game, in cleats and a blue-and-white jersey with *HUSKIES* on the front. She was tall for her age, with toothpick legs and long blond hair, wedged between Margo and Dumell. They looked happy and very much together, though Eve knew that they'd gone through a rough patch and had been broken up for most of the summer.

There was also a small contingent from the Senior Center, among them Hannah Gleezen, the popular new events coordinator, whose energy and positivity felt like a force of nature, and the Gray-Aires, an a cappella group she'd created and coached over the course of the spring and summer. Eve had heard them from inside the house, serenading the guests during cocktail hour, harmonizing on "Going to the Chapel" and "Walking on Sunshine," as well as an out-of-left-field version of "Beat It" that got a big round of applause.

The only person on Eve's list who'd sent her regrets was Amanda, but she'd been so touched by the invitation that she took Eve out for a celebratory lunch the week before the wedding, the first time they'd seen each other since January. She was thriving, happy with her new job, and deeply in love with one of her co-workers, an excommunicated Mormon research librarian named Betsy.

Unlike Eve, Amanda had kept in touch with Julian. She reported that he'd transferred to the University of Vermont and was really excited about starting the next chapter of his life, and especially about living away from home for the first time.

"Good for him," Eve said. "He's a sweet kid."

Amanda did something sardonic with her eyebrows—just a subtle lift-and-lower, a brief acknowledgment of the inadequacy or absurdity of the bland phrase Eve had used—but it was enough to bring it all back into the open, the strange and intense half hour the three of them had spent together in Brendan's bedroom, and the impossibility of integrating that episode into any sensible narrative of her life. Mostly she dealt with it by not thinking about it at all, or treating it like an erotic dream she'd had, an embarrassing one that refused to dislodge itself from her memory.

"So this is a little weird." Amanda leaned forward, dropping her voice into a more confidential register. "Julian and I . . . we kinda hung out for a while. Back in the springtime."

"Hung out?"

Amanda's face had turned a pretty shade of pink.

"It was totally casual. He came over once or twice a week, after his night class. Just for a month or two, when I really needed the company. But then I started to get to know Betsy . . . Anyway, he was really cool about it."

Eve was surprised to feel a slight pang of jealousy, or maybe just possessiveness, as if Amanda had gotten hold of something that rightfully belonged to her. But it was a ridiculous, greedy feeling, and she banished it from her mind.

"I'm just curious," she said. "Did he ever show you any pictures of me?"

Amanda opened her mouth, mock scandalized.

"Ursula! Did you send him some pictures?"

"Just one. I asked him not to show anyone."

"Well, I never saw it." Amanda shrugged, as if it were her loss. "Not that I would have minded."

Eve wasn't sure if she was relieved or disappointed.

"Next time you talk to him," she said, "tell him I said hi."

"I'll do that," Amanda promised.

Hannah Gleezen tooted on her pitch pipe and held up one finger, as if she were about to scold the singers. Then she brought it down and the Gray-Aires launched into "Here, There and Everywhere," the song that had been selected as the wedding processional. Eve thought it was a little excessive, as if the woman in the song were a goddess—*making each day of the year/changing my life with the wave of her hand*—but George had put his foot down.

*Please humor me on this,* he'd said, and of course she'd agreed, because she was flattered, and because he didn't ask for much.

Eve still marveled on a daily basis at the speed with which her own life had changed. A year ago, she'd been lost and flailing, and now she was found. She wanted to call it a miracle, but it was simpler than that, and a lot more ordinary; she'd met a kind and decent man who loved her. He was standing there at the end of the red carpet, handsome in a dark blue suit, a tear rolling down his cheek as he smiled at her and mouthed the words, *You're beautiful.* His best man, Brendan, was standing right beside him, supportively squeezing his shoulder. It was almost like a fairy tale, Eve thought, a little too good to be true, and certainly more than she deserved.

Of course, she hadn't exactly *met* him. It was more accurate to say that she'd tracked him down, engineering a "chance meeting" at Royal Serenity Yoga a week after he'd fixed the toilet in the accessible bathroom. She'd acted like it was an unexpected treat to see him there—as if he hadn't informed her that he was a Wednesday night regular—but he didn't call her on the lie. He just told her how happy he was to see her, and apologized for his baggy gym shorts.

*If I'd known you were coming,* he said, *I woulda worn my lululemons.*

They went on their first date two nights later. The Hollywell Tavern was booked solid, so they ended up at Enzo, which was just as romantic as she remembered. Only a few months had passed since she'd gone there with Amanda, but it felt a lot longer than that, as if their ill-fated kiss in the parking lot belonged to the distant past, a youthful indiscretion she could look back on with grown-up, head-shaking nostalgia. It felt so much more solid—so much more *real*—to be sharing a meal with an eligible man close to her own age, a man with whom she was already, improbably, beginning to sense the possibility of a future.

George had dressed up for the occasion—khakis, Oxford shirt, tweed jacket—and the outfit gave him a surprisingly academic aura, especially when he put on his reading glasses to study the menu.

"You don't look like a plumber," she said, realizing even before the words were out of her mouth that it was a stupid and condescending thing to say.

"Thanks," he said, though he didn't sound especially grateful.

"I'm sorry." Eve felt like a fool. "All I meant is that normally when I see you, you're—"

"Filthy."

"No, not filthy. Just not quite as handsome as you are right now."

"I clean up nice," he said, forcing a smile. "It's a necessity in my line of work."

He took a sip of the Chilean Malbec he'd selected after an in-depth consultation with the waiter. He clearly knew his way around a wine list, which was another thing Eve hadn't expected. It was humbling and illuminating, coming face-to-face with her own snobbery.

"Actually," he told her, "I'm thinking about retiring in a couple of years, as soon as Katie graduates. Just sell the business and be done with it. I'd like to travel a little, maybe live near the ocean. I've been doing the same thing for thirty years. I think that's enough."

He said he'd never really wanted to be a plumber in the first place. He'd gone to BU for Communications, but he liked partying a lot more than he liked studying, and had only lasted three semesters. He was nineteen years old, living at home, and of course he drifted into the family business, becoming his father's apprentice, not so much choosing a trade as accepting his fate, which turned out to be not such a terrible way to go.

"The pay was good and I liked working with my dad. I bought a nice house, had a beautiful family. The years go by and all the sudden I'm the boss." He bit the tip of his thumb, then took a moment to inspect the toothmark. "It all made sense until Lorraine got sick."

Her illness was a four-year ordeal—diagnosis, surgery, chemo, radiation, fingers crossed. A brief period of hope, a bad scan, and the whole cycle all over again. His older daughter, Maeve, got married right out of college, moved to Denver with her husband. She was launched. It was Katie he worried about, a moody teenager, really close to her mom. She was a wreck. On top of all that, George's own mother died, and all the crap started up with his father.

"This past year was a nightmare. I didn't handle it very well. I was trying to keep the business running and take care of everybody else. I wasn't sleeping too well, so I started drinking to slow my mind down, and you know how that goes. It got to be a problem."

"It's hard being a caregiver," Eve told him. "You muddle through however you can."

He said he'd had some difficulty controlling his emotions. He was angry all the time—at God, at himself, at the doctors, all of which was okay, as far as he was concerned. But he was also angry at his wife for being sick, which was unforgivable.

"You know what I was mad about? I was mad because I didn't have a sex life anymore. Like she was inconveniencing me. The poor woman can't eat, she's in terrible pain, but what about me, you know?" He released a soft, bitter chuckle. "I watched a lotta porn while she was dying. I mean, *a lot*. My wife was upstairs, wasting away, and I'm down in the office watching Spring Break Hotties, or whatever they call it." He delivered the bulk of this confession to the tablecloth, but now he looked up with a slightly bewildered expression. "I don't know why I'm telling you all this."

Eve was wondering the same thing. It wasn't the kind of story you expected to hear on a first date. But she was touched by his trust, and relieved to know that their experiences had overlapped in this one peculiar arena, not that she would ever tell him about that.

"You're a good man." She reached across the table and patted the back of his hand. "You took care of your family when they needed you. I remember that day you came to the Center. I saw how much you loved your dad."

He managed a weak smile. "I'm sorry if I was rude to you. That was probably the worst weekend of my life. Up to that point, anyway."

"You don't have to apologize. It was a sad situation. We all did the best we could."

He cheered up after that, told her about the trip to Hawaii he'd been fantasizing about, if he could work up the courage to go alone. He thought he might like to learn how to scuba dive, even though it terrified him.

"It's a whole other world down there. You're like an astronaut on a spacewalk."

She told him about Brendan and the rough patch he was going through, and talked a little about her Gender and Society class at ECC. George was more interested than she'd expected, explaining that Katie was big into all that stuff, queer this and trans that. She'd had a girlfriend her freshman year, but now she was dating a guy.

"She says she's attracted to the person, not the gender. I guess it doubles your chances of getting lucky."

"That's a very enlightened way of looking at it."

"Whatever makes her happy," he said. "That's the only thing that matters to me."

He drove her home and walked her to her front door. He asked if he could kiss her and she said yes. It was a nice kiss, though a little more polite than it needed to be. Brendan was away that weekend, visiting Wade at UConn, and Eve decided to seize the day.

"You want to come in for a drink?"

George wrinkled his brow like she'd asked him to solve a tricky riddle.

"I'd like to. But I think maybe we should take it slow."

He kissed her a second time, an apologetic peck on the cheek, and then headed back to his car. Eve went inside, feeling like she'd somehow snatched defeat from the jaws of victory, and poured herself a glass of consolation wine. She'd only taken one sip when her phone chimed, a text that made her close her eyes and thank a God she didn't believe in.

*Is it too late to change my mind?*

Things moved quickly after that. Why shouldn't they spend their weekends together? And why wouldn't he drop by for dinner on a Tuesday night, and maybe stick around and watch some TV? And if he got a little sleepy on the couch, which he tended to do, who said he had to go home? Her bed was a queen, and she discovered that she slept a lot better with him lying next to her, snoring very softly, as if he were making an unconscious effort not to disturb her.

Everything was better when George was around. Even Brendan liked him, which was the biggest surprise of all, given how grumpy and territorial her son could be. They bantered easily, employing a half-affectionate, half-mocking style that Brendan had previously reserved for his favorite teammates and closest buddies.

"Oh shit," he'd say, returning home from CrossFit. "This guy again? Don't you have a TV at home?"

"I have a nice one," George would say. "Lot nicer than this piece of crap. But your mom has Netflix and she's really pretty."

"Whatever, dude. I just hope you left me some food this time."

"I finished off the steak, but I left you lots of that zucchini you like."

Eve was deeply frustrated with Brendan in those days—he was the problem she couldn't solve—but George insisted her son was just going through a rough patch, that tricky transition between high school and the real world.

"He'll be fine, Eve. Not everyone's a Rhodes Scholar."

"I'm not asking him to be a Rhodes Scholar. I'm just asking him to do his homework every once in a while."

They'd probably had a dozen versions of this conversation before the night George laid his hand on her stomach and said, "You know, he can always come work for me. Just for the summer. If he doesn't like it, no big deal. He can try something else."

Eve was silent for a while, trying on the idea of her son holding a big wrench, wearing dirty Carhartt pants. It wasn't a life she'd ever imagined for him, but it seemed oddly plausible, certainly easier to picture than Brendan as a financial analyst or CPA. And she knew George would be a good boss and a patient teacher.

"You should talk to him," she said.

A week later, Brendan withdrew from ECC and started working full-time as a plumber's apprentice. He took to it right away. He enjoyed the physicality of the work, the tools and the terminology, the sense of accomplishment he felt at the end of the day. It could definitely be gross, but he said you got used to that pretty quick. The starting pay wasn't bad—way better than minimum wage—and it would get a lot better in a few years, after he passed his exams and got his journeyman's license. A six-figure salary by the time he was thirty was definitely not out of the question. It was even possible that he could someday take over the business, be the Son in Rafferty & Son.

Eve told him not to get ahead of himself, to just take things one step at a time. She was disappointed by his decision to give up on his education, but she was relieved to see him so upbeat and purposeful, with some of his old confidence restored. It was a huge improvement on the sullen, beaten-down version of her son she'd gotten used to living with over the past winter and much of the spring.

\*   \*   \*

I was hungover pretty bad on the day of my mom's wedding, but at least I had a good excuse. After the rehearsal dinner, I went to George's house and stayed up really late, drinking vodka shots with his daughter Katie and her boyfriend, Gareth, this tall, skinny dude who seemed about ninety-five percent gay.

"We're gonna be stepsiblings," Katie said. "Might as well get to know each other."

It was weird that I'd never met her until the night before the wedding, considering how much time I'd spent with her father, way more time than I spent with my own. George and I were like family already. But she'd been living in Ithaca for the summer, tutoring underserved youth, and it was too long a drive to just pop home for the weekend.

"I don't know." She glanced around the living room, which was full of family pictures that included her dead mother, and gave a little shudder. "It's just really hard to be here. I feel like crying every time I walk through the door."

"It's a grief museum," muttered Gareth. He had a goth thing going on, hair that was really short on one side and really long on the other. The long side just kinda flopped over his face, covering one eye.

"Yeah," I said. "I'm sorry about your mom."

"Thanks." Katie tried to smile. She showed me the inside of her forearm, her mother's name tattooed in graceful cursive letters. "She was a great person. You would've liked her. Though I guess if she was alive, you two would never have met."

"Probably not," I said.

Gareth poured shots and we all drank to Katie's mom.

"It's kind of amazing," she said. "She hasn't even been gone for a year, and here's my dad getting married again."

I asked if that bothered her, and she shook her head, no hesitation at all.

"I was worried about him over the winter. He was a real mess. But he's been a lot better since he met your mom. I think he just needs a woman to take care of him. He doesn't do that well on his own."

That made sense to me. I remembered how George had just kinda showed up at our house in the spring and made himself a fixture. Right from the start, it seemed like he belonged there, like he filled an empty space in our lives. But I guess we'd done the same for him.

"You know what?" Gareth said, as if an idea had just occurred to him. "Fuck cancer."

"I'll drink to that," Katie said, and we did.

Cancer was too depressing to think about, so I asked them how long they'd been together. They traded a quick look, like maybe this was a more complicated question than it appeared to be.

"We're, uh . . . not really together together," Gareth said.

"Yes we are." Katie sounded a little annoyed. "We live together."

"Yeah," Gareth conceded. "But we don't have sex."

Katie nodded, maybe a little sadly.

"Gareth is an ace," she told me.

"A what?"

"Asexual," he explained. "I want to *be* with people. I just don't want to *do* anything with them." He made a face, like he was thinking about a food that grossed him out. "I never got what all the fuss was about."

"That's cool," I said. "To each his own."

We drank a shot to that, to people being whatever the fuck they wanted. I was feeling pretty loose by then, so I looked at Katie.

"So . . . are you like that, too? Asexual?"

"Only with Gareth," she said. "If I'm attracted to a person, I tend to mold myself to whatever they are."

They were sitting together on the couch, and she dropped her head affectionately on his shoulder. After a few seconds, he reached up with his hand and started rubbing her back in a circular motion, kind of like he was cleaning a window.

"We do a lot of cuddling," Katie told me. "That's the best part anyway."

She was prettier than I'd expected—in the pictures I'd seen, she looked kinda plain—with her red hair and freckles, and kind of a soft, earth-mother body. Actually, she reminded me a lot of Amber, which was weird, because Amber had just sent me a long email a couple of days earlier, totally out of the blue. It was the first time I'd heard from her since I'd come home in the fall.

She said she'd just gotten back from Haiti, where she'd spent her summer volunteering in a women's shelter in the capital city. It had been an amazing and humbling experience, trying to help women who were so much braver and more resilient than she could ever be. Women who had so little to begin with, and had to struggle just to survive—to feed their kids, to keep them healthy, and, maybe, if they were very lucky, to send them to school so they could learn to read and write and maybe someday have a shot at a better life. It was a transformative experience for her, an experience that made her realize how trivial her own life had been, especially her life at college.

She said she was dreading the thought of going back to BSU, getting sucked into *that meaningless vortex* again—the parties, the softball team, the social media, the dining halls, with all that food getting thrown away every day.

She said she'd been meaning to write to me for a few months, but kept putting it off, because part of her had wanted to apologize and part of her thought that other part was insane. She certainly didn't want to apologize for anything *she'd* done—not for punching me, which I'd totally deserved, or kicking me out of her room, or ignoring the messages I'd sent her—but only for Cat's painting, which didn't accurately reflect her own feelings.

> *I'm not saying you weren't a disappointment to me, Brendan. But so many guys have disappointed me, I don't think it's fair to single you out.*
>
> *Also, if you were going to be up on that wall, I should have been up there with you. Because I'm the one who gave you the power to disappoint me. In that sense, I disappointed myself, which is just as bad, if not worse.*
>
> *I'm not going to let that happen again.*
>
> *I hope you had an okay summer,*
>
> *Amber*

I didn't really know what to make of the email, though I guess it was somewhat comforting to know that she didn't hate me as much as I'd thought she did. I was tempted to tell Katie the whole story, just to hear what she had to say. I had a feeling she was somebody you could turn to for advice in situations like that. But Gareth had started to give her a neck massage, and she was totally distracted by how good it felt, wincing and groaning like a porn star as he kneaded her traps.

"So Brendan," he said, squinting at me while he worked his magic fingers. "Are you really gonna be a plumber?"

"I'm just an apprentice," I told him. "It takes a long time to get your license."

Katie opened her eyes. "My dad says you might take over the business someday."

"Maybe," I said. "Unless I decide to go back to school."

It was weird—until I said those words, I hadn't even realized that I was thinking about maybe giving college another try. But I'd been feeling kinda down these past few weeks, listening to Wade and Troy and all my other buddies talk about how excited they were to get back to their dorms, back to their friends and their classes and the parties. It was hard to believe they'd just pack up their shit and leave me stranded in Haddington, doomed to a lifetime of installing water heaters and fixing leaky U-joints.

"You should definitely go back," Gareth said. "I transferred three times before I got to Ithaca. You just gotta find the right fit."

"I don't know what my dad tells you," Katie said, "but he never liked his job. He always said that he wished he'd gotten his bachelor's."

"Maybe I'll fill out some applications," I said. "Just to see what happens."

"You'll get in somewhere decent," Katie said, and we all drank to that, and then to some other stuff, and we kept going until the bottle was empty and everything was pretty much a blur.

\* \* \*

The guests continued to smile at Eve, beaming that united front of love and approval, but some confusion had begun to creep into their expressions, a collective unspoken question: *Is something wrong?* The Gray-Aires had been singing for a while now, so why wasn't she moving? Why was she still standing on the patio, strangling that bouquet with her fists? What was she waiting for?

*Go,* she told herself, but her feet remained rooted in place.

The singers forged ahead with the second verse, though they sounded a little less confident than they had on the first. The quizzical look on George's face had deepened into outright worry, and maybe even fear.

*He's a good man,* Eve reminded herself.

There had been only one genuinely troubling moment in their relationship, a tiny blip on an otherwise unblemished record of happiness. It had happened a few months ago, maybe the fourth or fifth time they'd slept together, and it was not something she wanted to be thinking about right now, with the sun shining and everyone dressed so beautifully, and the rented minister trying so hard not to look impatient.

The sex had been especially good that night, Eve on top, which was the way they preferred it. They'd found a groove, sweet and slow, and their eyes were locked together. It seemed to her that they'd moved beyond physical pleasure to a place of deeper intimacy, a place where their truest selves connected.

*Oh, God,* he told her. *I can't believe this is really happening.*

*It's amazing,* she agreed.

*Eve,* he said. *I've been dreaming about you for so long.*

*About me?*

*Fuck yeah,* he grunted, in a voice that seemed jarring to her. It was harsher than usual, and maybe even a little angry, as if he were speaking through gritted teeth. *You're my MILF!*

Eve stopped moving. A chill spread through her body, the memory of something unpleasant.

*Excuse me?* she said. *What did you say?*

He opened his mouth to reply, but then caught himself.

*Nothing,* he told her. *It's not important.*

That was the whole incident, just a few words in the middle of some otherwise great sex. It broke their rhythm for a few seconds, but then they found it again. When they were done, Eve thought about revisiting the matter, but what was she going to do, ask him point-blank if he'd sent her a creepy anonymous text back when they barely knew each other, back when his wife was dying and his father was losing his mind? And what if he'd said, *Yes, that was me.* What would she have done then? Where would she be now?

It was nothing, really, just a passing shadow, and Eve had lived long enough to know that it was foolish to worry about a shadow. Everybody had one; it was just the shape your body made when the sun came out. Her own was visible at that very moment, a familiar dark figure skimming the ground, moving slowly over the length of the shimmering carpet, leading her to the man she loved.

# Acknowledgments

*Mrs. Fletcher* and I would like to thank Liese Mayer and Nan Graham for their probing questions and excellent advice; Maria Massie and Sylvie Rabineau for their unflagging guidance and support; and Lyn Bond and Carolyn J. Davis for illuminating conversations that gave me momentum when I needed it the most. Nina and Luke Perrotta made the book better with their careful readings and thoughtful comments, and Mary Granfield helped in too many ways to list here.